Maybe it's You

Maybe it's You

CHRISTY
HAYES

Maybe it's You

By Christy Hayes

Trade paperback ISBN 978-1-62572-016-0

Book Cover Design by ebooklaunch.com

Edited by Iola Goulton, Christian Editing Services

Formatting by E.M. Tippetts

E.M. TIPPETTS BOOK DESIGNS

Chapter One

Reagan Bellamy picked the wrong night to wear the right boots. Every step she took in her heeled boots shot an arrow of galvanized steel up her calves, past her internal organs, and straight into her cranial membrane. She stopped walking, placed a steadying hand on a nearby tree, and closed her eyes on a deep breath of morning air.

Birds tucked into their cozy nests mocked her walk of shame across Addison State University's otherwise peaceful campus, determined to condemn her with their shrill accusations: Sinner. Hussy. Trash. Reagan shot a regretful glance at the overhead branches, mustered her strength, and limped on.

The predawn sky painted the sidewalk and stucco buildings of ASU with a dull film not unlike the one coating her mouth and her memories. Fitting punishments for her night of debauchery. Why had she inhaled more shots than she had fingers on one hand? More disturbingly, why had her best friends and roommates let her leave the bar with her worst nightmare and freshman mistake? Only now, in a frightening replay of events, the same boy had become her junior mistake. Fool her once, shame on him. Fool her twice …

Reagan was the world's biggest fool.

Some days, like this one, when the morning fog held everything in a tight vise, the sourness of the distant paper mill along Georgia's coastline hung in the air. Off in the distance, the cloud cover was giving way to a headache-inducing glare that would eventually burn away the scent, but not before she'd returned home. She followed the sidewalk into the entrance of her apartment complex and prayed to make it inside before anyone caught a glimpse of her in last night's clothes.

The squeaky hinges of a second-story door proved Reagan had wasted her prayers. She squared her shoulders, flipped her hair behind her back, and winced as the searing edge of the morning's hangover almost brought her to her knees. She tugged on the hem of her sweater dress and tried to pass for heading to church early Sunday morning.

When a pair of scarred leather boots appeared at the top of the stairwell, Reagan bit back a groan. Dash Carter was the last person she wanted to face when feeling her worst. She caught him giving her a full body appraisal before he hiked his guitar case onto his shoulder and descended the stairs with a loose-limbed gait she could only describe as a swagger.

"Rough night?" He eyed her as she worked up the nerve to tackle the staircase, more exposed than if he'd plopped her under a microscope.

"Late night." A wave of nausea pummeled her shaky stomach. She grabbed hold of the handrail, swallowed back the bile, and closed her eyes.

Within seconds, his minty fresh breath brushed her face. She pried her lids open, but quickly looked away. She couldn't stare into his hazel eyes for more than a second. He had a way of looking at her—with absolute focus—that stripped her bare.

"Whoa there." His tone oozed sympathy, sympathy she didn't deserve. "You okay?"

The gentle hand he placed on her lower back set every nerve ending ablaze. She forced herself to take the next step, and the one after, dislodging his hand and creating some distance. He smelled of soap and sandalwood, while she reeked like a garbage bag left at an abandoned tailgate. "I'm fine. Just got a little dizzy." The throbbing in her head kept her from sprinting up the stairs.

"You need some Pedialyte," Dash said.

She stopped at the top of the staircase and carefully turned in his direction. "What?"

"Pedialyte." Instead of looking at her like a cheap piece of trash, he flicked a lock of chestnut hair from his forehead and pierced her with his calm stare. "It's an electrolyte replacement, like Gatorade. You find it on the baby aisle in the grocery store. It'll help the headache."

"I'm fine." She did little to hide the snark in her voice. Couldn't he just leave her alone?

"No sense hurting when you don't have to."

She'd never disliked him more, and her aversion ran as deep as the string of women who probably fell at his feet. She hoped her closed-mouth smile conveyed her annoyance. She turned around, unlocked the door, and promptly slammed it, sending a shock wave of pain through her skull. What a jerk. He would have been less obvious if he'd asked who she'd hooked up with the night before.

"Will you please stop making so much noise?"

Reagan took two steps forward and found her roommate, Kayla, sprawled on their L-shaped couch wearing a tank top and underpants, her favorite crocheted throw twisted around her legs. Her arm lay over her eyes and she still wore a butterfly barrette in her messy blond hair.

"What happened last night?" Reagan asked Kayla.

"Shh." Kayla held a finger to her lips before gripping her temple with both palms. "Not so loud. It's like an echo chamber in here."

Reagan lowered carefully onto the couch to remove her boots. "At least you made it home. Alone."

Kayla gave a noncommittal grunt before propping up on her elbow. "You're the one who insisted we leave without you."

Reagan's pulse pounded, and her stomach vibrated in response. Leaning back into the cushions, she resisted the urge to pace and argue against Kayla's insanity. "Come again?"

Kayla groaned as she attempted to sit up. "Shelby tried to drag you away from the sweater vest, but you refused."

"Oh no." She dropped her head in her hands as an image of Chad Ferguson the night before fluttered through Reagan's mind like a puff of smoke. He hadn't been wearing the sweater vest that morning, or anything else as far as she could tell when she'd slithered out of his bed. She could barely stand to look at him with his pale chest, spindly arms, and the hair he kept perfectly gelled shooting like bamboo reeds against the stark white pillow. "Why? Why didn't I listen?"

"The same reason I'm lying here in my underwear. The devil alcohol."

"Never listen to me when I'm drunk and insisting I stay with someone you know I detest."

"You're more convincing when you're drunk and lapping him up like an ice cream cone."

"Tell me you're exaggerating."

"I would," Kayla said. "But I'd be lying."

Reagan's head fell back until it nestled against the soft cushion, her eyes drifting closed. Yes, she'd intentionally sought Chad out when she'd found him at the bar. As Professor Atkins's graduate assistant, he had pull in who became the professor's next undergraduate research assistant. Reagan was willing to do just about anything to make inroads with Professor Atkins, but she never thought she'd stoop that low. What a nightmare. "How could I go home with the jerk who took my virginity my freshman year and then acted like he didn't know me the next day?"

"Is he ignoring you now?"

"I got out of his apartment as soon as I woke up."

"Did you ...?"

The bowling ball in her stomach nose-dived into the gutter as shame flamed her cheeks. "I don't know."

Kayla's eyebrows disappeared into her bangs. "You don't know?"

"I was wearing my clothes, so I hope not."

Kayla reached a hand over and patted Reagan's arm. "Assume nothing happened and purge it from your mind."

"My mind *is* purged. I can't remember leaving the bar with him. What happened after is a total mystery. All I know is I'm never drinking again."

"Me neither. Let's make a pact."

She shook Kayla's hand, and used her roommate's grip to lever herself off the couch.

"Where are you going?" Kayla asked.

"To scrub every trace of Chad Ferguson from my body."

Reagan clutched the side of the shower, lightheaded from the steam. Or from lack of sleep. She stumbled to her bed and burrowed under the covers but found sleep as evasive as the details of the night before. She'd made a mistake. A big one. She didn't know whether she needed to apologize to Chad or act like the whole thing never happened.

Reagan hated not knowing what to do or how to act after spending her whole life walking on eggshells around her volatile mother and the men who waltzed in and out of their lives. Finally living life on her terms, surrounded by friends, the last feeling she wanted to relive was the sickening dread of not knowing what the next day held. She had a plan, she stuck to the plan, and everything she did was according to the plan. Getting blisteringly drunk and going home with Chad Ferguson wasn't a part of her plan. It wasn't even scribbled in the margins.

Hours later, after a nap and a bowl of leftover spaghetti, Reagan sat cross-legged at the kitchen table, contentedly engrossed in a paper disproving Keynesian economics. She glanced over when the apartment door opened and her roommate Emily walked inside carrying a bottle of red liquid.

Still dressed in last night's clothes, Emily lacked both the hangover and the embarrassment of a night spent away from home thanks to her boyfriend, Dylan. Reagan was still sober enough to remember when Dylan pried the beer from Emily's hand and whisked her out the door. They were disgustingly in love and nauseatingly dependent on one another. Reagan never wanted a man to order her around, but it would have been nice to have someone to run interference for her last night.

"What is this?" Emily set the bottle on the table before breezing past to the refrigerator.

Reagan struggled to remember the point of her half-typed sentence. "What's what?"

"It was on the doormat," Emily said over her shoulder.

Reagan reached for the bottle, turned it around, and nearly choked on the shame of last night's debacle. It had taken hours to expunge her reckless behavior from her mind and find solace in the safety of schoolwork, and the bottle of Pedialyte pulled her back to the present where humiliation ruled.

Her feet hit the floor with a resounding thud, she grabbed the plastic container, and rocketed out of the apartment. Somebody was going to pay.

Chapter Two

Dash gripped the neck of his guitar, his right hand hovering over the strings as the spark of anticipation pulsed under his skin. He caressed the stings like a lover, sank deeper into the soft leather chair, and let the tension seep from his body.

Strumming an out-of-tune chord, Dash earned a glare from Seth, drummer of their newly formed band, Evergreen, where he sat slumped on a folding chair in Dash's den. Seth resumed tapping out a beat on his portable kneepad as Dash adjusted the tuning pegs and thought of all the times he'd turned to music to start over.

During his rebellious adolescence when he'd been hell-bent on standing apart from his too-perfect siblings. Throughout his last year of high school and early years of college, when music was the only reason he hadn't taken the final plunge into hard drugs and alcohol. He tested a note, tuned some more. Eighteen months ago, he spent his days and nights shouting lyrics and pounding chords in a mindless haze of discontent. And now, cruising toward his degree and back to a place where he could look his parents and himself in the eye, music grounded him and provided an escape.

He drummed his fingers on the soundboard and glanced at the three guys lounging in his apartment, each embracing their instrument and a past as varied as his own. Jacob, the band's keyboard player and wordsmith. He sprawled on Dash's couch, thumping a chewed pencil against the sheet music on his lap, struggling with the beginning verse of the song they'd attempted to create in the few hours since their last performance. Eli sat next to Jacob, eyes closed, plucking out notes on his bass guitar that would eventually become the chorus. Though he couldn't read music, Eli's uncanny ear and bluesy soul made him a natural composer.

A new band meant a new beginning. Though they'd only been an official group for a few weeks, their sound was coming together. Dash scooted to the edge of his chair, the old leather grumbling, and readied himself for the magic. His pulse quickened to match the beat, the vibration of the strings swam through his blood, and Jacob's mumbled words nourished his soul. His foot tapped, and his fingers twitched over the sound hole as the tune began to take shape in his mind. Oh, yeah. They were coming together just fine.

It took him a few seconds to recognize the offbeat thwack as someone banging on his door. Lost in their musical haze, none of his bandmates caught the incessant thumping. They continued tapping beats, strumming chords, and scribbling words on paper.

Dash stood up, leaned his guitar on the coffee table, wiped his palms on the thighs of his jeans, and opened the door.

"What is this?" Reagan, red faced and ready for a fight, shoved the bottle of Pedialyte Dash had left on her doormat into his chest. He stumbled back from the unexpected force, grabbed the bottle before it tumbled to the floor, and stared at the girl who'd invaded his mind for the better part of the day. The better part of the year, if he was honest.

She'd showered—he could smell the soap on her skin—and dressed in yoga pants and a long-sleeved t-shirt. Her long brown hair hung from a ponytail that swung like a pendulum from her head. She was seriously beautiful, and seriously upset.

"We've been over this," he said. "It's an electrolyte replacement that helps with a hangover."

"I don't want your baby drink!"

"You're not hung over?"

"I'm …" She latched onto the doorframe with a white-knuckled grip, buried her face into the sleeve of her arm and inhaled deeply.

Dash stifled the impulse to comfort her, and instead crossed his arms over his chest and considered his options. The music behind him had stopped, which meant he and his neighbor had an audience. Reagan was mad, clearly, but also trying her best to keep the contents of her stomach in place, just as she had early that morning in the parking lot. He'd admired her strength then, and as he watched the rise and fall of her chest, he knew she was fighting a losing battle. She'd feel better when she finally let it out. He knew that from experience.

She lifted her head, swallowed hard, and pinned him with weary brown eyes. Every ounce of color had drained from her face. "I need to use your bathroom."

Dash stepped back as way of invitation, and she blew past him at a run. She only managed to crack the bathroom door before whatever was in her stomach made a violent return. He winced and prayed she hit the toilet.

Dash closed his apartment door and glanced from Seth to Jacob to Eli. They sat spellbound by Reagan's appearance. The stillness of his band mates only magnified the retching from the bathroom.

"Friend of yours?" Jacob asked around the pencil in his mouth.

Dash shrugged. She wasn't a friend, but he couldn't call her a stranger. He'd spent most of the past year watching her and forming an image in his mind. Serious Reagan always hustled wherever she went with her overstuffed backpack slung over her shoulder. Without the bag, she'd sprint along the running path that wound beside their complex, her earbuds hanging on for dear life. "Neighbor."

"She's hot." Seth used his drumsticks to tap a beat on his pad and winced when the heaving started up again. "Too bad she doesn't like you."

Dash gripped the bottle of Pedialyte in his fist when water began running in the bathroom. Perhaps Reagan would accept his gift now that her stomach was empty.

"She'll need that now for sure." Eli pointed to the bottle with the neck of his guitar.

Dash turned around when his friends, who'd resumed their tapping, humming, and strumming, quieted their instruments. Reagan emerged from the bathroom and fiddled with the hem of her shirt. Color rushed to her cheeks when she realized they weren't alone.

"You okay?" Dash stepped closer and blocked her from the prying eyes of his friends.

She nodded and sent her ponytail swinging. "I'm sorry about that."

"It happens. I'll bet you feel better."

"I do."

Dash stepped back and jerked his head in the direction of his friends. "This is Seth, Jacob, and Eli."

"Oh. Hello." Reagan lifted her hand in a half-hearted wave before shifting her eyes to the closed apartment door.

Dash moved fast, the Pedialyte in one hand, Reagan's arm in the other, and ushered her into his kitchen. He filled a glass with ice, poured the red liquid, and jiggled the glass in her face. "Drink."

She huffed out a sigh. "Fine, but only because I blew chunks in your bathroom."

Dash rubbed the back of his neck. "In the bathroom … or in the toilet?"

"The toilet." She swallowed a tiny sip, then took another through colorless lips. "I thought this would taste awful, but it's not bad." She took a long gulp, watching him over the rim of the glass. "Your bathroom was spotless. Thank you, posthumously, for being so clean."

He liked the sweet tea sound of her voice, and the way it seeped into him when she used fancy words like posthumously. "You're welcome."

She set the empty cup on the counter before looking up at him with her big brown eyes. Her early morning retreat had left him singed. Smelling like a distillery, the glint in her dark eyes could have brought him to his knees. But standing in his kitchen, soft and contrite? The girl should come with a warning.

"I came over here to give this back, not throw up in your bathroom in front of your friends and have you serve me like a waiter—or a nurse."

Considering what little he knew of her pesky nature, and the way she usually looked at him with the disdain given to a piece of chewing gum attached to the heel of her shoe, that was as close to an olive branch as he was going to get. What was it about her condescending attitude that summoned every dormant need to life? Even that morning, unsteady on her feet with the lingering scent of a random hookup on her skin, she'd still made him want.

"Life rarely goes according to plan."

Her eyes grew even larger before she cleared her expression and deliberately blinked. "Anyway, thanks for letting me heave in your bathroom." She pointed to the bottle. "Do you mind if I take this?" She stared at him as if bracing for a comeback or a lecture on drinking responsibly.

Dash had so little opportunity to study her at close range, he wasn't going to waste it with idle chatter. After a long moment where she met him stare for stare, he said, "It was always yours."

She lifted the Pedialyte from the counter, nodded her head, and swiveled toward the door.

"Reagan?" When she turned back, Dash had the pleasure of watching emotions wash over her face like a three-act play: annoyance, curiosity, acquiescence.

"Yes?"

"I'll see you around."

She looked her fill slowly, from his sock-covered feet to the tips of his hand-combed hair, like a cat scrutinizing its prey. "Yes, I suppose you will."

He stared at her retreating backside, rubbing a hand where the sharp punch of yearning ached deep in his abdomen. He didn't have time to linger over thoughts of his snarky neighbor with the sexy scowl and prickly attitude. He could have lots of women—any woman from the way they flocked to his shows and lingered after the last note had faded into the hum of the crowd. But he'd made a promise to himself, a promise he intended to keep. Nine months into his yearlong sabbatical and the only woman who'd ever tempted him was fresh off a hookup and could barely stand the sight of him. Figured.

Chapter Three

Reagan shoved her laptop into her backpack and mentally scrolled through her day. She had an eight o'clock appointment with Professor Atkins to discuss the research assistant position before her nine and eleven o'clock classes. Despite an embarrassing run-in with Chad in Professor Atkins's office where she'd mumbled hello and avoided eye contact, she'd somehow talked herself into an interview for the RA position, and she couldn't afford to be late.

"Shelby, I'm leaving," Reagan hollered down the hall of her apartment. "If you want a ride, let's go."

"I'm coming, I'm coming," Shelby called from the bowels of her room.

Reagan slung her backpack over her shoulder and went to the door, tapping her foot in annoyance. If she left in the next five minutes, she'd find a parking spot in the closest lot. Any later, and she'd be lucky to find a parking spot in any lot on campus. "I'm leaving now."

"Just hold your horses!" From the sound of Shelby's voice, she was still in her room, most likely rooting under the bed for a missing shoe or a matching sock. Of the many words to describe Shelby, neat and organized weren't among the choices. "Ready." Shelby appeared in the den, mocking Reagan's impatience with her singsong voice.

"It's about time." Reagan wrenched open the door and waited for Shelby to exit before closing it behind her.

Shelby scooted past, kicking her feet in front of her to avoid stepping on the untied laces of her wedge booties. "Unlike you, I try to look presentable for class."

"Unlike you, I don't have an image to maintain." Not that Shelby had to maintain anything. She was by far the most beautiful girl on campus.

Shelby snorted. "I just don't have to be the first one to class." She reached out and fingered Reagan's long-sleeved peasant top. "Although you do look rather nice today."

"I have an interview at eight, and I don't want to be late."

"Which is why you're not driving to the party tonight." Shelby clomped down the stairs. "Early for school is one thing, but early to a frat party is another animal all together."

"I'm not going to the party," Reagan said. "I've got to study."

Reagan knew Shelby had stopped walking when her heels stopped clicking. She turned around to face her roommate's narrowed eyes.

"The biggest frat party of the century, and you're not going? Why not?"

"I have a paper due Monday, and I need to work on it tonight and study for finals."

"But you've got all weekend."

Reagan started walking to her car. Yes, she had all weekend, but a night out meant more than taking a few hours to burn off some steam with friends. It meant drinking and a hangover and a late night that would set her behind.

"You know Dash's band Caliber is playing the party," Shelby said. "They're expecting a monster crowd."

Reagan weaved her way through the parking lot. "So?"

"So I thought we'd all go, like a last hoorah before Christmas break."

"Shelby, I can't. This paper is a big part of my grade, and my GPA matters."

"Are you insinuating that my GPA doesn't matter?"

Reagan slowed her pace and faced her roommate, squinting into the cool morning sun. Shelby managed a delicate balance between school, work, and partying better than anyone. "My GPA matters in terms of the assistantship. Of course your GPA matters. Everyone's GPA matters."

"Not everyone." Shelby placed a hand on Reagan's arm, stopping her forward progress. "Just because you drank too much last time we all went out doesn't mean it has to happen again. That was over a month ago."

The memory of that night still caused Reagan's stomach to burn with shame. "I didn't intend to drink too much last time, I didn't intend to spend the night out, and I sure didn't intend to let the whole world know I'd messed up."

"The whole world?" Shelby smirked knowingly. "Or our very hot neighbor?"

Reagan rolled her eyes and turned her back on Shelby, quickening her step. "What is with you and Kayla and Emily and this obsession you have with Dash Carter?"

"Are you humiliated that he caught you walking home after a night out and still thought enough to bring you something for your hangover?"

"It humiliates me that I'd get drunk and go anywhere near Chad Ferguson." She could barely stand the taste of his name on her lips. "The walk of shame and Dash's 'gift' were merely salt in my wounds."

"He didn't have to help."

"No, he didn't. And I thanked him." After throwing up in his apartment, but Shelby didn't need to know that part of the story. "Can we please stop talking about Dash?"

"Why does he bother you so much?"

Reagan sighed as she unlocked the car. She had too much on her plate to waste time on something—someone—she desperately wanted to forget. "He's a nice enough guy, and if I had loads of free time and were looking for a pot-smoking dropout with visions of musical grandeur, I'm sure he'd top my list. But why, exactly, does everyone think I should be tripping all over myself to get his attention?"

Shelby smirked at something in the distance. "He's hot, he's nice, and for some crazy reason, you've already got his attention."

"Oh, I see." Reagan opened the rear driver's side door and shucked her backpack inside. "You're jealous that someone finds me attractive."

"Jealous? Please." Shelby began searching the contents of her purse. "I think I left my ID on my desk." Shelby pivoted and sauntered toward the stairs.

"Shelby!"

"Just go on without me. I'll get a ride from Kayla."

Reagan scowled at the watch on her wrist. Even if she made it to campus in record time, she'd never find a parking spot. She gasped and jerked around in surprise when someone cleared his throat behind her.

Instead of a guitar case slung over his shoulder, Dash gripped a sporty black backpack that would have made him look more like a peer than a budding rock star if he weren't wearing a black leather jacket over a crisp navy t-shirt and combat boots. "Not going to the biggest frat party of the century?"

How did someone so big approach without making a sound? And if he'd heard her comment about the party, what else had he overheard? "It doesn't interest me." Reagan willed her heartbeat to settle. She'd seen him since she'd blown chunks in his apartment, but not up close. And not alone.

"Oh, yeah?" He cocked his head and studied her with his too intense stare. "What does interest you?"

She'd been searching for a way to shake him and his long lingering stares. The truth and all its boring details would accomplish that goal better than anything. "History, politics, law."

"Aah." He nodded his head, his shaggy hair bouncing in response.

"Aah?" Reagan was shocked his eyes hadn't already glazed over. She must have hit him on a day he hadn't toked up before noon.

"Let me guess. Your future includes law school, a clerkship, and a fast-track to partner before thirty?"

He was annoyingly close and she'd planned to lie and say it wasn't true, but before she could phrase her denial, her chin shot into the air and an arrogant sniff escaped. "Maybe. Something like that." Or exactly that. Sort of. "What difference does it make?"

"I'm simply making assumptions about you based on circumstantial evidence. Like you made assumptions about me."

"You're assuming I think about you. And I don't."

"Really?" His brows winged beneath the fringe of his hair. "You didn't just tell your roommate I'm a pot-smoking dropout with musical pipe dreams?"

Great. He'd heard her, and he wasn't going to be a gentleman and let it slide. "Okay … I'm sorry. I have no idea if you smoke pot or go to school or what your hopes and dreams are for your music. I was just trying to shut her up, which is not an easy task."

He stepped closer and she stepped back, slamming against the door of her car. She was forced to crane her neck and look up into his gorgeous eyes. "Do I make you uncomfortable?"

Reagan wanted to swallow, or take a breath, but neither was possible with his eyes boring into her from close range and his scent filling her nostrils. "Yes, you do. And I think you enjoy it."

When he grinned, she couldn't help but admire his pearly whites. She ran her tongue along her crooked bottom teeth and swallowed the sting of envy at his flawless smile.

"Maybe a little," he said.

Reagan expressed her dissatisfaction at being pressed between a four-thousand-pound car and a hundred and eighty-pound jerk by hardening her voice. "I have to go."

"And yet you can't."

"Excuse me?" She would have crossed her arms if he hadn't been standing so close.

He dipped his head, his feather light hair tickling her face, and tsked at her shoes. Or maybe it was her car. Since every working brain cell had evaporated into thin air, it was hard to tell.

"Your tire's flat."

The sunlight set his blue green eyes aflame, and the tremor of his voice in her ear sent a shiver down her spine. "What?"

"Your back tire. It's got a leak."

Reagan shook free of his spell and glanced down. Her once taught tire had formed a muffin top against the road. "What the—argh! Now I'm definitely going to be late."

"I can give you a ride. I'm heading to campus anyway."

"You're a student?"

"Occasionally. When I'm not high or fantasizing about stardom."

She deserved that, yet it stung. "You're making fun of me."

"Look." He ran a hand through his hair. "I've got an eight o'clock class. I'm going to campus and I'm happy to drop you wherever you need to go. Take it or leave it, I don't care either way."

She looked at her tire, up at her apartment, and back at Dash. He was being nice—again—and she needed a ride, but something made her hesitate. Was it the fluttering in her belly or the I-dare-you glint in his stare? "Fine. I mean yes, I'd like a ride." She retrieved her backpack from the back seat of her car and locked the door, snarling at her flat tire.

One corner of Dash's mouth kicked upward before he turned around and started walking along the domino of cars. She refused to look at his backside as he strode down the lot. He already knew his effect on women, and now he knew his effect on her. He stopped between a small SUV and an olive-green sedan, only to pull a helmet from the back of a black motorcycle hidden from sight between the two.

"Waaait a minute," Reagan said. "A motorcycle?"

Dash gave a one-shoulder shrug. "Seth borrowed my truck to haul our equipment, so I'm taking the bike." He held out the helmet. "You got a problem with that?"

Reagan choked back a sarcastic retort. She had so many problems that there wasn't time to list all the problems she had.

Was he serious? She took the helmet from his outstretched hand, cradling it against her chest. "This doesn't even look big enough for two. And don't you need a helmet?"

He unzipped a side pouch, pulled out a smaller helmet, and slipped it on his head, buckling the straps under his chin. "You're going to have to put that on, because it doesn't work if you hold it."

"I …" Dash pried the helmet from her grasp and plopped it on her head, lifting her chin and buckling the straps. Surrounded by his subtle cologne and clean soap scent and the sound of creaking of leather when he moved lulled her into compliance. It was hard to argue with someone who smelled so in charge.

He rested his hands on her shoulders. "It's a five-minute ride to campus. Use both the straps on your backpack, don't lean when we turn, and you'll be fine." He let her go, climbed atop, and leveled the machine so she had a steady surface to mount. With one smack of his boot, he dislodged the kickstand. Another kick brought the machine to life with a deafening roar.

Without the stabilizing force of his hands on her shoulders, she wobbled like a bobblehead doll. She watched him pull a pair of aviator glasses from the pocket of his shirt, slide them onto his face, and stare at her as if challenging her to climb aboard. With a deep breath, she snaked her arm through the other side of the backpack, found purchase on the seat, swung her leg over, and gripped his shoulders in a vise.

Dash used his legs to back out of the space and stabbed her with a taunting glance over his shoulder before revving the engine. "You're going to want to hold on."

Chapter Four

Bad idea. Bad idea. Bad idea.

Dash repeated the chant in his head from the first turn of the handles when Reagan latched her arms around his waist and molded herself to his backside like bread in a Panini press. He should have left her standing in the parking lot wondering what to do about the flat tire instead of trying to play white knight to her damsel in distress. She clearly had no interest in being rescued.

Why had he offered her a ride, especially after her snarky judgments about him as a pot-smoking musical wannabe? Instead of hurting his feelings, she'd made him laugh—and cringe. A year ago, she'd have hit the bull's-eye with her description. A year ago, he never would've been up at seven-thirty in the morning. A year ago, he'd have been sleeping off a hangover or waking up in a stranger's bed, trying his best to piece together the night before.

Those days were over, and Reagan was partly to blame.

A sharp turn had her snuggling closer. Dash gritted his teeth and tried to stay focused on the road. He couldn't afford to get distracted by the way her chest crushed against his back or the feel of her legs clamped around his thighs. As if the smell of her wasn't maddening enough, that frilly perfume that filled his head with images of wildflowers and naked skin.

Over the last ten months, when a cold shower or a good, sweaty workout wasn't enough to quell his hunger, Dash would hit the back roads on his motorcycle. Feasting on the power of the machine beneath his legs, the vibrations pulsing through his skin, and the heady rush of wind pelting his face, finding relief where speed and motion collide.

He wasn't feeling particularly comforted with Reagan wrapped around him like a vine. When she yelped, Dash slowed his pace through campus. Although eager to have her disembark, the last thing he wanted was to scare her.

He glided to a stop in front of the Humbolt building, assuming she had a class, a study group, or a meeting in the business center of the quad. She loosened her grip and unwrapped her arms with electrifying slowness. He felt every millimeter of distance as she disembarked, simultaneously mourning and celebrating her dismount. As he stood with his feet on either side of the bike, the machine thrumming between his legs, she unhooked the helmet, shook out her hair, and pinged him with a look he'd never seen on her striking face: joy. Either she'd had the time of her life on the short ride to campus, or he was so turned on he imagined the glow of her skin, the quirking of her lips, and the delight dancing in her dark eyes. He was stunned into silence.

"Thanks for the ride." She held out the helmet. He grabbed the straps and rested it atop his lap. "That was … fun."

"Fun?"

"I've never been on a motorcycle before. It's exhilarating."

"Exhilarating?"

"I bet it feels like flying when you open her up on the highway."

She'd never spoken to him with anything but derision in her voice, and her enthusiasm for the motorcycle left him stupefied. He needed to snap out of it, and fast. "Yeah. It's nice. I'll take you out some time."

She nodded, glanced at her watch, and gasped. "I gotta go." She bolted for the stairs. "Thanks again."

"Yeah, no problem," he said as she walked away. "No problem at all." Except his plan had backfired. Offer her a ride, get her to school as quick as possible, and get on with his day. No harm, no foul. But she'd turned the tables. He knew how to handle cynical Reagan with her mocking glares and whispered insults, but nice Reagan? Smiling Reagan? Eager-for-another-turn-on-his-motorcycle Reagan? That Reagan could cripple him.

The frat party of the century lived up to its billing. Hours before the first set, kids were everywhere, marking their territory in front of the stage, spilling out of the doorways, and leaning out the windows. How they managed to placate the cops, the adjacent houses, and the neighborhood was a mystery, but the band had strict orders to end the show by one a.m., and Dash was glad for it.

It didn't take long to remember all the ways he hated his old life, and Cee Cee Collins dancing her fingers up his arm and planting a wet kiss on his downturned lips brought everything front and center.

"Well, well, well," she drawled in her sugar-coated southern accent. "Look what the cat dragged in."

"Cee Cee." He gave her the once over, noting her dilated pupils and the way her barely-there dress hung from her body. "You're looking thin."

She smiled and glanced down at her see-through outfit before looking back at him from lowered lashes, no doubt thinking he'd paid her a compliment. It was a look he knew well, a look that signaled she was his for the taking. He'd never pitied her more. "I try. How're things on the dark side?"

"Things are good. Very good. I like the new band, and it feels good to wake up in the morning and know exactly where I am and what I did the night before."

She pursed her lips and started playing with the button on his shirt. "Where's the fun in that?"

He gripped her hands and gave them a gentle squeeze before placing them back by her side. It was like holding a skeleton. "You should try it sometime. I think you'd like it."

"I like you. I always did. Even before you became such a stick-in-the-mud."

"You need to lay off the hard stuff."

Her flirtatious smile dissolved. "And you need to lay off the lectures." When she shoved her hands onto her bony hips, he braced for her temper. "Why are you back, anyway?"

"Just doing a favor for the band." Though he'd moved on from Caliber, he couldn't turn his back on his friends—old friends who'd done nothing wrong but to continue with a way of life that was killing him.

"They miss you, you know. Brae's good, but he's not you. He doesn't seduce the crowd the way you can, and Caliber are suffering because of it. Do you even care?"

"I'm here, aren't I?"

"Yes, and so is everyone on campus. To see you."

"I'm still performing."

She sputtered a laugh. "That's not performing. And it's sure not going to get your face on Rolling Stone."

It was his turn to laugh. Rolling Stone? "Come on, Cee. We were good for a college band, but you're dreaming if you think we were that good. And even if we were, I'd have been too strung out to enjoy it."

"You act like you were a junkie. Like we all are."

"I was headed that way when I quit."

"Oh, my. You really are a bore." She took a sudden interest in her nails, if only to look up at him through her fake lashes. "Is that what dating a respectable girl has gotten you?"

She knew just where to poke. "I'm not dating anyone."

"Really? I didn't see you breeze through campus the other day with that little bookworm on your bike?"

He never considered what others would think of Reagan on his bike, and now he worried about Reagan. Ribbing from her friends was likely to place him back on her list of people to detest. Safer ground, for sure, but not where he wanted to be. "I was giving her a ride to campus."

"Yeah. I bet you were. The ride of her life. I'll bet she's never …" She leaned into him and the smell of her, the metallic scent of gasoline that meant she'd recently done a line of coke, had him holding his breath as she whispered dirty deeds in his ear.

"I wouldn't know." He shook his head to clear the image she'd placed in his head. "It was good to see you, but I gotta get ready."

As if on cue, he spotted Reagan's roommates walking across the lawn. Dark gorgeous Shelby, tall blond Emily, and sweet Kayla who smiled at everyone she passed. They were each beautiful in their own way, but none of them made his heart flare or caused him a second's pause. Now Reagan … just the thought of her lounging in her apartment with her hair in a messy bun had him aching. If she had any idea how she'd tied him in knots, she'd have a long laugh at his expense.

"You get bored with the good girls," Cee Cee called over her shoulder, "you know where to find me."

He knew all right. He knew exactly where he'd been and where he never intended to go again.

Chapter Five

"Reagan?"

Reagan bolted to a stop, fisted her backpack as if a safety net, and turned around as nerves skittered across her skin. Professor Adkins stood in the hallway, his hands tucked into the pockets of his khaki slacks. A wrinkled oxford shirt and neon green undershirt completed his ensemble. No matter how laughably he dressed, and no matter how well she thought her interview had gone, a week had passed and he'd yet to disclose her fate.

"Professor Adkins." She pulled at the hem of her t-shirt, wishing she'd made more of an effort to dress for campus.

"Do you have a minute?" he asked. "I'd like to discuss the research position."

Reagan willed herself to smile as if she hadn't a care in the world. "Of course."

She followed him down the marble hallway and into his office, a crowded and disheveled workspace that sent her OCD into overdrive. Her teeth ached at the sight of his desk, littered with files, a laptop, and yellow legal pads. On the day of her interview, she thought she'd caught him on a bad morning, but the current state of his office proved otherwise.

"Have a seat," he said. "Just toss those files in the chair onto the pile next to the credenza."

Instead of asking which pile, she chose one at random, setting the files from the chair atop the pile least likely to tumble over with the added weight. She sat down, folded her hands in her lap, and tried to calm her breathing.

"Welcome aboard, if you're still interested in joining me."

"Of course I'm still interested." The words tumbled out on a shaky breath. "Thank you so much for the opportunity."

"You might not thank me once you get started and realize what a mess the project is in right now."

She held his gaze, refusing to let her eyes wander to the reams of papers and books on the floor. "Oh, no sir. I'm up for the challenge."

"That's good." He leaned back, and the old wooden desk chair creaked in response. "Reagan, you're more than qualified, and I can tell by the way you cringe when you enter my office that you're dying to get a crack at this place."

"Aah…" Her face flamed.

"It's okay. That's a totally normal reaction to the chaos, but I need you to understand a few things." He leaned forward, took a sip of coffee from a mug decorated with pictures of a boy and a girl aged somewhere between five and ten, and reclined back. "I'm a disorganized person, obviously, but a good bit of the mess feeds my creativity. I simply can't function in an overly tidy space." A small dimple appeared when he smiled that took at least a decade off his mid-thirties face. "There's something about a clutter-free environment that renders me useless. It drives my wife crazy."

"Understood." She gave in and glanced around.

"Having said that, I'm not a complete idiot. I know I'm a few miles past disorganized and heading toward disaster. Chad's great at compiling information for the study—which adds to the clutter—but he's as useless as I am when it comes to getting a handle on the sheer volume of material we've amassed. That's where you come in."

"You need me to organize and consolidate your research, but not in a way that stifles your ability to work."

"Exactly. I just wish I knew how to get you started."

"I have no trouble diving right in."

"I like that about you, Reagan. I think you, me, and Chad are going to make a great team."

Chad. His name was like a blight on her past, an F on her report card, a felony on her rap sheet.

Professor Adkins sat forward and linked his hands on the desk blotter covered with scribbles. "I promise, over winter break, I'll do my best to go through the files and come up with a system so you can hit the ground running when you get back."

"I'm here over the break, Professor Adkins." She scooted to the edge of her seat and gripped the armrests tight to keep from steamrolling around the office. "I've got one more final and them I'm ready to get started."

Professor Adkins sat up straight in his chair and cocked his head to the side. "I didn't realize you live local."

"I don't." Reagan scratched her neck, bewildered by his frown. "But home isn't far, and I'd rather stay in town and get a jump on this."

She couldn't read the expression that settled over his face, a mixture of skepticism and curiosity. She prayed he didn't dig any further into her personal life. "It's not required," he said. "You're free to go home, get some rest, spend some time with your family. I expect a lot of my research assistants but working over break isn't necessary."

"I'd consider it a privilege."

He let out a lengthy breath, his brows arching skyward. "Okay. Then I guess there's something else you need to understand." He leaned back again and linked his hands behind his head, testing the limits of the springs in his chair. "I firmly believe in time off. The body and mind need periods of rest in order to function best, and a physically exhausted, mentally drained research assistant is of no use to me or the project."

She nearly rolled her eyes. As much as she loved school, she'd come to realize that academia was filled with people who couldn't survive in the real world. Although a brilliant mind, Professor Adkins could never hack the grinding pace of a law practice. Reagan could and would, when the time was right. "I'm not tired—physically or mentally—and I thrive on work."

"Look, Reagan, I get it. You're young and eager. But this is my break too. I've made plans with my family. I won't be here every day over break."

"That's fine. I can work from home or, if you're okay with it, come in when the building's open."

"I don't think they leave the buildings open over break." He scratched the back of his neck, and flicked his mop of red hair out of his eyes. "If you're determined to get started over the break, I can let you know when I plan to be at the office. Maybe I can send some files home with you."

"I'd appreciate that, Professor. I'm here, regardless, and I'd like to get started."

The sight of that dimple eased her heart rate. For a second, she thought she'd pushed too hard and scared him away from bringing her on board. "All right. I suppose if you want to work over break I shouldn't quell your enthusiasm. But do me a favor and don't tell Chad. That kid's so eager to please, he'd alter his plans just so I didn't think he was slacking."

Eager to please? Hardly. Chad Ferguson was a total butt kisser. She mimed twisting a key to her lips. "Mum's the word."

"Good." He stood, stuck out his hand. "Congratulations, Reagan, and welcome aboard. I hope you don't regret it."

"Thank you, Professor Adkins. I won't let you down."

Reagan was on cloud nine. Cloud one hundred and nine. Cloud one thousand and nine. Cloud one million and—

She stopped walking through the parking lot, looked up at her apartment, and glanced two doors down. She owed someone a long-overdue thank you. And, if she were being honest with herself, she wanted to share her good news. She climbed the stairs, humming a song from the radio, and gave Dash's door an enthusiastic knock.

Her mind blanked when Dash answered wearing only a pair of sweats dangling from his narrow hips. She stared at him stammering, "I …"

He had the gall to stand casually in his doorway, running his hand through his wet hair and then along his naked chest. "Sorry. I thought you were the delivery guy."

"I …" She cleared her throat and tried not to stare at the water clinging to the hairs of his chiseled chest and glistening in his hair. He'd rendered her stupid. "I'm sorry to bother you."

"It's no bother." He stood back and opened the door, ushering her inside with the wave of his hand. "Come on in and have a seat. I'll be just a sec."

Before she could refuse, he'd disappeared down the hallway. She stood inside his tidy den inhaling the clean smell of soap, fascinated by the small tattoo she'd spotted on his left shoulder. There was no musty wet towel smell or eau du locker room as expected, just the new carpet smell that permeated her own apartment and the subtle hint of lemon. She swallowed, eyed the door, and considered leaving. Thanking Dash for his part in her position didn't seem like such a good idea.

Reagan glanced around the den shaped just like hers. Instead of the L-shaped couch, matching pillows and designer throws in her apartment, Dash had a rust-colored, high-backed couch with the big roll-over arms that could have come straight out the 90s, and a worn leather chair. Two unframed movie posters—*A Few Good Men* and *Rudy*—softened the stark whiteness of the walls. The coffee table had fluted legs and a heavily glossed surface. He'd either raided his parent's basement or gotten a great deal at someone's garage sale.

She'd just started inching toward the door when Dash reappeared, wearing a worn t-shirt with the sweatpants. His feet were bare. Despite his casual attire and the finger tracks through his wet hair, an electrical charge heated the air and made coherent thought and communication impossible.

"Do you want to sit?" he asked when she just stood and stared. "Can I get you a drink?"

"No, thank you. I'm fine." She rubbed the chill from her arms when the air conditioner whooshed through the vents, pebbling her skin. Every few seconds a delicate ding rang from the dishwasher in the adjoining kitchen. She stood, staring at the small white scar dividing his left eyebrow.

"So ..." Her throat was impossibly dry. "I ... I wanted to thank you for the ride last week. I got the research assistant position in large part because I wasn't late."

A smile exploded across his face so quickly, so unexpectedly, her own lips curved in response. He had a truly fantastic smile. "Congratulations. That's awesome. I'm glad I could help."

"You were a lifesaver, on more than one occasion of late, and I'm grateful." She began shuffling her feet as he continued to stare at her with his megawatt smile. "I'd love to return the favor. If you ever need anything—a cup of sugar, a dozen eggs, your laundry done, whatever—please think of me first."

He was shaking his head before she'd gotten halfway through her list. "I think of you often, but there's nothing to repay. I'm happy for you and glad I could help."

Her stomach pitched as his casual comment hit home, just as he'd intended. Why did their conversations always feel like duel? "I'd feel better if you'd let me do something for you. I could clean your apartment." She looked around and realized that was like offering to clean a sterilized surgery center. The guy was compulsively neat. "Or buy you lunch, pay for your gas—"

She jerked her head toward the door at the knock. "Delivery," came a male voice from the other side.

"You're not a maid." Dash reached for his wallet on the end table. "And if I can't keep a one-bedroom apartment clean, then shame on me. Besides, my lunch is already here and there's no need to pay for my gas when the whole trip took five minutes, and I was headed to campus anyway."

"There has to be something." She swiveled around as he moved to open the door.

"Hey, man." Dash pulled a ten from his wallet. "Keep the change."

"Thanks." The delivery guy passed Dash the pizza box, crammed the money in his pocket, and saluted Reagan before making a mad dash for the stairs and the car idling in the parking lot with a screaming metal tune blaring from its speakers.

"How about we spilt the pizza as a thank you?" Dash offered.

Reagan huffed. "You just paid for lunch, so that doesn't qualify as me paying you back."

"Keeping me company would."

She was tempted, more tempted than she ever thought she'd be. She was starving, the pizza smelled divine, and Dash with his wet hair and pleading eyes painted an appealing picture. "I can't. I've got my last final tomorrow and I need every available minute to study."

"You're not eating until after the final?" He tilted his head in challenge.

"Of course I'm eating, but I'll be studying while I eat."

"You can study here." He pointed to his couch, all comfy and inviting, and the books spread across the coffee table. "I live alone, and I've got a final to study for too."

"I'm not hungry." She made a beeline for the door before her stomach rumbled. Saliva pooled in her mouth, and she could practically taste the cheesy dough and ripe tomato sauce emanating from the box. "I'll think of something."

She had the door open and had nearly escaped when he said her name. She turned back, and her stomach clamored for a whole different reason at the sight of him and the hungry look in his eyes.

"I know how you can pay me back," he said. "Come to my next gig."

"Your next gig?" Her hand fell from the doorknob and rested on her hip. "How does that pay you back?"

"I'm a musician. Musicians have fragile egos." He gave an aw-shucks grin. "If I look into the crowd and see you there that's all the payment I need."

It felt like a trap. She'd seen him perform a handful of times and he'd never appeared anything but confidently at ease on stage. "You don't strike me as the fragile type."

"I'm as fragile as the next guy." He set the pizza on the coffee table and faced her. "Your choice, but it would mean a lot to me, and we'd wipe the slate clean."

She narrowed her eyes and gave him a look that never failed to make her roommates squirm. He appeared unfazed. "When's your next gig?"

"Next weekend."

"And that's all you want?"

"Yep. Come watch me play."

"Okay …" Suspicion danced up her spine. "I'll be your number one fan."

Chapter Six

Saturday came and went with no word from Dash. Reagan should have been relieved, but with finals over and the campus nearly deserted, the anticipation of seeing him perform at his request had her blood humming. Even though he wasn't her type on any level—except the basest of levels—Dash's invitation gave her something to look forward to while her roommates were home with their families.

Someone to look forward to.

Despite the improbability of his attraction, Reagan wasn't a fool. A blind woman could sense the weight of his stare. He'd been harder to shake than most, and truth be told, she respected him for it. So instead of spending the holidays alone and lonely, as hour stretched to hour, and day stretched to day, she decided an innocent flirtation with her unconventional neighbor sounded like the perfect way to while away her Christmas blues.

But when he didn't call or let her know any details about his gig, she assumed he'd forgotten and stewed in disappointment. Had it all been a game to feed his ego? Had he enjoyed stringing along the nerdy girl down the hall—the only girl down the hall—while she twisted in the wind?

Figured. Men were pigs.

Instead of dressing in her favorite jeans and sweater (which she'd spent more time than she'd ever admit picking out), putting on makeup (which she rarely wore), and straightening her (sometimes unruly) hair, she spent Saturday night alone in her apartment, brooding and watching reruns on cable.

She woke early Sunday morning and after a quick breakfast and a punishing run through the solitary campus, Reagan showered and dressed in old sweats. Her run had cleared her head and helped her focus on what was important: organizing the three boxes of files she'd picked up from Professor Adkins the day before and getting through the holidays with minimal drama.

The whole reason she didn't go home over breaks was to avoid her mother's questions about Reagan's love life and endless droning of small-town gossip. Yet she'd welcomed a different kind of theatrics into her life by getting her hopes up over Dash. Despite his outward appearance, his smoldering gazes and shameless pursuit made her feel feminine and desired. She was female, after all, and he *was* attractive in a bad boy kind of way. Reagan had never been attracted to bad boys. The contradiction of him had her spinning fantasies that could only lead to disaster. Had she learned nothing from years of watching her mother?

With a shake of her head, she dove into the boxes, pulling out files—some with labels and some without—and organizing them into her own stacks not unlike the ones littering the professor's office floor. But Reagan's stacks wouldn't linger like land mines. They'd be individually labeled and placed inside the waiting accordion files she'd purchased after leaving Professor Adkins.

Knee-deep in paper, she jolted upright by a loud banging on her door. Reagan blew the hair from her eyes, sat up, and reached for her phone. It was two o'clock in the afternoon.

"Reagan?" She recognized that voice.

She got to her feet and padded to the door, squinting into the peephole at the jerk who'd stood her up. She cleared the irritation from her throat. "What do you want?"

"It's time to go."

"Go where?"

"My gig. You said you'd come."

"Your gig?" She wrenched the deadbolt free and yanked open the door. Dash stood at the entrance to her apartment wearing jeans and a t-shirt under his leather jacket, damp hair and his typical teasing smile. "It's Sunday afternoon."

"I know. But you said you'd go with me, and it's time to leave."

The anger she'd vanquished from her mind sparked to a flame at his flippant remark. "I'm not ready now. I was ready last night, but not now!"

He had the sense to appear remorseful, dropping his chin and glancing up at her from lowered lids, causing her stomach to flutter. "Couldn't be helped." He nudged his way inside and closed the door at his back. "Go change and run a brush through your hair so we can hit the road."

She growled at him and shoved at the hair she'd let air dry into a wavy mess. "I wasn't expecting you."

"I know, and you look pretty, but I think you'll be more comfortable wearing something a little less casual."

"I know how to dress for a concert, thank you very much." She shuffled down the hallway, slammed her bedroom door, and stood in the middle of her room fuming. Who was he to barge into her apartment and demand she get dressed, especially after he'd stood her up the night before? And who was she, marching back to her room to change her clothes as ordered when she'd just started to make progress on the files?

Reagan cringed when she looked down at her ratty sweat pants and an old t-shirt. She grabbed her jeans and sweater from the foot of the bed, changed into last night's outfit, brushed her teeth in the bathroom, and combed her hair into a high bun. If she looked upset and not her best, it was only because he'd made her mad and not given her any notice.

She stomped into the den with her hand on her hips, her lips pouted in a sneering frown. "Better?"

"Much better. Ready to go?" He appeared very pleased with himself, swallowing a grin as she grumbled and rammed her arms into a coat. "My, my. Someone's in a good mood." He reached for her hand and gently tugged her out the door.

"Someone was in the middle of something." Reagan used her key to lock the deadbolt and once again found her hand clasped in his. She ignored the tingling in her belly from the feel of his calloused fingertips rubbing against her palm. "Where are we going at this hour?"

"*At this hour* asks the girl I saw running through campus at daybreak."

"That's different."

He tightened his grip as they descended the stairs. "How?"

"I'm a morning person, and I love running before everyone's up. Concerts are usually at night."

"Entertainment happens at all hours of the day." He swung left at the bottom of the staircase and approached the motorcycle. "Your chariot awaits."

Reagan yanked her hand from his. "The motorcycle?"

"I thought you liked it?"

"I do," she said. "But … where's your equipment?"

"At the venue." He lifted an amused brow. "We can take my truck if you're scared."

It should have irritated that he knew her well enough to dare her into submission while not really knowing her at all. She crossed her arms over her chest. "I'm not scared."

"Good." He reached up and tugged on the ponytail holding her bun in place. She raised her hands to stop him, but he was too quick. Her hair tumbled out of the bun, past her shoulders, and bounced against her back. Dash's mischievous gleam disappeared for a second before he shook his head and presented the elastic band in his palm. "The helmet won't fit with all that hair piled on top of your head." His voice sounded lower and more dangerous than before. "And I've always wanted to do that."

He was too charming for his own good, and she was too vulnerable when not fully prepared. She shook the hair from her face and placed the helmet on her head, masking her blush in a scowl. Dash pulled the clasp tight against her chin, mounted the bike, and gave her a mouth-watering glance over his shoulder, goading her to climb aboard.

Abandoning all pretenses, Reagan placed a hand on his shoulder and obliged. She thrilled at the prospect of riding the bike with him again, snuggled close as the world zoomed by at lighting speed. The machine blared to life beneath them, molding them closer, and forced a laugh to bubble free from her chest. She wrapped her arms around his rock-hard abdomen as the cool

December air pelted her face. Despite all logic, she was having the time of her life.

Dash reveled in the feel of Reagan around him, knowing full well it would probably be the last time. He knew he was being tested. The first month of his yearlong dating sabbatical had been hard. Along with the high-speed motorcycle rides, he'd pound out punishing guitar riffs in his room and exhaust himself with grueling workouts in an off-campus gym. And he'd gotten through.

Reagan's sudden willingness to explore their connection was just another level of torment. He'd never felt about another woman the way he felt about her—intrigued, challenged, and turned on by her brain and outrageous curves. The same curves that pressed against his back and made it close to impossible to concentrate on the road.

Unlike her first ride on his bike, it only took moments for her to relax against him. The mid-sixties temperature had been delightful when he knocked on her door but blown into their faces at fifty miles an hour, it was downright crisp. Reagan zipped her jacket before climbing aboard, but he knew she was cold by the way she burrowed against him. At a stoplight, he balanced the bike with his feet and gathered her hands from the front of his jacket. Her fingers were as cold as ice.

"You cold?" he asked.

"A little." Dash unzipped the pockets of his leather bomber and placed her hands inside, wrapping his palms around hers until the light changed. She murmured and shimmied against his back as he goosed the engine.

Knowing the only layers between his bare chest and her hands were thin pocket liners and a t-shirt was nothing short of torture. He'd gone ten months without the touch of a woman, and other than the first agonizing month, he'd coasted through the past nine. Until now.

Enjoy it, he told himself. He memorized the feel of her pressed against him, the smell of her perfume, and the way the ends of her long hair twisted in the wind to tickle his face. He ached to stop the bike, fist his hands in all that chocolate hair, and prove to everyone—himself, Reagan, and the only one who mattered—that despite their differences, they had something worth pursuing. But ten months wasn't a year, and Dash wasn't a quitter. Come hell or high water, he was keeping his word. Even if it killed him.

As expected, she tensed as he made the turn into the parking lot, her hands fisting against his skin. Her body went rigid, and the air at his back where she'd pulled away foreshadowed an icy blast of coming attractions. He eased the motorcycle into a spot by the entrance, set his feet on the ground, and waited for the explosion.

Chapter Seven

Reagan couldn't remember ever being so mad, so deceived, so ambushed. Of all the places he could have taken her to feel belittled and out of her element, he'd made the perfect choice.

"Is this some kind of joke?" She shoved away from him and hurtled off the bike, tugging fruitlessly at the straps on her helmet.

Dash lowered the kickstand and dismounted. After setting his helmet aside, he watched her struggle with the clasp from a deliberate distance.

Temper and impatience surged through her veins, leaving her cold hands clumsy and useless. She huffed out a breath and flung her arms to her sides. "Would you get this off of me, please?"

With a step forward and with one flick of his finger, Dash loosened the clasp. Reagan wrenched the helmet free and her hair rippled against her overheated face. She clutched the helmet against her stomach and stared at him through narrowed eyes. "Why did you bring me to church?"

Dash stood in front of her, his expression guarded. "You agreed to come to my next gig."

Reagan glanced at the building and the surrounding landscape. Despite the bright sun and cloudless sky, chills tangled with the panic bubbling in her gut. The only times she'd gone to church was when her grandmother was alive. Reagan would sit in the backseat of her grandmother's car with wide and worried eyes while her mother fought the outing as if her grandmother were driving them straight to jail. She felt just as helpless now. "You tricked me."

He shrugged, the picture of innocence. "I suppose I could have been clearer." He wrestled the helmet from her grasp and led her toward the entrance. "You're here now, and I've got to get inside and warm up with the band."

She stopped walking and waved her hands in the air. "I can't go in there dressed like this." She looked down at her jeans and boots.

"Yes, you can. This church doesn't care what you look like, only that you're here."

Of course they cared what she looked like. This was church. Church people always cared. And judged.

"Look at how I'm dressed."

"But … but what am I supposed to do while you warm up with the band?"

He pulled the glass door open with one hand and led her inside with the other. The atrium screamed welcome with its floor to ceiling windows, tile floor, and exposed brick walls. It was so different from the blood-red carpet and stained-glass church back home. Even the air smelled clean and fresh, unlike the musty, carpet-worn scent of her grandmother's church. The people mingling around the vestibule wore casual clothing and happy smiles.

"There's a coffee bar in the bookstore." Dash ushered her along. "I'll buy you a cup."

"Caffeine will not help."

Dash stopped, turned to face her, and leaned in close enough to have her heart racing for a different reason. "If nothing else, it'll warm you up. As an aside, shouting in church is generally frowned upon."

"Which is exactly why you brought me here without telling me first." She wrenched her arm free of his grasp. He'd obviously plotted this entire venture knowing full well she'd be stuck.

"I'm sorry for not telling you the truth, but I had a feeling you wouldn't come if I told you."

She folded her arms across her chest. "You were right."

He glanced at the clock above a set of double doors. "I've only got a couple of minutes before the band sends out a search crew." His eyes, so alluring with their sunflower center, pleaded for mercy. "Let me buy you a cup of coffee and show you around."

Reagan huffed like a spoiled child and hoped her annoyance masked her alarm. She hated not being in control, and it was impossible to stay in control in an environment she'd never understood. "I don't have much choice."

She begrudgingly followed him into a coffee bar nestled into a corner of a sprawling bookstore with titles like, *God Is Life*, *Give Your Marriage to God*, and *How to Lead a Christian Life in a Heathen World* displayed on distressed bookshelves. Despite always feeling comfortable in a library or bookstore, Reagan's skin pebbled and her nerves frayed. She jolted when Dash touched her arm and asked what she wanted.

"Regular coffee." Reagan scowled at the pile of books stacked on the counter and the title facing out on top, *God's Healing Grace*. Where had her grandmother's God been while her mother worked three jobs and hooked herself to any man willing to warm her bed at night?

She accepted the cup he offered and followed him to the nearby bar where she watched him dump two tablespoons of sugar into his coffee. "Got a sweet tooth?"

"Goes down better sweet." The corner of his mouth jerked into a cocky grin, the same cocky grin that landed her right where she stood—the last place she ever wanted to be. "Most things do."

How could he feel so at ease in a place that made her feel like a degenerate? And how had he expected her to react when dragged to church against her will? Grateful? "Isn't flirting in church considered a sin?"

"The Bible's pretty clear on relationships between a man and a woman." He eyed her over the lip of his cup. "Talking falls under basic communication."

Reagan snorted as she added a packet of sugar and a splash of cream to her coffee, hoping the task would calm her nerves. "Then you'd better turn the wattage down on all that charm. What does the Bible say about kidnapping?"

His grin was quick and lethal. "Spreading the gospel is encouraged."

She rolled her eyes and forced herself to look away. All that smug confidence she'd attributed to his rock-star persona and the adoration of his legions of adoring female fans was really a cover for his holier-than-though censure of her lifestyle. She'd be darned if she'd let him use his good looks and charm to distract her from his web of lies.

Dash affixed a lid to her cup and led her back through the bookstore and out into the wide corridor, pointing to a row of double doors. "Inside's the main chapel. Two stories." He clasped her hand in his, tugged her along the hallway and motioned with his cup to a colorful wall outfitted with palm trees, a bright sun, and people milling about wearing matching t-shirts. "That's the tiny tots spot." He led her further into the church, raised his cup to another entrance with a checkerboard pattern. "That's for the older kids. The pre-teens are straight ahead, and teenagers are around the corner."

The grouping appealed to her sense of organization, plus she imagined the bold colors and friendly characters eased kids' apprehension at being left by their parents. He steered her in the opposite direction of the kids' areas toward a side hallway, but they were stopped by a couple of teenaged boys.

"Dash!" One of the boys called out and lifted his fist in greeting.

"Hey, Noah. Josh." Dash bumped their fists in turn, managing to do so without spilling his coffee. "You guys are early."

"My dad had a meeting," Noah said, "and Josh spent the night last night."

They both eyed Reagan as if she were an alien or a blow-up doll, their gazes zooming in to where Dash held her hand in his.

"This is my friend, Reagan," Dash said. "These knuckleheads are in my Axis group."

She stared at him, puzzled.

"It's the middle school ministry. We meet after church most Sundays and at least once during the week."

Of course they did. He sang in the church band and mentored youth. How very noble of him.

The best she could muster was a close-mouthed smile for fear her thoughts would tumble out of her mouth unbidden.

"We'll see you guys later." Dash tugged on her arm.

He stopped next to an unmarked set of double doors and turned to face her.

"Do you remember how to get back to the main chapel?" he asked.

A spark of panic zipped along her spine. "Wait … you're leaving me?"

He jerked his thumb at the door to his back. "I have to get inside and warm up with the band."

"I'll go with you." Even Reagan heard the alarm in her voice. The idea of him leaving her—alone—brought back the time her mother dropped her at a "co-worker's" house for the weekend. Despite her tears and begging, seven-year-old Reagan spent three days on a fold-out couch with a chain-smoking stranger who fed her nothing but cereal.

He loosened her fingers where they'd clung to his jacket, rubbing her hand and speaking in a hushed tone as if calming a spooked animal. "It'll be chaos in there, especially since I'm late. I won't have time to get you back inside the chapel and you may not find a seat."

"That's okay. I'll watch from backstage."

He shook his head. "Not allowed."

"What am I supposed to do?"

"Go back to the chapel hallway and drink your coffee. Talk to people. Play on your phone. Whatever. The service starts in less than an hour."

An hour? She had to entertain herself—in church, of all places—for nearly an hour? "Dash—"

"I'm going to be onstage, backstage, and then onstage again at the end." He opened the door to his back. "You'll be fine, I promise. Wait for me in the atrium after." He chucked her chin with his knuckle. "Try to enjoy it." He scooted inside and left her standing in the hallway gripping her coffee and seized by fear.

Before the door eased shut in her face, she spied all the things that would appeal to someone like Dash. Guitars lined an entire wall—acoustic and electric—along with drum kits of varying dimensions, single and double decker keyboards, and a ragtag assortment of musicians in skinny jeans and flannel shirts—the kind of people who made Reagan feel stiff and conservative. Dash was greeted by smiles and knuckle bumps while she stood outside and the air drained from her lungs.

Panic coated her throat and her hands tingled at the idea of sauntering into church as if it was normal, grabbing a seat up front so everyone could see how uncomfortable she was, and making small talk with total strangers. Not. But smart man that he was, Dash left her fuming and joined his band—the same guys who witnessed her puking in his bathroom weeks ago. Fantastic.

Oh no. She was alone in church, it wasn't Easter or Christmas, and her mother wasn't nearby, plotting their escape. She stared at the closed door and took one, two, three shallow breaths before turning around and putting one foot in front of the other. As she glanced around at the friendly people and cozy setting, she realized she'd have preferred Dash take her to some smoky dive bar than a building full of martyrs.

Walking back through the halls, she nodded to an anxious teenager with braces and a goofy grin and refused to consider what that said about her. All she had to do was find a seat in the chapel and sit through a boring church service for an hour, ride home on the motorcycle, and walk away from Dash for good.

It was easier to focus on her anger and let it mix into a raging brew than to let the anxiety take over. How dare he judge her! When had he concocted this ridiculous outing? When he discovered her creeping home after a night out? When she'd thrown up in his apartment from drinking too much alcohol? What a hypocrite! She'd seen him sipping drinks between sets at local bars. She even remembered a time her freshman year when Dash seemed baked and could barely remember the lyrics to his songs.

The chapel doors remained shut and she wasn't about to be the one to open them, so she made her way back to the bookstore and pretended to peruse the shelves. Bible studies lined one wall, some based on books of the Bible, some on stages of life—teenagers, young adults, singles. Married life took up a large section, as if marriage and parenting required an extra dose of God. When she thought about it, it probably did for those who believed. People of all ages milled about the space, talking with others about their weekend, their kids, their jobs. It would have appeared normal if they hadn't been standing in a house of worship.

Reagan rubbed at the pain in her chest and found yet another reason to blame her mother. If she'd been brought to church like the young families who stood around her, she'd have known what was in the Bible, she'd have understood the references she'd heard growing up about David and Goliath, Adam and Eve, and Noah's Ark. She remembered the snickers and whispers behind her back at school when she'd asked a classmate about communion. There were countless other stories and countless other times when she felt like the only person on earth who didn't have a clue about religion.

Reagan wasn't sure what her feelings were about God. She liked the idea of someone looking out for her, but the likelihood seemed improbable. She glanced around at the people sharing her space. They appeared normal and yet somehow, they believed. She didn't know what to think. She'd been tempted to read the Bible on her own, but as much as she liked to study, the Bible and its wafer-thin pages had always appeared too daunting.

When the chapel doors opened, Reagan waded into the crowd to find a seat in the back. In keeping with everything she'd seen thus far, the chapel was unlike any church space she'd ever encountered. Rows of auditorium seats replaced wooden pews. No lectern sat waiting for the preacher. Instead, the front held a darkened stage complete with rigging and theater lights. Was she waiting to watch a concert or a religious service?

Even though Dash had manipulated her into attending this alternate universe he called church, she resolved to sit through the service immune. She could sit through one hour and not burst into flames—she'd done it before. But she didn't have to talk to anyone and she sure didn't have to like it.

Chapter Eight

"Dude," Dash fist-bumped his keyboard player while eyeing his bandmate's newly spiked hair. "New cut?"

Jacob beamed before returning his fingers to the keyboard. "You like?"

"I do, and you'll save some wear and tear on your neck not having to flip hair out of your eyes."

"I know." Jacob flashed a wicked grin. "I keep doing it out of habit." He winked and then played the opening bars of what Dash recognized as a popular love song while wiggling his eyebrows. "Was that your hot neighbor I spied?"

Dash nodded and turned to grab an acoustic guitar from the wall.

"Sabbatical's over?" Jacob prodded.

"Still on." Dash tested the strings and tried to focus on the music and not the girl he'd stranded in the hallway. "Since this will probably be the last time she speaks to me, there's no conflict."

Both guys glanced at Seth when he pounded on his drums. "Are we going to do a run-through or talk about Dash's love life?"

Grateful for the distraction, Dash performed a quick sound check, and the band talked through the service's playlist. When Seth tapped off a count for the first song, the guys took their places and Dash approached the mic, playing his guitar by rote.

The opening song with its cheerful lyrics was one of his favorites, and a tune he'd performed many times. Thankfully. His concentration was shot. He couldn't get the horrified expression on Reagan's face out of his head. She seemed more than annoyed he'd misled her, more than angry he'd disrupted her day—she'd looked afraid. No matter how well intentioned his motives had been in tricking her into coming to church, he'd never meant to scare her or cause that panicked look in her eyes. He'd miscalculated. He wouldn't put it past her to bolt, and after witnessing her reaction, he wouldn't blame her.

Following the run through and some pacing adjustments, the band made their way to the auditorium's backstage area, Dash and Eli carrying their tuned guitars. "What'd you do to make the hot neighbor mad?" Eli asked.

"Her name is Reagan, and she didn't know I was bringing her to church."

"Where did she think you were bringing her on a Sunday afternoon?"

The guys shook hands with the minister as he passed and continued crisscrossing their way to the stage. "I asked her to come to my next gig, and she wasn't thrilled when I pulled up to the building."

"Why didn't you just tell her?" Jacob asked.

"I should have." He'd followed his gut instead of thinking out a plan. "I figured she wouldn't have come."

Seth twirled his drumsticks through his fingers. "Is she an atheist?"

Dash took a calming breath and loosened his grip on the neck of the guitar before he snapped it in two. His friends weren't being nosey or trying to upset him with their questions. They understood how isolated some Christian students felt among the socially liberal college population, as well as the judgment some faced when discussing their faith. "I have no idea, but I should have asked her to come instead of pulling a bait and switch."

"What now?" Jacob asked. "Wow her with your musical chops and ask her to dinner?"

Dash shook his head, firming his resolve. "I've got two months before I can date again, I seriously doubt she'd go out with me. Not after this."

Seth mimicked tapping his sticks against Dash's temple. "So why'd you bring her?"

"I like her, and I'm definitely attracted." The band stopped just beyond the curtain to wait for the lights to dim. From the sound of the chatter, the auditorium was getting full. "Maybe I wanted to test myself."

"Or maybe you wanted to test her," Eli said.

"What do you mean?" Dash loved the honest back-and-forth between his bandmates almost as much as he loved making music with them.

Eli shrugged. "You seem happy where you are in your life right now and, as far as I can tell, you're doing fine with the sabbatical." He adjusted the guitar strap around his neck and continued. "I think you can see the end, and at the end … you see her. I think you've always seen her."

Dash hoped the shadowed backstage lighting hid the heat that coursed along his neck. He never realized how transparent he'd been in his crush on his neighbor.

"She's the one, right?" Eli asked. "The one you changed for, or however the book said."

"Become the one the one you want to date wants to date." Dash echoed the catchphrase from the book that inspired his sabbatical.

Eli smirked. "I'll take that to mean I'm correct."

"Yeah, she's the one." Dash rubbed his neck. "But I changed for me. She's just the one I'd like to date once I'm free."

"Don't feel embarrassed, dude. We've all been there. And knowing who she is doesn't change anything. We all know what she thought about your old lifestyle, and it makes sense that you'd want her to know you've changed and find out what she thinks about the new you."

Jacob pointed at Dash. "So, this is about dating her?"

"Kind of, I guess. But I also felt God pushing me to get her here—don't look at me like that," he said to Jacob. "I know how that sounds after admitting I'm interested in her, but she seems … I don't know. A little lost and lonely. She's not from here and yet here she is, still in town when every other student has gone home to spend the holidays with their family."

"Except us," Eli whispered as the auditorium went dark, their cue to take the stage. He slapped Dash on the shoulder. "Let's show her some wow."

Reagan fidgeted in her seat as the congregation advanced inside the chapel. She'd tried to claim an aisle seat but was politely asked to move to an interior seat to make room for others, choking off her plans for a quick getaway. Anyone glancing at her would assume she sat enthralled by the church flyer she'd all but crumpled in her sweaty palms, not steadfastly refusing to make eye contact with the people who pressed closer. Or so she hoped.

She eased out of her jacket as the flush of embarrassment heated her skin to unbearable levels and risked a peek at the darkened stage complete with keyboards and drums in the back, microphones and amps in the front. It appeared as if all that was lacking were the musicians themselves. Her heart rate stuttered when the lights dimmed and a video played on the large screens on either side of the stage.

Reagan took great pains to relax, breathing in and out the air that smelled as clean and fresh as a roomful of newly showered people spritzed with high-class fragrance. No one would know how humiliated and out of place she felt among the hundreds of churchgoers in the auditorium as long as she acted normal and didn't give into the urge to run screaming from the building.

The video's Christmas themed music and dancing letters spelled out H-A-P-P-Y H-O-L-I-D-A-Y-S while cartoon characters straight from a Norman Rockwell painting fluttered around a traditional living room. Reagan crossed her arms against her chest and prepared for boredom to set in. An illustrated video of the perfect family Christmas was an unexpected development.

The animated newlyweds woke early on Christmas morning and exchanged gifts—a first edition book for him, and a gold bracelet for her. The scene moved to the window where the morning sun shone brightly off the freshly fallen snow. The story time lapsed to later that day as the happy couple prepared food in the kitchen. The oven dinged, and fearless wife opened the oven door for the happy husband to place the stuffed turkey inside to cook. Much to their horror, the picture-perfect turkey was too big for the oven.

Fearless wife adjusted the racks, and happy husband tried again, but with no luck. No matter how they tried, the turkey wouldn't fit in the oven. With panicked glances at the clock on the wall, both fearful wife and unhappy husband realized their first Christmas dinner wouldn't be as picture-perfect as they'd planned. The music faded as the first of the happy couple's guests pulled up the driveway. The letters H-A-P-P-Y H-O-L-I-D-A-Y-S danced on the screen as the words "Not so" crashed into the word "Happy," and all the letters toppled like dominoes.

Reagan admired the clever introduction to the not-so happy holidays. She could relate to Christmas disaster, but her cartoon version would feature an inebriated mother, a loser boyfriend, and a bucket of fried chicken left over from the day before. Her musing through Christmases past halted with the first beat of drums, the strum of a guitar, and the blast of Dash's voice singing a soulful version of *Holly, Jolly Christmas*. She hadn't seen them enter and realized the band must have taken the stage during the video.

The man had a gift. That was all Reagan could think as the lights danced around the stage and Dash's bandmates joined in the fun. The drums thumped through her chest, the bass swam through her blood, and at the center of it all stood her neighbor—dazzling, commanding, and completely off-limits.

The crowd sprung to their feet and Reagan followed so as not to stand out, gripping the seat in front of her instead of clapping her hands or waiving her arms in the air like so many sitting around her. She didn't have room in her brain to feel self-conscious. All she saw, all she heard, was Dash.

That voice, like honey over gravel, took an innocent Christmas carol and turned it into a personal chant, a willful pleading. Be jolly and all your dreams will come true. Be jolly and find peace. Be jolly and have faith. He made it sound as easy as believing in Santa Claus. If she'd spent the last few minutes stewing in her seat wondering how a hardened rocker could possibly humble himself in front of this lily-white crowd, she questioned no more. His appeal, that innate charm he wielded like a weapon, was on full display. Grandmothers, skin-headed gym rats, and twelve-year-old boys were equally entranced.

And, darn it, so was she.

Chapter Nine

Reagan watched Dash and his band bring the service to a close with a final song. The *Wonderful Christmastime* cover served as a balm to the thought-provoking sermon that had, despite her best efforts, pierced Reagan's resolve. She'd never heard anything even remotely similar to the minister's message about the true meaning of Christmas.

She'd tried her best not to listen to the thirty-something man dressed in jeans who took the stage after Dash and his band had treated them to a number of festive Christmas songs. The minister wore tennis shoes, closely cropped hair, and could have been any number of people she'd passed in the hallway on her way inside the chapel. Between the wireless headpiece and his conversational tone, he managed to make Reagan forget she sat in church. Preacher Stan talked about the birth of the Savior and delivered a powerful message about how we can chase perfection but never measure up that Reagan knew resonated with everyone. Not once did he call his audience sinners or make anyone in attendance feel anything but normal for trying to create a "perfect" holiday when Christ's birth was anything but.

Reagan scowled at Dash, again crooning to his captive audience. Not only had he kidnapped her and brought her to church against her will, but he'd manipulated her into paying attention and had in turn piqued her curiosity about God in the process. The scoundrel! She wouldn't give him the satisfaction of knowing the sermon had affected her. No. She'd act as mad as if she'd sat listening to the preacher cast judgement, and hopefully leave Dash hopefully feeling guilty for his machinations. If he was even capable of feeling guilt.

The audience applauded at the end of the song and the lights intensified, illuminating the chapel. Every seat was taken, both top and bottom levels, and carefree smiles adorned everyone's faces. Well, not hers. She would show her nosy neighbor just what she thought of him dictating her life.

The woman beside her smiled warmly and wished her a blessed day before turning to exit their row. When she reached the end of the line, an older man stopped in the aisle to let her out despite his wife clamoring that she had to use the restroom. Reagan clenched her teeth. It would be a lot easier to maintain her anger if people would stop being so nice.

They exited the chapel like a herd of cattle, narrowing to walk two by two through the double doors. She looked around the filling atrium where Dash had instructed her to wait. The space was huge, and every available spot along the wall was occupied by clusters of people content to dissect the pastor's message and deliberate its truth. After a meandering search, she found a gap, leaned against the wall in a casual pose she hoped rendered her invisible, and pulled out her phone.

As she scrolled through emails, she couldn't help but watch those around her. They seemed normal, if not abnormal, in their serenity. She felt a perverse sense of kinship with the only person she spotted who wasn't blinding her with joy—a sullen teenage boy who appeared to be in trouble with his parents if the look on their faces were any indication. *Good for you. Let's you and I bring and little bit of reality into this Disney World creation.*

Reagan's little game of people watching grew boring as the crowd thinned and the likelihood of her truly being invisible lessened. Where was Dash? Signing autographs and plugging numbers into his phone? No sooner had the thought materialized than the man himself strutted around the corner, band in tow, as if every step were taken on an endless unfurling red carpet. His expression changed when he spotted her in her hiding spot against the wall—a subtle hardening of his jaw, a tightening around his eyes. She straightened, crossed her arms over her chest, and purposefully kept her expression bland.

It took every ounce of will not to roll her eyes as he waved at and shook hands with those who lingered in the hallway as if he were Jesus Christ himself. *Move along and let the man pass. He's just a man with a gift for music, like a judicious accountant or a crafty lawyer. Nothing to get so worked up over.*

And then he drilled her with his gaze and that little voice inside her head went eerily quiet.

"Reagan." Dash jerked his head at the band. "You remember Seth, Jacob, and Eli."

Reagan smiled without teeth and held her hand out to shake each man's in turn. Seth nodded, his long hair tucked neatly behind his ears in sharp juxtaposition of the way he'd thrashed his head while pounding on the drums during their performance. Jacob was much taller than he appeared onstage huddling over his keyboard. And Eli, with the crooked teeth and winning smile, shook her hand between both of hers. "It's a pleasure to see you again, Reagan."

"Y'all were great," Reagan said. She could admit the truth to the band if not to Dash. "I've never heard Christmas music performed that way before."

Eli's grin grew. "We try to put our own spin on every song we perform—original or not."

"I'd say you spun tired Christmas music into magic."

Each band member—Seth, Eli, and Jacob—gave her a small nod of approval before slapping Dash on the back or arm and easing toward the exit, forcing Reagan to look at Dash for the first time since he'd approached.

Dash rocked back on his heels. "Did you enjoy the service?"

Reagan shifted her weight and crossed her arms. She wouldn't give him the satisfaction of knowing the truth now that they were alone. "It was different from anything I've ever seen."

"Is that good or bad?"

"It's different."

He studied her with an inscrutable expression that left her wondering if he was judging her. Either way, she found him maddening. She lifted her brows and pasted on a fake smile. "You ready to go?"

"Dash!"

Dash turned to see who'd called his name. Reagan peeked over his shoulder and bit back a groan as her worlds collided. With red hair gelled into submission and a cute blond at his side, Professor Adkins approached Dash with his hand outstretched and his dimples on full display.

"Mark," Dash said.

Reagan blinked as Dash shook the professor's hand. When he turned to the cute blond beside Professor Adkins and gave her a full-on I-know-you-well embrace, the coffee in Reagan's belly turned to acid.

This. Couldn't. Be. Happening.

As Dash introduced Reagan, Professor Adkins face registered surprise. "Reagan, I'm glad to see you aren't buried under all that paperwork I gave you yesterday."

Reagan gave her best self-depreciating smile while sneaking a glance at Dash. His startled look seemed more contemplative. "I'm happy to help." Truth be told, she'd do almost anything to be back in her apartment buried under all that paperwork instead of standing in a church atrium.

"Connie," Professor Adkins tucked his arm around the waist of the blond, "This is my new RA, Reagan Bellamy." Professor Adkins lifted his brows at Dash. "How do you two know each other?"

"Reagan and I are neighbors." Dash pinged the good professor with a pointed look that made it seem as if an entire conversation was going on between the two of them with just their eyes. Interesting.

"And the two of you?" Reagan asked. "How do you know one another?"

Dash rubbed the back of his neck. "Mark's my small group leader."

"Small group leader?" Reagan asked. He may as well have said Mark was his circus trainer.

"A big part of the church's mission is to get people connected in small groups outside of church." Connie faced Reagan, blinding her with a snow-white smile. "Mark leads a group of young men at our house on Tuesday nights."

"And Connie leads a group of young women on Thursdays." Mark beamed at his wife.

How very Christian of them, and how very out of Reagan's comfort zone. This conversation couldn't end fast enough. "How lovely."

"You should join us, Reagan. It's a great group, although some are out of town for the holidays."

"I …" Reagan nearly swallowed her tongue as her thoughts whirled. Professor Adkins knew she was staying in town, and he also knew that she'd quit her part-time job at the grocery store when given the opportunity to be his RA. Her only option seemed to be the truth. "I'm not really a churchgoer, so I doubt I'd have much to offer."

Connie's smile grew. Reagan spied Connie's white chicklet teeth and knew there'd be no escape. "Small group is a place of learning and sharing. Regular church attendance isn't a requirement, I promise." As if to show her sincerity, she crossed her hands over her heart.

Reagan flashed Dash a look of appeal, but he stood watching her the way a mother eyes a toddler on the brink of a tantrum. He obviously wasn't going to be her knight in shining armor and get her out of this mess. Perfect. She was going to kill him.

"I … I don't know."

"Why don't you come this week—Dash can give you our address—and give it a try. If you don't like it, you don't have to come back."

"Connie makes the best cookies for small group." Professor Adkins must love sweets if he thought cookies were reason enough for Reagan to attend. She'd rather peel her skin off than sit around their living room with a bunch of goody-two-shoes.

"Um …" She looked again at Dash, then Professor Adkins, and finally to Connie with her hopeful smile and pleading eyes. Had Reagan thought her cute? Cute as a fox. "Okay. I … guess I can give it a try."

Connie's mile-wide smile grew positively feral as she leaned in to give Reagan a hug, marking the entire conversation the weirdest and most uncomfortable of her lifetime. "Great. I'll see you Thursday."

"Thursday." Reagan mumbled under her breath as the happy couple wandered off toward the kids' area. As soon as their backs were turned, Reagan spun on Dash and zapped him with her most lethal stare. "You set me up."

His hands sprung toward the ceiling as if being held at gunpoint. "I had no idea you were working for Mark."

"I'm talking about the way you stood there and watched me walk right into that trap."

"What trap? You could have said no."

"Oh, please. How am I supposed to turn down an invitation from Little Miss Sunshine when I just started working for Professor Adkins? I need him to like me."

Dash had the nerve to chuckle. "He would like you even if you didn't attend the Bible study."

Reagan's throat shriveled as the saliva in her mouth disappeared. "Bible study? She called it a group. You called it a group."

"It's a group of people who study the Bible."

Panic, razor sharp and bristling, seared her spine and frazzled her brain. "I told her I didn't go to church." Her breath hitched. "I told her."

"Reagan, relax." Dash touched her shoulder but quickly removed his hand at her withering stare. "It's just Connie and a couple of ladies. They'll feed you some cookies, give you some milk, and make you feel as if you belong. Trust me, you'll survive. And you might even like it."

Reagan pointed an accusing finger at his smug face. "This is your fault. I would never have been in this position if you hadn't tricked me into coming to church." She looked up, blew out a breath, and closed her eyes. "Bible study? What's next? A séance? Tarot reading? Exorcism?"

Dash nudged her toward the entrance with a gentle tug on her arm. "I think you're confusing Christianity with spiritualism and possibly devil worship. Trust me, they're different."

"How would I know." She grumbled and followed him outside. The cold air did nothing to cool her shame or her fury. She couldn't believe what a total nightmare her day had become. And it was just the beginning.

Chapter Ten

Dash sucked in breath of crisp evening air and relished the burn. His hamstrings screamed as he barreled his way along the sloping path, his thoughts as scattered as the grit beneath his running shoes. His attention refused to focus on anything except the punishing run he'd begun over an hour ago. He'd pay tomorrow, but for now all he could do was purge.

Reagan hadn't spoken to him after they left church. She'd simply put the helmet on her head, mounted the bike, and sat rigidly behind him on the ride home. He would have forgotten she was onboard if it wasn't for her hair tickling his face every so often. Once home, she countered his apology by slamming the door in his face. Dash couldn't muster the energy to blame her.

He'd done exactly as she'd accused—manipulated her into attending church—and put her in an awkward position with

Mark. As he rounded the turn back toward campus, he conceded a brutal run wouldn't solve his problem any better than his earlier meeting with the Axis group. The boys, their antics and their questions about Reagan only magnified his worry. The storm of recriminations he'd hoped his trek would clear continued to drench his brain and left him even more confused. How would he face her? How could he apologize?

After stretching, chugging two bottles of water, and showering, he knew it was time to call an expert.

"Mom," Dash said. "I messed up."

On a quick intake of breath, she asked, "Are you in jail?"

"No, no. I'm sorry. I'm fine. I'm not in jail. Everything is fine."

"You said you messed up."

Silly of him to assume his mother wouldn't jump to the conclusion that he'd done something predictably stupid. His track record was enough to justify her reaction. "It's about a girl." After a short pause, he yanked the phone away from his ear.

"William Daniel Carter! Don't you ever start a conversation with those words unless you are incarcerated or in the hospital. Are we clear?"

"Yes, Ma'am." Dash was batting 0 for 2 today with the ladies.

"Now, let me sit down and calm my heart rate before you tell me how you messed up with a girl. And might I remind you that you gave up that particular sex not so long ago."

"No reminder necessary."

"But?"

"This one is different."

His guilt lessened when he heard her soft chuckle.

"That's what they all say." The volume of the nightly news decreased to a murmur and he waited patiently as she shooed the dog off the couch. "Tell me no one's pregnant."

"Mom!"

"What do you expect me to ask when you start a conversation with 'I messed up'?"

"Touché." He really needed to work on his opening lines. "No one is pregnant. I'm not in jail or in the hospital."

"Good. What's going on?"

Dash relaxed at the thoughtful tone of her voice. She would ease his worry and tell him exactly what he needed to do to make things right.

"This girl—a neighbor—is in town over the holidays. I kind of tricked her into going church with me where she got roped into attending a small group and now she's upset with me."

"Whoa, whoa, whoa. Can we backup a few steps and start from the beginning? Does this girl have a name?"

"Her name is Reagan. Reagan Bellamy."

"And who is Reagan Bellamy to you exactly?"

"I told you. She's my neighbor."

"Dash ..." Her tone advised him to slow down. "Tell me about Reagan."

He blew out a breath and ran a hand over his face. He'd gone to her for a reason and he needed to be honest. "She's a student at ASU. She's a junior."

"Go on."

"She's smart and driven and beautiful."

"I see."

"No, you don't see. But I can tell you. She lives in the apartment down from mine with three gorgeous roommates—and Mom, when I say gorgeous, I mean drop-dead gorgeous. There's a tall regal blond, a short pixie blond, and this Italian stunner who might be the most attractive girl I've ever seen in person."

"Sounds like you got lucky with the neighbors," she said. "But that can't be good for your dating sabbatical."

"The only temptation is Reagan."

"Reagan's the Italian, I presume?"

"No, the blonds and the Italian are her roommates. Reagan's the all-American girl next door." The weight on Dash's shoulders lifted by telling his mom about Reagan. She'd been his secret crush for so long and the reason behind many of his decisions. Admitting his feelings for her—or about her—eased his mind. "She has the cutest southern accent she does her best to hide."

"So why did you trick the all-American Reagan into going to church?"

He wouldn't have to explain to his mom. She knew better than anyone how he'd been before he changed his life for the better. "She never liked me, from before."

"She's got some sense in her head, then?"

Dash snorted. "She had me pegged, that's for sure. But I've changed, and I guess I wanted her to know."

"Why didn't you just tell her?"

The million-dollar question. "I don't know. She was so sure I was a loser that I knew she wouldn't believe me unless she saw with her own eyes."

"And?"

"And it was the absolute wrong approach. She was mad and then …"

"Then what?"

"She's not religious and she's terrified of going to small group."

"I'm sorry to keep backing you up, but logistically, how did you get her into a small group so quickly?"

Dash explained in detail, and his mom listened, only interrupting to ask questions when he wasn't clear. By the end of the story, his path forward seemed as murky as ever.

"Well, honey, you certainly painted her into a corner."

"I didn't mean to."

"Your intentions don't matter to her right now. Poor thing is probably panicked."

Dash cringed as the knife dug deeper. "You're not making me feel any better. What should I do?"

His mom sighed once and clicked her tongue. "I suppose the best you can do is help her prepare."

"Prepare how? I already told her Connie's harmless."

"It's not Connie she's worried about, honey. It's the Bible and all the stuff she doesn't know. For someone as academic as you've described, walking into that small group without knowing the Bible is like walking into an exam without studying."

"Okay." Dash stood up to pace. "I get that, but how do I help her get ready? Should I get her a study Bible?"

"You could, and all she'd have to do is speed read over a thousand pages in a couple of days."

Dash groaned and sank back onto the couch.

"I do have a suggestion," his mom said.

"Spill it. I'm floundering here."

"Do you remember those thumbprint cookies we used to make when you were little? The peanut ones with the raspberry jam?"

"Yes, of course I do, but what does that have to do with helping Reagan?"

"When you kids wanted to help me in the kitchen, I taught y'all to make those cookies because there were only a few ingredients."

"Meaning?"

"Meaning you don't start with soufflé when you learn how to bake."

His patience threatened to snap. He needed a plan, not a recipe. "Mom, please speak English. I'm too tired for riddles."

"Dumb it down for her, sweetie. Start with the basics."

"How do I dumb down the Bible for a smart educated woman?"

"Jesus asks us to come to him with a childlike faith."

"But she's not a child, and as far as I can tell, she has no faith at all."

"If she doesn't know the Bible or anything about religion, she's as childlike as a kid on her first day of Sunday school."

Dash tried to rub the worry from his mind by smoothing out the lines on his forehead. His mom's tone conveyed enough conviction to make him want to believe it could be that simple, but he wasn't convinced she was right. But what choice did he have?

"Will you do me a favor please?" he asked after a moment of contemplation.

"What is it?"

"Make me some of those peanut butter and jelly cookies. I could use a little childlike faith myself."

Chapter Eleven

"What do you want?" Reagan asked. The last person she wanted to find on her doorstep was Dash Carter. He had the nerve to grin, as if finding her irritated and disheveled on a cold Monday morning was something to smile about.

"I come bearing gifts."

"Go away." She didn't want him standing before her looking well-rested and smug while she'd spent the entire night tossing and turning in bed. How dare he pretend to be a perfectly harmless student in jeans and a hoodie. Reagan knew better. She knew hiding beneath that sweatshirt was a heartless hypocrite.

When she tried to close the door in his face, he anticipated her moves and stepped inside the threshold, blocking the entry with his foot. "Reagan, please. I've come to help."

"Help? You want to help me after everything you did yesterday? I don't think I can survive any more of your help."

Dash stood his ground, one hand on the door, the other gripping a couple of books at his waist.

Reagan sneered at him without blinking, willing him to wither under her stare and slink back to his apartment. He was responsible for her sleepless night—and not in a good way—and certainly not in the way he had before their Sunday outing to church. He was the one who upended her life in one afternoon. Disaster ensued every time she opened the door to him, and she'd be darned if she'd let it happen again.

The devil that he was, he held tight to the door, determination apparent in the steely set of his jaw and the sparks emanating from his green-blue eyes. Weren't musicians supposed to be weak and scrawny? Dash's athletic build made him too strong to physically push away from the door and out of her life.

"Ugh!" His rigid stance, dogged expression, and her inability to shoo him away set Reagan's simmering ire to flame, catapulting her into motion. She spun around and strode through the den, sending the neat stacks of research she'd spent most of the morning arranging airborne. She knew she'd destroyed hours of careful work, but she couldn't stop herself from prowling around the room like a caged lion. Her nerves were shot, and she was spoiling for a fight. If he thought himself so able to help, she'd do her part to set him straight. "What is it with you?"

Dash stepped through the door, closed it behind him, and stood near the entrance—blocking her escape or ensuring his? She couldn't be sure. Once inside, he didn't seem as confident about his decision to enter. He hugged the books to his chest and stared at her with wary eyes.

Good. Let him feel a fraction of the anxiety and stress she'd experienced for the past eighteen hours and see how he liked it.

Dash cleared his throat. "First, let me apologize again for yesterday. I'm sorry I took you to church without asking, and I'm sorry you now feel obligated to attend Connie's small group."

Reagan's mouth dropped open. "Seriously? You think I feel *obligated* to attend? There's the understatement of the year." She was beating a dead horse, as he'd made clear he thought she could have said no to her professor's wife. As if.

"Be that as it may, I'm sorry for my part."

"You mean your part as puppet master?" Reagan tapped a finger to her lips, "Or, speaking in Biblical terms, God?"

When Dash grit his teeth, Reagan's insides warmed. She was more than pleased to witness Mr. Cool, Calm, and Pious fight his temper. A few more well-placed jabs and she'd get the screaming match she was angling for.

"Are you still planning to go?" he asked.

"What choice do I have?"

He lifted the books from his waist and held them in front of him like a pizza box. "Maybe these can help."

Reagan couldn't make out the books from across the apartment and she feared if she inched closer she'd lose control and slug him in the face. "What are they?"

"Books. Study material." He shrugged in an oddly discomforting way. "I'm guessing, but I think the reason you're so freaked out about going to small group is because you don't know the Bible."

"Thank you, Captain Obvious. You're quite the genius."

After a few moments of teeth gnashing and nostril flaring, Dash took a tentative step forward and set the books on the coffee table. He moved back before she could strike. "I'll leave these here for you to look over if you want."

"Great." Reagan muttered at his retreating back. "More work. Just what I need."

"It's easy reading—probably too easy, but you've got to start somewhere if you don't want to go into this blind."

She didn't want to go into it at all, but she'd practically tattooed that across her forehead. Besides, he was leaving, and she feared further conversation would delay his departure.

With the door open, Dash turned as if to say something, but appraised her instead. Reagan couldn't fathom what he thought as he looked at her—anywhere from a heathen loser to a bitter bimbo. His face gave nothing away. "If you need anything or have any questions, I'm right next door."

She ignored him, gave in to curiosity, and made a beeline for the books. She lifted the first and gaped at the cover. "Are you kidding me?"

"Is there a problem?" he asked.

Shame—familiar and cloying—enveloped her like the scent of a skunk. No matter how far she traveled or how hard she tried, she couldn't escape the stench of ignorance. "These are study materials?"

"Yes."

"For me?"

Dash nodded, and Reagan could tell he expected some blowback by the way he straightened and faced her head-on.

"Are you trying to make me feel stupid or just embarrassed?"

His shoulders hunched, and he took a tentative step in her direction, nudging the door closed behind him. The impassive expression on his face morphed into pity. She preferred his anger.

"Neither. I'm trying to help without overwhelming you."

Reagan stared between him and the cartoon characters gracing the covers of both books. "You think the only way I can comprehend the nuances of the Bible is by reading a children's book?"

"No. There are no nuances in children's books. That's the point."

"Dumb it down for the dummy, is that the point?"

"Of course not. Reagan …" He stopped walking toward her when a noise escaped her mouth that sounded a little like a snarl. "Have you ever read the Bible?"

"No," she said. "And that doesn't make me a bad person."

"I never said anything about you being a bad person."

"Carting me off to church like some lost soul is all but calling me worthless."

"You're putting words in my mouth and assigning a motive that never existed." He clamped his mouth shut, inhaled a large breath through his nose and exhaled slowly before continuing.

Reagan stood stiff and bit her bottom lip to keep from shouting back. Dash seemed to be fighting a war within himself and she would do nothing to intervene, even if staying quiet meant battling every one of her instincts.

"I took you to church because that's where I was performing. That's where I perform now—generally—and I wanted you to know where and how I spend my time."

"Why?"

Dash shot his hip to the side, dug his fingers into his jeans, and pursed his lips as if she'd shoved a lemon in his mouth. "You seemed pretty set on believing every rumor you've ever heard and every stereotype of guys in a band. I wanted you to know the truth."

"Okay, I admit I was wrong about you." Incredibly wrong, and she wasn't sure she was happy about it. "But, again, why were you so eager to set me straight?"

"Mostly because you're judgmental."

That should have stung, but he wasn't that far off the mark. She was judgmental. She couldn't help it. Survival depended on making quick and definitive judgments of people and situations. It always had. "Fine. What's the other reason?"

A firm crease appeared between his brows and his mouth twisted into a grimace. She enjoyed plowing right through his charm and watching confusion prevail. "What other reason?"

"You said, 'mostly.' What's the rest of the reason?"

His expression lost all vigor and he dropped his hands to his sides. "Come on, Reagan."

"Come on, what? What am I missing?"

He stared at her for a beat, his eyes probing. "You're too smart to play dumb."

"And apparently you're nothing like I assumed. So spell it out for me, since I'm so stupid when it comes to you."

This time Dash growled, and along with a throaty grumble his temper flared to life. "I said you were judgmental. I never said you were stupid. But you're acting stupid when you stand there and pretend as if you never knew I like you."

"You like me?"

"Yes," he said, his tone louder. "Call me a masochist, but yes, I like you."

Reagan's brain buzzed, and her knees trembled. Who was this guy who waltzed into her life and spoke his mind without any regard for social norms? And why did his pronouncement make her heart flutter even knowing they were as different as heaven and hell? "You do realize you don't actually know me that well."

"Of course. But what I know of you—what I've observed over the past year—I like." He shrugged as if his words weren't shredding her defenses—and his. "Because I like you, I wanted you to judge me based on reality and not my past or some stereotype in your head. Unfortunately, in doing so, I took you to church against your will, got you roped into a small group you're terrified to attend, and now I'd like to help you get through it with your dignity intact."

Reagan decided to take a wide berth around his startling admission—he liked her!?!—and get back to the real question, one she could inspect without feeling as if her skin were on fire. "And the children's books?"

"Are the best way to get a quick overview of the main points in the Bible. The smaller book with all the illustrations is like a SparkNotes version of the Old and New Testament. The larger book goes into more detail on most of the topics covered in the smaller one. I wasn't sure how much time you had to read before Thursday, which is why I brought them both."

She looked between the book in her hand, the one on the coffee table, and the imposing man her apartment. "You just happened to have a couple of children's Bibles sitting around your apartment?"

"No, I went to the library." As he stared at her, his lips twitching, she watched his charming mask return. "Do me a favor please and refrain from shredding them when I leave, so I don't have to replace them."

He'd gone to a good bit of effort to help her out of the mess she was in. At some point, when he and his overwhelming persona wasn't staring at her, she'd have to take a moment or ten and digest everything he'd revealed in the past few minutes. "I respect library books too much to deface them."

Dash snorted. "Well, at least that's something."

Satisfied they'd reached a tentative peace, he turned to leave. Reagan looked up from the books in time to appreciate his narrow hips in the low-slung jeans. He really was too good-looking, and darn it, she liked him too.

"Thank you for the books."

He turned at the door and smirked. "You're welcome."

Chapter Twelve

Reagan sat on her couch, thumbing through the books Dash left. She'd spent the afternoon fixing the research she'd upended, and after a brisk run through the deserted campus, settled in for a different kind of research. Of all the revelations Dash dropped at her doorstep this morning, the most pressing and the only one she could wrap her head around was her need to prepare for Bible study.

She cracked the cover of the toddler-like version, complete with animated drawings and large font. On the first page, a gray-bearded character named Moses welcomed her to read the first five books of the Old Testament—the books God told him to write. She had to take a giant leap of faith to accept God spoke to this Moses fellow, but for the sake of research, she'd try to keep an open mind. Determined to learn about the Bible and arm herself with knowledge, she decided to tuck her cynical self away, if only for a little while.

God created everything in seven days, including Adam and Eve. They ate the forbidden fruit when a snake told Eve it was okay even after God told them not to eat from the tree of knowledge of good and evil. Snakes could talk? Oh, brother ... Reagan changed positions on the couch and slapped her inner cynic back into submission. If every page required her to suspend logic, reading a kids' book was going to be a bigger challenge than she'd imagined.

When the phone rang, Reagan tossed the book aside, grateful for the reprieve. She smiled when her roommate Kayla's name and picture graced her cell phone. "Hey there."

"Yay!" Kayla said. "I was hoping you'd answer."

"The odds were pretty good considering this place is a ghost town and there's nothing to do."

"Is it that bad? I was worried about you staying by yourself."

"It's been okay. To be honest, I'm kind of enjoying the quiet. How are things at home?"

Kayla swallowed a grumble. "Uh, okay. I wish we didn't have such a long break. I'm bored already. I should have gotten a job."

"I told you."

"I know you did, and I should have listened. Or maybe stayed at school with you. I feel bad you're all alone."

Reagan was relieved Kayla wasn't present to witness her cheeks flame red. "There are a few people around, but not many." And only one who made her world feel very crowded at the moment. "It's not that bad."

"So what are you doing?"

Reagan glanced at the book next to her and chuckled. It was too good not to share—especially with her most fanciful roommate. "Right now, I'm reading the Bible."

The silence on the other end spoke volumes. Reagan rolled her lips between her teeth to keep from chuckling.

"Um, did you say you're reading the Bible?"

"Actually, I'm reading a children's Bible."

"A children's Bible? Explain, please."

Reagan did, leaving out the most critical and vexing aspect of the story—Dash's surprise admission that morning.

"So he took you to church, you ran into Professor Adkins, and now you have to go to a Bible study at his wife's house?"

"Yes. Which is why I'm reading the Bible."

"Oh, Reagan." Kayla chuckled. "Only you would make that sound like capital punishment."

"It is punishment! Come on, Kayla. I have to suspend disbelief to get through the very first page of a children's Bible. Do you know how hard it is for me to suspend disbelief?"

"I think trying to accept religion as an adult is difficult for most people who weren't raised with faith. But for you? Nearly impossible."

"Exactly!" Thankfully Kayla understood. Having this conversation, even the beginnings of it, released an enormous amount of pressure in Reagan's head. She should have called Kayla as soon as Dash brought her home from church. "How do you actually believe this stuff?"

"I haven't put a lot of thought into my religious beliefs in a long time, but I guess because it's what I was taught from a very young age."

Reagan stared at the cartoon picture of Eve talking to a snake. "It's so ridiculous."

"It's called faith for a reason. It takes a good amount of faith to believe something you can't see or something that challenges common sense."

"What you call faith, I call ignorance. How in the world can any logical thinking person believe God created an entire universe out of nothing? Call me shortsighted or intolerant, but I can't."

"Or won't. Faith is a choice."

"Whatever."

"What part are you on?" Kayla asked.

"The part where a snake talks to Eve and tells her it's okay to eat from the tree of knowledge."

"For goodness sake, Reagan, you've only just begun."

"I know, and I already can't believe the stupidity of it."

"Well, if you're determined to go to this Bible study, you're going to want to approach the Bible and the people there as something other than stupid. Because I love you, but when you think someone is stupid, it's written all over your face."

Reagan sighed at the prudence of Kayla's statement. Not only did she have to suspend disbelief, but she had to pretend to be something she wasn't in order to impress—or not insult—people who mattered. "I know, I know. And I can't look at Professor Adkins's wife—or Professor Adkins, for that matter—like they're stupid. That'll be career suicide."

"Stop trying to disprove what you're reading and just read it like a story."

"I'm trying, but it's hard."

"Oh, please. When you put your mind to something there's nothing that'll stand in your way."

Reagan hummed her approval at Kayla's compliment. She was nothing if not determined.

"But enough about work," Kayla said. "Tell me about Dash."

Uh oh. She should have known Kayla wouldn't let her get away with glossing over the details of their neighbor. The same neighbor her roommates had been trying fruitlessly to get her to notice. "What about him?"

"Sounds like you're spending a good bit of time together."

"Well, he's one of the only ones left in the apartment complex and he's right down the hall."

"Is he staying in town for the holidays?"

"I have no idea."

"Why haven't you asked him?"

"I don't know, Kay. Maybe because whenever I'm around him he's been too busy shoving his religion down my throat."

"Okay, fine. I can tell you aren't ready to discuss Dash. But know I expect details when I get back to town."

Of course she would. And a small part of Reagan wanted to share every detail of what he'd said that morning, but the pragmatic Reagan knew sharing with Kayla would do nothing but pour fuel on the fire. When the time was right, she'd let Kayla in on the entirety of the situation, but for now it was best to keep it simple. "Why are you so interested in Dash? Do you have a thing for him?" And why did saying that out loud—even though she knew it wasn't anywhere close to true—make her stomach deflate and slither to the floor?

"Oh, Reagan. These deflection techniques are so cute. Enjoy your book and let me know when you're ready to spill the juicy stuff."

Her roommate was too smart for her own good. The juicy stuff? She wasn't sure there was anything juicy about knowing her next-door neighbor liked her and wanted to change her opinion of him. Why did he care what she thought, even if he did like her?

And how could he like her when he didn't even know her? He'd change his mind when he did know her. Because no matter how much he'd messed up his life, hidden under that reformed bad boy was an all-American guy with a mom and a dad and probably a sibling or two who loved and supported him through thick and thin. That kind of guy would run from someone like Reagan.

Chapter Thirteen

Dash turned the TV on in time for the opening bars of the Monday Night Football jingle. The familiarity of it, the image it conjured of his dad sitting in his leather club chair tuning in at home had Dash smiling. Maybe he'd call his dad at halftime and dissect the game. If he could pay attention to the game.

Restless and sore from his run the night before, Dash had taken his truck for a drive to the beach, fiddled with the guitar with his toes in the chilly sand, and made it home in time to shower and settle in for kickoff. He hoped the football game could do what nothing else had been able to do—get his mind off Reagan.

He'd been honest with her. He did like her, and he had for a long time, even though the real Reagan was vastly different from the Reagan he'd imagined. He'd pictured her as a serious student, an amateur athlete, and an all-around good girl. What little he knew of her so far had shifted his image.

She was a serious student and a phenomenal runner, as he'd confirmed when he saw her sprinting out of the complex. But the choirgirl aspect didn't exist. Considering all the changes he'd made in his life—for himself, for his family, and for the relationship he wanted to have with a woman in the future—he should've at least considered the possibility she was different than he'd envisioned. In fact, he'd made assumptions of her the same way she'd made assumptions of him—and they'd both been wrong. What he couldn't figure out was why he didn't feel disappointed.

Those flashes of vulnerability and self-doubt she couldn't mask with her tough exterior did him in. Every. Single. Time. Did she realize how every feeling washed over her face in vivid color? He doubted she did, because she would have tried to cover her emotions the same way she tried her best to hide that southern twang he found so endearing.

The conundrum of her, the way she'd change and reveal something new and mysterious about herself at every turn, kept him longing to know more. Like peeling an onion, every layer revealed something new. Her unpredictability was as addictive as the drugs he used to sample.

Had he really thought it would be easy to change his life and the perfect girl would magically appear, ready and willing for his pursuit? His mom would say it was the dreamer in him, the same head-in-the-clouds quality that fed his musical aspirations leading him to confuse fantasy with reality. He shook his head when he realized he'd missed over five minutes of the game while brooding about the very girl he was trying to forget for a little while.

A knock at his door had him fumbling for the remote to turn down the volume. He jogged to the entrance and opened it, unable to stop the smile from splitting his face at the sight of Reagan on his doormat, huddled beneath a thick wool sweater.

"Come in and get out of the cold." He pulled her in with one hand and shut the door with the other. "I can't believe how much the temperature dropped since yesterday."

"Tell me about it," she said. "I about froze on my run this afternoon."

"I saw you sprinting out of here like your butt was on fire. You must have been some kind of track star in high school."

Reagan sputtered, rolling her dark eyes. "Not likely."

"Why in the world not?"

"I was too busy working to play sports."

Though she'd revealed another clue, he'd tuck it away for further discussion at a better time. "What brings you by?"

She pulled out the basic children's Bible he'd delivered to her apartment earlier that day as her eyes met the television. "Oh … I didn't mean to interrupt. I can ask you another time."

"No." He reached out and grabbed her arm to stop her retreat, instantly letting go when her stare landed where his hand rested on her arm. "Stay. I don't care about this game at all."

Her eyes narrowed, but she seemed to believe the earnest expression he tried his best to exhibit. "If you're sure …"

"Absolutely. Do you have a question?"

Her face morphed from timid to earnest in a nanosecond, like a windup toy cranked tight and finally set free. "Yes, I have a question." She marched in front of his coffee table and turned around sharply. "Child sacrifice? Really? This is the God you believe in?"

Dash wracked his brain and came up empty. If only he'd spent time reviewing the Bible instead of daydreaming. "Uh … there's no child sacrifice in the Bible."

"Hello!" She flipped through the beginning of the children's Bible and held the pages open so he could see. "Right here. God told this Abraham guy to kill his only son, and he was going to do it!"

Dash fought the urge to smile. Her passionate response meant she'd not only read the words but tried to connect with them as well. He needed to tread lightly so as not to send her off the rails. "I get where you'd have some trouble with that one."

"This book is made for children—young, impressionable children who probably can't even read—and it tells them God instructed a parent to kill a child! Worst of all, God glorified the parent for his willingness to do it!" She dropped the book on the coffee table and her voice grew somber. "If my mother had read this story to me, I'd have been horrified, and scared to death that God would ask her to do the same."

Dash couldn't look at her accusing stare while he racked his brain for the meaning behind the passage he hadn't given much thought to in years. "I think the point of the story is Abraham's obedience to God."

"By asking him to murder his eight-year-old son? If your dad tied you up and almost shoved a knife in your stomach, would you be able to forgive and forget just because God asked him to do it?"

Dash rubbed the back of his neck. "Probably not, but I assume Abraham talked to Isaac afterward and explained."

"Oh, please. Eight-year-olds are young enough and naïve enough to believe their parents have their best interests at heart.

They're also old enough to remember every time they hurt them or let them down."

She'd dropped so many hints about her life he wasn't sure where to start, but he knew her well enough to realize she wouldn't appreciate him poking into her past. Before he could try to calm her down she waved her arms in the air.

"And the other book doesn't even mention the story of Abraham trying to kill Isaac, so I think maybe they thought better to leave that little gem out of their version."

Proceed with caution, his brain warned. *Proceed with caution. Proceed with caution!* "Before you get more upset, why don't you have a seat. I'll get my study Bible and see what it has to say."

She stood still, her feet planted, an adorable crease splitting her brows. "What is your Bible going to say that's different from this one? How can child sacrifice be justified?"

He eased in front of her and placed his hands on her shoulders, backing her up until her knees hit the couch and she tumbled into the seat. "Give me just a second and we'll have a look."

He nearly chuckled on the way to his room. Of all the reactions he'd expected from her—from indifference to complete dismissal—he hadn't expected this. Her questions meant the Bible had captured her attention. Maybe not in the best way, but any way was fine by him. Now he needed to feed her innate curiosity in a way that compelled her into reading more.

When he returned to the den, Reagan sat with her hands clasped between her knees and her eyes on the television. "Denver just scored."

"You like football?"

She shrugged. "Not really. I know the teams and the basic principles, but I've no idea about the positions other than quarterback, receiver, and the two lines."

"That's more than most." Dash sat next to her and flipped open to the book of Genesis. "Is your dad a fan?"

"I don't know my dad."

Dash looked up to find her glaring at him. As much as he wanted to probe into the statement she'd mumbled as if telling him the score, her stare advised him not to. He dropped his gaze and grappled to find the offending passage with all the noise in his head. "You're referring to Genesis 22. You mind if I read the chapter and the notes?"

"What notes?" she asked.

"A study Bible has notes to certain passages for clarity. They give context to the verses."

"Knock yourself out."

She sat quietly while he read, the only sound the muffled murmurings of the football announcers. "It states in Genesis 22:1 that God was testing Abraham's faith. And in 22:2, He asks Abraham to sacrifice his only son—the son he loves so much. God understands how much Abraham loves his son, so He knows asking him to sacrifice his son is the ultimate test of his faith."

"That's great for God, but not so great for Isaac."

"True, but God's not asking Abraham to do something He's not willing to do. He sacrificed His only son for the sins of humanity."

Reagan narrowed her eyes. "You're talking about Jesus?"

"Yes."

"When do I get to the Jesus part? Right now, this just seems cruel."

Dash chuckled and flipped through the pages until he found the beginning of the New Testament. "Not for a while. Genesis is the first book of the Old Testament. Jesus doesn't come around until the New Testament." He held the book up and showed her the thickness of the Old Testament as compared to the New. "The New Testament begins here, with the book of Matthew."

Reagan scowled. "If Jesus is the whole point of Christianity, why isn't he mentioned until the second half of the bible? That makes no sense."

"It's important to understand how people lived and how they believed before God sent Jesus to save us. Without that history and context, what Jesus did and how people reacted to him wouldn't mean much. And Jesus is referenced in the Old Testament—just not by name."

Reagan leaned forward and picked up the children's Bible, scrolling through until she found the New Testament, and studied the two parts of the book as Dash had done to his. "So most of this is backstory?"

"Pretty much. Some of it's boring and hard to understand, but some is exciting and violent and fascinating."

"It reads like fantasy. I can't read this and believe it happened the way it says it did."

"You don't like a good fantasy every now and then?" Dash rested the Bible on his knee and sat back into the cushions, relieved when Reagan did the same.

"Not especially."

"You're not a Star Wars fan?"

"I've seen the movies. They're pretty good."

"Pretty good?"

He got the eye roll he expected. "You're such a guy. The movies are entertaining if you're into that kind of thing."

"And you're not?"

"I like movies, but I understand they're a fun escape from reality." She swiveled on the couch to face him. "Are you suggesting I approach the Bible the same way I do movies?"

"If you're having trouble reconciling the reality of it, then yes. I think that's a good way to look at it. You go to the movies willing to suspend reality for the sake of entertainment, right?"

"Yes."

"So read the Bible. Just read it. Whether you believe it or not is up to you, but I think you may be trying too hard to understand it. Just let it be and read."

Reagan inhaled a big breath and let it out, slumping against the couch. "I suppose I could try." She looked him up and down, wrinkled her nose, and scowled.

"Is there a problem?" he asked.

"You always smell good."

Dash let out a sputtering laugh. "You say that like it's offensive."

"It's just … distracting."

Knowing he'd gotten to her the way she'd gotten to him tasted sweet on his tongue. "That's seems fair. You've been distracting me for a while."

Reagan dropped her eyes and flushed an appealing shade of pink. "Why is that?"

"Excuse me?"

She fastened her eyes on his, even as the blush crept up her neck. That right there—her courage in the face of embarrassment—was what he found so fascinating.

"Why am I a distraction? I live with three gorgeous women—including one who physically renders men stupid—and you're distracted by me? That makes no sense."

He should have expected her to question him after his earlier admission, but she'd still caught him off guard. He preferred honesty. "I've noticed your roommates, and you're right—they're beautiful in their own way." He fidgeted in his seat.

"But?"

"But I'm not attracted to them."

She choked on his words. "You're attracted to me?"

"Yes."

Regan swallowed and stared at her hands before lifting her eyes to his. "I swear I'm not fishing for compliments, but why me?"

Could she be any cuter or more oblivious to her appeal? And what would it hurt to tell her the truth when it seemed best to be authentic? "For starters, you're smart and independent and not afraid to say what's on your mind. You care about school and your grades in a way that makes you stand out amongst other students, because you don't take this opportunity for granted. And that's attractive. Beside that, you're beautiful and infuriating."

She scrunched her face and looked away, the pink in her cheeks flaming red. "I don't know what to say."

"You don't have to say anything. But you also don't have to worry about me making a move on you."

Her eyes zipped to his and her brows arched. "I don't?"

Was that disappointment he detected in her stare? Why did even the hint of regret on her part make him feel so good? "I'm in the middle of a date-free year."

"You gave up dating? For a year?" Her brows lowered over narrowed eyes. "Why?"

"This may shock someone so completely immune to my charm, but I've had more unhealthy relationships then I care to admit."

Reagan shrugged. "I've seen you on stage. I get the appeal."

"It's not something I'm proud of. When I decided to make some changes, it made sense to work on myself without any ... distractions."

"And I'm a distraction."

He needed to be honest no matter how she'd react. "You're more a temptation."

"Umm." She nodded and then dropped her head to her hands. "This is the weirdest conversation I've ever had."

"Considering how I bungled things before, I think it's best to be up-front."

"In the honestly department, you've certainly made up for the bungling."

"I'm trying."

"So." She tipped her head to the side, "Where does that leave us?"

"Friends?" When he reached his hand out for her to shake, she slid her fingers along his, warm and soft and inviting.

"Friends." They smiled at one another with their hands entwined.

He let go when she stood up to leave. "I'm around if you have any more questions."

She chewed her bottom lip and smirked. "I'm always full of questions."

Chapter Fourteen

Mark Adkins's couch could double as a therapy chair—had doubled as a therapy chair—more times than Dash could count. The soft leather withstood the antics of the Adkins kids, currently squirrelled away with Connie, and the ups and downs of a twenty-one-year-old coming to grips with his life as a Christian.

"Yay, mom," Mark said in the middle of Dash's play-by-play of the past few days. "The children's books were a great idea."

Dash stood up and began to pace. "I feel like I'm betraying Reagan's confidence. She's working for you, and your wife runs the small group."

"Yes, but I've been your small group leader and—dare I say—mentor for a lot longer. We can pretend I don't know who you've been talking about all this time, or we can face reality and move on."

Dash stopped and narrowed his eyes at Mark. "You just want to know what happened."

"Yeah." Mark's quick smile told Dash he understood his sarcasm. "All kidding aside, you've come a long way in a short period of time and I feel partly responsible for your progress. But if you'd rather talk to someone else about this so as not to feel uncomfortable, that's fine."

"No, I don't want to talk to anyone else. You're my mentor and I need you—now more than ever."

"Okay. Then understand what you say to me is confidential and won't in any way affect my relationship with Reagan."

"Understood." Dash sat back on the therapy couch and continued with the events of the day before. When finished, he looked expectantly at Mark.

"I'm glad you were honest with her about your dating sabbatical." Mark's expression sobered.

"But?"

Mark shook his head and brought his linked fingers to his chin. "I'm not so sure sharing your feelings is a good thing. I don't want you to get your hopes up."

"About what?"

"About having a relationship with her. The girl you've just described sounds a long way from the Christ-centered woman you've made a lot of changes to eventually find."

"I know she's not a Christian. But I'm excited she's willing to read the Bible and give it a try."

"So am I. But she's giving it a try because she feels she has no other choice. You have to be prepared for the prospect that she may go through the motions and dismiss it altogether. That's not the kind of woman you've been telling me you want to spend your life with."

"You sound pretty cynical for a man of faith. And considering the way you met your wife, a tad hypocritical." Dash knew Mark was trying to protect him, but he couldn't help but get defensive.

"I pray this is her first step to becoming a Christian. That would be the best-case scenario for her. As your friend and mentor, I have to caution you to not get your hopes up in case that doesn't happen. I don't want to see you get hurt or have her derail your momentum."

"Because I'm attracted to her?"

"Because it sounds like you're developing a relationship with her before the end of your sabbatical. I don't think that's a good idea."

"The only relationship we're developing is a friendship. Come on, Mark. I thought you were a good listener."

"Dash, all I'm saying is you need to tread lightly." Mark leaned over and squeezed Dash's shoulder. Despite knowing Mark meant it in an encouraging way and not in the condescending way it came across, the gesture annoyed. "You've had it bad for this girl for a long time and becoming friends with someone you're already attracted to could lead to trouble."

"Just because I'm attracted to her doesn't mean she's attracted to me."

"Dude." Mark sat back and chuckled. "I'm probably going to lose my man card for saying this, but you're not exactly hard on the eyes."

Dash clutched his heart in an effort to mask the sting of embarrassment. "Why, Professor Adkins, are you flirting with me?" He dropped his voice to a whisper. "Does Connie know about your crush?"

"Shut up. I'm serious. You're already attracted, and on some level, she probably is too."

"You don't know that."

"In my experience, girls react one of two ways when they know a boy likes them. They either entertain the idea, or they avoid the boy at all costs. She's still talking to you, so I'd say she's open to the idea. And I'm not telling you something you don't already know. She likes you, and she's willing to consider a relationship."

Dash schooled his face so as not to express delight at Mark's assessment of Reagan's interest. "She knows I'm unavailable."

"Yes—for a short time. That probably makes you more attractive. It gives her time to get to know you and to get herself out of the mess you got her into."

"What are you saying? We shouldn't be friends?"

"I'm not saying you shouldn't be friends. Most stable relationships begin as friendships. I'm simply cautioning you not to put the cart before the horse. This year was about getting closer to God, understanding how best to serve Him using your gifts, and becoming the kind of person a nice, Christian girl wants to date. I don't think it's a good idea to bide your time until the year is over and then jump into a relationship full throttle with someone who might not be what you want her to be."

Dash's annoyance with Mark doubled. "You're assuming that after we get to know each other as friends, we're going to want to be in a relationship. There's no way to know if that's true."

"What if it is?"

Dash sighed. It was what he wanted. Unless and until she proved otherwise, he wanted to know her, to know her past, to know what drove her, to know everything about her. Darn, he hated when Mark was right. "Then I guess we'll take it slow."

A knock sounded at the door, meaning the others had arrived for Bible study. Mark stood, put his hands on Dash's shoulders and squeezed. "God has a plan for all our lives. He put you in Reagan's path for a reason and it might have been to bring her to God. If that's all it is, you have to be okay with that. In fact, you should be thrilled to have instigated a relationship between her and her Heavenly Father."

"I know. If that's all my role is meant to be in her life, I'll be okay with it. That would be huge."

Mark made his way to the door, nodding. Dash hoped that meant Mark was satisfied with his answer.

Dash blew out a breath and sat down on the couch. He meant what he said to Mark—he would be more than okay if his only role were to bring Reagan to a relationship with God. If anyone could take the baton and run with it, Connie was the woman for the job. But no matter how far he'd come in his own walk with faith and how skeptical Mark seemed, Dash couldn't shake the feeling he and Reagan were meant to be more.

Chapter Fifteen

Reagan lifted her hand to knock on the door and cringed when she saw her fingers tremble. She balled her hand into a fist and told herself to get a grip. She'd read the entire toddler Bible and most of the children's Bible. She had a fleeting knowledge of the major points of the story and had talked herself into believing she could fool them into thinking she wasn't totally ignorant.

But she didn't know who *they* were, and that alone would justify giving into fear and walking away without a backward glance. Forget Dash, forget Professor Adkins and his sugary-sweet wife Connie and her Bible-toting friends. Forget them all! But walking away meant acting like a coward, and Reagan Bellamy was no coward. With a fortifying breath, she knocked on the door.

Connie answered so abruptly, Reagan almost retreated a step. Almost.

"Hi, Reagan! I'm so glad you could make it." Connie swooped in and gathered her into a bone-crushing hug.

The only reason Reagan didn't bolt from the porch was that the tiny woman had rendered her stupefied. Fortunately, or unfortunately, common sense intervened before Reagan could disengage and take the first backward step toward freedom.

Before Reagan could respond, Connie shut the door, took her coat, and ushered her into a room filled with the kind of furniture and knickknacks displayed in the magazines her roommate Emily devoured daily. Reagan didn't know what to expect, but after witnessing the disaster of Professor Adkins's office, the tidy den filled with neutral colors and stylish pops of color surpassed her expectations.

A woman either slightly pregnant or slightly overweight wiped cookie crumbs from her lap as she stood.

Reagan felt Connie's hand at her back. "Reagan, this is Alana Pickens. Alana, this is Reagan Bellamy. She's a student at ASU and Mark's new research assistant."

Alana held out her hand to shake. "Hi, Reagan. It's nice to meet you."

"Likewise." Reagan took in Alana's leggings and oversized shirt. Her hair, a honey blond that reminded Reagan of Kayla, shined with health.

Alana placed a hand on her belly. "I'm pregnant. I like to qualify my attire and stomach just so there's no confusion. I'm at that awkward stage where my clothes don't fit and I'm not showing enough for maternity wear."

"Congratulations." Was the woman a mind reader? "Is it your first?"

"Second." She glanced at her watch. "My first better be getting bathed, if his dad knows what's good for him."

Connie ran a reassuring hand down Alana's arm. "Spending time with Luke is good for Dave. They'll be just fine."

"I know, I know. I'm just a little afraid of what I'll come home to."

"A messy house can be cleaned. They need this time together as much as you need a night out."

Reagan suppressed a groan. She couldn't spend an entire night listening to discontented housewives complain about their husbands. At least she had a husband and a home to raise her kids. Instead of letting her thoughts leak out her mouth, she reached for a cookie and took a seat on the couch.

Alana followed suit when Connie excused herself to answer the door. "So, Reagan, where are you from?"

"Cottersville."

Alana's pretty brow furrowed. "I've never heard of it. We're not from around here. We moved to the area for Dave's job."

"Cottersville's about an hour and a half southwest of here. It's a tiny blip on the map."

Alana's smile grated on Reagan's nerves. "That must have been fun, growing up in a small town."

Fun? Living in a place where everyone knew every detail of your life—from conception to present day—and never let you forget? Not exactly. "More fun to leave and never look back."

"Oh." Alana's lips twitched, and her smile faltered. Maybe it would be wiser to say what they wanted to hear rather than tell the truth. The truth could lead to questions better left unanswered.

They both stood when another woman entered wearing a wrinkled pencil skirt, a fitted jacket, and droopy smile. "I'm sorry I'm late." Her crisp voice belied her haggard appearance. "I had a deposition in Savannah and there was an accident on the highway."

Alana reached out and gave the woman a hug. "You're not late. We haven't even started."

Reagan's ears began to tingle. With just one word—deposition—the stranger had become the most interesting woman in the room. She held out her hand in greeting. "I'm Stephanie Sellars."

"Reagan Bellamy."

"Pleasure to meet you." Stephanie gave Reagan an up down appraisal. "You must be a college student."

Reagan nodded, studying the woman with interest. Her brown hair was cut in a shoulder length bob and her blue eyes sparkled with intelligence. "I'm a junior. Pre-law."

"Oh, you poor soul." Stephanie laughed and slipped out of her blazer. "Quick. Change your major while you still have time."

Reagan deflated like a balloon stabbed with a needle. "Excuse me?"

"I'm kidding." Stephanie tapped Reagan's shoulder. "It's been a long day and I'm tired. Forgive my sarcasm."

Connie bustled in with a plate of what smelled like pumpkin bread. "Stephanie works at the DA's office." She set the plate on the coffee table. "And Reagan is Mark's new RA."

Stephanie collapsed onto the couch and toed off her pretty heels. "If you can successfully navigate Mark's office, I'll hire you when you graduate."

Was she serious? A job in a tiny DA's office with low pay and long hours held little appeal. "I'll keep that in mind."

"Y'all ready to get started?" Connie asked. "We're all here. Marg texted yesterday. She's at her daughter's house, helping with the baby for a few days."

Alana cradled her bump. "Is everything okay with the baby?"

"Everything's fine. Cindy's husband is out of town on business, and it was a good excuse for Marg to spend some time pampering." Connie sat in a chair that formed a horseshoe around the coffee table. "Let's pray ourselves in." She extended her hands to the women on either side before dropping her head.

Reagan hesitantly took Alana's fingers while her stomach twisted in knots. She bowed her head and stared at her tennis shoes as Connie began to speak.

"Heavenly Father, thank you for the blessings of this evening, bringing us all here together in Your name. Please be with us as we study Your word and help us to bring You into our everyday lives, especially during this very busy season. Please keep us focused on the birth of Our Savior and the wonderful blessing of His life you bestowed to us so long ago. May we never forget His life and sacrifice. In Jesus's name we pray, Amen."

Reagan swallowed the dust in her mouth and bobbed her head between the three women in the room. The air in the cozy den evaporated with each passing second.

Connie broke the silence. "Since we're missing Marg, Kendra, and Fallon—" Connie looked at Reagan. "Kendra and Fallon are the two college students I told you about who've gone home for the break. Anyway, since they're not here, I thought we'd each give a brief testimony of our faith journey before we get started to help Reagan get to know us better and feel comfortable in the group."

Faith journey? Dash never said anything about a faith journey. If Connie dared to ask Reagan to go first she was out of there without a backward glance—no matter what that meant for her assistantship.

"I'll start," Connie announced.

Connie's declaration did little to calm the blood raging through Reagan's veins. She didn't know what a faith journey was much less what to say when all eyes turned to her.

"Two things first. As most of y'all know, whatever we say in this group is confidential. The only way we can be open with one another is to trust that what's said here stays here. Second, y'all know I like to talk, so cut me off if I'm dragging this out too long." Connie cleared her throat and met each woman's eyes before taking a deep breath.

"I wasn't raised a Christian. My parents divorced when I was four and we supposedly went to church when I was little, but I don't remember. My dad moved in with another woman and her two kids right away, and they quickly married. My half-brother came along a few months later."

Whoa. Whoa. Whoa. Reagan sat up in her seat as reality blurred. Connie wasn't raised a Christian by perfect parents who showered her with love and affection? That was the last thing she expected from little Miss Perfect Pants.

"My sister Becca and I lived with my mom. My dad provided child support but wasn't a part of our lives in any meaningful way. My mother was angry at my dad for leaving and hurt that he'd obviously been having an affair. She stayed angry. My parents had and still have a hate-filled relationship that scared Becca and I for years. Church was the last thing we had time for, and I never thought I was missing anything by not going."

Reagan noted the sadness behind Connie's eyes and the way she kept kneading her hands tightly in her lap. She knew all too well the pain of a parent who never put her first.

"I met Mark at my first job after graduation. He was a part of a group who went to church together on Sundays and he asked me to go. I didn't really want to go to church—I'd lived for twenty-three years, I'd survived the breakup of my family, and I knew right from wrong. Sure, I'd had a string of relationships that went from bad to worse and had pretty much sworn off men—especially nice men who had big plans and a squeaky-clean reputation. But they were my friends—the only friends I had in the city—and I didn't want to be left out. So I started going with them to church and to brunch after. Mark made me laugh and kept making me think about him when all I wanted to be was friends. We were so different, and deep down I knew I wasn't good enough for him."

Connie's words landed like a sucker punch. How could Connie Adkins, who oozed happiness and left a trail of unicorns and rainbows in her wake, have had the upbringing she'd described?

"The church wasn't what I expected, and neither was Mark. I had fun, so I agreed to go the next weekend and it became a regular outing for me. When I realized I was developing feelings for him, I told him the truth about my past and figured it would scare him off, but it didn't. He called me brave and encouraged me to read about the different women in the Bible he thought I'd identify with, women like Ruth, Esther, and Abigail. Little by little I began to believe in our Heavenly Father's unconditional love. Knowing that and truly believing it changed my life."

Connie had, sometime during her story, unclasped her hands and the sparkle of contentment had returned to her brown eyes. She blinked at the women seated around her with a goofy smile on her face. "That's it. Who'd like to go next?"

Reagan reached for a cookie, averting her eyes in the process. She couldn't choke down a single bite with her mouth bone dry and her heart pounding in her ears, but it gave her something to do with her hands.

Alana shrugged. "I'll go. My story's pretty boring. I was raised in a Christian home with two parents who loved and doted on my brother and me. I accepted Christ as my Savior in elementary school and I never questioned my faith. It was always just a part of me. Dave and I met in college and we got married after graduation. He was also a believer and we've attended church regularly ever since. Luke came along two years ago and …"

Alana paused, her brows disappearing beneath her glossy bangs, and looked at Connie. After an encouraging nod of Connie's head, Alana continued.

Here we go. Complain, complain, complain.

"Things are different now. Harder. Dave and I used to make dinner together and talk about our days, but everything's about Luke and now the baby." Alana cradled her baby bump. "I feel … not quite worthy of his attention. I quit work when Luke came along—I was in sales for a small printing company and my salary didn't even cover daycare—and staying at home was what I wanted. It is what I want, what we both want." She nodded as if to convince herself. "But being at home is socially isolating, and I'm a slave to Luke's schedule, and Dave doesn't really want to hear how many diapers I changed or about our trip to the grocery store."

Reagan nearly rolled her eyes when she spied Alana's lip quivering and the sheen of tears in her eyes. "We're excited about the baby—of course we're excited—but a part of me is afraid I'm going to lose even more of myself and that another baby is going to push us farther apart."

Alana forced an annoying giggle as if to brush off her bleak little story. "Sorry," she said. "I think it's the pregnancy hormones. My life is good—great—and I'm very grateful I get to stay home with Luke and the baby."

"You're in a challenging stage of life," Connie said. "I remember how lonely it was when Lily and Jackson were babies and I was at home alone all day. Mark worked long hours, and we were like two strangers passing in the night."

Alana nodded. "How did you get through? You and Mark are so close, so in synch."

"Honesty. Communication. We butted heads a lot back then. He missed the physical intimacy we'd always shared, and I was so tired from the kids hanging on me all day long I just wanted to be left alone."

"Yes," Alana said. "Dave doesn't get that I don't want to be intimate with someone who can't be bothered to have a conversation with me."

"Talk to him," Connie urged. "Tell him how you feel. Get a babysitter one night a week and reconnect with your husband."

"Luke's in a stage right now where he throws a fit when we leave."

Oh brother...

"A good babysitter can handle a little fussing," Stephanie said. "I had some doozies back in the day and they turned out fine."

"I feel guilty leaving him."

"How good will it be for Luke if your marriage crumbles because you never take time for yourselves?" Connie asked.

Alana sighed. "You're right. I'll talk to Dave." She looked at Reagan and Stephanie. "Sorry. I didn't mean for that to turn into a therapy session."

Stephanie chuckled. "Don't apologize. If I ever get married and have kids, I'll know what to expect and who to come to for advice."

Reagan fidgeted in her seat. Did Alana expect her to say something to lighten the mood? What did Reagan know about raising kids and being married?

"I guess it's my turn," Stephanie said. "I was raised in a Christian home, had a great upbringing outside Atlanta. I'm the middle child—I have an older and younger sisters, and my parents are still married. I did my undergraduate work at Addison State, got my law degree from Southeastern, and started at one of the big firms in DC after graduation. I went to church occasionally while at ASU, stopped completely in law school, and my hours at the firm were so crazy long I barely had time to eat, much less go to church."

Reagan hung on Stephanie's every word. Law school at Southeastern was Reagan's goal and working in DC or any large city in America would be the icing on the cake. How did Stephanie go from Reagan's dream job to working in the DA's office in nowhere Georgia? And why?

"I got caught up in the rat race. I worked every second of every day. When I wasn't working, I was thinking about work and feeling guilty for sleeping when I should have been working." She closed her eyes and shook her head with obvious regret. "I started having panic attacks. The first time, I thought I was having a heart attack. I was at the office late, maybe ten o'clock, and working on a big case coming up for trial. One minute I was looking over my notes, and the next it felt like someone was choking me. I couldn't breathe, and my limbs got all tingly, and my heart started racing."

Reagan scooched back after leaning too far forward and almost slipping off the couch.

"I thought I was dying. I finally got my breath back and, believe it or not, I went right back to work. The same thing happened two days later, only this time I was in the conference room with three other attorneys. Someone called 911. An embarrassing hour later I was sent home to 'rest' and taken off the case. I returned the next day and pleaded with my boss to let me back on. I assured him I was fine, and whatever happened the day before wouldn't affect my work. He begrudgingly let me back on the case. I felt pressured to catch up and prove my worth, so I barely slept and worked myself into another attack a week later."

Stephanie dropped her head, shook out her hair, and continued relaying the painful story. "This time I couldn't talk myself out of the ambulance ride, or out of the week-long break the firm insisted I take. I was miserable and convinced my career was over. I got a visit from one of the partners, a man I'd barely spoken to in my almost two years at the office. He was nearing retirement and not all that involved in the day-to-day. He sat down on my couch. Instead of firing me like I thought he was going to do, he told me about his life. He told me about how he worked himself out of a good marriage, worked right through his kids growing up. He explained how he missed everything that was important, and how when work becomes the focus of your life to the exclusion of everything else, you don't realize until it's too late that what really matters is everything you ignored while climbing to the top.

"He asked me if I was happy." Stephanie let out a strangled laugh. "I couldn't even remember the last time I felt happy. He told me to take the panic attacks as a sign to get my priorities together. 'God's trying to tell you something,' he said before he left.

"Numb and more confused than ever, I got down on my knees and prayed. I prayed every day and by the end of the week, I couldn't go back to work. Not only was I embarrassed by what had happened, but I couldn't shake what he'd said to me. And I realized the last time I was happy was at ASU. So I quit my job, moved back here, and started working at the DA's office. Now, no matter how much work is on my plate, I make myself leave at six every night and I don't let myself get to work before eight. I started back at church, met Connie, joined this group, and with God's help, I'm figuring out how to be happy."

Reagan was so caught up in Stephanie's story, she didn't realize all eyes were on her and waiting for her to speak. She took a shaky breath and tried to think. She couldn't look at the women in the room while she tried to organize her thoughts. They'd bared their souls, telling painful truths she never expected to witness, and the thought of doing the same left her tongue tied and petrified.

"If you're not ready to share, you don't have to." Connie shrugged as Reagan sat mummified in fright.

"I …" What? What was she going to say? Admit she wasn't a Christian, that she didn't even know what that meant. Tell them she'd read a children's Bible and thought it a fantastical story only fools believe? "I'm not really a Christian." The words were out of her mouth before she knew what happened.

"That's okay," Connie said. "Everyone's welcome."

"My grandmother was." Reagan tried to wipe away the shame. "She took me to church a few times, but I thought it was boring and I hated the stiff dress and tights she made me wear. My mom hated the way people judged her." Why had she said that about her mom? Why did she even bring up her mom?

Connie flashed a pitying smile. "Not everyone who attends church has their hearts tuned to God."

"I didn't understand the purpose of church, the rituals and the fancy words everyone knew by heart but me. Mom said we had to go to keep Grandma off our backs, and once she died—my grandmother—we never returned. I didn't miss it."

"Of course you didn't, if you didn't understand."

"I still don't understand." Oh, boy. Now she'd done it. Now she'd gone and said something she couldn't take back.

"It's a foreign concept—praying to a God you can't see, believing in a higher power, especially if you've never been taught." Connie nodded in support. It made sense she'd understand Reagan's confusion. She'd just admitted as much. "That's why they call it faith. Believing in God and Jesus doesn't happen overnight. It takes time and learning. I'm glad you're here, Reagan, and that, for whatever reason, you're willing to take a step toward understanding."

She wouldn't have been there if she could have thought of a way out. Everyone stared at her with stupid sympathetic smiles on their faces. She didn't want pity from Stephanie who couldn't handle a little stress, or Alana who had it all and couldn't face a conversation with her husband. Good grief. These people were pathetic.

Connie handed Reagan a thin hardback book with a shiny red cover. "This is the book we're studying. We read the first two chapters last week. They're short and it won't take too long to catch up if you want to join us. This book tells the story of three women involved in Jesus's birth—the Christmas story—in a way that mixes the words of the Bible with the author's interpretation."

"Okay …" Reagan gripped the book as resentment oozed all the way down to her toes. She was stuck alright. Stuck as mud.

Chapter Sixteen

Dash's mouth watered at the smell of buttered popcorn. He stretched his arm across Josh in the darkened theater. "Noah, pass the bag."

The boy did so without looking away from the movie screen and nearly dumped the tub of popcorn into his best friend's lap. Dash made a quick grab and saved both a grease stain and an obscene amount of money from littering the floor. His wallet weighed considerably lighter after bringing four of his Axis guys to see the latest comic hero movie.

He loved spending time with his guys, watching movies, bowling, and playing Frisbee golf when the temperature wasn't so cold. This week's outing served two purposes—mentoring his boys and keeping his mind off Reagan. Dash hadn't heard from her since before her Bible study. He'd seen her, running in or out of the apartment complex. He waited patiently—or not so patiently—for her to come to him, tell him about the Bible study, if she'd kept her word and attended, and if and how she planned to proceed.

Because waiting around for her to come to him was as frustrating as watching paint dry, he suggested a movie when only a handful of guys showed up for Axis on Friday night. After the closing credits rolled, Dash did his best to corral his guys toward the bathroom to relieve their bladders and wash their butter-sticky hands before he drove them home. Once he'd gotten them all in the car and buckled up, the movie talk started in earnest.

"I liked it." Drew spoke from the backseat, his curly dark hair flopped over his eyes. "Even though I've seen all the others, I thought this one was the best."

"The graphics on the older movies suck," Josh said.

Dash cleared his throat. "Let's try not to say 'suck,' okay?"

"Sorry." Josh pulled the strings of his hoodie sweatshirt. "But they do."

"It's the technology," Drew said. The kid had an impressive knowledge of graphic technology, because his parents were art professors at the college. "Ten years from now, the movie we just saw will look as old as the original comic movies."

"Why do they always have to have a love interest?" Timmy smacked on a piece of gum. His mom had gelled his stick-straight hair into a vertical swoop away from his forehead. "I mean, these movies are for guys. Guys don't care about girls."

"Give it time," Dash said under his breath. Timmy had the baby face and chubby middle of a kid on the verge of an impressive growth spurt. Dash's brother had been chubby in middle school, yet was taller than their dad by his freshman year of high school. As soon as that happened, the girls appeared from out of nowhere and his awkward brother became the big man on campus in every possible way, sealing Dash's fate as Brent Carter's disappointing little brother.

"Dash cares about girls." Noah twisted from the passenger seat to face the guys in the back and sent a waft of eau de prepubescent boy stench in Dash's direction. The kid needed to freshen his deodorant every couple of hours. "Josh and I saw him holding a girl's hand last weekend."

Dash inwardly groaned as a chorus of ooh's, aah's, and kissing noises lasted for almost a mile. He chewed his lip and took the ribbing like a man. His goal was to forget his neighbor, not explain her to a bunch of twelve-year-old boys.

"That's enough, guys."

"Who's your girlfriend?" Timmy asked in a singsong voice.

"She's not my girlfriend," Dash said. "She's just a friend."

"You were holding hands," Josh said. "I don't hold hands with my friends."

Dash blew out a frustrated breath as the giggles started up again. How could he explain Reagan to a bunch of middle school kids when he could hardly explain her to himself? "She's a girl, she's my friend, and I was showing her around the church. I grabbed her hand because I was late for band practice and I wanted her to keep up." He grinned out the front windshield at the logic of his response, certain that would shut them up.

He should have known better.

"She's pretty," Noah said. Even in the darkened car surrounded by hoots and giggles, Dash spied Noah's red tipped ears. "I think you should ask her out."

Dash loosened his jaw to unclench his teeth. They were just kids. They wouldn't understand a dating sabbatical, and he sure didn't want to explain the concept to them. "Just friends, guys."

"You don't want a girlfriend?" Drew asked. "My brother's in high school and he says you become a man when you have a girlfriend."

Oh, brother. "You legally become a man when you turn eighteen, but even then, there's a lot to learn."

"Like what?" Drew asked. The kid wanted to know the ins and outs of everything.

"Well … life, I guess. Experience. Making mistakes and learning from them. Being responsible for yourself in terms of gainful employment. Respecting yourself and others. All the stuff we talk about at church."

"No," Drew said. "I mean what specifically makes us a man?"

"It's different for everyone. Your path will be different from Timmy's and his will be different from Noah and Josh."

"How do we follow our path?"

"We pray," Josh said. "Right, Dash?"

"Exactly right, Josh. Prayer and thankfulness are at the heart of letting God lead."

"I can't wait to tell my brother he's not a man yet," Drew said. "I knew his stupid girlfriend didn't make him a man."

"First of all, let's not call his girlfriend—or any girl—stupid. God made all of us in His image, so He wouldn't appreciate you calling her stupid. Second, if your brother likes and respects his girlfriend, he'll pray for her and for himself, and ask God to lead their relationship in a way that honors Him."

Drew pushed the hair from his eyes and stifled a chuckle. "You're talking about sex."

"Well …" Dash rubbed at the knot forming at the base of his skull. How had their conversation veered so far off course? "Part of honoring God means saving sex for when we get married."

"Have you had sex?" Drew asked.

Dash squeezed the steering wheel because it was physically impossible for him to go back in time and avoid the conversation all together. Or tape Drew's mouth shut. "I'm not married, am I?" He prayed his vague answer would satisfy their over-inquisitive minds.

"You don't have to be married to have sex," Josh said. "Guys brag about it all the time at school."

Dash remembered all too well the misery of middle school and the larger-than-life stories boys told to fit in or feel validated. As fast as some of his classmates ran during his junior high years, he imagined it ten times worse for these guys. He said a small prayer for help in explaining a delicate subject to inquisitive minds. "In my experience, most of those guys are lying."

"Even some of the girls talk about it," Noah said. "I don't think they'd lie. Do you?"

Noah's thoughtful question and earnest expression meant Dash had to tiptoe carefully. How appreciative would their parents feel if they knew the current the topic of discussion? "Girls lie just like boys do. Truth be told, I don't know if your classmates are having sex and neither do you. I would counsel any boy or girl your age not to have sex for a multitude of reasons, but mostly because it goes against God's plan for our lives. If you believe your friends are having sex, I would pray for them."

"That's your answer for everything," Timmy said.

"Prayer *is* the answer to everything—especially when the answer is complicated."

The only sound for the next few miles was the rumble of the tires along the rutted blacktop and Timmy blowing bubbles and letting them smack against his cheeks. The spell burst when Dash applied the brakes at a four-way stop, and the boys began talking about the movie, to Dash's immense relief. Any more questions about sex would've sent him careening into a ditch.

As his shoulders relaxed and he twisted his head from side to side to loosen the kinks in his neck, Dash thought it time to take his own advice. Instead of worrying about Reagan and the Bible study, he resolved to pray for her instead. He glanced at Noah sitting next to him and into the rearview mirror at his guys in the back seat, moved by a wave of love and gratitude for his Heavenly Father. Whoever would have guessed that a carful of stinky preteens would teaching him the real meaning of life?

Reagan didn't want to go back to church. She really didn't. After sitting through Bible study and listening to the ladies talk about the Christmas story and the women who played the biggest part—mostly someone named Elizabeth, who Reagan had to look up in her kid's Bible—she was once again forced to step outside reality and believe Elizabeth's husband was struck mute by an angel who announced his wife would be having a baby in her old age. Seriously, these Bible stories would be so much easier to believe if they weren't so preposterous and repetitive—hello, Sarah and Abraham!

She'd read the first two chapters of the Christmas book, and the next two for the upcoming study. She didn't have to go back to church to understand the homework, but what if she missed something important that the ladies wanted to discuss at Bible study? She'd have to admit she hadn't gone. With school closed for break and Professor Adkins taking "family time," there wasn't much work to do other than read the Bible study and finish the longer of the two books Dash had dropped off.

She didn't go to church to see Dash play and she sure didn't go to see him. If she'd wanted, she could have walked the fifteen steps from her door to his and seen him all week long. She'd spied him coming and going, and she'd been careful to time her exits from the apartment so he wasn't around.

They'd established a friendship, and while amused and flattered by his attraction, she couldn't let go of the lingering resentment at having to attend Bible study. Because of him, the weeks she'd intended to spend making inroads with the professor and taking a breather from her hectic school schedule had morphed into reading the Bible and eating cookies with her professor's wife. Reagan despised unscheduled adjustments to her plans, even though Professor Adkins's "family time" meant she didn't have much work to accomplish anyway.

She snuck in the chapel as the lights dimmed and took a seat in the back. The room smelled as pure and clean as the people around her, and a knot formed at the base of her skull. When the same Christmas jingle started playing over the church's impressive sound system and the H-A-P-P-Y H-O-L-I-D-A-Y-S letters began dancing on the screens beside the stage, Reagan took a deep breath and settled in for another cartoon. This time the characters were older, with young children and a cute little puppy. The happy family spent a snowy evening decorating the Christmas tree with a roaring fire blazing in the fireplace adorned with stockings for Mom, Dad, Charlie, and Lauren.

Mom and Dad placed the delicate glass ornaments near the top of the tree, while Charlie and toddler Lauren were in charge of putting the more durable ornaments on the lower half. Little Lauren perched atop her dad's shoulders and placed the star at the top of the tree, and it looked magazine perfect. The family settled in for games and popcorn, while the nameless puppy slept by the hearth with a stuffed black and white kitty under his paw.

Yawns had the little ones scurrying off to bed, and later Mom and Dad snuggled on the couch, presumably discussing world events and the cosmic fate of their ideal life. Before bed, dad let puppy out to use the bathroom and watched in amusement as puppy shook off the freshly fallen snow. Off to bed they went, puppy in tow.

Later that night, lit only by moonlight steaming through the windows, puppy meandered to the tree, sniffing the low-hanging ornaments one by one. When he approached a stuffed ornament eerily similar to his kitty toy, he cocked his head. A few in the church audience chuckled in anticipation.

The puppy swiped the kitty with his paw, but kitty only dangled teasingly from the branch, inciting the determined puppy. Next, he used his teeth, pulling on "his" kitty as if playing a game of tug-of-war with the tree. Fraser fir was no match for nameless puppy. After a few hearty yanks, the perfect tree came tumbling down. Ornaments smashed into tiny pieces and the star Lauren had placed atop the tree only hours ago cracked in two. Puppy, with kitty in his mouth, scurried into the arms of a sleepy Dad, ready to accost an intruder with a baseball bat. The scene faded to black as Dad looked over his shoulder at Mom and the kids on the stairs, a tiny tear rolling down Lauren's chubby cheek.

As the "Not so" fell between H-A-P-P-Y and H-O-L-I-D-A-Y-S and the letters tumbled, Reagan's stomach clenched and the knot at her skull slid down to the base of her spine. Last week, the band followed immediately after the video, and she steeled herself for the impact, refusing to let her infuriating neighbor turn her into a swooning idiot.

Lights blazed, Seth lifted his arms to strike the drums, the crowd sprang to their feet and Reagan followed. The beat was raucous, and the tune unfamiliar. The chords pierced her chest and vibrated through her bones. In the center of the chaos stood Dash, bobbing his head, his eyes closed, commanding the strings of his guitar. Swept into the violence of the notes, Reagan could only gape at Dash as he sang about sin, redemption, and God's grace.

Unlike last week's Christmas tune, the opening song was a far cry from anything she'd ever heard in church. If it weren't for the lyrics, she could have been in a bar listening to a band of polished and accomplished musicians sing of love lost and found. But she was in church, and she was as entertained as if she were watching a favorite band perform, so captivated she forgot to be angry.

On the chorus, Dash opened his eyes and impaled the audience with his stare. Buried inside the bowels of a house of worship, Reagan watched and wanted. She wanted the dark hair, the raw desire, the passionate artist who looked at her the way a starving man eyed a feast.

I'm in church! He's unavailable! I'm mad at him! The warnings drifted away with every beat, every strum, every second he spent on stage. Knowing what she knew about his past, the changes he'd made in his life, and his feelings toward her only magnified his appeal. Reagan never should have been attracted to someone like him. It defied logic and went against every plan she'd ever made for her life. But standing in the dark with the beat of his music pulsing through her chest, she acknowledged the truth.

She liked him every bit as much as he liked her.

Dash let loose on the stage in a way that made her attraction feel even more inconvenient. After getting to know him, she'd never peg him as a guy looking to garner approval. Yet Dash was perfectly at ease as the center of attention, illuminated in a single beam of light as colored strobes swam around the chapel. Reagan couldn't imagine anything worse than hundreds of eyes on her all at once. A shiver shot along her spine at the idea, and a question clamored in her head: how would it feel to throw caution to the wind and get lost in the very thing that gave her joy?

More important, what did a guy like Dash find even remotely attractive about a girl content to disappear into the shadows?

Chapter Seventeen

Dash sat in his den with the guys from Evergreen, working on the church's remaining Christmas services and brainstorming future gigs. When they'd first formed the band, moving away from the moneymaking mindset of a secular band like Caliber into the missionary mindset of Evergreen had been a struggle for Dash. Never before had the purpose and the glory gone to God instead of the bottom line.

While the guys in Caliber would lie, steal, and cheat to get a toe in the door of any venue, Evergreen operated on a different level—developing relationships with church secretaries, festival organizers, and booking agents. He never thought he'd ask a stranger if he could pray for something in their lives as a way to end a booking request—and actually do it. The more Evergreen played together and prayed together, the better they got, and the more people they could lead to Jesus.

Seth set his laptop beside him on the couch and stretched his legs atop Dash's coffee table. He'd pulled his shoulder-length hair into a man bun at the base of his skull and repeatedly tucked the loose strands behind his ears, reminding Dash of all the reasons he'd never let his hair grow that long. "I did a little research and I don't think going through the student activities center is a good idea."

Eli stopped tapping his pencil against the notebook in his hand. "Why not?"

"There are all kinds of upfront-fees we'd have to pay to join associations. Then we'd have to spend more money on producing a top-notch video to qualify for this showcase where college booking agents choose the acts for their venues."

"Don't you think the church would help us create an awesome video?" Eli asked. "Stan mentioned the other week how he thought Evergreen had helped increase their attendance."

"Asking the church to pay for a video that might make us less available to play at church doesn't make much sense," Dash said. "And Stan's been awesome with helping us get our foot in the door."

Seth cocked his head to the side. "I thought Mark Adkins got our foot in the door?"

"Mark made the introduction. Stan's approval got us on stage."

Jacob swiveled his neck from side to side before looking up at Seth. "So we'd have to pay upfront for a video for something that's basically a shot in the dark?"

"An expensive shot in the dark." Dash said. "And I don't think the performing arts center is any better. We'd have to dumb down the God-speak just to be considered, and that's not why we started this band."

"Exactly," Seth said. "As much as I hate to admit this, the college part of our college band isn't much of an advantage."

"Except college towns are music meccas." Jacob ran his hands over his short hair before thrusting them in the air. "That's our ace in the hole."

Dash hated to quell their youngest member's enthusiasm, but hours on the phone and the computer doing research had brought reality front and center. "There's no ace in the hole, even if we weren't a Christian band. But we are, so we're especially limited on venues because of our message."

"Can't we dilute the message to get some better bookings?"

"Dilute our message or change our mission?" Seth jerked his feet to the floor. "That's a slippery slope. If we dilute the message too much, we may lose our church appeal. We started as a Christian band for a reason."

Dash looked around the den at the guys in turn. Each one of them had their motivations for forming Evergreen, and at the heart of it was spreading the gospel. Just because finding gigs meant more legwork and a little creativity didn't mean it wasn't worth pursuing. "I've contacted both the chamber, and the convention and visitor's bureau and requested their media files and events calendar. I'll get moving on those and see if we can make some inroads."

Eli stood up and stretched his back before sitting back down on the couch. "I talked to the sound guy after service on Sunday. He suggested we call the local prison and offer to play their services."

"The prison?" Jacob's eyes widened, and his voice cracked. "Are you serious?"

Eli shrugged. "I imagine they need ministering to more than most."

Jacob wrinkled his nose. "But still."

"It's a lead," Dash said. "We need to explore every option. In that same vein, I think it's worth the time to approach the local homeless shelters and nursing homes. As Jesus told the Pharisees, the healthy don't need a doctor."

Seth nodded. "It's hard to argue with Jesus."

"What about the campus ministry programs?" Jacob asked. "That seems more up our alley."

"More up *your* alley." Seth's nostrils flared as he glowered at Jacob. "Look, dude, I'd love to play at campus ministries, and we will—with time. But we talked about what we'd be willing to do to get the band off the ground, and you agreed."

Seth, in particular, had expressed to each member his experiences with booking the Christian market. Dash knew how hard it was to book secular gigs, and the Christian element made that task even more difficult.

"I know I did, but prisons? Nursing homes? I mean, that seems like a waste of our time."

Eli clasped the pencil in a white-knuckle grasp. When the most carefree member of Evergreen became frustrated with Jacob, the kid treaded on a thin patch of ice. "What's our mission, Jacob?"

"I know, I know. To bring people closer to God."

"And who needs God more in their life? A bunch of cute coeds, or those folks on the fringe of society?"

Jacob sighed. "I'm not trying to be difficult, but I also don't want to work for free. I told my parents being in a band wouldn't cost me money. If I don't make enough to cover my expenses, I'm going to have to get a paying job."

"Playing low or no revenue venues is the best way to get ahead," Seth said. "We're relatively new to the Christian scene.

Just because we play almost every week at Stan's church doesn't mean we're a huge draw. It's church—people go there for the sermon, not the band."

Dash understood Jacob's concerns and Seth's frustrations, which was why he'd done his best to barter services. "I've got my friend Steve all set to record our show at the animal benefit in January, and Connie said she'd help with the website. It should be up and running soon." He shuffled through his notes and logo sketches. "We're just in a phase where we have to spend a little to get established. But dude, if you need to get a job, get a job. Just try to find something flexible where you don't have to work on nights or weekends."

A knock had all heads swiveling toward the apartment door, and then back to Dash.

"Expecting someone?" Eli asked.

Dash stood, his heart skittering against his ribs in a series of expectant flutters. It could be anyone knocking on his door—a salesman, a wrong address—but his gut told him otherwise. He combed his fingers through his hair and wished he'd worn something other than sweats and a ratty t-shirt.

When he opened the door, Reagan stood on his threshold holding the library books against her chest. "Hi." Her smile appeared wary and a little bit shy.

"Hey." Swamped by relief and delight at her presence brought Mark's warnings front and center, but he pushed them out the open door with the same enthusiasm as he motioned her in with the wave of his hand. "Come on in."

She took one step inside and came to an abrupt halt when she spotted the band in the den watching her with smirking smiles. Dash nearly rolled his eyes. Could they be more obvious?

"Oh, I'm sorry." Her pale face tinged peach. "I'm always interrupting."

"You're not interrupting." Seth stood up, gathered his laptop, and stuffed his drumsticks into the back pocket of his jeans. "We were just leaving." He shot the others a pointed look and wagged his head at the door.

"Please don't leave on my account." Reagan waved the books at the band as exhibit A. "I'm just returning some books."

"We're done," Eli said. He stopped and gave her a hug on his way out. Dash grit his teeth at Eli and the smarmy grin he bared to Dash behind her back. "Good to see you again."

Jacob, still irritated, bobbed his head at Reagan as he followed the others out.

She frowned at the door as it closed behind the guys. "Well, I certainly know how to clear a room."

She looked so pretty standing there wearing a sweater and jeans. He wanted to run his hands along the soft material and sniff her hair, so he stuffed his hands behind his back and took a step in retreat. "We were edging toward an argument, so you did us a favor."

"An argument? Over what?"

"Oh, you name it. There's a lot to iron out with a new band."

She raised her brows and considered him before saying, "Y'all didn't sound like a new band at church on Sunday."

Her admission left him reeling. She attended the service without his prompting *and* she'd enjoyed the worship music? "You were there?"

"I couldn't have the Bible study ladies thinking I'm not a regular attender."

Her comment, despite the snarky delivery, amused him and served as the perfect opening to the question he was dying to ask. "How was Bible study?"

"It was ..." Reagan set the books on the table and straightened into a thoughtful pose. "... enlightening."

"Interesting word choice." Dash sat down on the couch and looked up at her with pleading eyes. *Sit. Talk to me. Tell me everything.* When she hesitated, he quirked an eyebrow and issued his most challenging stare.

"What do you want me to say?"

He should have expected her to layer the pretty cream sweater with a coat of armor. Dash recognized the tactic and decided it best to remain dispassionate. "I don't know." He shrugged. "Tell me how it went."

Her shoulders drooped as she sat on the edge of the couch and tucked her hands between her knees. "Everyone was nice. There were only two people besides me and Connie. The two college students went home for break and another woman was visiting her grandkid."

"So you weren't overwhelmed?"

Her lips twitched and she bounced a shoulder, billowing her scent in his direction. Despite her best attempt at nonchalance, Dash could tell by the line between her brows she found his question irksome and he expected her to dodge. "It was weird."

"Define weird."

"Connie asked everyone to give their testimony, so I learned a few things about the group."

"And?"

She appeared conflicted, chewing on her bottom lip and watching him with pensive eyes. "Connie wasn't raised a Christian," she said as if disclosing a shameful secret.

"I know." Dash drew out the words. Telling him something he already knew hadn't breached Connie's trust.

Her brows arched skyward. "You know? How do you know? Does she tell everyone or wear a little star on her chest like the Jews in Nazi Germany?"

Hidden beneath her sarcasm was a curiosity as obvious as Drew's desire to understand how everything worked. "Connie's my friend. We've shared our stories."

She only huffed and picked at a loose string on her sweater. She appeared embarrassed and a little forlorn.

"It's not a sin, not being raised a Christian."

She lifted her eyes to his, a sparkle of humor illuminating her dark brown pools. "I figured it was required for a leadership position."

"She doesn't get paid to lead Bible study"

"I know. It just surprised me. She seems like she has a pretty sweet life. They all do."

"Who?"

"The ladies. One's a stay-at-home mom, the other works for the DA here in town." She leaned back, her shoulders still hung in defeat. "They were a little whiney—not Connie—but the other two. One's worried about her marriage after baby number two and the other couldn't handle a job at one of the big firms in DC." Her lips curled in displeasure. "I'm not supposed to talk about specifics, but that's the gist. Do me a favor and don't tell Connie I told you."

"My lips are sealed, but it sounds to me like they were being real. That's what a testimony is for—to lay your true self before God and those who seek to help."

Dash cringed when she straightened her spine and slipped her armor into place. "I know you think I'm judgey."

Keep talking. He grinned and shifted on the couch, setting his foot atop his opposite knee and stretching his arm along the back of the couch, inches from her silky hair. *I'm relaxed and listening without judgment.* "We've established that."

"What am I supposed to do? Sit there and feel nothing?"

"What did you feel?"

"Honestly? Like an intruder. Why were they telling me intimate details about their lives? They don't know me, and I don't want them judging me. The whole thing seemed weird."

"Did they judge you?"

"No. I don't think so. I don't know. Maybe. How could they not?"

Dizzy from her ping-pong emotions, Dash smothered a smile. She looked cute sitting there as tortured as his middle schoolers trying to wrap their minds around a foreign concept. "Part of becoming a Christian is learning about grace and forgiveness—of others and yourself. Jesus teaches some powerful lessons."

From the disgusted look on her face, he'd pushed the Godspeak too far. He searched for a way to dial it back and get her talking again, but she saved him by changing the subject.

"What's this?" she asked, pointing to his sketches.

"Oh." He leaned forward, picked up the papers, and handed her the notes. "We're working on a website. I'm just goofing around with our logo."

She flipped through the pages. "What are you going for? These designs are all over the place."

Dash sighed. "I know. I can't conceptualize what I have in my mind."

"Shelby can probably help. She's a graphic art major."

"She is?" He pictured her stunning roommate, aloof and untouchable, and wondered how good she'd be at bringing his ideas to life.

"Yeah, and she's good. I can ask, but I'm sure she'd do it."

"We can't afford to pay her. That's why I'm trying to create one on my own."

Reagan set the drawings on the table. "She'll do it for me."

"You'd do that for us?"

"Ask her a favor? I'd say I owe you at least that much."

"You owe me?"

"Well." She smirked. "I supposed after this whole Bible study debacle we're technically even, but I don't mind asking for a favor. She's probably as bored as I am."

Emboldened by her admission and desperate to make some progress for the band, Dash said, "If you're bored …"

"Don't push your luck."

"I could really use some help with the website." He held up his hands when she narrowed her eyes. "You said you were bored, and I'm not the creative type."

She crossed her arms. "Oh really, rock star. You're not creative?"

"Okay, fine. I could write a song about creating a website easier than I could actually make one."

"It's not that hard. I made one for an econ project last semester."

Bingo. He smiled and blinked his eyes in his most cartoonish attempt at flattery. "Then it shouldn't take us long."

After the expected eye rolls and an audible huff, she finally relented. "Hand me your laptop."

Chapter Eighteen

Reagan should have known better than to enter Dash's lair while still buzzing from his performance at church. She should have stayed inside her apartment and spent the evening with her old friend, the TV, and given her hormones time to settle. She'd made the mistake of checking the library books for their return date and smarted when she saw they were due the next day. Sometimes the ardent rule follower in her made life more than a little inconvenient.

That's why she sat scowling at her handsome neighbor as he reclined on his couch, sucking on a candy cane that stained his tongue red. The cad. She tore her eyes away from his mouth and zoned in on the laptop. "There are plenty of free website platforms that are super easy to set up and maintain, but you're going to need to pay for a domain name and a hosting site."

"How much is that?"

"Not much. Maybe five bucks a month."

"That's doable."

"What do you want to name your domain? Evergreen dot com?" She chewed her lip and opened a new window. "That's probably taken."

"I suppose we should use the word 'band' in the name so people know what we are."

"Evergreen dot com is taken, and … oh, look at that. Evergreen band dot com is some kind of folk music group from overseas."

"Ah, no thanks." He crunched the tip of the candy cane and chewed loudly. "What do we call it then?"

"Let's check a domain registry and see what's open." As she typed the search terms and found a site listing available names, Dash scooted closer on the couch, so close the entire side of his body nestled against the side of hers. She bloomed with heat at the intimacy of their position and the feel of his peppermint breath on her skin. Their mutual attraction simmered below the surface, ready to scorch them both at the smallest provocation. In that moment, she wished she hadn't agreed to help. She cleared her throat. "How about evergreen dash band dot com?" she said. "Or we could do a dot net search."

Her voice sounded different—high and breathy. Dash must have noticed because he leaned away and stared at her with crinkled brows. "You okay?"

She shoved him with her knee. "I'm fine. Scoot over please. You're making me hot."

Oh no. Why did she say that? And why did he have to grin from ear to ear as her embarrassment turned her redder than his candy cane tongue. "Temperature hot! Get your mind out of the gutter."

"Sorry." He looked anything but. "I'm a guy. My mind tends to dwell in the gutter, especially when you're around."

His offhand comment only made her skin flame brighter. "You said you wouldn't hit on me."

"I'm not hitting on you. I'm simply reacting to your statement." He twisted the rest of the candy cane in the wrapper and tossed it onto the coffee table, giving them a moment to retreat. "If you're temperature hot, I can turn the heat down."

She'd worn a sweater because he kept his apartment chilly. If he turned the heat down, she feared he'd freeze in his sleep or they'd soon see their breath when talking. "No, don't touch the heat. I'm okay. Just give me some space."

He nodded and stood. "You want something to drink?"

"I wouldn't turn down a water."

"Coming right up."

When he disappeared into the kitchen, Reagan collapsed against the couch. What was she doing? What were they doing, talking in doublespeak about taboo topics and taking every opportunity to flirt? She wanted to help him with his website. He clearly needed help, she was bored, and she was more than happy to assist, but not as a way for them to get closer. Everything inside of her warned that getting to know him better was a mistake of colossal proportions. She was already attracted—too attracted—and stepping back seemed the wisest course. But now they'd started the website …

"Hello?" Dash waved his hand in front of her face. She'd been so lost in thought she hadn't heard him return.

"Oh." She straightened and blinked her mind clear. "Sorry."

He set a bottle of water in front of her and took a swig of his own before sitting down with a good foot of space between them.

"Thanks." She reached for the bottle, took a sip, and set it back down. "So, what about 'evergreen dash band dot com?'" She loosened her grip when he tilted the laptop in his direction.

"I suppose that'll work. We'll just have to emphasize the dash in our promo materials."

She secured the domain name, relieved their conversation had veered away from the serpent in the room. He stretched his legs out and crossed his ankles atop the coffee table. His feet were bare. Something about that flash of skin had her skin pebbling.

"Thanks for your help with all this," he said. "This saves me from pestering Connie."

"Connie was going to set up the website?"

"When she had some free time."

Reagan snorted. "Considering Professor Adkins devotion to 'family time' over the holidays, that should be sometime next year." She handed Dash the laptop. "You need to fill in your information for the domain name. Then we'll get you set up on a hosting site."

She watched him type, his long fingers striking keys with graceful efficiency, and wondered what those hands would feel like on her skin. *Stop! You're your own worst enemy!*

"You okay?" Dash asked.

"Yeah. Why?"

"You were mumbling. I didn't know if you were talking to me."

"Sorry." She rubbed her temple to hide her embarrassment. "Just thinking out loud."

He handed the laptop back to Reagan and stood up. "I need to get my wallet for the payment. Be right back."

She glanced at the screen and couldn't believe her eyes.

"What's so funny?" He skirted the coffee table and sat on the couch. His eyes narrowed with suspicion.

"Your name is William?"

"Yes." He cocked his head. "Why is that funny?"

"I just never pictured you as a William. Or Bill. Or Billy."

"Ha ha. Did you think Dash was my real name?"

She shrugged. "I don't know. Is Dash your stage name?"

"Seriously?" he said, pulling at the collar of his shirt. "You think I'd make up a stage name? What do you take me for? Sting?"

"Your name is William, but everybody calls you Dash. What's a girl to think?"

"I'm a fast runner, okay. Mom and Dad have called me Dash forever and it stuck." He shook his head, grinning. "I can't believe you think I'd make up a stage name."

"Why? Lots of people do."

"It's so pretentious. Who am I protecting myself from? Fans?"

"I'm sure you've got a few."

"Maybe."

She'd embarrassed him. Hidden beneath that sexy stubble, his cheeks had darkened to the color of her mother's Barbie-pink spritzer. How interesting. "Whatever, Billy. Just put the information in so we can move on."

He refused to take the laptop from her when she tried to pass it back. "Don't call me that."

"Why not? It's your name, right?"

"Do I look like a Billy?"

She wanted to say yes. The thought of him answering to Billy was laughable, but she couldn't say it with a straight face. "No, you don't look like a Billy. Maybe a Will, but not a Billy."

He growled and ripped the laptop from her grip. "It's Dash, now and always. Got it."

She gave him a mock salute and delighted at his annoyance. Somehow, frustrating him made her happy for the first time in weeks. He handed the laptop back and pocketed his credit card.

"What's next?"

"Hosting site." She keyed in the site and turned the laptop so he could see. "I've used them before and I like them because of the security. Hacking can be a problem, and they backup and protect your site automatically for about ten bucks a year."

"That sounds good."

They passed the computer back and forth—to Dash for the personal information and payment—to Reagan for the selections. With the domain name and hosting site up and running, the fun part came next. "Now we pick a theme and start personalizing the site."

"What kind of theme?"

"There are hundreds of website templates that we can personalize." She pulled up the browser and, despite the warning siren in her head, scooted next to Dash, careful to leave an inch of space so their legs didn't touch. She scrolled through the many options. "You probably want something pretty generic with pictures and maybe a blog."

"A blog? What are we supposed to write about?"

"Whatever you're working on, funny stories from the road, whatever."

"The road?"

"You know what I mean. Anecdotes from practice or stage performances. The point is for visitors to get to know you on a personal level."

"I don't really want to put a bunch of personal information out there for anyone to see."

"It doesn't have to be too personal, but the point is to humanize the band. Show your funny side, your serious side, your friendship with each other. The more people connect with you all on a personal level, the more invested they'll feel in your music and want to see you perform."

"That makes sense. I just never thought about what that might look like."

"I'd start with a blog to really let people dive deep, and then move on to smaller social media posts when you're better known. You should also have some videos on the site or link to them. I can embed a few small clips into your site, but the more you have on the internet with your name and website, the better your SEO."

"SEO?" he asked.

"Search engine optimization. SEO helps your site stay on the first page when someone searches for the band."

"Okay. I hadn't thought about that. But we don't have any video yet."

She stopped typing and looked him in the eye. "It doesn't have to be fancy. Even a clip of a song from a phone would work."

He scratched the back of his neck and ducked his head. "None of that, either."

"Really? Why not?"

Dash shrugged. "I guess we never thought about it. We've been so busy trying to book live shows that we overlooked the obvious."

"If you can get someone to film you, I can upload it to the site."

"Other than church, we don't have any gigs lined up until January."

"What about practice?"

"Well, yeah, but that's not very professional."

"It'll look raw and edgy. Honestly, it'll be something for people to discover. You're unknown and basically underground at this point."

He blew out a breath. "You're right. I should have done this a long time ago."

This time she shrugged, happy to have moved into safer territory. "No worries. We'll get it up and running in no time. What's your favorite band?"

He lowered his brows and scowled at her as if she'd asked him to pick his favorite child. "That's a hard question. I have more than one favorite."

"Okay, pick *a* favorite."

"I like Deadman Dead."

"The rock band?"

"Yeah. Why are you surprised?"

"I don't know." The lyrics from their most memorable song, Hellfire, floated through her head. *You'll find me in the space between heaven and hell, licking my chops at the liberty bell, chasing the devil inside my soul, feeding the monster for population control.* "That doesn't seem like the kind of music you'd listen to."

"Because I'm a Christian?"

"Surely you see the irony?"

"The guitar riffs are amazing, even if the lyrics are a bit morbid. They created some of the most classic melodies of all time."

"I agree. I like them too. I just didn't figure you as a fan."

"I like all kinds of music."

"Okay, name another band."

He twisted his lips as his eyes roamed the room. "I've always liked Sweetgrass Butcher."

"The swing group?"

"I'm surprised you've heard of them."

"My mama likes their music."

"She has good taste."

Reagan snorted. Saying her mother had good taste was like saying Elizabeth Taylor could really pick the men. "In music, maybe." Desperate not to talk about her mother, she pulled both band's websites up on screen, side by side. "Take a look at their websites and tell me what you like and don't like."

He leaned closer, using the touch pad to scroll through both sites. The peppermint smell of his breath lingered. As they both scanned the websites, their bodies relaxed into one another until the space between them disappeared. Reagan felt his thigh muscles against her jeans and heat from his body warmed her skin.

"I like them both." He sat back and turned his head in her direction. Their faces were close—too close. "I see what you mean about personalizing their story. I think Sweetgrass Butcher does a better job of creating interest in the music with their 'About Us' page."

He appeared unfazed by their proximity, his voice normal, his posture casual, but his pupils dilated, and his muscles tensed as they stared at one another. Her brain seemed to operate on a sphere immune to his magnetic pull. "They're not so well known, so they need it more. You'd have to live under a rock not to know Deadman Dead and their colorful backstory." She glanced away to break the spell when she drifted toward him and his heat. *Focus. Maintain control.* "Give me the name of a band you've heard of but don't know much about."

He blew out a breath and it wafted between them, a siren's song pulling her under. "Um, how about Treadway."

"Never heard of them." She keyed in the name, grateful her fingers functioned, and pulled up their website.

Dash scratched his neck. "They're from Ireland, I think." He used his finger on the pad to read the "About the Band" page. "Scotland and Ireland." He chewed his lip as he read, scrolling down the page quickly. Either he skimmed the passage, or he'd mastered the art of speedreading, or their proximity was getting to him too. "I see what you mean. Reading their backstory makes me want to know more."

She shooed his hand and touched the "Social Media" page. "They update the blog regularly to keep fans interested. And they're active on social media."

"The topics aren't what I expected to find."

"Bands are a dime a dozen. It's the people that make them different."

He swung his eyes to her, their gazes locked, held. What was it about the way he looked at her that made her want to be reckless for the first time in her life?

"People are full of surprises." His fingers touched her hair and her fight or flight instincts kicked into gear. She squirmed, squealed, and slammed the laptop shut, shoving it into his gut.

"Okay, website's done. Now work on the content and let me know if you have any questions."

He didn't smirk at her or flash that dimple she knew he wielded like a weapon but stared at her with an earnestness that had her pulse thrashing in her ears. "Just like you, Reagan, I'm full of questions."

Chapter Nineteen

Dash paused on the porch after small group when Mark tapped him on the shoulder. "Hey," Mark asked. "Do you have a minute?"

"Sure," Dash stepped back inside, let the door close, and turned to face his friend. "What's up?"

"Nothing. I haven't talked to you this week and I wanted to see how you're doing."

"Sorry about that. I'm good. Hanging with the kids a lot. Working on the website."

Mark shoved his hands in his back pockets and tipped his head to the side, giving Dash a quizzical stare. "I thought Connie was helping with the website."

"She was supposed to, but Reagan came over and had it up and running in one night. I'm working with the guys on content and videos."

Mark nodded and narrowed his eyes in a look that conveyed both skepticism and interest. "You're spending a lot of time with Reagan?"

They'd just finished a discussion on righteousness and Mark—who'd led the discussion and explained eloquently about how God judges our hearts and not our deeds—seemed bent on seeing only the worst in Dash's motives. "I wouldn't call it a lot of time. She returned some books I loaned her, and we got to talking. She's a whiz with the computer and really understands marketing. Picking her brain is helping the band."

"The band." Mark bobbed his head, stared at Dash with his lips rolled between his teeth. "Right."

Dash counted to ten before letting out a breath. Mark didn't even try to hide his disapproval. "What?"

"Nothing."

Dash rolled his eyes, wished Mark's interest didn't feel like a rebuke. "Just say whatever it is you want to say."

This time it was Mark who sucked in a breath before pacing into the den and away from the front door. Dash followed, ready to defend himself against whatever Mark accused. "She's getting awfully involved in your life."

"Because she helped me set up a website? If that's your standard, shouldn't you be concerned your wife offered to help?"

"It's not the same thing and you know it."

"Really? Connie offered to help because we're friends. Reagan offered to help because we're friends. What's the difference?"

"Don't be obtuse." Mark crossed his arms, narrowed his eyes. "You only want to sleep with one of them."

"Who said I don't want to sleep with Connie?"

Mark's head jerked back, and his mouth dropped open.

"Kidding." Dash's quick-witted comment scored with Mark—throwing him off course enough to mollify his anger.

"You said yourself the hardest part of the dating sabbatical was not having sex." Mark sat down on the couch and rested his elbows on his knees, linking his fingers as if in prayer. By the rigidness of his posture and the tightness of his face, Mark's anger may have waned, but not his concern.

"How do you make the leap from helping with a website to having sex? I don't see the connection."

"You don't want to have sex with Reagan?"

Dash flicked his gaze upward.

"Don't get angry," Mark said. "I'm just asking a question."

"What do you want me to say?" Of course he wanted to have sex with Reagan. She was smart, witty, beautiful. And that body, her outrageous curves—when he let himself think of them—drove him to madness. "I like women. I miss women. I miss sex most of all. I never realized how much validation I got from women, but I've gotten to know myself better and I don't need that anymore. I'm comfortable with who I am without anyone else."

"You didn't answer my question."

"If you're asking me if Reagan stirs up feelings of lust and wonder, then yes, she does. But that's okay. I miss sex, but I want something I never had—a real connection with a woman outside of sex."

"And you want that with Reagan?"

"Haven't we been through this already?"

"I'm trying to keep you accountable. That's what you asked me to do when you started this thing."

Dash sat down on the couch, defeated and frustrated at having to defend himself. "Putting aside the sexual attraction, I like her. I don't see why it's such a big deal to spend time with her when all she's doing is helping with the website. It's not as if she's throwing herself at me."

"You don't think you're testing yourself?" Mark asked. "Just a little?"

He recalled Reagan sitting next to him so close he felt every muscle in her body constrict, heard every breath she took, smelled every inch of her milky skin. "What if I am? A little. Is that wrong?"

"It's not wrong as much as it is dangerous."

Dash thought of Mark and Connie, how they met, the classic friends-to-lovers story they both liked to tell. "Back when you and Connie were just friends working together and going to church together, didn't you want her?"

"Every second of every day." Mark's face sobered and he waved his hands in the air. "Why do you think I'm so worried about you?"

"I have no idea, considering how well that worked out for you."

"In the long run, yes, it did work out. But then?" He scrunched his face and shook his head from side to side. "It was torture, pure unadulterated torture. I prayed every day for patience. At the time, because we were working together, I couldn't escape her or the desire. I wouldn't wish that on anyone."

"Even though you got the girl in the end?"

"Here's the thing, Dash. I was older and much farther along on my journey with Christ. I leaned on Him more at that time than any other time of my life. You're still new to this—trusting God with everything—and I don't want to see you slip and regret it. Unlike my situation, you have a choice about whether or not to spend time with Reagan. For your own sanity, I urge you to dial it back. You can still be friends. Just don't look for ways to be near her."

"I'm not orchestrating anything. She's my neighbor. I loaned her some books. She gave them back. End of story."

"Not end of story. She set up the website, right?"

"Yeah."

"And when you've got some content and a few videos to embed, you planning to do that yourself?"

Dash sputtered. "Maybe."

"Maybe? That means no. That means you're going to go back to her and ask for help. Spend more time with her. Torturing yourself."

"I can handle spending time with her. I'm not that weak."

"You're also not that strong."

"Thanks for the vote of confidence."

They stared at one another, gunslinger vs. gunslinger, friend vs. friend. "Look, you count on me to be honest and that's all I'm trying to be." Honesty was the cornerstone of their relationship, the reason they'd become so close. Dash needed to remember that Mark wasn't his enemy so much as his conscience.

"As far as I can tell, you walked away from the drugs and the drinking and you've never looked back. Part of the reason is you're not hanging out with those guys and not performing in bars anymore."

"I've filled in a time or two when the old band needed me."

"But not regularly."

"No, but—"

"Seeing Reagan is a regular occurrence. She's tempting you almost every day."

"You make it sound like she's conspiring to get me alone. You couldn't be farther from the truth."

"I'm not—"

"Yes, you are, and I'm sick of it. She's not some floozy who's trying to get me into bed. She's a nice girl who's serious about school and her future. If I'm tempted by her on a regular basis it's because *I'm* tempted."

He ran his hands through his hair and gave a frustrated tug before letting go. Mark could be as honest as possible with Dash about his motives, but not Reagan's. She was off limits. "When I fill in for one of the guys in the old band, they give me grief all the time about the changes I've made in my life. They're drinking, popping pills, and the girls are still around, ready to go. So don't tell me I don't know the difference between befriending someone nice and putting myself in a tempting situation because I do."

Mark face and hands went limp. They stared at one another, deadlocked, as the cuckoo clock counted the seconds. "I'm sorry I upset you," he said after a lengthy pause. "I hope you know I'm only saying this because I care. You've come a long way in a short time, you're smart and talented, and I'm worried about you throwing all your progress away over a girl you barely know."

"I'm not—"

"And despite how it may sound, I like Reagan. I think she's a nice girl. I simply want you to see this through and come out stronger on the other side."

Mark's compassion sounded more like condemnation and an attack on an innocent girl but fighting about it would get them nowhere. "I know that, and I appreciate your concern."

Mark reached out and put a hand on Dash's shoulder, squeezed. "I'm praying for you, man. I really am."

Reagan looked over her Bible study in preparation for tonight's meeting. She wasn't sure why her stomach churned at the thought of facing the women again. They were harmless, and didn't pressure her to contribute. She wrestled between treating people with respect and living true to the common sense that had served her well throughout her life. Virgin births flew in the face of all logic, no matter how many normal level-headed people believed it happened.

Read it like a story. Dash's advice came back to her again and again. She wished those were the only words of his that rang through her head on a daily basis.

Life rarely goes according to plan was another. That had certainly proved true by the mere fact that she was reading a Bible study.

You're beautiful and infuriating. Back at ya, she wanted to say. Right back at ya.

You're a temptation. She was tempted to jump him, consequences be darned.

My mind tends to dwell in the gutter, especially when you're around. Her mind hadn't left the gutter since he'd wheedled his way into her life.

She needed to focus on the negative—like the Bible study—as a defense against his charms. Every time they were together, every conversation revealed more appealing aspects of his personality. He made her laugh, he made her blush, he made her think, and he appreciated her mind. He also made her daydream about him with alarming regularity. And speaking of Dash, she needed to call Shelby and ask a favor.

Her roommate answered on the second ring, sounding sluggish. "Hello?"

"Are you sleeping?" Reagan asked. "At two o'clock in the afternoon?"

"It's called a nap. Most of us mortals take them on occasion."

Reagan only grunted. She'd never been a napper. She never saw the point.

"Did you call for a reason or just to interrupt a perfectly good dream."

"I called to ask a favor."

"Then you might reconsider your opening line."

"Ha ha. How's your break been so far?"

Shelby let out a lazy, brazen yawn that reverberated through the phone. Reagan pictured her friend sprawled atop an unmade bed. A beauty queen in need of an audience. "Break's been boring. Now that I've caught up on my sleep from finals, I'm bored to death."

"Good. I have a project that might keep you busy."

"A paying project?" Shelby's voice rose an octave.

"No. Consider it charity."

"Is this something for the good professor?"

At Shelby's question, Reagan realized how much the favor would cost her pride. "I need your help with a logo."

"A logo for what?"

"A band. Evergreen."

"Who's Evergreen?"

She didn't want to elaborate but couldn't think of a way around the truth. "Dash Carter's band."

The pause on the line told Reagan everything she needed to know.

"Hmm. I take it your break's been anything but boring." There was a distinct purr in her voice.

"Oh no. I'm as bored as the rest of you."

"Doesn't sound like it, not when you're working closely with our sexy neighbor who happens to have a huge crush on you. How's that going, by the way?"

Reagan gritted her teeth. She should have known Shelby would dig. "We're not working closely. I'm simply helping with his website. They need a logo and you're a graphic artist. I figured you wouldn't mind."

"I don't mind. I'm happy to help." She cleared the sleep from her throat. "Interesting that you didn't deny the crush."

Reagan sucked in a breath. Asking a favor meant more than Dash would ever realize.

"You may as well spill the details," Shelby said. "I already talked to Kayla."

Oh, brother. Now her roommates were talking behind her back. "Then you know there's nothing to tell."

"Really? It's not the least bit unusual for you to attend a Bible study?"

"If you talked to Kayla, you know I'm not going because I want to. I got roped into going because of Dash and his relationship with Professor Adkins."

"The very person you're asking a favor for? Interesting."

"Not interesting." She refused to indulge Shelby in her silly matchmaking. She'd been pushing her at Dash for months. "Are you going to help him or not?"

"Sure. I've got nothing better to do. But I need some information."

"Like?"

"Like what kind of music they play, their intended audience, color preferences, typefaces, brand messaging, other band logos they like, images they're considering."

"I didn't ask him about any of that." The ugly green-eyed monster coated her stomach, weighing her down. "Maybe you should call him."

Reagan pictured Shelby twirling a lock of hair with her fingers like she'd seen her do a thousand times. She pictured her roommate on the phone with Dash, a breathy, sex kitten sound to her voice as she giggled at Dash's responses. Their conversation would lead to a meeting, which would lead to Dash falling under Shelby's spell. Darn it, why did it matter?

"I'll type up a list of questions and email them to you," Shelby said.

"Wouldn't it be easier to talk to him?" Even as the words left her mouth, her stomach curdled. Her beautiful roommate who could—when she wanted to—charm the pants off of anyone and the guy who stirred up so many conflicting emotions Reagan couldn't find her footing. Why did the thought of them communicating, working together on a project, make her want to pull out her hair?

"Not necessarily. People like to think about their answers, and—as I assume there are others in the band—he's going to want to get their input as well. If I email you, you can pass it along to him and he'll have time to think about it and talk to the others before I start down a path that's all wrong."

That made sense, and it relieved the stretched-beyond-breaking sensation in her stomach. "This sounds like more work than I thought. Are you sure you don't mind?"

"I told you I'm bored, and I've never done a band logo before. If they hit it big, I could be famous."

Reagan snorted. Shelby was already famous for her looks and hated every second of it. "Okay. Send me the email and I'll get it to him."

"Perfect. I'll go ahead and do a little research of my own. What kind of music do they perform? Like Caliber?"

"Evergreen is a Christian band."

"Oh. I guess that makes sense, considering he pressured you into a Bible study. I don't know anything about Christian music. What's it like?"

Reagan recalled the band's performances at church. They were gritty, raw, and powerful. "Their music is really good—some is kind of like Caliber but with a clean message about God, and some stuff is more pop-like. None of the lyrics are in your face. I'm trying to get him to video a few practice sessions, and when he does I'll send them to you."

"That'd be great. Tell him not to think too long. Once break is over, I won't have much time with classes next semester."

"I'll get right on it."

"You do that. And Reagan?"

Uh oh. Here come the barbs. "Yes?"

"Don't do anything I wouldn't do. With Dash, I mean."

Reagan had no idea what Shelby would do—ignore him, tease him for her own purposes, and shut him down—and Reagan lacked the savvy to manipulate Dash. She rolled her eyes. "Whatever."

Chapter Twenty

Lightheaded with a sense of déjà vu, Reagan stood on Connie's doorstep on another crisp December evening. Despite the welcoming glow of the porch lanterns, Reagan felt anything but. *Fraud. Fake. Degenerate.* Those were the words flashing through her mind in the seconds it took for Connie to answer, blind Reagan with her full-wattage smile, and drag her inside as if leading a prisoner to execution.

Alana entered behind Reagan, pushing the door open with one hand while carrying a foil covered tray in the other. When she stripped off her dark gray pea coat, Reagan noted the drooping maternity overalls. Alana had obviously given up on regular clothes and plunged head first into mommy wear. God help her. On a certain level, Reagan could sympathize with Alana's struggle to find clothing that fit. While Reagan wasn't hiding a burgeoning belly, she did spend a great deal of time shopping for clothes that hid her embarrassingly large bust line.

Stephanie was already sitting in the den, wearing jeans and a sweater. She must have left work on time and made it home to change before Bible study. Without the power suit, Stephanie appeared younger, less impressive, and more like a regular person. Not someone Reagan would choose to emulate. Stephanie stood, and everyone exchanged hugs and greetings. After the requisite oohs and ahhs about the tasty treats on display, they got down to business.

"I'll pray us in," Connie said. "Heavenly Father, thank you for this day and for this time when we've come together to study Your word. Thank you, Father, for the preservation of those words, for those who choose to study the Bible and use their talents to help us better understand You and grow closer to You. We ask You to be with us tonight as we gather in Your name. Amen."

"Amen," Reagan muttered as the muscles in her stomach coiled. Could she sit here another night and pretend to believe? Was it even right to try?

"This week we read about Mary and the angel Gabriel who delivered some shocking news to the girl who would play a major part in Jesus' story. Did anything you read this week really strike a chord with you?" Connie looked expectantly from face to face.

Reagan cased the room—the artful bookshelves, the basket tucked into a corner filled to overflowing with folded blankets, the presents stacked under the pretty Christmas tree —anywhere but at Connie and her thirsty gaze.

Alana cleared her throat. "I was amazed at Mary's willingness to believe the angel and to accept what he said as from God without question. Never once did she doubt what he said or worry about the consequences."

"I liked the way the author showed us how different the responses were between Mary and Zacharias," Stephanie said. "Zacharias questioned God and was punished by God. Mary believed and was exalted by God but punished by society." She shook her head. "It's an interesting and still relevant conundrum."

Reagan sat still as a stone, stewing in resentment.

"I agree." Connie nodded. "It's one of the many ways the Bible is applicable to this day. How many times have each of us experienced the pull between doing what we know is right in the eyes of the Lord and doing what is socially acceptable?"

Reagan fidgeted in her seat, regretting the movement when Stephanie glanced her way.

"I experienced something like that just this week." Alana tucked her hands beneath her legs. "Our neighborhood had an open board meeting—we've got issues with a few of the more restrictive covenants and the creative ways people are skirting them—and this one lady on the board suggested creating a task force to roam the neighborhood in search of violators. She had the gall to suggest the stay-at-home moms should be the first to volunteer because we don't work and have so much time on our hands."

Stephanie scoffed. "She actually said that?"

"Yes." Alana nodded. "As if I have nothing better to do but throw Luke in the car and drive around looking for covenant violators."

"Things never change." Connie sighed. "I heard the same digs when the kids were younger. I hear them even more now that the kids are in school."

Reagan sat very still as words collided in her brain, clamoring for release. *What do you do all day? Would it be a big deal to put Luke in the car and drive around? Let's face it, you're home and not at work.* She rolled her lips between her teeth and did her best to appear neutral.

"Did you do it?" Stephanie asked. "Did you volunteer for the task force?"

"No. At first, no one raised their hands, but then one mom did and the others fell into line. The whole task force is made up of stay-at-home moms and report to the working folks. It turned my stomach."

"They got bullied," Stephanie said.

"Exactly." Alana ran her hands along her legs, up and down as her cheeks colored. "It would have been different if the moms had volunteered of their own volition, but they didn't. I'm not saying that volunteering wasn't right in the eyes of the Lord, but they didn't do it because they felt called to serve. They did it because they were called out."

"That's a great example. Reagan?" Connie asked. "Did anything stick out to you in the reading?

Oh, no. Reagan's gaze bounced from woman to woman. They sat in their seats, their chests rising and falling with easy breaths, inquisitive looks on their faces while Reagan began to sweat. Did she really expect an answer?

"I … I thought Gabriel's blessing to Mary sounded more like a curse. I thought her naïve to see it as anything but."

"Mary's naiveté could have factored into her willingness to accept Gabriel's announcement." Connie's voice held nothing but patience and consideration, but Reagan's back stiffened defensively. "Back then, girls married young. She may not have understood what would happen when word got out that she was pregnant."

"Her faith was stronger than her concerns," Stephanie said. "That's why God chose her."

"Was she faithful or foolish?" Reagan dared Stephanie before she could stop herself. "I didn't read anything that told me it wasn't ignorance that made her go along with Gabriel and God. What evidence did the Bible provide for Mary's faithfulness?"

Stephanie reached for her Bible, a well-used leather-bound edition. She thumbed through the pages and read aloud. "Luke 1:38 reads that Mary responded, 'I am the Lord's servant. May everything you have said about me come true. And then the angel left her.'"

Reagan fished the phone from her pocket and, as she'd done while reading the Bible study, found the passage before Luke 38. "Verse 34 reads, 'Mary asked the angel, But how can this happen? I am a virgin.' That's almost the same question Zacharias asked Gabriel, and he was turned into a deaf-mute until John was born."

"I think you've both made a decent argument," Connie said. "The answer may be that God knew each of their hearts just like he knows our hearts. What we say and what we mean are sometimes at odds."

It sounded like a warning. *God knows your heart's not in this for the right reasons. Connie, Alana, and Stephanie know too.*

Connie veered the discussion back to the week's reading and continued with questions. Alana and Stephanie answered eagerly, while Reagan did her best to avoid contributing, nodding in agreement when it seemed appropriate and avoiding eye contact at all cost. She wouldn't get trapped again. She spoke up on one other occasion, when Alana said something so stupid Reagan couldn't stop herself from shedding light on her ignorance and convincing the ladies she had in fact read the Bible verses referenced in the study guide. Her comments were met with blank stares. Was slovenly belief the only way to feel welcome in this group?

After a brief interruption from Lily wanting a kiss from her mommy before bed, the evening concluded. Connie prayed them out. Reagan stuffed her arms into her jacket and made a beeline for the door. Connie stopped her with a disarming smile. "Would you mind helping me carry these dishes into the kitchen?" she asked as Alana and Stephanie chattered out the door. Connie's innocent request seemed laced with something deeper, something dubious that tickled Reagan's nerves and sent alarm bells screeching along her scalp.

"Uh, sure." She picked up a serving dish still loaded with ginger cookies and followed Connie through a doorway into the kitchen. Like the rest of the house, the space was light and bright, with shiny stainless appliances and a muted countertop that called visitors to grab a seat at the island and stay awhile. The cluster of dishes in the sink should have eased Reagan's nerves—*see, real people live here*—but it only heightened her sense of feeling like an intruder in their happy home. She set the platter on the counter next to the sink and backed against the island.

"Sorry about the mess." Connie threw a stack of dirty paper plates into the trash and flashed her affable smile. "Mark is great with the kids, but not so great with cleanup."

"You live here. Life's messy sometimes."

The smile was back, but as Connie's lips slid downward into a contemplative pout, Reagan straightened and prepared for battle.

"That's the understatement of the year. Listen," Connie wiped her hands on a paper towel and tossed it into the trash. "I get the sense you're not totally comfortable in the group."

Bravo. Connie detected the obvious. What did she want, a medal? "I'm … okay."

Connie pursed her lips and glanced at her shoes before lifting her eyes to Reagan.

Here it comes. She knows you're a fraud.

"It's not just that you seem uncomfortable, but you're a bit defensive about our belief system."

By defensive did she mean unimpressed? "I would say I'm more questioning at this point. Isn't it okay to ask questions for clarity when the subjects run counter to common sense?"

"Asking questions is fine. I encourage you to ask questions, but your line of questioning comes across as dismissive. One of the rules of the group is to treat others with respect, but honestly, your questioning of Alana bordered on rude."

Rude? Connie thought it rude to question the woman about God's prudence in impregnating a twelve-year-old virgin? Reagan began to perspire in the warm kitchen and her thick down jacket. "I'm sorry if I came across as rude, but I'm having a hard time reconciling the Bible with reality."

"That's normal. You're looking at Mary's situation from a twenty-first century viewpoint. Times were different back then. It wasn't unusual for a girl to marry at twelve. That's just the way it was."

"Okay."

"I'm not saying it was right or wrong, but that's how it was. There are certain facts you have to accept as true before you can put the verses into context."

"Fine. Old men married kids. Got it."

"Reagan …" Connie reached across the space between them and placed her hand on Reagan's arm, squeezed. "I get where you're coming from. I do. I was you not that long ago. Full of disbelief, and lots and lots of questions."

"So surely you can understand my hesitation to believe what sounds like nonsense."

"I absolutely understand. But here's something you need to understand. We can't convince you that the Bible is an accurate account of the past, or that Jesus was real. No one can convince you. Only you can do that."

And the nonsense kept on rolling. "I'm supposed to convince myself?"

"Only God can reveal himself to you—when He's ready and you're ready. If you're at all serious about taking this journey, the first thing you need to do is open your mind to the possibility of Jesus."

As much as Reagan disliked Connie's confrontation, she had to appreciate how the woman didn't beat around the bush. "I don't know how to do that. Dash suggested I read the Bible like reading a fantasy story, but I can't. Fantasy isn't supposed to be real—that's why they call it fantasy. This is supposedly real, but it's so far-fetched, I can't believe it happened the way the Bible says it did."

"The only way to open your heart to the truth is to trust and to pray."

"I don't know how to pray." The words were out before she could snatch them back. Connie just stood there, a pitying smile on her pretty face. On a huff, Reagan turned and stormed around the island, needing distance.

"You know all those doubts you've got swirling around your head?" Connie asked, her voice quiet. "The ones I can practically see churning during Bible study? Tell God what you're thinking. Ask him to help you."

"Speak to God?" It sounded simple—too simple. "Tell God I think the Bible isn't true?"

"He's an all-powerful king. He can handle your doubts."

"I'd feel foolish."

Connie shrugged. "I'm sure you would, the first time or two. After that, you might get used to giving God your doubts instead of wrestling with them alone. Reagan, you're obviously an academic. Academics have the hardest time reconciling the good news of Jesus. Whole books have been written about academics who went in search of disproving Jesus. Do you know what happened?"

Reagan lifted a shoulder.

"Their research led them to believe in Christ."

She flung her arms in the air. "I don't have time to do any more research!"

"That's okay. You don't need to. The man I'm talking about was a journalist. He wrote a book about his journey and now it's a movie. Honestly, I'd recommend the movie. The book gets into the weeds of the Bible and—I'm not saying you're not bright enough to understand, but you're probably not familiar enough with Jesus's story to make it interesting."

Reagan purposely unclenched her jaw when her teeth began to ache. "I guess I can watch a movie."

"I'm not trying to talk you into anything, but I think it might help you decide whether or not you even want to explore your faith right now. It has to be up to you, Reagan. Not me. Not Mark. And not Dash."

Dash? Seriously. She wouldn't put herself through this for a man. "I'm not doing it for Dash."

"Whatever your reason, it needs to be yours."

What should she say? That she felt pressured into joining because of Connie's husband? Because she couldn't think of any way to explain that didn't make her sound weak or desperate, Reagan said nothing.

"When I started going to church," Connie said, "I didn't feel moved. I was entertained and curious, but I wasn't convinced. Someone suggested I pray, ask God to soften my heart. I did, and I can't explain how it happened, but that was the first time it got easier. I'm not saying you have to pray what I prayed or do what I did, but think about what you need from God in order to make the leap and ask Him to help you. God is always listening and willing to help."

Chapter Twenty-One

Dash gave a quick knock on the door and snuck inside. He was late for practice, and he figured the guys would be angry.

"Sorry I'm late." Dash stripped his jean jacket from his body and tossed it with the other jackets along Seth's bannister. He'd taken a run that morning, longer than intended, to ease the lingering sting of Mark's confrontation. His run had put him behind. He knew Mark wanted only the best for Dash, but he had gone about it in the wrong way. Attacking Reagan didn't do anything but make Dash mad and goad him to prove Mark wrong.

"You smell like greasy pizza." Eli wrinkled his nose.

"Sorry. I took my Axis boys to play Frisbee golf and then out for pizza. I didn't have time to shower."

Jacob began rooting through his bag and tossed something at Dash.

"You keep deodorant spray in your bag?"

"You never know when you might need to freshen up. You're welcome, by the way."

"Thank you." He fished the canister under his shirt and squirted the strong scent of woodchips and pie spice under each arm. "Wow. That's … powerful."

"The ladies like it."

Dash coughed as the potent fragrance assaulted his nose and coated his throat. "I'll bet."

"You've been spending a lot of time with those kids," Eli plucked at the strings of his bass.

"I like hanging out with them. They keep me young."

"Ha ha." Seth stood up, held his arm out in front of him with his fingers up, pulling his fingers back to stretch. After alternating arms, he dropped each hand behind his head and pushed down to stretch his shoulders—exercises he habitually performed before every set. "Eli's right. What gives?"

Dash carefully retrieved his guitar from the case, sat down on one of the folding chairs in Seth's house, and began playing frets on each string to warm up his fingers. "They're out for break and they're bored."

"Their parents must love you," Jacob said.

"It works for all of us. Spending time with them keeps them out of trouble and we have fun together. Besides, I think I'm making a difference in their lives and that makes me feel good."

"I think it's awesome," Eli said. "You're like my older brothers except you actually want to spend time with them. My brothers ditched me at every turn."

"My brother did too." He'd wanted to be just like Brent for so long—perfect Brent who had time for everyone but Dash. "Maybe that's part of it. I mean, who else is willing to play Frisbee golf with me on a cold winter day other than a bunch of twelve-year-olds?"

"I love Frisbee golf," Jacob said. "I'll play with you anytime."

Dash nodded, continued with the frets. "Noted." Once done, he stilled his hands. "Good news. Reagan's got the website set up. It's still private because we need some content. She wants some videos of us performing or practicing."

"We don't have any video," Eli said. "I knew I should have asked the church."

"She said practice video would work. The point is to humanize the band."

"Sounds logical." Seth twirled his sticks. "I've followed band blogs for years. I loved the personal stories from the road and anything behind the scenes."

"Speaking of blogs," Dash stood up and rested the guitar against the wall. "She wants us to write one."

"About what?" Jacob asked.

"Anything and everything. Our songs, inspiration, funny stories, whatever. The point is to create content that increases our SEO. She also asked her roommate to help us design a logo. She's a graphic artist."

"She's thinking like a manager." Eli wagged his brows. "I like it. I like her."

"Yeah." Dash folded his arms across his chest and narrowed his eyes at Eli. "I noticed."

"Look who's jealous," Eli said. "You can't date her anyway."

"I know I can't, but that doesn't mean I want you to date her."

"I'm just yanking your chain." He stilled his strings. "You want me to set my phone to record a song?" He nodded with his head at a plant stand in the corner of Seth's apartment. "I could lean it against that plant."

"Works for me. The sooner we get her some video, the sooner she can get the site live."

"And the blog?" Seth scowled at Eli as he pulled a limp leaf from the plant.

"I say we do one a week," Dash said. "Since there are four of us, that means we only have to do one a month. How does that sound?"

Seth shrugged. "That doesn't sound too bad."

"I'm glad you agree, because I'd like you to go first."

"Why me?"

Dash picked up his guitar and moved closer to the drum set when Eli waved him over. "Because you used to follow band blogs, so you're familiar with the content and style."

"Okay, but our first post needs to be about something specific."

Dash thought of Reagan's advice about making the blog personal. "You're right. Introduce the band, the reason we formed, and our mission, but go beyond the basics whenever you can. I'm told bands are a dime a dozen. It's the people that make them different."

"I can do that," Seth said.

"Good. I'll do the next one, and we can get a pattern going that works for everyone." He lifted the guitar strap over his head. "Is that camera ready to go?"

"Just the woman I wanted to see."

Reagan's back stiffened as Dash stepped inside her apartment uninvited, and he caught her sharp intake of breath. She closed the door before turning to face him. "I'm busy."

"This will only take a second. I've got the video for the website."

"Just email it to me and I can upload it later."

"I don't have your email, and I was hoping you'd show me how." When she glared at him, he gave her his most charming smile. "I can't depend on you for everything." And according to Mark, he shouldn't.

At her withering stare, he glanced around the apartment. It was like his … but not. Her walls weren't half empty but held framed pictures that complimented the pillows on the L-shaped couch. There were curtains on the windows and the whole place smelled like a spring meadow filled with wildflowers. "Nice place."

"Thanks. I can upload the video myself, but I'll have to show you how to do it later."

He looked at her, the messy hair, the yoga pants, the thin V-neck t-shirt, and did his best to make her smile. "Hot date?"

She snorted. "No."

"Why are you trying to get rid of me?"

"I'm not."

"Yes you are." And it irritated him more than he cared to admit. Every time they were together it was like starting over. Would she ever warm to him? "Why?"

She sighed and crossed her arms under her chest. He tried his best to ignore the way her breasts perched against her arms like a painting atop an easel, demanding his attention.

"I'm going home."

"Home?"

"I have one, ya know."

"Oh." He chuckled, shaking himself free of her spell. "I know you have a home. I thought you were staying here and working with Mark."

"He's too busy with 'family time.' Being here is a waste of time."

Ouch. Quit being petty. She wasn't talking about him. "What about the Bible study?"

"What about it?" She turned and walked toward the hallway, stopped and waved at him to follow her when he simply stood in the den and watched her go. "You may as well come on back if you're going to be awhile. I've got packing to do."

Dash's legs tingled. Was she seriously inviting him back to the inner sanctum, the Holy Grail, her bedroom? What did this mean? Could he be in her space, with her bed in close proximity and not jump her? His legs began moving before his mind could catch up and scream for him to stop, Stop, STOP!

The smell hit him first, that sweet and tangy scent that was pure Reagan. He would have known her room from the smell alone. It took every ounce of control not to whimper. She moved between the open suitcase on her bed—double bed, simple white comforter, three pillows in shades of blue artfully arranged on top—and her walk-in closet, holding jeans and sweaters, yoga pants and t-shirts and tossing them onto her bed.

"I thought you wanted to stay in the study to get closer to Mark." He didn't recognize his high-pitched voice or the urgent need to convince her to stay.

"I don't think it's working."

He cleared his throat to be sure he sounded as natural as possible. "What do you mean? Did something happen?"

She folded a shirt and set it down near—*good grief*—a frilly white bra and stared into the suitcase a moment too long. "Nothing happened. Why would you ask if something happened? Did Connie say something to you?"

Uh-oh. Something definitely happened. Mark's warnings swarmed in his brain, but he shoved them away. He'd deal with that later. "No, but you're leaving, and I thought you wanted to stay."

She sighed, her lips in a thoughtful frown. "It's too quiet here."

Enveloped in her scent, surrounded by her most intimate things, the need to comfort her left him dizzy. "You miss your roommates."

She straightened and looked him in the eye for the first time since entering her sacred space. "Yes, I miss them, even though I get a lot more work done in the quiet."

He could feel her relax, watched every inch of her yield at the mention of her friends. They were her safety net, the family of her making, and she was lonely without them. He tugged the chair from her small desk and straddled it, folding his arms across the seatback. "Y'all seem so different. How did you end up rooming together?"

"We met in the dorm freshman year and clicked." He watched her fold a sweater before placing it in the suitcase. "We're very different, but I love my roommates."

"Tell me about them."

She gave him a sidelong glance. "You know them already."

"I know who they are, but I don't *know* them."

Reagan rolled her eyes, but her lips curled up in a way that revealed she was more than happy to talk about her friends. "Fine. I'll give you the rundown. Emily's pretty and stylish and if you didn't know how sweet she was, you'd want to kill her with your bare hands."

Dash recalled the night he'd helped her drag Emily's very large and very drunk boyfriend into their apartment. "She's the one dating the football player?"

"She broke up with him, thank God, and now she's dating his brother."

"His brother? Interesting. You don't like him either?"

"No, he's great." She held a t-shirt against her chest, meticulously folded each sleeve toward the back, bent it in half lengthwise, and again before setting it inside the suitcase and reaching for another from the bed. How did women know how to fold laundry so perfectly? Was it in their DNA? "They're so disgustingly in love. I want to claw my eyes out if I'm around them too much."

Dash lifted his chin from where he'd settled it against his arms. "It bothers you that they're in love?"

"No, it's just … hard to watch."

"Why?"

She scrunched her face, and yanked a hair tie from her wrist, and wrestled her hair into a messy bun. He ached to run his lips along the column of neck she'd exposed and feel her melt against him.

"They're so in synch. He's very protective of her and she's giddy when they're together. I don't know. It's sort of like they're already married."

Why did she find the idea of love and protection so distasteful? "Sounds nice, having someone to count on."

"It is nice for them, but watching it makes my belly ache."

"Your belly ache?"

She waved her hands dismissively. "It's probably just hormones, and I can't explain it."

Perhaps her belly ached from envy. Lord knew he'd experienced a twinge or two around Mark and Connie. Their perfect love and adorable kids. He knew their marriage wasn't perfect—no relationship was—but Dash longed for something similar. Despite his need for Reagan to explain further, he knew she'd shut down if he pushed too hard, so he changed the subject. "What about Kayla?"

Her face softened into a smile. "Kayla's sweet and gullible. She'll do anything for anyone."

"She seems like the nicest person." He rested his chin atop his arms and watched her roll a pair of jeans against her bed.

"She is. She's got a bleeding heart and only sees the good in people."

"You say that like it's a bad thing."

"It's not a bad thing, but I worry about her." She reached for another pair of jeans. "She needs to toughen up a bit or she's going to get run over by life."

"Only you would think kindness a character flaw."

She flattened her lips and smirked, delighting him to no end. He enjoyed their banter and would miss it—and her—when she was gone.

"What about Shelby?"

"Shelby …" Her gaze drifted beyond him as she clutched a sweater to her chest. "Shelby's gorgeous, chaotic, street-smart. Personally, I think she's lonely."

Dash snorted. "She doesn't have to be. I know about a million guys who'd give their car away to go out with her."

She stopped short on her way to the closet and turned to face him, her brows bounding skyward. "You included?"

How many times did he have to tell her? "My attention lies elsewhere."

As predicted, her cheeks pulsed with color before she continued into the closet. "Shelby knows she could have anyone. I think that's the problem."

"How is that a problem?"

"Her looks are all anyone sees." She came out carrying a pair of tennis shoes in one hand and a pair of sexy heels in the other. "It defines her, and she uses it to her—and our—advantage whenever necessary, but most of the time she'd prefer to blend into a crowd and disappear."

"Really?" Dash shook his head and thought of Shelby. The whole world could be her catwalk. "I don't see that."

"That's what she wants you to see. It's a blessing and a curse to look the way she does. It's hard for people to see her for what's inside and not how pretty she is." She looked down at a pair of socks she'd fisted in her hands and then up at him, her lips twitching. "I suppose you have that in common."

"Are you calling me pretty?"

"If the shoe fits."

He grunted, embarrassed, but he'd take any compliment she'd offer. "Well, I'd say she's lucky to have friends like you who look beyond her beauty."

"That's just my take. She's a tough nut to crack." She tossed the socks into the suitcase and walked back to her closet. "As close as we all are, she keeps things pretty close to the vest, and I'm the last person to pry because I don't like people poking their nose into my business. She's an expert at evading even the most persistent admirers."

Dash grinned. "Well, you've got that in common."

She poked her head out of the closet in her most flirtatious move to date. "How am I evading? You're my most persistent admirer, and we're in my bedroom together."

He caught her grin before she disappeared back inside the closet.

"Anyway, our differences make us work." Her voice squeaked like an out of tune guitar. "No one is vying for the same guy or degree or lifestyle. We call each other out when we're being obnoxious or when we need to hear the truth."

"Those are good friends to have."

She stepped out with a pair of boots. "To be honest, of all the things I thought I'd find at college, friends like them were the biggest surprise."

"I like it when people surprise me. Most of them do, when you give them the chance." He wanted to touch her, yearned to feel her skin beneath his fingers.

Reagan set her boots in the suitcase, tucked a stray lock of hair behind her ear, and looked at him beneath lowered lashes. "Are you talking about me?"

He had to stop teasing her. He was confusing them both with his behavior. Or maybe Mark was right. Maybe he was testing them both. "You, and everybody else on the planet. No one is as two-dimensional as we assume."

"You sound like a psychology major." Her eyes widened. "*Are* you a psychology major?"

"No, I'm a business major, but I like psychology. I thought about it as a major, but it's too much school."

"You don't like school?"

He shrugged. "Not enough to get a doctorate."

"I like school. I like the predictability of it. I like learning new things every day."

Dash liked her. The unpredictability of her. Learning new things about her every time they talked. "You don't learn new things every day without school?"

"Not really." She leaned past him, her scent flitting in his face, and backed away with a leather journal, its edges worn with use. What he would give to have access to her innermost thoughts and musings. "I mean, I guess I do, but school is the intentional learning of new things. It's the goal of the day and that makes me happy."

He memorized her face, the delicate slope of her cheek, the crease in her lush bottom lip, those chocolate eyes that saw too much. How could he not feel attracted to someone dedicated to learning, innocent enough to be surprised by people, and curious by nature.

"Stop," she said.

"Stop what?"

"Stop looking at me like you're using every word I say to fill in some picture in your head."

He became very still and gave a slow, deliberate shake of his head. "Wow. I didn't realize I was that transparent."

She snorted. "You're not, believe me."

"And yet you knew what I was doing?"

"You have this way of looking at me that's disarming. You're trying to figure me out. Like a puzzle."

"I'm sorry that bothers you." He didn't want to make her uncomfortable or put her on edge. "You don't like to talk about yourself. I have to take the nibbles you reveal and put them together."

"And what do you see when you put the nibbles together?" She turned her back and walked into the bathroom.

He didn't think she was ready to hear what he saw. He knew he wasn't ready to be honest. "I see a very beautiful, very complicated woman."

Something rustled in the bathroom before she emerged carrying two coordinated zipper bags. "I could say the same about you." She nestled the bags into the suitcase. "You don't talk about yourself either."

"I'm an open book. Ask away."

She crossed her arms, considered him as he watched a glitter of mischief spark in her coffee eyes. "Tell me about your friends."

"My friends are the guys in the band, my Axis kids, Mark, and my small group."

"How long have you been with the band?"

"About five months."

She worked her lip, studying him the way he'd studied her. He was being evasive and she knew it. "And before?"

He tried to answer with as much honesty as she could stand. "I used to hang with a different crowd."

"Caliber?" she asked.

"Yes." He steeled himself with a fortifying breath. "If I hadn't been so messed up, I would have realized how bad we were together. We pushed each other into worse stuff and expected nothing but good music and good times." He shrugged, tried to rid himself of the weight of the guilt. "It's not a great way to get ahead in life."

"Is that why you live alone?"

"I took a semester off when I realized how bad my life had turned, and when I came back there weren't many options. I didn't want to live with a stranger and take the chance I could slip back into bad habits."

"So …" Reagan sat down on her bed and picked at a string on her comforter, her eyes downcast. "How bad did it get?"

"I skirted around the edges of bad for a long time. Since high school, really."

"A born rebel?"

"Not really born a rebel, but I slid there without much problem." He pictured Brent. Straight As, captain of the football and baseball teams, a string of beautiful girlfriends. "I was small for my age and a huge disappointment to my teachers and the coaches at school who thought I'd be the second coming of my older brother." Dash was upset when he got cut from the basketball team freshman year, but mostly because he overheard the coach tell one of his assistants he thought for sure he'd be better because he was Brent's younger brother. 'I guess they can't all be perfect,' he'd said.

"You're not exactly small now."

"No, but that's when I stopped caring about my grades, stopped trying out for sports, even after I had my growth spurt. I started hanging out with the wrong crowd so I'd garner a different kind of attention."

"You make your life sound like an afterschool special."

Dash snorted. "I suppose it does."

"What made you change?"

He debated how much to whitewash the truth. If he wanted any kind of future with her—friendship or otherwise—he'd be smart to tell her himself and not live in fear she'd discover his past on her own. "I woke up one morning, well, one afternoon, and realized I couldn't remember any details from the previous three days. The last memory I had was from four days prior when the band played at that bar downtown where the waitresses dress in their underwear."

"Batter Up?"

"That's it. We headlined that night to a packed house. I was high as a kite on whatever anyone put in front of me before we hit the stage. I don't remember much after that—including how I got back home or how I spent the next few days. It scared me, and it freaked my mom out when she drove down to find me passed out in my apartment after I hadn't returned her calls. There's nothing like disappointing your mom to make you want to do better. Be better. We packed my things and left."

"Wow."

"The worst part is the way I treated my family. I did stupid stuff, made them worried and angry just because I could. I was a jerk to the people who loved me the most."

"I'm sorry for your mom." Her voice sounded flat and bitter. "It really sucks when the people you love let you down, but she's lucky."

"Lucky how?"

"You know you let her down and made changes to fix your relationship. Some people let you down over and over again, and they never change."

He wanted to ask. The words were on the tip of his tongue. "I'm sorry." The sorriest chicken in the world.

"Hey." She zipped her suitcase and set it on the ground. "At least she's predictable."

She was talking about her mom. He didn't know what to say or how to ask her to elaborate.

She walked to her desk and reached around him to pick up her phone. "What's your number?"

He called out his number as a seed of hope bloomed. He stood and placed the chair in its slot under the desk.

"Shelby agreed to work on the logo. I just texted you my email. Send me the video, and I'll send you a list of questions she needs answered before she gets started."

"Fantastic. Seth agreed to write the first blog post. He said he'd have a draft to me in a couple of days."

"Send it to me when you're ready and I'll have your website live whenever you give the word."

"Should we go live before we have the logo?"

Reagan shrugged. "That's your call, but if you get the answers back to Shelby soon, it shouldn't take her long to get started."

"I'll get to work on those." They looked at one another, eye to eye, soul to soul. "So, I guess this is goodbye for a while?"

"I'll be back a day or so before school starts."

Dash absorbed the disappointment of not seeing her for weeks. He let it simmer and sink into his bones. Because he wanted to hug her, he shoved his hands into his pockets. "Have a Merry Christmas, Reagan."

"You too. When are you going home?"

"We're playing the Christmas eve service and I'll leave right after."

"Be careful on the road."

"You too." He couldn't stop his hand from reaching out, cupping her cheek in his palm. For a second, she relaxed into his hold and let him run his thumb along her buttery skin, her eyes heavy. He dropped his hand before she shrugged it away and ruined the moment. He was playing with fire and they both knew they could end up in flames. "I guess I'll see you next year."

Chapter Twenty-Two

The air smelled stale and achingly familiar. Despite her years serving food at the county's most popular diner, Reagan's mother wasn't a great cook. Throughout Reagan's childhood, her mother put Velveeta on everything she made to mask the taste. The scent of processed cheese lingered as if soaked into the scarred Formica countertop and absorbed into the fibers of the ancient rug beneath the sink. How fitting that her childhood home would forever smell like fake cheese.

Every time Reagan came home, the familiar sting of failure clung like cheap perfume. She'd worked so hard, was still working harder than ever, only to end up right back where she started. Reagan set her bag on the couch and looked around the small den. *It's only temporary. This is not your place any more. It will never be again.* Her mother's life represented the lowest depth of misery, hopping from one boyfriend to the next, working a minimum-wage job, pretending to be happy with her life when Reagan knew she had to be miserable.

The place never changed. The ancient television sat tucked into a console older than Reagan. Her pictures were everywhere—on the console, along the hallway to her bedroom, scattered around her mother's room—from kindergarten to graduation, from toddlerhood through the awkward years of middle school to the fresh-faced girl on the cusp of freedom. Reagan picked up a photo of her wearing her cap and gown and studied a face she knew all too well. What had Reagan expected of college at that age? What had that optimistic girl imagined her life would be like two and a half years after graduation?

What would her friends think of her hometown and the crumbling foundation of her youth? What would Dash think? She mentally slapped herself for the second he popped into her mind. Why did she care what Dash thought? Men were the problem, the root of all evil. Why would she ever go and put herself in the same position her mother did over and over and over again? Men were trouble. They could be a means to an end, and nothing more. Not for Reagan, anyway, at least not until she found success on her own.

The sound of keys in the lock startled Reagan from her musings and had her fumbling to replace the picture into its dusted hollow. She turned in time to watch cautious surprise flicker over her mother's once pretty face.

"Baby girl?"

Reagan cringed at her mother's endearment. "It's me."

Tammy Bellamy rushed to embrace her daughter, digging her keys into Reagan's back.

"Ouch, Mama, you're hurting me."

Her mother stepped back, her forced smile unable to mask the bitter pain in her eyes from Reagan's tone. "I didn't expect you home so soon."

Reagan moved to shut the door her mother had left ajar. She refused to feel guilty. "Disappointed?"

Tammy's brow creased. "I'm surprised but never disappointed. When did you get here? I wish you'd let me know you were coming so I could have tidied up a bit."

The place looked as dingy as ever, if not coated with its usual layer of dust. "No need on my account."

"I could have picked up dinner or brought something home from the diner. Sheldon made beef stew today. You love his stew."

"I'm not hungry." Reagan winced at the coldness of her tone and tried to sound less resigned. The least she could do was play along with her mother's manufactured excitement. "Go change. You must be tired from being on your feel all day."

Tammy blinked away a sheen of tears from her haggard eyes as if Reagan had offered her a foot massage instead of an invitation to sit on her very own couch at the end of a long day. "I'll do that. Then I'll see if I can't rustle up something for when you are hungry."

Reagan didn't think her stomach could handle one of her mother's cheese-covered concoctions. "I'm good, Mama. Really."

"Hush now, baby girl. Let me spoil you."

The only thing Mama would spoil was her appetite. "Go on and take your suitcase back to your room and get settled. I haven't touched it since you left."

The first time Reagan came home for break and found her mother had cleaned out her drawers and moved her books around in the bookcase, she'd pitched a fit. Tammy had tried to be helpful by organizing the books alphabetically by author, but all Reagan knew was that her stuff had been rifled through and her privacy invaded.

"Maybe there's a Christmas movie on TV we could watch. You always loved the Christmas movies."

Reagan took a breath to explain her tastes had changed since elementary school, but clamped her lips shut when her mother began humming on her way down the hall. What would it hurt to indulge Mama and sit through a movie? If anything, it would give her an excuse to be quiet and spare Reagan from answering a million questions about her life or listening to gossip about people in town. As if Reagan cared who was catting around on their spouse or tipping the bottle a little too much. Thank goodness she no longer had a reason to care what happened in her hometown.

Reagan lugged her suitcase down the hall, huffing as the wheels caught in the shaggy carpet strands, and heaved it onto her bed. A tornado of dust erupted from the bedspread and plumed into the air. Reagan coughed and waved a hand in front of her face. True to her word, her mother hadn't touched her daughter's room in months. Her blank walls still held the outline of long-ago posters, adding to the surreal feel of being home. Nothing had changed and yet everything had changed. She no longer looked at the tiny box room as her sanctuary, no longer needed her books to escape, and hardly recognized the girl who used to while away her life dreaming of the future.

She unzipped her suitcase, grabbed a handful of shirts, and turned around to put her clothes into the empty drawers of her dresser but her feet refused to move. Did she really want to unpack and fill her drawers as if coming home for good? Better, she decided, to keep her things in the suitcase for the short time she was home, ready and able to bolt at a moment's notice.

After carrying her cosmetic bags to the bathroom and arranging her toothbrush and toothpaste neatly on the counter, she returned to her room satisfied she'd unpacked. Before toeing off her shoes, she reached into the bottom of the case for her most precious possession, the leather-bound journal one of her teachers gave her for high school graduation. She'd never written a thing on its pages because she didn't want to sully the pretty ivory lined paper with useless daydreams and nonsense. Someday, when she'd amassed wisdom and a fair amount of life experience, she'd fill the pages with everything she'd learned.

"You coming, Baby Girl?" her mother called from the den.

Reagan rolled her eyes and tucked the journal under her pillow. "I'm coming."

The diner was packed for Monday lunch. Reagan should have known better than to enter the town's social center at the busiest time of day, but she couldn't stomach another moment within the walls of her childhood home. Her room was claustrophobic, with three hundred channels there was nothing to watch on television, and there was no place to go without driving an hour in any direction.

Sliding onto a cracked vinyl seat at the counter was like sliding back into the womb. Reagan probably spent more hours at Highway 5 Diner than she did anywhere else growing up. She ran her fingers over the initials she'd carved into the corner of the laminate surface, a feat that cost her hours of confinement in her room in addition to hundreds of dishes washed in Sheldon's kitchen. She'd never carved her initials—or any other graffiti—into another surface again.

Her mother stayed busy, refilling pebbled plastic cups with tea sweet enough to melt enamel. She sashayed through the tables, pitchers double fisted in her palms, and charmed the locals as if she hadn't seen every one of them the week before. Tammy inquired about babies born, commented on weight lost, and oozed southern hospitality like nobody's business. Despite Reagan's disapproval of her mother's life choices, she couldn't help but admire her geniality. Perhaps if Reagan had inherited her mother's graciousness instead of an innate petulance and inability to candy-coat the truth, she would have enjoyed a smoother path through life.

A man slipped onto the stool next to her, nodding and smiling with all his teeth in a way uncommon anywhere other than Small Town, USA. Reagan whispered a polite but guarded, "Hello," and scanned the menu as if she couldn't recite it in her sleep. Her mother sauntered up behind the counter, her perfume announcing her presence more than the faded pink uniform.

"Well, you two sure brighten my day." Tammy smiled at Reagan and winked at the man beside her.

Reagan blew out a frustrated breath. "Mama, he's a little young for you."

Tammy balled her hands and slammed them against her hips. "Reagan Elizabeth Bellamy. If you think for one second I'm hitting on the preacher, you've only got one oar in the water."

"The preacher?" Reagan's eyes slid sideways just long enough to catch a smile skate across the man's face and two cherries balloon on his baby fine cheeks. He couldn't have been a day over thirty. With shorn hair and an almost gaunt face, she would have guessed military before minister. "Sorry," she mumbled.

He held out his hand for Reagan to shake. "James Chatham, pleased to meet you."

“Please forgive my daughter, Reverend Chatham. She's got more horse sense than common sense.” She wiped the counter between them with a damp rag. “I'll let you two get acquainted while I fetch y'all some tea. Seems like y'all could use something cold to calm your skin.”

Reverend Chatham tugged his ear as his color began to recede. “So you're the famous Reagan Bellamy I've heard all about.”

What was with God and His constant need to humble her in front of His faithful? “Famous?”

“Well, sure. Your mama talks about you all the time. How's school going?”

“Uh, okay. I guess.”

“Congratulations on your new position. I hear those RA jobs are hard to get at Addison State.”

Reagan whipped around to face him. “You know about my RA position?”

“Your mama told me. She's very proud of you.” He jerked a shoulder, fighting the white button down he'd starched into submission.

Reagan bit her lip and counted to ten. How dare her mother share details of her life with a stranger—a preacher, no less. Did the woman have no sense? “Okay …”

“Look.” Reverend Chatham placed his hand on her arm. “Don't be mad at your mama. She's proud of you and all you've accomplished.”

“I'm not mad,” Reagan said through gritted teeth. When the reverend smiled knowingly, Reagan knew she'd been chided. “I didn't realize she telegraphed the details of my life to everyone in town.”

"We share good news about our loved ones. You're the light of her life, ya know. I'm glad to finally meet you. She didn't say you'd be home."

"I wasn't planning to be." And regretted the decision with every passing second.

Tammy walked up with a glass of tea in each hand, setting them down with a smile. "What can I get you both for lunch? Special today is meatloaf with a side of mac and cheese."

"I'll have the special," Reverend Chatham said.

"Figured you would." Tammy grinned at him before beaming at her daughter. "I've been trying to fatten him up since he showed up in town. How about you, sugar? Burger and fries with a milkshake on the side?"

That's what Reagan wanted, what she'd been craving the moment she'd stepped inside the place and inhaled the greasy scent of charred beef, but she wouldn't give her mother the satisfaction of being right. "I'll have a salad, please, and a cup of soup on the side."

"Oh, honey." Tammy let her face fall along with the order pad in her hands. "Don't tell me college has turned you into a health nut?"

"A balanced diet is the cornerstone of a healthy lifestyle." Reagan wanted to gag the moment the words left her lips. She sounded like one of the pretentious idiots she routinely made fun of on campus.

"Silly of me to think you'd want some comfort food on your first trip home in months." Tammy made no attempt to hide the derision in her voice. Poor Reverend Chatham, the innocent bystander, seemed taken aback by their behavior. He coughed and glanced at his lap, anywhere but at the two women hurling verbal barbs.

Reagan had to have the last word, audience or not. "Scarfing down a burger and fries isn't going to get me that husband you're hoping for now is it?"

The color in Tammy's cheeks sparked from ember to flame in seconds. "Well, I never …"

"Reagan," Reverend Chatham said in his most conciliatory voice, "in my humble opinion, Sheldon's macaroni and cheese is the purest form of comfort food. There's not a chance I'll eat it all myself. I'd be much obliged if you'd consider splitting it with me."

Reagan scowled at her mother, and Tammy scowled right back. Reagan could continue to make a scene in her mother's workplace or accept the reverend's best attempt at an olive branch. "Fine. I'll share his mac and cheese. Satisfied?"

Tammy shrugged. "It's your life, Reagan. You can do as you please. You always have." With that, she turned her back and walked into the kitchen, the swinging door swishing in her wake like a metronome.

"Well." Reagan's chin thumped against her chest and she tried but failed to take a cleansing breath through the grenade in her throat. What had happened to her legendary control? "Sorry about that." She fought the tears that threatened, pushing them back with practiced discipline. When she felt his hand on her back, she lost the battle and a single drop leaked out of her eye and skirted along her cheek. She wiped it away, embarrassed, and attempted to laugh the awkwardness away. Her chuckle emerged as a strangled sob. There wasn't much hope in resuscitating her impression now. She'd been rude to the woman the reverend called her biggest fan and topped it off by crying in shame.

"There, there," the reverend said. "It's okay. She's made of tough stuff, your mama. And so are you."

Reagan couldn't fight the smile she flashed or the tears that continued to trickle. "Oh, yeah. I'm as tough as a kitten."

"You learned how to get by like your mama. It's hard to take a different path. She's proud of you, but you confuse her. She doesn't understand your new world or your lack of excitement or willingness to share it with her."

"She told you that?"

He glanced at the kitchen door as if checking for Tammy's return. "I'm pretty good at reading people."

She pulled a napkin from the silver holder and blotted her face before blowing her nose. "I suppose that's handy in your line of work. I'd hate to hear what that little scene said about us."

"It said you're not a perfect family. Just like every other family in America."

"Not perfect? Yeah, we're definitely not perfect."

Tammy emerged from the back carrying a large tray crowded with plates, her gaze locked on the back of the diner, her manner as jovial and breezy as ever. Looking at her now, no one outside of earshot would ever guess she'd had a spat with her daughter.

"She wants things for me I don't want for myself. She can't understand my dreams."

"Have you told her?"

Had she? "She's always known my feelings about college and getting out of this town. I think she resents me for it."

"Parents want better for their kids, even when they don't understand."

"She thinks better is a husband." An image of Dash flashed through her mind, just a hint of him holding her cheek and looking at her as if she held the key to something he craved. She shook it away before it could take root. "I think better is a career and independence." She shrugged. "There's not much common ground."

"There rarely is."

Reagan sputtered a laugh. "Come on. I bet your parents are proud. You're a preacher, for goodness sake."

Reverend Chatham nodded. "Yes, in a nowhere town far from home, in a church with dwindling numbers, living alone near the poverty level. Not exactly their dream come true."

"Are you kidding me?" She studied him, his serious expression, the beginnings of crow's feet around his eyes, the ruddy complexion. How could someone so gentle disappoint his parents?

"Deadly serious. They'd take your dreams over mine in a heartbeat."

Well, well. Wasn't that just a kick in the pants? She was learning something new every day. "Maybe we should switch parents. Although Tammy's not too keen on church."

"I've tried my best to get her into the fold. She's a tough one."

"She doesn't like church people or their judgement. Present company excluded, of course."

He nodded, used to taking one for the team. "Of course. How about you?"

"My experience with church is rather limited, as I'm sure you can understand. We used to go to the Methodist church with my grandma but haven't been back since she passed. I did recently attend a couple of services at a church not far from ASU."

"And you lived to tell?"

She liked him, his humor, the kindness in his denim-blue eyes, and she enjoyed their easy banter. There was no other explanation for her next statement other than he'd lulled her into a sense of imperviousness. "I even joined a Bible study."

"Will wonders never cease?"

"Don't tell Tammy. I'd hate to disappoint her more than I already have."

"My lips are sealed."

They snickered and acted like a couple of kids caught with their hands in the cookie jar when Tammy returned to top off their tea glasses. "This looks like trouble."

"We're just getting acquainted," Reverend Chatham said.

Tammy slanted her eyes at him and then studied Reagan with a mischievous grin. The move was practiced and intended to gloss over their scene, but Reagan knew the hurt lingered. "Your food will be ready in a minute." She turned her back to greet a couple who'd entered the diner and slid into an empty booth behind them.

"What are you studying?" the reverend asked.

Reagan wrinkled her nose. "Some Christmas thing about the women of the Bible."

"You didn't enjoy it?"

"Let's just say the ladies in the group didn't appreciate my take on their interpretation."

"You're a pragmatic girl, Reagan. I can see where you'd have some doubts. It's hard to appreciate the Bible as a skeptic."

"So I've been told." Connie's rebuke still stung. Stung like a paper wasp.

"I'm happy to answer any questions you may have. Provide some material for clarification."

"I was told there's a movie I should watch." She shrugged, wished for a subject change. "I don't know. I may be curious and bored enough to do some research while I'm home."

"Why don't you come by my office after lunch? I can give you some reading material, a movie or two to watch, and perhaps I can pick your brain about that church at ASU." He scoped the room before turning back to Reagan and lowering his voice. "Making changes around here is like trying to herd cats. It doesn't happen easily."

"I don't know how much help I can be. I only went a few times."

The reverend nudged her arm with his elbow and wagged his brows. "You're curious and bored. I'm curious and frustrated." He chuckled. "We sound like a soap opera."

"A bad soap opera."

He looked at her with guileless eyes. "What do we have to lose?"

Chapter Twenty-Three

Dash stared at the images on his computer screen, scowling. Why couldn't he just pick a couple of logos and be done with it? They were all fantastic—simple yet inspired, distinctive yet appropriate. He growled in frustration. He needed to cull the eight choices Shelby had provided him before presenting some to the band for a vote. She'd been fantastic, so eager and helpful. She had an eye for detail, and she'd done her research. Together they'd come up with a plan and she'd implemented it quickly. Now she'd done her job, it was time for him to do his.

Every time Dash hovered his finger over the delete button he hesitated and cursed himself for being so indecisive. He needed help, and he knew who he wanted to ask. He had her number, and he'd been searching for an excuse to call. His inability to make a decision—an informal one at that—seemed as good as any to reach out, see how she fared at home, hear her voice. Feed his addiction.

Dash blew out a breath. Overthinking and obsessing had become his new drug of choice. He used to count on his instincts, go with his gut, and let the consequences unfold as they may. Everything about this—both the logo and Reagan—seemed too big, too impactful to leave to chance. He had to plan and consider all sides of the equation before formulating a solution. The problem was, in his mind, both the logo and Reagan were one in the same. She'd gotten the ball rolling with the website and she'd asked her roommate to help, so why shouldn't he ask her opinion when he wouldn't even have decisions to make in the first place if it weren't for her?

Before he could change his mind, he reached for his phone, pulled up her contact, and tapped her number. His heart gave a mild jolt, a warning across the bow, but he ignored it. Too late now. Even if he chickened out and hung up, she'd know he'd called. May as well face the music.

Dash envisioned Mark wagging a finger in his face, his lips pressed tight into a bitter sneer. *Uh huh*, imaginary Mark taunted Dash. *I knew you couldn't let her go*. Dash shooed his friend and mentor away as the phone rang a second and third time. His stomach knotted. What if she didn't answer? Should he leave a message? What would he say?

"Hello?"

The sound of Reagan's voice, curious and a little wary blanked his mind. She'd stretched the two syllables so thin he caught the tang in her voice. He'd missed that twang.

"Hey." He tried to act natural. "What's up?"

"Umm …"

He face-palmed into his free hand. *What's up? What's up? Is that the best you can come up with?* "It's Dash."

"Oh. Hi, Dash."

He'd spent every one of the last four days since she'd left thinking of her and she hadn't even programmed his number into her phone. Awesome. "How's it going?"

"Good. How's it going with you?"

She sounded different, like being at home had thickened her accent and the added distance had left her detached. He shouldn't have called, but he couldn't just hang up. "I wanted to thank you for hooking me up with Shelby."

"Oh."

"She's been great to work with and she's come up with some really good logos."

If it weren't for the sound of her breathing, he would have thought she'd hung up. "I told you she was good."

"Yes, you did. And you were right. So good, in fact, that I'm having trouble winnowing them down to just a few. The guys—the band—they'll get overwhelmed if I present too many choices, but I can't whittle them down on my own."

"How many are there?"

"Eight. I'd like to give the guys three or four to chew over. Three would be best so it doesn't end in a tie."

"You want to go from eight to three? No problem. You've still got my email, right?"

He had her email, her phone number, and the outline of her face imprinted on his soul. He was losing his mind and losing control of the conversation. He wasn't ready to hang up. "Yes, I do. Are you busy now?"

"Uh …"

"I mean, it's okay if you're busy, but if you're not, I'd love to get your first impressions."

"Hang on a sec and I'll get my laptop."

He heard shuffling— he couldn't tell if it was feet or items— and then the distinctive sound of keystrokes. His chest swelled, and his smile bloomed. No matter what she'd been doing, she'd stopped at his request.

"Okay. Did you send it?"

"Just now. It may take a few minutes to go through." And he'd use his time wisely. "How's it going at home?"

"It's okay. Kinda boring."

"Same here. The closer we get to Christmas, the quieter it gets around town." He cleared his throat when she didn't respond. "Is your tree up and decorated? Presents bought and wrapped?"

"Presents are bought but not wrapped. Decorating the tree happens Sunday."

"Interesting that y'all wait until right before Christmas. My mom has our tree up and decorated the day after Thanksgiving."

Reagan harrumphed. "That would require way too much effort."

"Is yours a designer tree or is it filled with cheesy ornaments you made in grade school?"

The sound of her chuckle set his skin ablaze. "If I'd known the ornaments I made back then would get pulled out year after year I would have spent more time on them."

"Which one is your favorite?"

"My favorite ornament?" She blew out a breath. "In first grade, the teacher arranged the class to look like a Christmas tree and we made ornaments from the picture. We were all supposed to wear green that day and of course my mama forgot. I'm wearing a bright yellow shirt. I look like the only ornament on the tree. I was so embarrassed and mad at my mom for years when she dragged the ornaments out."

"And now it's your favorite? Imagine that."

"Yeah." Her voice sounded misty and low. "It's funny how different things look from the rear view."

Something inside of Dash settled. He'd been as anxious to hear her voice as he'd been to find out how she'd coped at home. She rarely spoke of her mom, but whenever she did come up he hadn't detected any longing or emotion in her tone other than resentment. Listening to her now, soft and melancholy, he was glad she sounded as if she were making peace with her past. No matter what happened between them, he only wanted the best for her life.

"I got your email," she said. "Hang on while it pulls up."

Dash closed his eyes and imagined he were there next to her, breathing her breath, nestled close as they were the night they worked on the website. "Oh," she said. "They're all just the band name."

"Yeah. Shelby and I talked about using a graphic and we even played around with a few, but when you look at other Christian bands—both well-known and not—the logo is typically just their name. And we decided to keep it simple when we considered how much it would cost to reproduce a logo on promo materials."

She said nothing, and he resisted the urge to fill the silence. He needed her agile mind to process and think without distraction.

"They're all good, so I don't think you can go wrong with any of these."

"But …"

"But if you're asking for my uninformed and unenlightened opinion, I tend to like the second, fifth, and eighth the best. The font of each of those has a personality that fits your music and

I like the use of color. And maybe the third, but not as much as the others."

He flipped through the images on his screen and agreed with her assessment. He'd liked something about every one of the logos Shelby made, but Reagan hit the nail on the head about the fonts having a personality that fit the band. Like it or not, he was asking her to edit the copy for the homepage and the blog. "Personality, huh. I get what you mean."

"They're all good, but those stand out to me." She cleared her throat. "You and Shelby work well together."

Dash grinned at her salty tone but schooled his voice to sound casual. "Don't call yourself unenlightened when in two seconds you nailed which you liked and why when I've been staring at these for days and couldn't put a finger on my thoughts the way you just did."

"You're too close to the material to think objectively. And my opinion means squat if the guys can't agree."

Enlightened, pragmatic, and if his instincts were correct about her tone, jealous of him working with Shelby. Was it any wonder he was smitten? "I can't thank you enough."

"It was nothing. I told you I'm bored."

His call had garnered more than he'd hoped. She narrowed Shelby's logos down to three—the three best—and she'd sounded good. "Well, you were a big help and I appreciate it." Dash said goodbye and tossed his phone on the couch. His smile disappeared when Mark's face reappeared in his psyche. *Feel better?* Mark asked.

Yes, he told imaginary Mark. *I do.*

Fine. Now you have no more excuses to call her.

If Mark had been present, Dash would have stuck his tongue out at him like a toddler.

Chapter Twenty-Four

Reagan knocked on the office door, tapping the DVD on her thigh with impatience. James's car sat in front of the church and he'd suggested she stop by. Where was he? How long did he expect her to wait in a place that made her skin itch, a place whose dingy interior and outdated wallpaper were in desperate need of a makeover?

He rounded the corner and stopped short when he saw her. "Hey." He flashed an affable grin. "How long have you been here?"

"Just a minute."

"Sorry, I was in the restroom." When he passed her and opened his office door, she caught a whiff of his cologne. His fresh scent stood in direct contrast to the musty odor of the church and the sickeningly sweet potpourri used to mask its aroma. "What'd ya think of the movie?"

Reagan set *The Case for Christ* DVD on his bureau and sat in the chair facing him. He appeared older and wiser in this environment, between an old oak desk and shelving crowded with books. If she'd met him here, in his church office, wearing his crisply starched shirt, khakis, and worn loafers, she wouldn't have opened herself up to him, shown him her vulnerabilities, taken his counsel. He would have appeared too judgmental, too otherworldly to trust with her deepest secrets and dreams. As she reminded herself of his humility and his friendship, she didn't know whether to feel grateful for their meeting place or resentful that the church and his God kept butting into her orderly life.

"It wasn't the usual escape I watch movies for, but it wasn't half bad. Although the main character—the atheist—was portrayed as a selfish jerk while his wife came across as an innocent angel. But hey, I'm no movie critic."

"Challenging long-held beliefs is uncomfortable. When life's sacred truths are under attack, it makes people grumpy."

"Are you calling me grumpy?"

His bubblegum smile popped into place. "If the shoe fits."

She rolled her eyes and examined the paneled walls. A good coat of white paint would spiff his office up in no time but removing the books and the shelving appeared an obstacle too burdensome to overcome. She need go no further than his office to find more than enough research material. "So what's next?"

"You want more?"

She shrugged. "Why not? There's not much else to do in this backwoods town."

He swiveled his chair around and scanned the books, tapping his finger on his chin like an evil professor. When he turned around with a slim paperback in his grip, he appeared ready to pounce.

"Why do you look so pleased with yourself?" she asked.

His smile faded, and two thin lines emerged between his brows like quotation marks. "What do you mean?"

"You're enjoying this, and it makes me skeptical."

He chuckled and set the book on his desk. "You are possibly the most cynical person I've ever met."

Reagan wrinkled her nose and smiled widely. "Thank you."

"I like you, Reagan. You're the kind of person who makes this crazy job worthwhile."

"I make your job feel worthwhile?" She shook her head. "You need a new line of work."

"Probably," he muttered.

"Seriously. You need to explain."

"You're cynical but open to learning. You ask questions but don't impugn my motives."

"Are you getting hassled by the faithful?"

He blew out a breath. "As I said, when sacred truths are challenged, it makes people grumpy."

"You said your members weren't happy about you suggesting changes."

"I need to be patient and understand their concerns. Change is hard, and things happen on God's timeline, not mine."

"There's nothing you can do to speed God up a little bit?"

He chuckled. "It doesn't work that way."

"What are you faithful supposed to do when you're convinced something is good and there's resistance on all sides? Wait for God to swoop in and make everything right?"

"God knows our hearts. He knows I'm frustrated. He knows the congregation is resistant, and He knows why. Instead of me plowing forward with my plans, He asks me to give Him my frustration and let Him guide the progress."

"How does He do it?"

"If the changes I want to make align with His plans, he'll soften the hearts of the congregation. If not, He'll lead me in a different direction. He knows best, and I trust Him, but that doesn't mean I don't get frustrated and impatient."

"It sounds like a passive way to live your life."

James fluttered his hand on the desktop. "Where you say passive, I say peaceful. Think about it this way—how much in our lives can we really control?"

"A lot," she said. "I control every aspect of my life, and that suits me just fine."

"You think you do. In your wildest dreams, did you ever imagine you'd spend your Christmas break discussing divinity with the new preacher in town?"

Reagan relaxed her face when she realized she was scowling. *That angry face of yours is going to leave you looking like a prune at my age*, her mother always said. No matter how petty her mother's comment, she didn't want to look like a prune. "Don't throw logic in my face when I'm grumpy. What are you? A masochist?"

James shook his head at her, but his amusement quickly faded. He studied her intently. "What's going on with you? Did something happen with the boy?"

Prune face be darned, Reagan scowled at her new friend. She'd been forced to tell him about Dash in her explanation about going to church and joining a Bible study. In a moment of weakness, she'd confessed her feelings for him were complicated and confusing. She never thought he'd throw that confession in her face. "Why would you ask me that? Why does everything have to come back to Dash Carter? Can't I be grumpy because you and everyone else in my life are making me miserable?"

He simply continued to look at her with his kind and patient eyes. Reagan found it ironic that he could feel impatient with his congregation and yet so tolerant with her and her moods.

"Fine," she said. "I talked to him. He asked my opinion about the band logo and in doing so commented on the fabulousness of my roommate Shelby."

"Ah." James nodded. "You're jealous."

"I'm not jealous. He can't date, remember?"

"That never stopped him from flirting with you."

"Exactly! What if he flirts with everyone? What if he's tied me up in knots for nothing?"

"I don't think it's nothing. From what you told me, his interest in you sounds genuine."

"But you don't know Shelby. She's … the most beautiful person I know. Truly stunning. All she'd have to do is crook her finger in his direction and he'd go crawling."

"I see you hold the male gender in high esteem."

"Trust me on this one, preach, she's a man magnet. Even you'd be tempted."

"Possibly, considering my current dating pool, but that's neither here nor there. If you're jealous, Reagan, own it. Accept that you like him."

"I do like him. Too much. It's annoying. I have to focus on school. My mom got derailed by a charming man, and look what that got her."

"A beautiful daughter," James said. "Your mom is a classic example of God's plans overriding our own. I admire your mom. She didn't take the easy way out. She kept you, she raised you, and she loves you like the precious child of God you are. She sacrificed her own plans for God's—and for you."

"Oh, trust me, I know all about how she sacrificed. I've heard about it every day of my life." But as the words came gushing out of her mouth, something deep inside Reagan cracked open and a memory oozed forward, a memory from childhood that contradicted her words. Reagan stood on the playground of Cottersville Elementary School while fussy Shelly Morgan, whom everyone wanted to be friends with in second grade, made fun of Reagan for not having a father. Reagan didn't understand why she should feel ashamed of not having a dad—why would she want a man around all the time when men only distracted her mother and kept her from paying attention to Reagan? But when Shelly made a big deal out of it, Reagan started missing a parent who couldn't even be bothered to stick around until she was born. Instead, she blamed the parent who stuck for making her feel like an outcast.

"You seem troubled." James's tone was so gentle, so soothing. Tears threatened to leak out of Reagan's eyes, and she had to use every ounce of resolve to drive them back.

"I'm ..." What was she? Could it be she'd spent the last twenty years of her life so focused on herself that she'd failed to consider—even for a second—the hard choices her mother had made? For as long as she could remember, Reagan made it perfectly clear she'd leave town and never look back. Why wouldn't her mom spend a great deal of time looking for love when the one she sacrificed for had no intention of staying? "I'm being selfish."

"It's easier to recognize faults in others and much harder in ourselves. Forgive me for referring back to the Bible, but there's a passage that relates to your situation."

Reagan clenched her fists in her lap. "Of course there is. Go ahead. I know you're dying to." The last thing she needed was a passage from the Bible, but listening to James preach was easier than fighting the urge to cry.

He reached for a pad of notepaper, jotted something down with a pencil, and placed the paper between the pages of the book he'd selected for her to read. When he glanced up, she narrowed her eyes at his smirk.

"Aren't you going to tell me?" she asked.

"I could, but I think you're ready to do some research on your own."

"Why can't you just read it to me?"

He shrugged, and by the stubborn set of his shoulders, she knew he'd made up his mind. "Call it homework."

"I'm on break." Reagan leaned back and folded her arms. "I don't do homework."

"Fine. Call it research." He slid the book across the desk and folded his arms, daring her with his stare.

"You think you're so smart, but I know what you're doing. You can't make me read the Bible."

"You're right. I can't. But if you want answers and a little guidance, you might just find it in the last place you ever thought to look."

That night while her mama showered, Reagan slid her grandmother's Bible from the dusty bookshelf and hurried to her room, locking the door behind her. After sitting on her bed, she took a deep breath, ran her fingers along the cracked leather cover, and opened the pages, squinting at the tiny print in the dim light from her nightstand. She found the book labeled Matthew and flipped the pages until she found the passage James referenced, Matthew 7:1-5.

Do Not Judge Others (NLT)

7 Do not judge others, and you will not be judged. 2 For you will be treated as you treat others. The standard you use in judging is the standard by which you will be judged.

3 And why worry about a speck in your friend's eye when you have a log in your own? 4 How can you think of saying to your friend, 'Let me help you get rid of that speck in your eye,' when you can't see past the log in your own eye? 5 Hypocrite! First get rid of the log in your own eye; then you will see well enough to deal with the speck in your friend's eye.

Reagan leaned back against her headboard and let the sting of shame wash over her before closing her eyes with a heavy sigh. James, the sneaky devil, was too smart for his own good. She clasped her hands together and spoke her first words to the God she'd spent weeks rebutting.

Lord, if you can hear me, please please take this log out of my eye and help me know what's true. All the people I've come to respect believe in you—actively fight for you—and I'm tired of fighting them and myself. I don't even know why I'm fighting anymore. I want a better relationship with my mom, but I don't know how to make that happen. I want to stop feeling guilty all the time for making her life so miserable. I guess I want some of the peace everyone says only you can bring. Help me find the way, Lord. Amen.

The first thing Reagan saw when she opened her eyes was the bookshelf filled with her favorite stories arranged spine side out, alphabetical by author, just as she'd find in her favorite place—a library. How long had it taken her mama to organize the mess she'd left behind in her rush to bigger and better? When the water stopped running through the pipes she felt a desperate longing to talk. It was time—past time—to take the log out of her eye.

Chapter Twenty-Five

Reagan stood on Professor Adkins's porch watching her breath hover and fade into the cold January air. So much had changed since the last time Reagan stormed out of this house and swore never to return. Changes she couldn't have foretold. Changes that forced her to take a hard look in the mirror. Changes that demanded she humble herself and apologize.

"Reagan?" Connie answered the door wearing tights and an oversized ASU sweatshirt splattered with paint, her smile friendly but guarded. "How are you?"

"I'm good. I'm sorry to just show up on your doorstep, but do you have a minute to talk?"

"Uh … sure. The kids are working on an art project. Come on in and let me threaten them not to paint the house while we talk."

Reagan retreated. "I can come back later if it's not a good time. I should have called …"

"No, don't be silly. Come on in and make yourself at home. I'll be just a minute."

The family Christmas tree stood in the den, lonely and droopy without the presents underneath. The place felt lived-in with a blanket pooled on the leather couch and a used paperback fanned on the end table waiting for someone's return. Reagan took a deep breath and inched onto the soft leather, telling herself not to feel scared. How could she feel scared in a room that screamed for her to take her shoes off and cuddle, start a fire in the fireplace where stockings hung empty and slightly off center.

"Sorry about that." Connie returned with two bottles of water in her grip. She set each down on the coffee table, careful to place them on coasters with the kid's pictures emblazoned on their surface. "The kids are very ready to go back to school, and so am I."

"How was your Christmas?"

"Oh, it was wonderful. We drove down to Florida to see my mom and spent a few days in our bathing suits on the beach—believe it or not."

"Wow. That sounds nice, considering what you came home to."

"It's been cold this winter, hasn't it?" Connie clasped her hands and tucked them between her knees. "How was your Christmas? We missed you at Bible study."

The pit in Reagan's stomach threatened to swallow her whole. "My Christmas was different—in a good way—and I'd like to tell you about it, but first I want to apologize."

"Apologize?"

Reagan hoped the puzzled look on Connie's face was sincere. She couldn't stand the thought of playing games when she needed Connie's trust and authenticity more than ever. "The last time I was here for Bible study I was rude and short to you and the others. I'm sorry if I seemed dismissive. I *was* dismissive, and I realize how rude I was when you were only trying to be nice."

"Oh, well …" Connie's brows lifted, and a tiny smile graced her lips. "Thank you. I think you're being a little hard on yourself, but I appreciate your apology."

"It's warranted, if not for the things I said, for the way I acted and the things that went through my mind."

"Your thoughts are between you and God."

"I know, but my mama says I wear my mind on my face, so I suspect I owe Stephanie and Alana apologies too."

"That's up to you. You're welcome at Bible study anytime whether you apologize or not."

"I appreciate that, and I plan to take you up on it. I want to learn about the Bible. From you. From the others."

Connie reached over and placed her hand over Reagan's where she dug her nails into her jeans. "I'm glad. And I hope you keep asking questions. I don't profess to have all the answers, but I'll try my best. I find Bible study most rewarding when we question what we read instead of accepting it as absolute."

"I'm good at asking questions, and I'll try my best to speak up and ask without judgment."

"That's all we ask in the group." She pulled her hand back and relaxed into the couch, signaling her willingness to listen. Connie excelled at using body language to convey her emotions, a skill Reagan admired. "It sounds like you had an eventful Christmas. Do you want to share?"

Reagan gathered her courage the way a toddler readies to launch into their first steps. "I spent most of my break with the new preacher in town. His name's James and it all happened by accident." Reagan recounted the sequence of events that led her to reading everything she could get her hands on, including her grandmother's dusty Bible. "He helped open my eyes to a lot of things—about God, about Jesus, about me—and he helped heal my relationship with my mom. She raised me alone, since the day I was born, and I've given her nothing but grief ever since."

"You may think so, but you're wrong."

"More grief than she deserved, that's for sure. I blamed her for everything, including stuff that wasn't her fault. She loved me—she loves me—more than anyone, and I used her as my personal punching bag. I'm ashamed of the way I treated her."

"Did you apologize?"

"I did what you said. I prayed to God for help and I apologized. It was humbling and emotional—two things I detest—but it helped in a lot of ways and she was grateful. We talked like we never have before. She told me how hard it was to be a young mother alone. She explained how she grew up in church but stopped going when people there said hateful things when she got pregnant."

Reagan would never forget how shattered her mother looked, sitting on the couch in her fuzzy pink robe, tears streaking down her face. "We both decided to give church another try after James convinced her not to blame an entire congregation for a few bad apples. Before we went the first time I told her what you said about praying for God to soften our hearts. It worked, because we both made it through the service and went back for Christmas eve and the following Sunday. She's going to keep going and I think being a part of the church community is going to give her the family she's missed."

This time Connie's beaming smile didn't offend Reagan. Instead, it warmed her. "Oh, honey. That's so wonderful. I'm so happy for you and your mom." And this time, when Connie scooched along the couch and gathered Reagan into a hug, Reagan didn't flinch or pull away, but held on and accepted the gift of friendship.

When Connie pulled back, Reagan swiped the tears from her eyes with trembling fingers. "It's like somebody turned on the faucet, and I can't turn it off."

"Don't be embarrassed."

"Seriously." Reagan chuckled and accepted the tissue Connie offered. "The waterworks are a problem."

"Not for me." Connie cleared her throat. "May I ask what made you come here? I wasn't sure we'd connected."

"You were the first person to call me out. You, then James. You'd like him. He's sneaky nice like you. No one's ever called me on my attitude before—especially not my mom. She's danced around me for years in hopes I'd magically become nicer. Funny how the answer to both our prayers were found in a place neither of us thought to look."

"The Bible?"

"The Bible, and in people like you and James." Her cheeks heated but she said the name anyway. "And Dash."

"The Bible and believers are good places to go for answers, and I know God puts people in our path to lead us closer to Him."

"I feel good. I asked God to take control of my life and He has. Believing in Him and the Bible made everything feel settled in a way it never felt before."

"That's the crazy thing about submitting our will. There's so much peace in letting go. I'm glad you found it." Connie tilted her head and frowned. "Do you hear something?"

Reagan listened, but other than the hiss of the heat clicking on, she heard nothing. "No."

"Neither do I." Connie stood. "And that makes me nervous. Give me just a minute to peek in on the kids."

Reagan bolted upright. She'd been so comfortable talking to Connie she'd forgotten about the kids and the art project. "Oh my gosh, I've taken up too much of your time already."

"You don't have to leave. I'll be right back."

"No, I actually do have to go. My roommates are coming back today, and I want to clean the apartment before they get here."

"Okay," Connie followed Reagan to the foyer and opened the door. "I hope you'll be back. We start up on Thursday and it should be the full group. I think you'll really like everyone."

Reagan blanched. She'd forgotten about the other students and the grandmother who belonged to the group. Fear and instinct had her ready to make excuses, but she'd vowed to return to Bible study, face Stephanie and Alana, and quench her newfound thirst for information. If returning to Bible study meant being vulnerable in front of strangers, so be it. With God's help she could be brave.

"I plan to be here as long as school and work don't get in the way."

"Good," Connie said. "I'm glad you came by."

Chapter Twenty-Six

Shelby arrived first, dragging a bulging suitcase and asking Reagan for help with the others in the trunk of her car. After they wheeled and toted the last of the bags into the apartment, they collapsed onto the couch.

"You were gone five weeks," Reagan said. "Is your washing machine at home broken?"

"I like to have options, and one of those only has shoes."

Reagan glanced at the bags and rolled her eyes. "You have serious problems."

Shelby stuck her tongue out at Reagan. "I wore every pair, thank you very much."

"I thought you were bored."

"I was. Dreadfully bored. I'm glad to be back."

"Then how did you wear that many pairs of shoes?"

"I said I was bored, not bedridden. I went out. I saw people." She wrinkled her nose as if smelling something unpleasant. "I'm done with the high school crowd. How many times can I listen to gossip about people I don't care enough about to follow on Instagram? It's forced friendships. I don't care anymore."

"That's harsh."

Shelby shrugged and stood up. "It's true. They're not my friends. Not really. All they want to talk about is the calendar. I mean, come on. That was freshman year."

Reagan assumed Shelby posing for the cover of a hottest coed calendar the fall of their freshman year was her biggest regret in life. The money she received for posing paled in comparison to the grief she continued to receive from guys and girls at home and on campus. "They're just jealous."

"Of what? All the money went to tuition."

"They don't care about that. All they know is you were famous, and they weren't."

Shelby scoffed. "Famous? Please. The calendar used me to make money, and I used the calendar to get money. That's capitalism in practice. And it was years ago. The topic should have died."

"You live in infamy. They hate you because you're beautiful."

"And pretend to be my friends at the same time. Thank God I'm back where you three love me for my sparkling personality."

"Ha-ha." When Shelby turned toward the hallway, Reagan called her name, stopping her roommate in her tracks. "Don't be mad at them for being jealous. They're not the only ones."

"Excuse me?"

Reagan felt God nudging her to clear the air, be authentic in her relationships, and reap the rewards. She wasn't totally comfortable with the idea but decided she'd best not ignore God. "I was jealous of you over break."

"Jealous of what?"

"You and Dash creating the logo together."

"What?" Shelby gaped at Reagan.

"He called me and emailed the logos. They're awesome, by the way. He went on and on about how great you are." Reagan picked at the cuticle of her fingernail before glancing up and meeting Shelby's eyes. "I was jealous of you even though I love you."

"Reagan …" Shelby skirted the coffee table and sat next to Reagan on the couch. "He doesn't like me. When I was working with him, all he talked about was how great you are and how the band never would have had the website up and running so quick if it weren't for you."

"He did?"

"Yes. Listen, I know when a guy is into me. Dash Carter most definitely is not."

Relieved and embarrassed, Reagan waved a hand in front of her face. "It doesn't matter anyway. He can't date."

"Why not?"

"He's in the middle of a dating sabbatical."

Shelby cocked her head to the side, a furrow between her brows. "Why?"

"He's focusing on God." Reagan shrugged. "It's kinda like rehab. No sex, no drinking, no drugs. He's making changes to get his life in order."

"Huh. A dating sabbatical. Maybe that's what I'll do."

Reagan snorted. "You'd actually have to date before taking a sabbatical."

"Details. I like the way it sounds. 'It's not you. I'm on a dating sabbatical.'" She flashed a self-satisfied grin. "I like it!"

They turned their heads when Kayla walked in, sporting matching overnight bags in each hand. She squealed when she spotted Shelby and Reagan in the apartment. "My people! I'm so happy to be back!"

They hugged and helped Kayla carry her bags to her room where she plopped on her bed and let out a huge sigh. "All is right with the world."

Shelby shoved Kayla's feet to the side and sat on Kayla's bed. "It's crazy, isn't it? The first year of college we couldn't wait to go home for break, and now we can't wait to come back."

"We tasted freedom and we like it." Kayla toed off her shoes and linked her hands behind her head. "I love my family, but the rules and complaining are just too much. *Are you going to sleep the day away? I hope you don't keep your room at school as messy as you keep it at home.* Blah blah blah."

"I know," Shelby said. "My mom actually asked if I was a lesbian because everyone else my age has a serious boyfriend."

Reagan choked. "Are you kidding?"

"Nope. I told her I'm not a lesbian. I just sleep around."

"Shelby!" Kayla slapped a hand over her mouth. "You did not."

"I did too, and the sad part is I think she'd prefer me to sleep around."

"Why didn't you just tell her how picky you are?" Reagan asked.

"It was more fun to shock her, and I figured that would shut her up."

"Did it?" Kayla asked.

"For a day or two. Then she spent the rest of the break inviting old boyfriends over to the house."

"Yikes." Reagan shuddered. "No wonder you're glad to be home."

"Where's Em?" Kayla asked.

"Probably with Dylan," Reagan said. "They'll show up eventually."

Kayla patted the bed and crooked a finger at Reagan. "Come, sit, and tell us about your adventures with the fabulous Dash Carter."

Reagan rolled her eyes but obliged and sat on Kayla's bed. She expected this—the questions, the insatiable interest—from her closest friends. In a perverse way she looked forward to purging the story and letting them in on her newfound path. "There are no adventures, and what happened with Dash over break you both already know."

"He's still smitten with our little Reagan," Shelby told Kayla. "I can confirm that based on my interactions with him over break."

"How did you interact with Dash over break? Were you here too?"

"I helped his band with their logo, thanks to Reagan hooking us up." She shot an apologetic look at Reagan. "Sorry. Bad choice of words. She connected us, and I gave them a few logo options."

"He loves them, in case you weren't aware," Reagan said.

"I know. He told me, and he told me you helped him decide on the three to show the band."

"He needed an objective opinion." Reagan shrugged.

"And you were happy to oblige." Kayla's eyes sparkled with mirth. "What happened next?"

"Nothing happened next. I went home for break, he went home for break, end of story."

Kayla pouted comically. "He didn't call?"

"No, other than to ask my opinion about the logos."

"That's it?" she asked.

Reagan averted her eyes, studying Kayla's collection of teddy bears on her dresser. "We texted a little. Merry Christmas, Happy New Year, that kind of thing." When she glanced at her roommates, they were grinning at each other. "Don't read anything into a few texts, please. He's off-limits."

"Off-limits how?" Kayla asked.

"He's in the middle of a dating sabbatical," Shelby explained. "And yet still flirting with our little roommate."

Reagan rolled her eyes as heat inched from her neck to her cheeks. "Stop. Please stop. It's not funny."

"It's not funny," Kayla said. "It's perfect. He's liked you forever, and you're finally admitting you like him too."

"Did I admit that?" Reagan asked Shelby. "I didn't admit to anything."

"True, but you didn't stomp out of the room and slam the door in our faces like you would have done a few months ago," Shelby said. "And instead of calling him a waste of space in the universe like you used to do, you called him 'off-limits.' So don't sit here and tell us you don't like him when we know you do."

"Fine. I like him. Happy?"

"Are you?" Kayla asked. "Doesn't it feel good to admit your feelings? You can trust us, Reagan. We're not going to betray you."

"I know that. I do. But there's more." And she wasn't sure how either of them would feel about the rest.

Kayla and Shelby shared a furtive glance before locking their eyes onto Reagan. "Trust us," Shelby said. "We're not going to judge him."

"It's not about him." Reagan wiped her sweaty palms on her jeans. Why was it easier to admit her feelings for a boy than her feelings for God? "I mean, it started with him, but now it's more me."

"Stop being so cryptic and just spit it out," Shelby said. "You're making us worried."

"I found God." Reagan waited for a reaction, studying her roommates' narrowed eyes and skeptical expressions.

"What does that mean?" Shelby asked. "Did you trip over him or something?"

"Don't joke." Reagan clasped her hands into fists. "I'm serious."

"Is this about the Bible study?" Kayla asked.

"Yes and no." She took a deep breath and relaxed her hands. Even to Reagan, her seismic shift in perspective sounded odd. She needed to have patience with her roommates and explain from the beginning, even if the explanation made her appear weak. "I read the study and a couple of children's Bibles, but it seemed so out there, so unbelievable. I mean, how could logical reasoning people believe a virgin gave birth to God's son, who later died and was raised from the dead? It made no sense. But Dash believes. Kayla, you believe."

Kayla nodded. "I do."

"And the ladies at Bible study believe, and Professor Adkins and his wife believe. I felt attacked for not believing, as if common sense were a four-letter word. So I left Bible study and told myself I'd never go back. I went home where everything made sense. Until I met the local pastor at my mom's diner, and he challenged me to open my mind in a way that piqued my curiosity. I did some research, and that research led to more research, and that led to more questions, and I finally started to read the Bible."

"And?" Shelby asked.

"When I read the Bible with the possibility that it might be true, it kind of clicked. It's messy and violent and full of crazy messed-up stuff, but it's recorded history that many, many people have spent decades trying to dispute. Jesus is real and as much as I hate to admit being wrong, I was wrong. I believe He's God's son sent to die for our sins on the cross."

Kayla reached over and clasped Reagan into a hug. "That's awesome. I'm so happy for you."

Shelby continued to stare at Reagan, biting her lip and twisting her hands together.

"Trust me, no one is more surprised to hear those words come out of my mouth than me. Except maybe my mom."

"What does this mean?" Shelby asked.

"It means a lot to me."

"I get that, but what does this mean for us? For us living together?"

"I don't understand your question."

"Are you going to start judging us, condemning our behavior and our language? Just because you found God doesn't mean I want to live with some Jesus freak."

Reagan should have predicted Shelby's reaction and tried to quell her frustration. Hadn't she reacted the same way when learning about Dash? "Shelby, I understand how this sounds, but the truth is I don't know what it means. I don't know how to live as a believer, but I guess I'm going to find out."

When Shelby cringed, Reagan tried to explain. "I've changed, on the inside, and as weird as it sounds to admit this, I feel better. More at peace. My mom and I are on the best terms we've been on in years, and I'm not anxious about the future for the first time in a very long time."

Shelby straightened. "That's great and I'm happy for you, but don't shove your religious crap in my face." She stood up and looked at Kayla. "I've got to unpack."

Reagan let out a frustrated breath when Shelby shut the door.

"Give her some time." Kayla rubbed Reagan's leg. "You know she doesn't like change."

"What's changed for her?" Reagan asked. "I'm the one going through something monumental and she's mad? Give me a break."

"Okay." Kayla smoothed her tone. "Let's imagine if Shelby came back from break a changed woman, committed to Buddhism or … or in love with Lilly Pulitzer."

Reagan laughed. "I'm not even sure what Buddhism is, and Lilly Pulitzer? Can you even imagine?

"No, I can't, but you as a woman of faith is as crazy an idea as Shelby wearing neon paisley outfits all over campus."

She had a point. A valid point. "Okay. I get why she's freaked, but I don't think things will change between us. Do you?"

Kayla shrugged. "I don't know. But I'm not opposed to you making changes in your life. That's up to you. Just try to have a little patience with us if we need some time to adjust."

"I'm not going to go around spouting Bible quotes. I don't even know any!"

"Can I ask you a question?" Reagan nodded. "Is this about Dash?"

It was a fair question and one she'd asked herself a time or two, but that didn't erase the sting. "No. He surprised me—you know I didn't expect him to be someone I could respect. But he is, and I think religion played a big part in changing his life for the better. He thought I was someone I'm not, which is pretty ironic considering I thought he was someone he's not—or at least he's not anymore. Dash shoved his religion on me and I was furious, but he also put me in a position to face things I hadn't considered before."

"Like what?"

"I never understood how grown adults could believe nonsense, and meeting with them face to face at Bible study just made me dig my heels in harder. But when I met James—"

"Who's James?"

"He's the pastor at my hometown church. I met him over break and we clicked. He wasn't anything like I thought a preacher should be, and he didn't get mad at me for questioning his sanity for believing. If anything, he's the reason I decided to delve into Jesus. Dash is just the one who got my hackles up in the first place."

"And now?"

"I don't know. I'm going to keep going to Bible study. I like Connie—Professor Adkins's wife. She's easy to talk to and she understands my need for information."

"I mean with Dash."

Reagan sighed. "I don't know what happens with Dash. I do like him. He's amazingly talented. He's a good person—flawed but good at the core, and he's kind. We're friends who like each other and nothing more."

"Is that enough for you?"

"Considering a couple of months ago I hated his guts, I'd say that's pretty good."

"How long is he in this sabbatical?"

"I don't know and I'm not going to ask. He's working on himself and I need to work on me. It's hard enough being friends with him. I don't want to think how hard it would be if we decided to explore our feelings."

"Why would it be hard? It sounds wonderful."

Of course it sounded wonderful to the most romantic person on earth. Reagan couldn't explain how thinking about Dash, wanting him the way she did, felt heavier and more important than anything should at this stage in life. "Have you ever known me to date casually?"

"No. You don't really date at all."

"Exactly. I can't afford to get sidetracked from school because I won't be at school unless I keep my scholarship."

"What does that have to do with Dash?"

"He's a distraction. A very attractive distraction, but a distraction all the same. I can't get wrapped up in a relationship."

Kayla's brows lifted, and she bit her lip. "It feels a little too late for that."

"I just told you we're just friends."

"Yes, you and Dash are friends, but you and God are in a relationship. Relationships take time and work. So if you can devote the time and work to God without getting sidetracked from school, why not Dash?"

Could she be any more obtuse? "I'm monogamous. One relationship at a time. And God found me first." Not exactly true but pursuing a relationship with God felt safer than a pursuing a relationship with Dash.

Chapter Twenty-Seven

Dash tossed his phone in the air, caught it, and tossed it again. He set the phone on the table when his dad's voice echoed in his head. *Quit tossing that thing like it's a toy and not a two-hundred-dollar computer. If you break it, you pay to fix it, not me.* His dad was right, and he needed to break his habit. He glanced at his phone and noted the time. Where was Mark?

"Sorry I'm late." Mark scooted into the booth opposite Dash. "Jackson's soccer practice ran long."

"Soccer? In January?"

"Indoor league. It keeps him busy and focused at school."

"How was Christmas?" Dash asked.

"Good. The usual. The kids got three presents from us—if three was good enough for Jesus, it's good enough from us—but the grandparents load them up on tons of toys they don't need and will never play with once the novelty wears off." He plucked a menu from the salt and pepper caddy and scanned it. "How was yours?"

"Good. It was good to see the family. Brent's engaged—no shocker there."

"Engaged, huh? To business school Barbie?"

Dash nodded and weighed his food options. Chicken fingers or a burger? "Leave it to Brent to find a woman as plastic as he is."

"You don't think they're in love?"

"Who knows. They look good together, and that's all that matters." Dash decided on a burger and set the menu down. "I hope they're in love. I'm not sure Brent's doing this because he loves her or because she's pressured him into a ring. He said it's going to a be a long engagement, so maybe they'll come to their senses before they say, 'I do.'"

"We should pray for them."

"We should." After the waitress took their order and walked away, Dash looked at Mark. "So what's up? Why the dinner invitation?"

"I wanted to catch up, and I wanted to apologize."

"Apologize?"

"I was hard on you before you left—too hard—and I'm sorry."

Dash stared at Mark, his posture relaxed, his hands flicking the paper-covered straw from side to side on the table. Jackson needed constant motion because his dad did. "I accept your apology."

Mark lifted his brows, blinking once. "Thank you."

"You seem surprised."

Mark chuckled. "I am, a little. I didn't think you'd accept so easily."

"Life's too short to hold a grudge. You made me mad, but I know you're only looking out for me. I'm sorry for interrogating Connie before I left. Whatever happened at Bible study between her and Reagan is none of my business." Dash ran his finger over a chip on the table's surface. "I did some thinking over break."

"And?"

"And you were partly right. I was getting too close to Reagan. In some regards I'm no better than Brent—choosing a girl because she looks good by my side. Reagan's always intrigued me, partly because she so clearly disdained my former lifestyle. But liking her isn't fair to her or to me."

"Why's that?"

"I tried too hard to make her into something I wanted and needed her to be—a woman of God. She's not, and if I'm serious about changing my ways, I owe it to myself and to God to look for someone who shares my values."

Mark glanced away, inhaling in a breath as he scanned the room.

"What is it?" Dash asked.

"Nothing."

"I thought you'd be thrilled with my decision."

"I'm happy you've done some introspection." Mark glared at Dash with a pointed stare that had Dash's senses whirling. "So does this mean you're over your crush on Reagan?"

"I'm not over her, but I see her more clearly now. She's a friend. Right now, that's all she can be. Besides, I've got a tough schedule this semester and some important gigs lined up with the band. I won't have much time for anyone."

Mark nodded, his eyes downcast. "I see."

Dash wished he saw because the guarded look on Mark's face and the halting quality of his voice made him suspicious. "Are you sure—"

"Hey, guys." Eli appeared at the table and nudged Dash to scoot over. Dash complied but wished Eli had asked if he could join them instead of butting in uninvited. Dash would have said no. "You order yet?"

"Just did," Mark said. "Would you like to join us?"

Eli smiled, his lip hitching on his twisted incisor. "Uh, yeah. That'd be great."

Fantastic. Something was going on with Mark, and there was no way Dash would figure it out with Eli around.

"Was Santa good to everyone this Christmas?" Eli asked.

Dash shrugged, still irritated at his bandmate. "The usual. A few sweaters, some cash."

"Same for me." Mark seemed like his old self. "Except I've graduated from cash to cologne."

"Bummer." Eli nodded, looking between Mark and Dash, waiting for someone to ask about his Christmas. "I got that amp I've been jonesing over for months! It sounds awe-sum." The singsong pronunciation of the word made him sound like a fool.

"The Spider?" Dash asked.

He drummed his fingers on the table. "Yep."

"Wow. Your parents really love you."

"Or they were trying to shut me up, but who cares. I got it, and we can all enjoy."

"And we will," Dash said. A new amp would definitely help with the live gig at the fundraiser in a few weeks.

"If you guys are going to talk bandspeak, I'll get my order to go," Mark said.

"Don't leave on my account." Eli raised his hands. "I'm done talking about the band. I'm just stoked about the new amp."

"The equipment we use on the road is less than fantastic," Dash said. "Any upgrade makes our sound better, especially as we start to get bigger gigs."

"Interesting." Mark stretched the word out the way his dad did whenever his mom asked his opinion on decorating. "Any gigs in the works?"

"We're doing a fundraiser for the local pet shelter in a few weeks," Dash said. "And I'm filling in for the lead in my old band in March."

Mark's brows winged upward, the only outward sign of disapproval as far as Dash could tell. He knew if Eli weren't present, Mark would pepper him with questions and concerns.

"Caliber?" Eli asked. "Haven't they replaced you yet?"

"Yes, you know they have, but they were in a bind for some frat thing in Savannah."

Dash knew neither guys would like his answer. Eli said it didn't serve Evergreen when Dash fronted for another band, and Mark said putting himself in a dangerous situation wasn't good for Dash's recovery.

"We give Jacob grief for not fully committing to our mission and here you are performing for your old band," Eli said. "It doesn't seem right, especially since the Caliber audience will never cross over to the Christian market."

Dash lifted his hands from the table and turned to face his band mate. "It's the last time. I told them not to call me again, and I meant it."

"You want some company?" Mark asked. "I could always talk Connie into a weekend away."

Mark's offer wasn't for company and they both knew it. "I don't need a babysitter, thank you."

This time Mark lifted his hands. "I wasn't trying to overstep, but a weekend away is different than filling in for a night here in town. I imagine it will be harder to find refuge from the partying when you're staying at the same hotel."

"I'm not at the same hotel. I booked a room at the function site, and the band's staying at some motel close to River Street. Trust me, Mark, I'm not going to party with the band."

Mark nodded stiffly, only moderately appeased. "Sounds like a good plan."

It was a good plan, a considered plan that focused on easing his guilt over dumping the old band and his commitment to a new and improved lifestyle. He wished, just once, Mark would give him the benefit of the doubt instead of jumping to the worst conclusion. "It is. I feel bad for walking away from Caliber the way I did, but I've filled in enough to make amends. I'm not going to feel guilty anymore."

"You have nothing to feel guilty about." Mark paused as the waitress brought their food. "You've done right by them. A simple apology should have been enough."

"I know, and I've apologized. They booked this gig when I was with the band and that's the only reason I agreed. The frat was giving them a hard time about the lead being different." Dash shrugged and squeezed ketchup onto his plate. "They threatened to cancel, and I know they need the money."

"To buy drugs," Eli said, and Dash shot him a hard stare. "Kidding." Eli's digs didn't help Dash's case with Mark.

"Savannah's not far," Mark said. "I'm just a phone call away if you get in a bind or you need help in any way."

"Noted." Dash wiped his mouth and tried not to let resentment sour his meal. Mark was only trying to help, and Eli was just being Eli. Dash simply wished their comments didn't feel so judgmental. He knew the guys in Caliber, he knew how he used to live, and he knew better than anyone how to avoid the landmines he'd face at the event. As he washed his meal down with a soft drink and mindless chatter, he wished his mentor and current bandmate could trust him and have a little faith.

Chapter Twenty-Eight

Reagan gathered her books and stuffed them into her bulging backpack. She was heading to meet her classmates at the library, then to Connie's for Bible study. Reagan knew her roommates were going to talk about her the minute she left the apartment, so she tried to leave as unobtrusively as possible. Shelby remained guarded since Reagan's admission—to the point where the entire vibe of the apartment had changed. And not for the better.

"I'm going to meet my study group and then go to Bible study," Reagan said. "I'll see you guys later."

"What are you studying?" Emily asked, using the remote to turn down the volume on a talk show.

"Constitutional rights and liberties."

"No." She chuckled. "I mean at Bible study."

Shelby, who'd been painting her fingernails, scooped up her polish and disappeared into her room. Reagan watched her go, the burden of discord resting heavy upon her shoulders. She refused to give in and roll her eyes. "The Book of John."

Emily blew out a breath and spoke in a hushed tone. "Give her some time."

"What's the big deal? It's not like anything has changed for her. Has it?" she asked.

"No. Nothing has changed except Shelby and her bad mood."

"Exactly. I wish she'd talk to me instead of avoiding me all the time. I have to keep reminding myself I have nothing to feel guilty for."

"You don't. This is her issue, not yours."

"What's her issue? I can't even guess why she's so upset."

Emily shrugged her shoulders. "Whatever it is, she'll let you know eventually."

That cryptic answer meant Emily knew but didn't want to say, making Reagan feel even more like an outsider.

"Thanks." Reagan shoved her bag on her shoulder. "I gotta go or I'm going to be late."

"Happy studying." Emily turned back to the TV.

Reagan closed the door behind her and brooded as she glanced down the hallway to her neighbor's door. It would have been nice if she had time to talk to Dash about Shelby, ask him if he'd gotten any blowback from friends after he'd changed his ways. She knew he had—he'd admitted as much by telling her he'd basically made all new friends.

Reagan didn't want to make new friends. She loved her friends—well, mostly—and didn't want to start over. Why couldn't her roommates be happy for her and let it drop? It's not like she went around the apartment talking about Jesus all the time.

She descended the stairs to her car. Dash had stalked her before Christmas, appearing every time she exited her apartment even when she tried to avoid him. Since returning from break, he was MIA. She'd knocked on his door after break, hoping to fill him in on all that happened at home and ask about his Christmas. And, if she was being honest, to see him again, but he'd blown her off saying he had a big test to cram for. Ever since, she hadn't time to reach out and rarely spotted his car in the parking lot. If she did spot his truck or the motorcycle, it was late at night—too late to knock on his door and reconnect.

It bothered her, his absence and complete lack of communication. He'd always been the one to reach out to her, not the other way around. And now radio silence. What was with people anyway? This whole Jesus philosophy of loving others above yourself was next to impossible when people acted like jerks all the time.

She felt a nudge, rolled her eyes, and said a silent apology to God. Okay, maybe not jerks. Something was going on with Shelby, and she'd eventually get it out of her. But Dash? His absence might not be about her. He might be struggling or super busy or be having family problems. If she wanted to be friends with him, she had to put some effort into the friendship.

She settled behind the wheel but before turning on the car, she shot him a quick text.

Hey. Just checking in since I haven't seen you around. Hope all is well.

There. She'd done it. Since there weren't scrolling dots telling her he'd gotten her message and was anxiously typing a response, she set her phone down and got on with her night.

Connie hugged Reagan before ushering her inside the house. Everyone was there—Stephanie, Alana, Grandma Marg, Kendra, and Fallon. Reagan loved Marg and her stories of her granddaughter, even feeling a twinge of envy for the grandmother she'd lost and barely known. Kendra and Fallon were total opposites.

Reagan would have dismissed Kendra as a total sorority clone before meeting her a few weeks ago at their first study after break. Despite her outward appearance—blonde, petite, beautiful—she had a compassionate heart and a home life that made Reagan's seem normal. Fallon, with her pink-tinted hair and piercings, would have looked more at home at a concert than a Bible study. Both girls had a deep love of the Lord and a unique way of looking at the world that turned Reagan's stereotypes on their head.

"You look tired." Connie walked Reagan to the door after a spirited discussion on God's nudges and the stillness required to feel them.

"I came straight here from study group for my constitutional law class. The material is endless."

"Sounds riveting, but you've been distracted since you arrived. Is everything okay?"

What was with Connie and her super human powers of observation? "My roommates are … I don't know. They don't like the fact I'm a Christian now."

Connie nodded sagely, as if expecting the exact news Reagan delivered. "Change is hard for some to accept."

"What's changed? That's what I can't figure out. Nothing has changed for them. I would understand the tension if I were going around spouting Bible verses and condemning them for the way they dress or their foul language, but I'm not. I'm acting the same."

"But you're not the same. Not inside where it counts. I've seen the change in you, Reagan. You're not as wound up as you used to be. You're more relaxed and accepting of everyone."

Was she? Although tired from her heavy load of classes and extra hours spent working for Professor Adkins, the frantic need to prove herself had loosened its grip on her life. And she was trying to be more open-minded and accepting. "But aren't those good things? Am I missing something?"

"How many roommates do you have?" Connie asked.

"Three."

"And do all of you play a certain role in each of your lives? Is one of you the peacekeeper, another the drama queen, and so on?"

"I guess so. Kayla is the peacemaker, Shelby does tend to thrive on drama, and Emily is our own little domestic goddess. Is that what you mean?"

"That's exactly what I mean. Now, what's your role?"

"My role?" Reagan searched her mind. What did her roommates expect from her? "I don't know. I guess they'd say I'm the serious student, and maybe the realist."

"And would you admit your reality has changed since becoming a Christ follower?"

Reagan took a deep breath. Connie's statement hit her in the face as she let the air out of her lungs. "When you put it that way, I suppose it has."

"If I've noticed the changes in you—and believe me when I say they're positive changes—I would imagine your roommates have noticed too. It probably upsets them that by becoming a Christian you've changed what they've come to expect from you."

Wary and exhausted, Reagan sighed. "What am I supposed to do? Apologize?"

"No, you don't owe anyone an apology for choosing to follow Christ. Have you been at all sensitive to their feelings on the matter?"

Reagan recalled her earlier comment to Emily and her face flamed. *What's the big deal? It's not like anything has changed for her. Has it?* "No, I haven't. I didn't realize how much I've changed or how any change in me would upset them or the harmony we've established in the apartment."

"Don't look so sad," Connie said. "This isn't something you can't work out together. Talk to them, ask them about their feelings and listen—really listen—to what they have to say. If these are your best friends, you owe it to each other to work this out. I would hate for you to lose each other because you've made a positive change in your life."

"Did this happen to you? Did you lose friends?"

Connie glanced away, and a furrow appeared between her brows. "I had a roommate when I started going to church with Mark. She was an atheist, and she never liked him. She thought he was trying to brainwash me into becoming something I wasn't."

"Ouch. I bet that wasn't easy."

"We agreed to disagree until I declared Jesus as my Lord and Savior."

"What happened?" Reagan asked. "Did you move out?"

"No, but I thought about it. We argued a lot and there were some pretty tense moments, but we found a kind of truce until the lease came up."

"So you lost her as a friend?" Reagan hugged the study book to her chest. "I thought this was going to have a happy ending. Or at least a silver lining."

Connie laughed. "You've changed, but you're the same sarcastic Reagan I know and love. We're still friends. We keep in touch through social media."

"Social media? What are you saying? Am I going to have to get all new friends? I don't want to do that."

"You don't have to do anything. All you have to do is be yourself and the rest will sort itself out. Okay?"

Reagan huffed. "Fine. I'll talk to them, but as far as pep talks go, you really need to work on your material."

"Yep." Connie shoved her out the door. "Same old Reagan."

Chapter Twenty-Nine

Dash reread the text for the millionth time.

Hey. Just checking in since I haven't seen you around. Hope all is well.

He'd started to respond a dozen times and deleted all attempts, throwing his phone onto the couch and picking up his guitar instead. What came out were angry sounds, violent combinations of strings clashing, until his head hurt almost as much as his fingers.

The guilt lay heavy on his conscience. She'd reached out to him twice now. He needed to blow her off again so she'd get the message without him having to say the words. Why did doing the right thing by her feel so wrong?

Dash needed to respond to her in the same off-the-cuff tone, something flippant and meaningless, but what he wanted to say was, "Stop texting me because letting go of you is harder than I thought it would be. Avoiding you is what I'm trying to do in order to get over the idea of you and accept the reality that you're not who I'm supposed to be with."

He was acting like a teenage girl and he despised himself for feeling so torn up over someone as wrong for him as … celery. He hated celery, and yet his mother and every other woman in his life kept paring it with his favorite foods—peanut butter, pimento cheese, any and all dips including his favorite chili and the sour cream. It simply wasn't fair. And now he was hungry. And annoyed. And he still hadn't answered her text!

He grabbed his phone and responded.

All good. Busy with class and the band. See you around.

See you around? That was lame. He deleted it.

Talk soon.

He typed but deleted that as well. *Talk soon* sounded worse than *see you around. Talk soon* implied he welcomed the twang in her voice and was eager to listen to her complain about Mark and his disaster of an office and how she'd spent countless hours trying to organize his mess without causing him to have a stroke. Dash wouldn't have even known about Reagan's sneaky attempts to arrange Mark's piles into clearly marked files with individual labels and her own genius system if Mark didn't continually inform Dash of how valuable she'd been to his team and how much it irritated his annoying senior RA that she'd managed to do in a few weeks what he'd been unable to accomplish in over a year. He could only smile at the thought of Reagan outsmarting Chad. Dash had a deep and visceral dislike of Mark's pretentious senior RA.

He retyped

see you around

and hit send, noting for the first time the lateness of the hour and that he'd spent most of the night brooding over what to write and cursing the universe for putting her into his orbit in the first place.

He set his guitar in its case and sank to his knees, turning so he could brace his elbows on the couch and fold his hands together before closing his eyes. "Lord," Dash prayed aloud, "I need help. If Reagan is not the girl for me, if she's not the one I'm supposed to be with, please take this longing from me. Lord, please help me see her for what and who she is, a child of yours meant for someone else, meant for a different life than the one you've slated me for. Show me how to get to a place of friendship with her. Please take this attraction away and help me focus on you and all the glorious plans you have for my life. I trust you, Lord, and I'm trying to be patient and wait this out, but I'm not doing so good on my own. I give this to you, God. I give her to you—not that I ever had her or that she was ever mine—but I give her destiny to you and pray you set her on a good and healthy path that leads to happiness and leads to you. I ask this in the name of Jesus Christ, my Lord and Savior. Amen."

Satisfied he'd answered her text and asked for help from the only One who truly had a map of life's course, he turned out the lights and went to bed.

Reagan found Shelby laying on the couch when she got home, her newly painted pink toes peeking out from under Emily's cashmere throw and her long dark hair spiraling over the cushion. Was Shelby asleep, or faking sleep so she didn't have to speak to Reagan? She closed the door forcefully, too loud to sleep through yet not loud enough to wake the entire apartment. When Shelby stirred, Reagan decided now was as good a time as any to clear the air.

"Sorry," she said. "Didn't mean to wake you."

Shelby sat up and pushed the hair from her eyes. "It's okay." She clicked the TV to off and set the remote on the coffee table. "I need to go to bed anyway."

"Shel?"

Shelby stood up and turned to face Reagan, looking her in the eye for the first time in weeks. "Yeah?"

"Can we talk?"

Shelby pinched the bridge of her nose and squeezed her eyes tightly shut. "I'm really tired, Reagan. Can it wait?"

"I'd rather not, but if you're too tired, go on to bed. I'll see you in the morning."

Reagan turned her back and wiggled out of her backpack, leaning it against the wall by the door. Reagan could feel Shelby's eyes on her as she slipped her shoes off and massaged the knots in her neck. When she turned to go into the kitchen for a glass of water, she wasn't surprised to find Shelby standing in the same spot, the throw pooled in her arms. "I thought you were going to bed."

"What do you want to talk about?"

Reagan pivoted away from the kitchen and sat down on the couch, far enough from Shelby so she wouldn't feel hemmed in. "Us. What's going on in the apartment since I came back from break."

Shelby sighed, lifting her shoulders dramatically, and let them fall as she collapsed back onto the couch. "So talk."

She wasn't going to make it easy for Reagan to explain. That was okay. Easy didn't solve problems or mend friendships. "You're obviously upset about something."

"Yes, I am."

"Is it because of my faith? Are you upset because I'm a Christian now?"

"No." Shelby's voice dripped with contempt. "I don't care who you worship."

"Then what is it? And don't tell me nothing because you can hardly stand to be in the same room as me."

Shelby twisted the throw in her fists, one direction and then the other, back and forth as her face became more and more infused with color. "It's you. You're not the same person you used to be."

"Okay." How had Reagan missed what everyone saw so clearly? "That's true. I've changed on the inside. I only recently realized how different I must seem to those of you who know me best. I have changed, but I'm still the same. I want to get back to where we can be friends again. I want you to talk to me."

"I can't talk to you. I don't even know who you are anymore."

"I'm not sure what you mean. Can you give me an example of how I've changed, so I can understand why you're so upset?"

"You want an example?" Shelby tossed the throw aside and stood up, slapping her hands against her hips. "Last week, last Thursday to be exact, I came out of my room looking like a hooker, teetered past you on four-inch heels, and you said nothing. Nothing! Not one word about my outfit, my perfume, my hair, my makeup, nothing! You looked me up and down, and went back to reading your book. That is not normal behavior!"

Reagan remembered the moment. Shelby had come out of her room wearing red leather pants and a tube top, enough makeup to perform community theater, and smelling like she'd showered in the latest pop star perfume. It had taken every ounce of willpower to swallow the snarky comments that flooded her mouth. "I was trying to be nice."

"Nice? Nice? Since when is it nice to let your roommate strut around campus looking like a prostitute? Who are you?"

"Okay, look. You're right. You looked ridiculous, and I can't even count the number of sarcastic comments I wanted to say."

"Why didn't you say them?"

"If you want to dress up like a clown and go out at night, that's your business, not mine. I support you."

"That's not support! You used to support me, but now you're just this shell or robot or something. It's like you're not even here."

Ouch. That hurt enough for Reagan to want to flee to her room and cry, but nothing would change by running away.

"You probably don't know this since you haven't spoken to me lately, but my mom and I have gotten to a good place, a place we haven't been in a long time. I spent my whole life judging her and her choices and her lifestyle, and I couldn't find any reason to respect her because I never took the time to look at life from her perspective. The moment I did, the moment someone challenged me to, I realized how wrong I was. So I'm trying to look at everyone with an open mind and not be so judgmental. I don't want to make the same mistake with my friends, so if you wear an outfit I think is revealing or stupid or is asking for unwanted attention, I'm not going to comment because I don't know why you're dressed that way."

"Ask."

"Ask what?"

"Ask me why I'm dressed that way. Don't let me walk out the door looking like a fool. What if I didn't know how stupid I looked? You just let me do it when the old you—the Reagan I know and love—would have taken one look at me and laughed in my face. She's the one I trust to have my back. She's the one who would commiserate with me over the stupidity of the human race. This new kinder gentler version of you is a stranger. I don't like her. I don't trust her."

"Are you telling me you intentionally dressed provocatively to see what I'd do? Was that a test?"

"Yes," Shelby said. "And you failed. You proved I can't trust this new you. I want the old Reagan back. I liked her."

"I'm still the same old Reagan. I'm sorry I let you leave the apartment looking like a street walker. You looked ridiculous."

Shelby's lips quivered as she tried not to smile. "I did, didn't I?"

"If hooker was the look you were going for, you nailed it."

"And you failed it."

Reagan sighed. There were so many pitfalls to changing her ways she could hardly keep them straight. "I promise I'll be honest from now on. I may try to soften my response so as not to offend you or God, but I'll be honest. But Shelby, I need you to be honest with me as well. You've been pouting around the apartment for weeks, acting like a spoiled kid instead of talking to me. Were you ever going to say anything, or were you just going to sulk through the semester and never speak to me again?"

"I was going to say something after I'd let you suffer. And if that's not Christian enough for you, then so what. I'm not a Christian."

"That's fine. That's up to you. I'm not in the conversion business."

"You're not?"

"No. I'm too busy working on myself to have time to tackle a mess like you."

Shelby smiled, real and genuine this time. "That's my girl. I knew you were in there somewhere."

Reagan stood up and hugged her friend. "I'm still here and if I get annoying, call me on it. I don't want to lose you. I don't want to lose any of you."

"Fair enough. I'm asking you, as your friend and roommate to stop being so nice all the time. It's really annoying."

"Noted."

"I'm going to bed," Shelby said.

"Sweet dreams." Reagan laughed when Shelby growled. "I mean nightmares. Happy nightmares."

"That's better."

Reagan grabbed her backpack and shoes and headed down the hall to her room, relieved to have navigated at least one hazard. She tossed the backpack onto her bed and pulled her phone from a pocket. Dead. When she plugged it in to charge, it buzzed. There was a text from Dash.

> *All good. Busy with class and the band. See you around.*

Her good mood burst like a balloon stuck with a pin. The hurts just kept on coming. She'd finally gotten to a place where she could admit she liked him, but he was no longer interested if his text and disappearing act were any indication. She shouldn't feel like he'd broken up with her or led her on. He'd been up-front from the beginning. They were friends and that's all they could be until his dating sabbatical was over.

Time to focus on God and forget about her good-looking neighbor.

Chapter Thirty

Reagan sat on the coach, seething. "I can't believe you talked me into this," she said to Emily in the seat in front of her. Mike had gotten up to use the bathroom, either to pee or to puke, and she was finally free to vent. "He's trashed already!"

Emily twisted around and stuck her head between the seats. "I'm sorry, Rea. He's just blowing off steam."

More like blowing brain cells. "If he's like this the whole trip, I'm going to kill you. Both of you."

Dylan's head appeared above Emily's. "I'll talk to him if he gets out of hand."

"He's already out of hand. Seriously, who gets drunk at ten in the morning?"

"He's a total sweetheart, Rea. He's just hurting right now. Karen did a real number on him."

Reagan understood why. Dylan's roommate was harmless—an affable, friendly, typical frat boy. He'd turned into a total douche bag the moment he started chugging beers on the way to Savannah and inching closer and closer to her while getting blisteringly drunk.

When Emily had begged her to accompany Mike to their frat formal because his girlfriend had broken up with him, she'd said no. She was too busy and had zero interest in being his last-minute plus one. Emily had actually gotten down on her knees and given her some sob story about his girlfriend breaking his heart and how embarrassed he'd be if he didn't have a date. What a fool Reagan had been to believe her.

"My sympathy for him is just about over." She'd skipped a class for this? She'd rather sit in a lecture hall listening to her professor drone on about philosophy of law than ride shotgun with a drunk broken-hearted frat boy. Emily owed her big time. She glanced to the back of the bus and saw Mike holding a long tube. "Oh my gosh, Em. He's funneling a beer!"

Dylan stood up, scooted past Emily, and looked down at Reagan. "I'll talk to him."

"Thank you." But she knew it was too late for talk.

Emily watched Dylan work his way to the back of the bus then met Reagan's glare. "I'm sorry, Reagan. Dylan will talk some sense into him."

"I hope so, because I'm not babysitting him all weekend."

"You won't have to. I promise. Once we get him to the hotel, he'll pass out and sleep it off."

"Speaking of sleeping," Reagan said. "Did you talk to Dylan about the sleeping arrangements this weekend?"

"Yes, and he's fine with sharing a room with Mike. He knows the only way you agreed to come was if we shared a room."

"Good. I don't want to get in your way if you and Dylan want some time together this weekend, but I won't sleep in the same room as Mike. That wouldn't look good for either one of us."

"I know. It's no problem. We understand."

Good, because the more Mike drank, the more handsy he became. She refused to spend the weekend fending off advances from a guy just because some girl stomped on his heart at an inopportune moment.

Dylan returned with three beers in his hand and passed one to Reagan.

"So?" Reagan took the beer because she had no other choice.

"He's beyond reason right now. The best advice I can give is to drink up and let him have some fun with the guys. Once we get to the hotel, I'll put him to bed and let him sleep it off."

Fantastic. She sighed and scowled at the warm beer, resolving to never get herself in these situations again.

"Once we get him in bed, we can walk around City Market and have some fun," Emily said. "The fraternity rented out a bar on River Street tonight, and that will be a blast."

Reagan could do this. She could walk around Savannah with one of her best friends and have fun at a bar. She'd done it before. No matter how mad she was at her date, she didn't want to ruin Emily and Dylan's fun. "Sounds like a plan."

She managed to enjoy the remainder of the bus ride after Mike returned and fell asleep. True to his word, Dylan half-walked, half-carried Mike to their room and ordered him to bed while Reagan and Emily took a cab to explore the galleries and shops of City Market. They strolled through gift shops and nibbled on treats from a cookie store. She picked up a birthday gift for Kayla and a Mother's Day gift for her mom before they headed back to shower and get ready for the evening.

By the time they met in the lobby for a short ride to the bar, Mike was sober, showered, and apologetic. He complimented Reagan on her outfit—a pair of jeans, heeled boots, and a plum-colored sweater that flattered her complexion and kept her warm—and promised she wouldn't have to babysit him the rest of the weekend. Reagan appreciated his apology and tried her best to give him the benefit of the doubt.

The Irish pub on River Street was as much fun as it was quaint. A troubadour band complete with fiddle, banjo, and mandolin played traditional Irish music that encouraged sing-a-longs and dancing. Reagan wished she'd worn a lighter shirt when the sweat began to drip down her back while dancing with a group of girls to the heel-tapping music. It was impossible to not have fun in such a festive environment. Mike kept to his word, sipping Irish beer and keeping tabs on her throughout the night. When they finally made it back to the hotel, she was happy she came.

Mike walked her to her hotel door, hugged her goodnight, and walked back to the elevator to his room on the floor above them.

Reagan and Emily slept in the next day, waking up after eleven and spending the next hour giggling and telling stories from the night before.

"I'm glad you talked me into coming," Reagan said. "Yesterday was fun and last night was a blast."

"Mike's a nice guy."

"He is," Reagan said. "I appreciated his apology and he was a perfect gentleman. He's a great dancer."

"So." Emily sat up and propped two pillows behind her head before leaning back and grinning at Reagan. "Is there any chance for a love connection?"

"Aah … no. Why would you ask?"

She shrugged. "Mike may have mentioned something to Dylan about how pretty and cool you are. I think he's hoping for a hookup tonight."

Reagan choked on a sip of water. "He's what? What did Dylan say?"

"Dylan agreed that you are indeed very cool and very pretty, but the chance of a hookup was slim to none."

"Less than none, as in not going to happen. What is it with guys? You have one nice night and they want to jump into bed. I thought he was distraught over his breakup?"

"He is, but he's a guy. Most guys use sex as a Band-Aid."

"I'm nobody's Band-Aid, thank you very much."

Emily laughed. "I think Mike took it as a challenge. If I were you, I'd expect the full court press tonight."

"Fantastic. That's exactly how I don't want to spend the evening."

"Don't worry. Once you shut him down, we can dance the night away and have fun."

Reagan didn't share Emily's optimism and decided to change the subject. "What's on the agenda for today?"

"Well, my super wonderful boyfriend has arranged a mani-pedi and a facial for the two of us at the hotel spa."

"For me?" Reagan asked.

"Of course." She glanced at the clock. "We'd better get ourselves dressed if we want to grab a bite to eat before our appointments."

"I feel bad." Reagan pulled on a pair of yoga pants and a workout top. "Why is Dylan paying for a spa day for me?"

"Because he's a great guy, and he wanted us to feel pampered."

Reagan joined Emily in the bathroom. She ran a brush through her hair and piled it on top of her head in a messy bun. "That boyfriend of yours is pretty awesome. I think he's a keeper."

Emily giggled as she spit toothpaste from her mouth. "I think you're right." Reagan rolled her eyes as white suds ran down Emily's chin. Her roommate was stupidly in love. Reagan accepted the annoying pang in her heart for what it was—a mixture of jealousy and gratitude. Reagan's time would come and only God knew when, but even Reagan knew it wouldn't be tonight, and it wouldn't be with Mike Dempsey.

With hot pink nails and a tingling complexion, Reagan exited the elevator and made her way to her room. The mani-pedi and facial had been just what the doctor ordered after a night of fun. She'd left Emily on the elevator, on her way up to Dylan's room to thank him properly for the pampering. Those two were perfect for one another. After letting herself into the room, Reagan thought she recognized Dash's voice humming an unfamiliar tune. She peeked her head into the hallway and did a double take when she saw a dark-headed guy about his height enter the room two doors down from her own.

Dash? In Savannah? It couldn't be. Why would he be in Savannah this weekend, staying in the same hotel as a fraternity formal? It didn't make sense. She shook her head and called it wishful thinking before closing the door to her room. She needed a shower, and she needed to forget about the crush she hadn't seen in weeks.

Chapter Thirty-One

They were high as a kite and it wasn't even five. Dash could tell his former bandmates had started partying earlier than usual by the elongated syllables, the mumbled umms and aahs, and the intermittent giggles.

Freaking fantastic.

He declined an offer to join them at their hotel for a 'pregame party,' took their ribbing like a man, and tried in vain to confirm the time they'd meet. Dash would be ready. His band? Maybe not. He said goodbye, hung up the phone, and laid his head on the desk before getting up to stalk around the room.

Mark was right. It had been a mistake to fill in for the lead. He no longer had the patience for Caliber's nonsense, their 'whatever' attitude, and their mocking of his changed ways. No matter what, this was the absolute last time he did a favor for his former friends.

He sat down on the bed and fell back, staring at the ceiling while marinating in disgust. What a loser he'd been. What an absolute waste of space. How many years of his life had been wasted on good times in an altered state of mind? No wonder Reagan thought him a loser. If it hadn't been for God's grace and his parents' love, he would still be right where they were—zoned out with no plans beyond the after-party.

One night. Four or five hours tops. He could do this. He could sing his old songs, charm a hundred or so drunk coeds, and go home to his better life. Days like today when the old life crashed against the new he was most grateful to God. That Jesus gave his life on a cross for losers like him was a freaking miracle. He'd spend the rest of his days trying to live up to that sacrifice, doing his best to follow in the footsteps of the only perfect person to walk the earth.

With nothing to do and hours to kill before the party, Dash decided to take advantage of the hotel's gym. He changed into shorts and a t-shirt, grabbed his phone and some headphones, and left the room. As the elevator dinged and the doors opened, his spine tingled as Reagan's roommate, Emily, emerged, her blond hair pulled back into a ponytail and her cheeks flushed with color. She gave him a fleeting smile before her eyes grew large and recognition hit.

"Dash?"

"Hi, Emily."

"What are you doing here?"

"I'm playing at the fraternity formal tonight. I guess you're attending?"

"Ah, yeah. It's my boyfriend's frat." She glanced around. "Are you … are you here alone?"

"Yes … I mean, I'm with the band. They're not here yet. At the hotel, I mean." Why was he rambling and having so much trouble answering a simple question?

"Does Reagan know you're here?"

"Ah, no." He cocked his head in question. "Why would she?"

"She's here. At the formal. With Dylan's roommate."

He sucked in a breath and hoped his face didn't give away his surprise. He had no right to feel upset that she'd moved on. He was the one who'd cut off communication.

"Okay. Great." He stuck his hand out when the doors began to close without him. He needed the time alone to wrap his mind around what she'd just revealed. "I guess I'll see you tonight."

She gave him a wave goodbye. Dash punched the button for the lobby level and leaned back against the elevator as the doors began to close. Reagan was here. With a date. While he played with his old band. Who were using. Talk about worlds colliding. When the doors opened, he stumbled into the hallway and made his way to the gym. He needed a workout more than ever.

"Oh my gosh!" Emily chirped as soon as she entered the room. "You're never going to believe who I just ran into!"

Reagan stepped out of the bathroom, her wet hair wrapped in a towel, cinching the hotel robe tightly around her waist. "Who?"

"Dash Carter." Emily stared at Reagan, blinking her eyes, her hands clasped in front of her. "He's playing with the band at the formal tonight. Isn't that exciting?"

"Evergreen is playing the fraternity formal?"

"No, silly. Caliber."

"Dash is playing with Caliber?" Reagan absently rubbed at the ache in her chest. She shouldn't care. She shouldn't feel concerned about him spending time with his former band even though she knew how wrong his life had been when they hung out on a regular basis. He'd told her about the drugs and the women. Why would he put himself in that position again? Had his absence from her life meant he'd gone back to his old ways?

"Why don't you sound surprised?" Emily asked. "Did you know he was coming?"

"What? No. I saw him—I thought I saw him earlier. I thought I was wrong, but I guess he's really here."

"Why do you look like that?"

"Like what?"

"Like your puppy just got hit by a car."

Reagan sat down on the bed. "I'm worried for him. His old bandmates aren't good for him to be around." She should have followed up with him. She should have checked in to make sure he was okay, instead of feeling insulted he'd lost interest.

"What do you mean, not good for him?"

"You know, the whole sex, drugs, and rock 'n' roll culture. He made a change, or at least I thought he did."

"Well, he looked fine to me. He was on his way to work out, so that doesn't sound like rock 'n' roll behavior."

No, it didn't, but it also didn't mean he couldn't work out before getting lit with his bandmates before the show. "I guess."

"I told him you were here with a date."

Reagan's stomach quivered. "You didn't."

"What better way to make him jealous? I know you still like him."

"Emily …" She closed her eyes wishing her roommate had kept her mouth shut. "What did he say?"

"He didn't say anything, but he didn't look happy."

No, he wouldn't be happy. Reagan was one of the few people who knew how much he'd changed—and was one of the few people who'd be disappointed in him for going back to his old ways. "You'd better shower." Reagan wanted to end the conversation and changed the subject. "We don't want to be late for dinner."

"Please don't be mad at me." Emily gave Reagan a hug before disappearing into the bathroom and closing the door behind her.

Reagan wasn't mad. She wasn't sure how to describe the numb and empty feeling settling into her bones, but it definitely wasn't anger.

The chicken Reagan ate for dinner sat in her belly like a brick. She excused herself from the table to escape to the restroom before they left for the ballroom. She wanted to freshen her lipstick and arm herself for the inevitable encounter with Dash. After washing her hands in the sink, Reagan appraised her appearance in the mirror. The wide-strapped plunge-neck dress in coal black fit her like a second skin. The delicate silver necklace dangled down her cleavage like an arrow. She applied a fresh coat of lipstick and ran her hand over the hair she'd meticulously curled into waves that hung down her back.

Reagan should have been self-conscious in the revealing dress and three-inch heels. Instead, she felt powerful. If Mike's reaction were any indication, she'd accomplished her goal. But it wasn't Mike she'd primped for. It wasn't Mike's attention she'd hoped to snare. She wasn't sure why or how making Dash want her again was a good thing. All she knew was she wanted his attention. Maybe if she had his attention, he'd turn his back on his bandmates and she could talk some sense into him, get him back on track. It was the only thing she could think to do.

Mike leaned against the wall outside the restroom waiting for his date to emerge. While grateful for his courtesy, her stomach thrashed with nerves as he slipped his arm around her waist and led her into the ballroom. The dim lighting made it seem as if they were entering a dream. The band's equipment sat on stage minus the musicians. Reagan wiped her sweaty palms onto her dress and in doing so knocked Mike's hand from her hip. He led them to a group of guys near the bar and asked what she wanted to drink.

"Club soda with lime please." She scanned the stage.

"You sure? I'm paying," Mike said.

"Positive. Just trying to pace myself."

He nodded, confused by her refusal of free alcohol, and moved closer to the bar to order. One of the girls she'd met at the Irish pub approached and complimented her dress. As they talked, Dash appeared out of nowhere along with a motley assortment of guys who took their place on the stage. Dash stepped into the spotlight wearing loose jeans and a black t-shirt, his hair sexily mussed. He didn't appear stoned or otherwise intoxicated, but who was she to tell?

"I'm so excited they got Caliber to play," Tina said. "They're so good with Dash Carter back in the lead."

Reagan's stomach dropped. Back in the lead meant he'd left Evergreen. She couldn't understand his sudden change of heart.

"Good evening, everybody," Dash spoke into the microphone, his deep baritone rumbling through her chest, sending her heart aflutter. "How we doin' tonight?"

She watched him intently as the crowd catcalled and whistled. Energized by their enthusiasm, Dash strummed his guitar once, twice before speaking again. "Here's an oldie but a goodie. Y'all come on out to the dance floor and show us how it's done."

Mike returned with her drink and resumed his position, one hand around a glass filled with amber liquid, the other around her waist. She stepped back and away, smiling over the lip of her drink, nodding to the tune. Mike scooted closer so their arms touched, but she couldn't take her eyes off Dash. By the second song, he had the crowd jumping around, arms in the air, a frenzy of grinding movement. If she wanted to get a better look at Dash, she had to get closer. That meant dragging her date to the dance floor and letting him touch her as she wound and slithered her way to the front.

Reagan hated being in the middle of the throng with no space to move and almost no air to breath. She and Mike were attached to one another through sheer necessity. Their bodies moving in tandem, his hands finding purchase on her hips, his head inching lower and lower to the base of her neck had Reagan jerking away, intensifying her dance moves so as not to feel captive in his arms. An onlooker would see Reagan and her date dancing enthusiastically to the music. Anyone who knew her would see her frantic movements as a desperate attempt to free herself of his zealous advances. Thankfully no one in close proximity, including Mike, knew her well.

While she danced, her gaze followed the band's lead singer. For most of the vocals, Dash's eyes stayed closed or downcast, perhaps blinded by the bright lights. When it came time for a drum or guitar solo, he bounded out of the spotlight to the side of the stage where he appeared to survey the pack of moving bodies. Right before the chorus started on his third or fourth jaunt out of the spotlight, Reagan caught his eye and held it for a beat.

Okay. He's spotted me.

Unfortunately, at the exact moment she locked eyes with Dash, Mike's hands latched onto her hips and he yanked her against his body. Despite Reagan's best attempt to push him away, Mike wouldn't budge.

Dash gave nothing away—he showed no sign of intoxication and not an ounce of jealousy before lunging back to the microphone to finish the song. Reagan's knees wobbled and her eyes stung when he continued performing as if nothing had happened, as if their stares hadn't collided. Disappointed at his indifference and her physical reaction, she danced out of Mike's reach until he screamed in her ear he was headed for the bar and left her alone to dance with a group of girls gathered by the stage.

For the next hour or so, she danced, blew at the hair in her face, and observed Dash on the platform. Perspiration dripped along his temples, soaking the collar of his t-shirt, and glistening off the hair on his arms. With every twist of his head, droplets flew and pelted the fans worshipping at his feet.

Reagan followed the arc of the beads and watched them land on his female admirers. She fought the overwhelming urge to ram through those up close and lick those pieces of him off strangers. What was wrong with her? He was probably using drugs again the way he bounded around the stage, jumping up and down and wielding the guitar like a weapon. And he would probably take one of the girls to bed that very night.

Heavy with disappointment, she turned and weaved through the crowd to the back of the room in need of air and water. After downing a glass from the bartender, she spotted Emily talking to a group of girls.

"Hey." Reagan joined their circle.

"Heeeey," Emily squealed.

Uh-oh. Her roommate had, in the span of a few hours, gotten stupidly drunk. "Are you okay?"

"I'm fiiiine. Are you okay?"

"Where's Dylan?"

Emily lifted her drink to point at the bar. "He went to get me some water."

Good idea. Reagan hoped it wasn't too late.

"The band's awesome," Emily loud whispered into Reagan's ear. "Dash is really good, and so sexy on stage."

Reagan cringed at Emily's slurred words and envy panged in her gut. If stupid-in-love-with-her-boyfriend Emily had noticed Dash's appeal, what must the other girls think? Silly question. She'd seen him seduce more than one audience with his voice alone, including an entire church congregation.

Reagan intercepted Mike on his way to join her, squeezing his arm as she slowed. "I'll be right back." If he figured out she was avoiding him, so be it. He shrugged and returned to the bar while Reagan made a beeline to the restroom.

She needed to escape and figure out what to do next.

Chapter Thirty-Two

Dash watched Reagan turn her back to the stage and merge into the throng of dancers, zigzagging in and out before she disappeared into the blinding glare of the stage lights. He couldn't get the look on her face when he'd spotted her out of his head. Why had she glared at him with solemn eyes and a downturned pout on her lips? She was the one with some guy's hands all over her, thrusting her luscious curves in his face to the beat Dash created. Between the two of them, he was the one having the worst night of his life—babysitting his former band while watching her bump and grind with some random 'friend.'

Why did her dress have to dip nearly to her navel and show off every curve and valley? He couldn't blame the guy for trying pull her close, but everything in Dash wanted to jump down from the stage and punch the guy in the face. What was wrong with her? Didn't she know the effect she had on men? On him? He'd found her hard to resist in the past, but now? With the image of her hands in the air and her body moving to the beat, he'd be hard pressed to sleep a wink that night. Or any night thereafter.

He glanced back at Colin and signaled for a change in the set, moving from the pop music favored by fraternities to harder tunes, edgier songs that didn't encourage dancing. Who'd complain if he messed with the playset? His band was too strung out to care and everyone else too drunk or too engrossed in conversation to notice.

As they wound down the set with a mixture of covers and originals, Dash gave his farewell performance everything he had left to give. Reagan was out there somewhere with her date and her friends, proving once and for all how wrong they were for one another. She was parties, good times, and full steam ahead with school. He was one foot in front of the other, eyes on God, future unknown.

With one last strum of his guitar and one final, "Goodnight," every ounce of energy drained from his body. He carried his guitar to the staging area in the back of the ballroom and collapsed onto a chair while his bandmates high-fived and made plans for the after-party that would begin in the van back to the hotel. Thank goodness he'd booked a room at the convention center so he could collect his things and disappear. Despite a shared history, he'd paid his debt in full. Dash Carter had just performed his last set with Caliber. Ever.

He placed his guitar into the case, wiped the sweat from his brow, and slipped away from his past like a ghost. All he wanted was a shower and some sleep. Then he could get on the road at daybreak and end the nightmare once and for all.

Reagan spotted the fabric on the doorknob the moment she rounded the curve in the hallway and approached the door to her room. Once there, she placed her ear against the faux wood surface and caught the unmistakable sound of Emily and Dylan together. Oh, brother. What were they doing in her room when Emily knew full well she had no intention of hooking up with Mike?

Mike … just thinking of him made her eyes roll and had her slumping against the wall. She couldn't avoid her date after the band finished playing and couples began exiting the ballroom hand in hand or mouth to mouth. Lids drooping and coordination shot, he'd spotted her as she approached and propositioned her loudly—with an audience—and stepped on her foot in the process. He'd made it easy to say no.

But saying no now meant she had nowhere to sleep when all she wanted to do was rest her aching feet and forget about her fruitless attempt to get Dash's attention.

Dash.

She'd spotted him earlier. Only two doors down.

She couldn't. Could she? He was probably out partying with the band …

A bang and giggles sounded from inside her room. Reagan sighed, straightened her dress, and approached Dash's door. Really, what choice did she have?

After three quick knocks, the door opened a crack.

Dash appeared in the gap, his eyes narrowed, his posture stiff. "What are you doing here?"

Reagan swallowed the urge to turn and run away. "Sorry. I didn't know where else to go."

"What's wrong?"

"Emily's in our room with Dylan … not sleeping." She could only see half of him from his position behind the door. Half his bare chest, half his navy boxers, one of his legs.

No shirt.

No shoes.

Big problem.

"Where's your date?" he asked.

She twisted the necklace at her throat and chewed her lip. *Where's my date?* Did he really want her to spend the night with some random guy? "Last time I saw him he was doing a round of shots and using the bar to keep himself vertical."

"Oh." He held the door like a shield in a white-knuckle grasp. "Let me …" He cleared the gravel from his throat, loosened his hold, and backed away from the door. "Let me get some clothes on."

Clothes seemed unnecessary since the image of him in boxers had already imprinted her brain. She could no more stop herself from stepping into the room than she could click her heals and return home. Reagan entered his space and her breath caught when the door clicked shut at her back.

She inhaled the crisp tang of soap, spied the king-sized bed looming in the distance, and tasted the unmistakable flavor of want. When he turned, she bit her tongue to keep from whimpering. The cross, two nails with a wire wrap, adorned the back of one sculpted shoulder. Powerful in simplicity, stunning in presentation, perfectly befitting the man. She was a goner.

He yanked a t-shirt over his head and stepped into athletic shorts before turning to face her. "So …"

"Yeah, I know this is a huge inconvenience, but I didn't know where else to go."

"Hey." He waved a hand in front of his face as if welcoming her into his room in the middle of the night were no big deal. "It's no problem."

"Really? I guess this happens a lot."

His brow crinkled adorably. "What?"

"Random girls showing up at your door." Her attempt at humor fell flat.

"Not recently."

They both glanced at the bed before slanting their eyes at each other and away.

"I'll sleep on the floor," Dash said.

"Uh, no. You're not sleeping on the floor. That's ridiculous since I'm the one who barged in on you. And it's unsanitary. It's a big bed. In fact, a king is nothing more than two twins put together, so there's plenty of room for two people. Without touching." She cringed inwardly at the insinuation that drifted out as she babbled on. Of course there'd be no touching. He'd barely looked her in the eye since she'd entered the room.

She lowered herself onto the edge of the bed and removed her shoes one at a time, unable to stand another second in her heels. She let out a satisfied groan as she flexed her toes.

"No arguments. I'm sleeping on the floor."

"No way. If you sleep on the floor, I'm leaving. I won't kick you out of your bed." She limped to stand.

"It's not a big deal."

"Yes, it is. I can go back to my room or … go find Mike."

"You're not wandering around the hotel in the middle of the night."

"Then I guess we're going to have to compromise." She glanced around the room, stepped to the door between the bathroom and the bed, and flung it open. "Aha." She reached up on tippy toes and pulled two extra pillows from the otherwise empty shelf. "We'll make a pillow barrier. They do that all the time in the movies."

"A pillow barrier?"

"Either that, or I'm leaving."

He huffed out a sigh, rubbing the back of his neck. "Fine."

She felt the weight of his stare like a laser before the blast.

"Long night?" He stood on the opposite side of the room. If he backed up any farther he'd disappear into the curtains.

"No longer than yours." She felt cold air hit he back of her thighs and knew her dress had inched dangerously high when she leaned a knee on the bed to arrange the pillows. She shuffled backward and peeked at him while righting her dress. "That was quite a show you put on tonight."

He shrugged and inched closer to the bed. "I try to give them what they pay for."

"I guess Evergreen didn't work out, since you're back with Caliber."

His eyebrows pinched, and he ran a hand over his face. He looked tired to the core. "That was me paying my debt to Caliber once and for all. Evergreen is my only band from now on."

"What debt? I thought you left them last year?"

"I did, but they asked a favor and I stupidly said yes. I won't be filling in again."

"Oh." While relieved his appearance with Caliber was only temporary, there was something about him, the way he rubbed his arm and the empty look in his eyes that told her there was more to the story. "Well, that's good news. I was worried you'd … gone back to them."

"Never." The vehemence of his tone sent a chill up her spine. She took a step toward him before the look in his eye had her screeching to a halt.

She knew that look, that vacant, haunted stare she found in the mirror whenever she thought about her know-it-all past and the years she'd spent resenting her mom. "You're not like them anymore. You don't have to hate yourself now for what you did in the past. You've moved on."

His stare shot to hers and held. His eyes widened, and his lips twitched before the shadow of a smile touched his face. How could someone so confident and gorgeous appear so vulnerable? Dash stood every inch a man in the small room, but that unguarded look on his face had her imagining him as a boy and melted her defenses.

"I have moved on." His shoulders drooped as he sighed. "Being with them tonight was like being transported into the past. And it was ugly."

"You weren't tempted?"

He snorted. "I was disgusted."

"Good. Disgusted is good. That's what you want to feel, right? I mean, disgusted is better than longing for what you gave up."

"Well, yeah, but it's hard to appreciate how far I've come after slipping back into my former life."

"You said yourself you're done with them and your old lifestyle. There's no need to look back ever again."

He shrugged and pulled out the desk chair, sat down. "Looking back keeps you humble. It's hard to get all high and mighty when the past is there to remind you where you came from. It's just difficult to relive it and still feel good about myself."

"Then maybe it's a good thing I'm here, because I can tell you how proud I am of you for walking away from a successful band and the only friends you knew to change your life for the better."

He stared at her, still a looking little bit defeated and a whole lot vulnerable. "There's nothing to be proud of. I played the gig and got out of there as fast as I could. I should have talked to them and tried to convince them to get clean. At the rate they're going, one of them will end up dead. It's only a matter of time."

"That's not your responsibility, Dash. You can't put all that on your shoulders."

"You couldn't have paid me a million dollars to spend another hour with them. If I've changed so much, I would have used that time to try and make a difference. Instead, I ran like a coward."

"That's called self-preservation and there's nothing wrong with feeling that way. Maybe sometime in the future you'll be in a place where you can counsel them, but now's not the time. I don't think you can help others until you're ready. God's still working on you. It's like the airline thing. You have to put your mask on first before assisting others. You're still putting on your mask."

And maybe that's why he'd been avoiding her. Dash was in the middle of his date-free year and being around her was too much temptation. Instead of feeling hurt because he'd cut off communication, she should respect his right to make it to the finish line in any way possible. He'd called her tempting more than once, and she'd been flattered. Now, watching him stew in self-loathing, she felt guilty for causing him pain.

"I guess I am." He smiled at her, flirty and sly, and her apprehension eased at the change in his tone. She prayed she'd helped a little in putting that spark back in his eye. "You're pretty smart, you know?"

She rolled her eyes. "I wouldn't exactly say—"

"For someone so smart, you sure make some pretty dumb decisions."

Chapter Thirty-Three

Dash shocked himself by being so blunt. By the way Reagan's mouth fell open and her head jerked back comically, he suspected he shocked her as well.

"What is that supposed to mean?" she asked.

If she could barge in on him nearly naked and completely defenseless, turnabout seemed fair play. He wasn't the only one who'd put himself in a bad situation that weekend.

"It means you have all the confidence in the world when it comes to academics. No one knows more or is willing to work harder than you to solve a problem or ace a test. But when it comes to your physical and emotional safety, you've got no confidence at all. You expect people to hurt you, you expect them to let you down, and you're absolutely fine when they do. You're a beautiful woman worthy of someone's time and attention, but you constantly settle for less. Why is that?"

Her mouth worked. "What are you talking about?" Her words were more choked than spoken.

"I'm talking about your date! You go away with a guy for the weekend, bump and grind all over him on the dance floor, and then wander around the hotel with nowhere to spend the night. What would you have done with Dylan's roommate if I hadn't been here? Do you have any idea how stupid it is to trust some guy at a frat formal?"

She inhaled a huge breath and thrust her hands onto her hips. "First of all, the only reason we were on top of each other on the dance floor was because there wasn't enough room to take a breath without touching, much less a step. And second of all, how dare you?"

How dare he? Did she have any idea how she looked and what it did to him to see her wrapped around someone else? "You've got to be more careful. I mean, come on." His eyes lingered on places better left alone. "Look at that dress."

Her head bobbed down, and her frown deepened before she lifted her head. All the while, her arms went around herself as if anything could cover her dangerous curves. That tiny scrap of fabric certainly didn't. "What's wrong with this dress?"

"Nothing, if you're trying to put everything you've got on display."

She gasped, and that breathy sound reined in his tempter quick. He may as well have slapped her. When he saw her chin quiver the knife in his gut twisted painfully.

"Reagan, I'm sorry. That's not fair."

"I'm not looking for attention." Her voice shook, her face aflame.

"I know you're not." He ran a hand through his hair and wondered how he could have turned on her when she'd just done everything she could to make him feel better about the way he used to live his life. What kind of friend was he? "It was hard to watch. I'm sorry."

"I wanted to get close to the stage to see if you'd been using again. I was worried about you. He … came along for the ride."

And didn't Dash feel like a jerk. She'd been looking out for him? That explained the look on her face.

"And if we're being honest with each other," she continued with her chin in the air. "I could say the same about you strutting around the stage, winking at all the girls who screamed your name. If that wasn't you putting yourself on display, I don't know what is."

Touché. They could while away the rest of the night drawing blood from each other instead of dealing with the elephant in the room. It was time to face reality and time for a truce. "You're right. I'm sorry I made assumptions."

He'd ignited her anger and she stood ready, fists balled, for battle. His simple apology caught her by surprise and yanked the target away.

"Okay." Her hands relaxed at her sides. "Thank you. Just for the record, I don't expect people to hurt me. Mike's a friend, and he's drunk."

"Drunk or not, you deserve better."

She stared at him, a crinkle between her brows. "You shouldn't make me mad and then be nice to me. It's confusing. And I'm sorry for assuming the worst about you."

He nodded, appeased and relieved she'd forgiven him. Knowing what he knew of her, he didn't think she'd back down so soon. "Listen, I'm tired and I know you are as well." He stood up and rummaged through his suitcase, finding his last clean t-shirt.

He tossed it to her. "You can sleep in this if you want. There's an extra toothbrush in my case in the bathroom."

She caught the shirt and held it against her chest. "Are you sure? I can probably wait Emily and Dylan out and go back to my room."

She could, but what kind of jerk would he be to let her? "It's a big bed. I'll fix the pillow barrier. Go change and let's get some sleep."

As if.

She licked her lips and then pulled them into a tight line, as unconvinced as he was about either of them getting a wink of sleep. "Okay. Thank you."

"No problem." As the bathroom door shut Dash sank onto the bed and let his head drop into his hands. Where had that anger come from? Why had he attacked her like that? He was mad at her for putting herself in a bad situation with a drunk frat guy—any guy—and instead of feeling grateful she'd sought him out for refuge, he'd berated her instead. He wouldn't blame her if she'd walked out and slammed the door in his face.

Dash took a deep breath and closed his eyes. *Are you testing me, Lord? If so, this one's a doozy. Playing with the band was nothing compared to this. I just wish I had as much faith in me as you do, because spending the night with Reagan may be the death of me.*

Reagan stared at her reflection in the mirror and cringed. She'd done the best she could to remove her makeup, but she still had crescent-shaped smudges under her eyes and tinted lips. At least her teeth were clean. So, too, was his bathroom. She'd never known anyone so tidy. The only hint he'd used the bathroom was the damp towel hanging neatly on the rack and the lingering smell of soap. His toiletries sat neatly tucked into the monogrammed leather case where she'd found the extra toothbrush.

She turned around and surveyed her backside in the mirror. Despite the shirt hanging halfway down her legs, she didn't want to leave the bathroom. *Man up. You saw him in his underwear.* She scrunched her eyes closed. *No! Bad idea.* She tried to banish the memory from her mind. No need to think about Dash's muscles rippling as he pulled on his shirt, his super-sexy cross tattoo, or the way his boxers clung to his narrow hips. Nope. That would be a mistake to think about that before she crawled into bed with him. Especially after he'd made her feel cheap and easy.

Why had he been so angry? She'd never seen him so upset. He'd practically been shaking as the temper coursed through him. And over what? Mike Dempsey? Please. She'd never kiss him, much less spend the night in his bed.

She closed the toilet lid and sat down, putting her hands together and closing her eyes. *Dear God. Please help me. I want to be good. I do. I want to go to sleep next to Dash and not think inappropriate thoughts about him and me together. In bed. Touching. Please help me go to sleep so I can look him in the eye in the morning without regret and look myself in the mirror. Amen.*

She stood up, looked at her reflection, and whispered, "You can do this," before turning the knob.

Dash lay under the covers, his arms outside the blanket, his head propped up by a folded over pillow. He'd arranged the other two pillows down the center of the bed and turned a basketball game on the TV with the volume set low. He jerked his head in her direction when she came out of the bathroom.

"You okay?" he asked.

A loaded question. "Yep. Thank you." She lifted the covers and settled on the farthest edge of the bed. She could barely think above the clamor of her heart slamming against her chest as she stared at the ceiling. She looked at him when the sheets rustled.

Dash lay facing her, his cheek cradled in his palm. "You don't have to sleep on the edge of the bed, Reagan. I'm not going to attack you."

She chortled. "I know. I just … don't want to disrupt your sleep."

"I'm sorry I got angry with you. The thought of you having to fend off some drunk guy made me crazy."

"I wasn't going to sleep with him. I'd have barged in on Emily and Dylan before I put myself in that situation." She shifted on the bed to face him when her neck began to ache. "Mike's a nice guy. He's drunk and heartbroken, but I don't think he would have forced himself on me."

"Guys are pigs. Don't ever assume otherwise."

"I don't. Believe me." Their silence hung heavy in the air along with something else. Something more powerful. "You're not a pig."

She smelled the minty toothpaste when he sighed. "Don't test me, Reagan."

"I mean you're clean." She prayed he couldn't see her turn a hundred shades of red in the muted television light. "The bathroom's spotless, your clothes are neatly packed in your suitcase, and this t-shirt smells like flowers."

"Fabric softener." His shoulder hitched, and the sheet shimmied lower. "It makes my clothes soft and it smells good."

"You're quite the conundrum." She couldn't rein in her smile.

He reached over the pillow barrier and tugged a lock of her hair. "Explain, please?"

"Who would have guessed the sexy rocker on stage is a neat freak who uses fabric softener? Most guys don't even know what fabric softener is."

"My mom taught me right. And look who's calling who sexy. You made every girl in that ballroom look like kids playing dress up."

Her heart lurched and her eyes shot to his mouth. His lips, those perfectly formed lips, were only inches away. With everything in her, she wanted to lean closer and touch her mouth to his. Despite her thickened blood, she knew they were wading into dangerous territory, and she needed to stop. It wasn't fair to tease him when they both knew it would be a mistake. "Dash …"

"Sorry, but it's true."

"Why do you say things like that when we're lying in bed with each other?"

Dash shrugged. "I'm my own worst enemy."

Reagan chose to stare at the covers between them. His eyes, those ever-changing eyes, saw too much and she didn't want to see his reaction when she admitted the truth. "I'm not exactly immune to you."

"Why do you make that sound so distasteful?"

"Should I be happy about our attraction? You're on a dating sabbatical, and despite appearances to the contrary, I'm trying to make smarter decisions in my personal life."

The flicker of hurt passed over his face, but she noticed. The hints of vulnerability only made him more attractive. "And being with me isn't a smart decision?"

"It isn't an option." She narrowed her eyes. "Or is your sabbatical in name only?"

"I'm not super human." When he reached across the distance and tucked a strand of hair behind her ear, his fingers grazed the sensitive skin of her neck. "If you wanted to break me, you could. So easily."

Their entire conversation felt like a trap, or maybe a dare. "And you'd hate me in the morning."

He drew in a thick breath and blew it out slowly. "I'd probably hate us both."

"So …" She cleared the longing from her throat and tried to squelch her fickle heart. "We sleep?"

"We sleep." He nodded once and turned to stare at the ceiling before clicking off the TV and plunging the room into darkness. He didn't sound convinced.

Chapter Thirty-Four

Dash had had his fair amount of vivid dreams, especially over the past year, but this one took the cake. Without thought, without waking, his mouth sought the object of his desire. As lips touched lips, heart stirred heart, he lost himself in sensation.

The ringing sound grated, pulling him away from of the warmth and forced his eyes open. It wasn't a dream or a pillow he lay entwined with but Reagan Bellamy. In the flesh. Lips swollen, eyes dim and unfocused. He shook his head, scrunched his eyes closed and open again. Still Reagan, still her arms and legs tangled with his.

"Reagan." Dash lifted himself away, her body protesting. "Reagan, your phone."

She groaned. If he lived to be a hundred he'd never forget the raspy sound of her voice.

"My phone? My phone …" She sat up and reached for her cell on the nightstand. "Hello? Hello?" She stared at the display before glancing his way and quickly averting her eyes. "It was Emily. I missed her call."

Dash eased into a sitting position, grabbed a pillow, and jammed it against his lap. He stared at Reagan, in the middle of the bed where they'd somehow drifted during the night. He dragged his hands through his hair and called himself every kind of fool. He should have slept on the floor or driven home last night. Did he really think he could spend the night inches from her and behave? "Reagan, I'm so sorry …"

"No, no it's … not your fault." She lifted the covers and scooched over to step out of bed, flashing the edges of her lacy black underwear and the expanse of her lean legs. He smothered a groan and averted his eyes. "I shouldn't have come here last night."

"It's not your fault," he said. "I was asleep, dreaming. It wasn't the first time I'd dreamed of you. I'm sorry."

She stopped searching for her dress and stared at him, her sleepy eyes huge, her face flushed. "Why would you say that to me when I can still feel you against me?"

He closed his eyes and let that sink deep into his psyche.

"You're not the only one who has needs." She flung her arms in the air. "What do you think I'm made of? Plastic? I have no idea how that happened, but I've dreamed of you too, so don't go putting all the blame on yourself. I'm the one who came to you when you were vulnerable and alone. I'm also not the one with everything to lose."

She shook her head violently, her eyes seeking, and appeared ready to bolt from the room. He needed to calm her down and fast before she left wearing only his t-shirt and blaming herself for something he'd done. "What are you talking about?"

"Your sabbatical! I know how much it means to you." She found her dress draped over the chair and hauled it against her chest, turning toward the bathroom. He knew he should let her go, he knew they both needed time to settle down and digest what happened, but he also understood nothing would be settled until she knew the truth.

Dash rubbed the heels of his hands against his eyes and cleared his throat. "It's over."

Reagan turned, her hand on the bathroom door, a crease between her brows. "What's over?"

"My sabbatical."

Her fingers slid from the knob and her face went pale and slack. "It's over?"

Dash nodded and glanced away. He couldn't stand to see the hurt on her face, the wounded look in her eyes and know he'd done that to her.

"When?"

"Two weeks ago."

"Two weeks ago?" she asked. "I don't understand. If your sabbatical is over and you want me the way you say you do, why have you been avoiding me? Why didn't you tell me?"

"I ..." He wouldn't lie to her. Not to Reagan. He'd done enough damage already. "I didn't want to get your hopes up."

She sucked in a breath and narrowed her eyes, rubbing her temple as if he'd asked her a complicated math problem instead of slashing her confidence. Her warm chocolate eyes turned as frosty as a root beer float. "My hopes up?"

"About us. About the two of us."

He stared at her, seeking, desperately wanting her to read his intentions so he didn't have to say the words out loud. When her forehead cleared and her eyes shuttered, he knew his smart, intuitive neighbor had connected the dots.

"Oh. I see." Everything about her dimmed—her frantic movements, her high-pitched voice—everything went dull and lifeless. "I'm not good enough for you, for this new and improved version of you."

"Reagan ..."

"No, it's okay. I get it. You've come too far to go back and slum around with someone like me."

"It wouldn't be slumming. That's not what I meant."

"Then what did you mean?"

"It wouldn't be fair to either one of us to start something with you I can't finish."

She simply stared at him, her dark eyes taking him in. She saw him, warts and all, and she accepted him for who and what he was. Had he done the right thing in pushing her away? "I went through all of the past year, all the changes, all the confessions, all the commitments, so I could find someone with the same beliefs."

She stared at him, her teeth nibbling away on her bottom lip as if she were sampling something distasteful. "Then it's a good thing Emily called and stopped us from making a big mistake." She turned to go into the bathroom. "I'll be out of your way in a minute."

When the bathroom door closed, Dash collapsed against the pillows and covered his face with his hands. *If I've done the right thing, Lord, why does it feel so wrong?*

Dash sat up when she came out of the bathroom, watched as she gathered her shoes and pushed the hair from her face. She wouldn't look him in the eyes.

"Thanks for letting me crash here last night," she said. "I'll see you around."

Dash opened his mouth to say something, anything to ease the sting of the truth, but he couldn't find the words. As she disappeared through the door, he lay back and stared at the ceiling, heart aching and mind numb. He wanted to go after her and try to make things right, but what could he say to make her feel better? What did he want her to do other than what she'd done by accepting the limitations on their friendship?

Reagan knocked and fell into Emily's arms as soon as the door opened, unable to hold back the tears another second.

"What happened?" Emily asked. "Where have you been?"

Reagan couldn't speak, could barely breathe through the brick in her throat.

"Did Mike …?"

Reagan shook her head when Emily pulled her back to search her face. "No. Not Mike."

Dylan stepped forward, barefoot and wearing his shirt and pants from the night before, his hands clenched into fists at his side. "What happened?" His voice sounded ominous and low. "Who did this to you?"

"No one touched me." But that was a lie. She'd been touched. If only she could forget the feel of Dash's calloused hands, his agile, hungry mouth. "I'm sorry. Give me just a second."

Reagan moved past Emily and sat down on the made bed she should have slept in the night before. When Emily emerged from the bathroom with a box of tissues, Reagan grabbed them greedily and blew her nose to clear an airway. In and out, in and out. She sucked in air and tried to calm her stuttering breaths.

Emily sat next to her and began rubbing her back. "It's okay." Her manner and rhythmic touch soothed. "It's all right. You're safe now."

"I was never in danger." She dropped her head into her hands as a wave of shame threatened to crash. "Oh, Em, I'm so stupid."

"Reagan," Emily said. "What happened?"

She dropped her hands but kept her head down and stared at the pattern in the rug. She couldn't look at Emily and Dylan when she relayed the humiliating tale. "When I came up last night you two were already here." She glanced at them expectantly, waiting for … an embarrassed admission, an apology, anything. When they remained where they were—Emily on the bed rubbing her back and Dylan looming over them, the muscles in his neck corded like rope—she continued.

"I didn't know what to do or where to go. And then I remembered watching Dash go into a room two doors down."

Emily dropped her hand. "You were with Dash last night?"

"Did he hurt you?" Dylan's teeth were clenched so tight she expected him to spit dust. "I swear if he put a hand on you …"

"No." She shook her head. "It wasn't like that. He let me in, gave me a shirt to sleep in, and we went to sleep."

When Reagan paused to gather her thoughts, Emily squeezed her shoulder. "It's okay. You can tell us."

"We woke up when you called. We were … making out." She covered her face and wanted to hide in the bathroom. She had no problem telling Emily about her embarrassing night, but Dylan?

"I don't know how it started or even how long it had been going on, but we were both pretty worked up. I jumped out of bed because, well, I was mortified, but mostly because I felt horrible about Dash and his sabbatical."

"Sabbatical?" Dylan asked.

Reagan pleaded with her eyes for Emily to explain. "He's not dating for a year while he gets his life in order," Emily said.

"Oh." Dylan nodded, his lips in a thoughtful frown. "Okay."

"What did he say?" Emily asked. "Did he accuse you of something?"

"No. I don't think either one of us was conscious of what we were doing. I started apologizing for going to him last night and for ruining his sabbatical when he told me it wasn't my fault."

"Of course it wasn't your fault," Emily said. "He's a guy." She shot an apologetic smirk at Dylan. "He probably started it."

"Why didn't you just come in the room last night?" Dylan asked. "Just because we were in here doesn't mean we … Oh, you thought we were …" He lifted his brows and nodded.

"I heard you," Reagan said. "I know you were …" She raised her brows and smirked at him. "Besides, I saw something on the doorknob."

"We weren't," Emily said. "I got plastered and Dylan brought me up and put me to bed. I ripped my new dress." She frowned. "And I don't even remember coming to the room."

"She was totally out of it. Whatever you heard was me trying to wrestle her out of her dress and into bed. I fell asleep not long after. I'm sorry. I should have gone down and looked for you."

"So you weren't …"

"Nope." Dylan shook his head. "I like my woman lucid."

Emily rolled her eyes. "I was a mess. I owe you both an apology for getting so drunk. I'm not even sure how it happened."

"Liquor," Dylan said. "It's not your friend, baby. Never again, okay?"

Emily nodded. "Agreed."

They smiled at each other, all sappy grins and adorable eyes, and Reagan wanted to slap them in the face and scream. *Don't be happy now! Can't you see how miserable I am? How dare you two ooze love and affection when I'm in the middle of a crisis!*

"So what happened?" Emily asked, breaking her gaze away from Dylan. "Why the tears?"

"His sabbatical is over. It's been over for two weeks."

"I don't get it," Dylan said. "If he's done with his sabbatical, what's the big deal? I thought you two liked each other."

"You didn't know his sabbatical was over?" Emily voice was like a soft cotton blanket over Reagan's battered heart. "He didn't tell you?"

Reagan's chin quivered, and the waterworks threatened a comeback. "Not a word. He's been avoiding me for weeks."

"After all you did for him? After all the flirting?"

"I know," Reagan admitted. "I didn't get it at first, so he had to spell it out for me."

"Spell what out?" Dylan asked. "I'm confused."

"I'm not good enough for him."

Emily stood up, her hands gripping her waist. "He said that?"

"He didn't have to," Reagan said. "He's changed, Em. He's not the same person he used to be. He's not the type of guy who'd hook up with a girl simply because he can."

"Neither are you. So what if he's changed? You've changed too. You've changed a lot. Maybe if he'd made any attempt to contact you, he'd have known."

But he hadn't made contact. At least now she knew why. "He doesn't know, and I'm not going to tell him."

"I'm still confused …" Dylan lifted his brows and eyed her with pursed lips.

Emily turned to him. "He's a practicing Christian now. He thinks Reagan's not."

"So tell him." Dylan, like most guys, didn't understand the fine print on the page in front of him.

"I can't," Reagan said.

Emily and Dylan swapped worried glances before zooming back in on Reagan. "Why not?" Emily asked. Dylan wasn't the only one not thinking this through.

"Why would he believe me? Would you?" she asked Dylan. "If we'd made out and you'd stopped because I wasn't the type of girl you wanted in your life, would you believe me if in that moment I told you I'd changed?"

"Probably," Dylan said. "Because I'd want to make out."

"Exactly." Reagan plopped back on the bed. "If I'd told him, I'd have sounded desperate."

"Or willing." Dylan grinned.

Emily swatted him with her hand. "That's not helping."

"Sorry." Dylan lifted his hands. "I don't see what the big deal is. Why don't you shower, change, and go back and tell him? You wouldn't be making it up on the spot and you can talk about everything without all the sexy getting in the way."

"All the sexy?" Emily asked.

"Sure." Dylan shrugged. "When he told you, I'm guessing you were still in his room, still wearing his shirt, and still buzzing from the make-out session, right?"

Reagan nodded.

"So, take a shower, and give him some time to think things through. If you tell him later, after all the heat has fizzled, he'll know you're not making it up to scratch an itch."

Reagan was either too tired or too fragile because Dylan's plan sounded like a good idea. The only idea that made sense. She had changed, and Dash deserved to know—if for no other reason than because he'd been the catalyst. "That's not a half bad idea."

Emily stood up and framed his face in her hands. "You're a genius." She covered his lips with hers.

Ugh. Reagan rolled her eyes and made a puking sound. "You two make me sick. Why aren't you mad at her for getting drunk?"

Dylan tucked Emily into his side and smirked at Reagan. "The benefit of her getting drunk is hearing how much she loves me. She's very effusive with her praise when she's hammered."

"So is your roommate," Reagan said. "You may want to check on him too."

Dylan cringed. "Was it bad?"

Reagan shrugged. "I'd be shocked if he remembers, and that's probably a good thing."

Emily grabbed Reagan by the shoulders when she stood up to take a shower. "Next time, just knock on the door."

Reagan sighed. "Let's hope there's never a next time."

Chapter Thirty-Five

Dash didn't answer her knock, and the desk clerk confirmed what Reagan feared. He'd checked out and was probably halfway home. Reagan slumped against the wall, waiting for the elevator, disappointment sinking clear to her toes. She'd practiced what she would say, how she would say it, and had run every possible scenario through her mind. She hadn't thought he'd run.

What a mess. Really, she didn't have time for this. Between a Bible study, full load of classes, and keeping Professor Adkins on task, she had zero free time to pursue a relationship. Just the word made her hands clammy and her stomach cramp. She'd just come to accept the freedom of giving her fears and dreams to an almighty God. Giving those same insecurities to a flesh and blood man who had the power to crush her was a million times more dangerous.

He could hurt her. Opening herself up to Dash put her in a position she swore she'd never be in. It was safer to walk away and chalk him up to someone who led her to Christ. He'd move on—probably had ladies lining up to date him—and he'd be fine. He'd certainly brushed her off easily enough. But then her mind wandered back to his touch, to the feel of his hands on her skin, and the brush of his lips and she knew she was being a coward. She knew.

There was something between them, no matter how hard they tried to fight it. She deserved to lay her cards on the table and Dash deserved to know all the facts before walking away. She'd simply have to bide her time and talk to him back at school. She mentally berated him for leaving. It would have been so much easier to speak to him now, while the moment was fresh and before she had time to marinate in doubt.

What if he rejected her even after he knew the truth? It could happen. There could be a multitude of reasons why he wouldn't want to date her. She was difficult, judgmental—he'd certainly pointed that out on more than one occasion—and focused on school. They were from different parts of the state, had vastly different home lives, and probably had opposing goals for the future. Her goals were … fluid, if she were being honest. Finding God, trusting Him with her future had lifted the urgent edge to her studies and her quest for perfection.

She had no idea what Dash's plans were. Pursue music? He'd be a fool not to see where his gift could take him. As a business major, he could do anything under the sun and go wherever he wanted to go. Perhaps it would calm her heart and her fears if she'd take a step back and realize spending time with him wouldn't automatically mean a relationship. They could take their time, get to know one another, and explore their attraction.

Resigned, she returned to her room to gather her things. Emily and Dylan sprang apart when Reagan entered, rolling away from each other on the bed where they lay fully clothed.

"Seriously?" Reagan asked. "I can't leave you for five minutes without you two molesting each other. It's not like you never get alone time at home."

"Sorry." Emily stood up and straightened her shirt. "We didn't think you'd be back so soon. What happened?"

"He's gone. Checked out an hour ago."

Dylan glanced at his watch. "He'll be home before we even get on the bus."

Reagan tucked her tooth brush into her toiletry bag and placed the bag in her suitcase. The last thing she wanted to endure was the bus ride home. "Kill me now. I don't want to get back on that bus."

"I talked to Mike," Dylan said. "You were right. He doesn't remember much past dancing with you."

"Told ya." Reagan zipped her suitcase closed. "How's he feeling?"

"Not good, but he won't admit it. He's stubborn about hangovers."

"Why?"

"I don't know. I think he thinks it's weak to admit he feels bad after tying one on."

"That would make him super human. Although …" Reagan appraised her roommate. Her color normal, her makeup in place, her posture straight. "You don't seem too worse for wear."

"I've felt better, but I did it to myself. I'm trying not to complain. Besides, Dylan bought me some coffee so I'm feeling a bit better."

Of course he'd seen to her every need. Reagan tried to imagine a man catering to her every desire. Did she even want that? She shook the thought away. *Stop putting the cart before the horse!* At the rate her mind was spinning, she'd have her and Dash married off in a matter of weeks.

"Alrighty then." Reagan tried a cheerful tone to mask her unease. "The dreaded bus ride begins in forty-five minutes. Who wants breakfast?"

Dash intended the bruising run to quell his dark mood, and while he may have exhausted his body, he couldn't silence his mind. Everywhere he glanced he saw the look on Reagan's face. By trying to do the right thing, he'd hurt her more than he'd ever thought possible. He'd brought all of her pain on himself by shamelessly flirting with her when they never had a chance to become more than friends.

He rounded the corner and slowed his pace, scanning the parking lot for her car. Relieved she wasn't home, he took the stairs two at a time and escaped inside his apartment instead of stretching outside like he usually did. He didn't want to face her if she drove up and caught him unaware. He performed a few half-hearted lunges and calf stretches before stepping into the shower.

If only the water could wash away the guilt as well as the sweat. He had to make things right. But how could he convince her she was worth any guy's time and attention with the caveat that he was the exception to that rule? He couldn't. He couldn't do anything but stay away and pray for her to meet someone special who could. Yet his hands balled into fists just thinking about her with someone else.

The tile cooled his forehead where it rested. Dash let the water go cold against his back as he wracked his brain for ways he could renew her self-esteem without giving her false hope. He couldn't think of a single way except one, one that would prove to her he wasn't worth her time. She could walk away with her head held high if he were the one not worthy of her time and attention. It was the only valid plan that could help them both in the long run. Resigned, he shut off the tap. It was time to get busy.

"Just go talk to him." Shelby said.

Reagan stared out the kitchen window at two students trying to light an old charcoal grill with matches. Their laughter echoed off the enclosed courtyard like kids on a playground. "I can't take you moping around the apartment another second."

"I'm not moping." Reagan turned to face her roommate. "I'm just waiting for the right time to approach him."

"You've been home for days. Spring break and Easter are right around the corner. If you don't talk to him now you never will, and you avoiding him is making the rest of us miserable. If you're determined to let Christ lead your life, then listen to Him. I'm pretty sure He's keen on honesty."

"That's rich, coming from you."

"I know about God," Shelby said. "I just don't want him in my day-to-day life. You say you do, so prove it. Tell Dash about your newfound way of life and see what happens. Unless you're afraid."

Of course Reagan was afraid. Of course she'd been avoiding talking to him since she'd gotten home. Instead, she'd thrown herself back into school. School was safe. She knew how to study.

She understood her responsibilities with Professor Adkins. She enjoyed her time at Bible study. Maybe she hadn't shared her latest fiasco with Connie and the others, but so what? That didn't mean she was chicken. She simply didn't want her new friends to judge Emily and Dylan and all the students who lived their lives differently.

"I'm not afraid," she lied. "I'm busy."

"Not too busy to hide out here like some sort of lovesick loser."

"Shelby!" Kayla said from her seat on the couch. "That's a little harsh."

"Maybe so," Shelby said, "but I never thought Reagan would run from a challenge."

"First of all ..." If Shelby's wanted to rouse Reagan into action, she'd succeeded. "I'm not lovesick. I like him, but we hardly know one another. Second of all, he's never around."

"Have you knocked on his door?"

Reagan's cursed her pale skin as her cheeks flared. "I'm keeping an eye out for his truck. When I don't see it, I assume he's not home."

"You know what they say about assumptions?"

"Don't say it." Reagan pointed a finger in her direction. "Don't be that girl."

"They make an ass out of u and me."

"You proud of yourself?" Reagan asked. "How does it feel to be a walking cliché?"

"I don't know. How does it feel to be a yellow-bellied chicken?"

Kayla stood up and put herself between Reagan and Shelby, her arms outstretched. "Enough digs. Shelby, this isn't helping.

And Reagan," Kayla turned up the volume on her pleading eyes, "She does have a point."

Reagan threw her arms in the air. "What is it with you two? Haven't I been hurt enough?"

"Look." Shelby softened her tone. "If you go over there and plead your case and he dumps you, I'll be the first one to wrap my arms around you before kicking his butt. Until then, you're quitting before the last out. The Reagan I know and love is not a quitter."

Why were they pushing so hard? What did it matter to them if Dash knew the truth? "He could reject me anyway," she said before she could think better.

"He could," Kayla said. "But then he'd be the fool, and not you. I know it's hard to lay your cards on the table. But if he matters the way I think he matters, you're a fool if you don't at least try."

Reagan took deep breath and let it out. Would she rather be a foolish quitter or a broken mess? Two all-around lovely choices. "Fine. I'll knock on his door and tell him the truth if it will get you two off my back."

"Make that three," Emily called from her bedroom. "I'm trying to stay out of it because you scare me when you're mad, but I agree with Shelby and Kayla. You need to tell him, or you'll spend forever wondering what could have been."

Reagan wanted to be mad at her roommates for butting into her life, but she'd certainly butted into theirs—especially Emily when they'd manipulated her into facing her feelings for Dylan. If Emily could break up with one brother then boldly date the other while facing their family in the process, the least Reagan could do was tell Dash about accepting Christ. No matter the outcome, he deserved to know the role he played in her journey.

Reagan marched to the front door and opened it. When she turned around to ask her roommates to wish her luck, they collided into her back like falling dominoes. "I'm going, I'm going. You don't have to push me."

Shelby gave her a shove out the door in answer. The laughter died from Reagan's lips at the same time as the floor gave way. Reagan grabbed hold of the railing to stay upright. Dash swaggered his way up the stairs, his hand against the lower back of a gorgeous redhead wearing a shoulder-baring sweater, painted on jeans, and fabulous leather boots. When Dash mumbled something that made the redhead giggle, Reagan's lunch threatened to make a return appearance with a sound somewhere between a gag and a gasp.

Dash glanced her way. His eyes widened before he brazenly winked and continued to his apartment, twisting the knife in her belly when he linked his fingers with the girl. Reagan's insides leaked out her pores and pooled on the ground below her ugly yellow tennis shoes. Shelby yanked Reagan's arm and pulled her inside the apartment and away from Dash and his date.

"Maybe it wasn't as bad as it looked." Shelby closed the door. She didn't sound convinced.

Reagan could only nod. It wasn't as bad as it looked—it was worse. Way, way worse. "It's okay. I'm okay." She'd say anything so she could slip inside her room and relieve the pressure in her chest. She'd never wanted to be alone more.

Kayla glared at them both. "What? What happened?"

"Dash was outside," Shelby said. "With a girl."

"What girl? Where?"

"It doesn't matter," Reagan said. She shoved away from the wall and tried to escape.

"Just because he's with a girl doesn't mean he's on a date. They could be studying or working on his music." Kayla stepped in her path.

"They were together," Shelby said.

"It's okay. It's fine. His sabbatical is over and he's ready to date. He just doesn't want to date me." Reagan tried to swallow the pain while her ribs constricted. "No big deal. This makes it easy to move on. He did me a favor, really."

"But …"

Whatever Kayla was going to say slipped from her tongue at Reagan's warning stare. Couldn't they tell she wanted—needed—to be left alone?

"I'm fine, and this proves I was right about not telling him. It wouldn't have made a difference, and I saved myself a humiliating conversation."

Emily stood in her doorway as Reagan passed on her way to her room. "It's his loss," she said.

Maybe so, but Reagan was the one who was lost.

Reagan did something she'd never done before—she called her mama and balled her eyes out to the woman she knew would understand. Tammy soothed the worst of her pain, reminding her men were stupid, and telling Reagan she deserved a man who would cherish her. She considered calling James and thanking him for reuniting her with her mom, but she feared she'd be tempted to tell him about Dash. Or worse, he'd ask. That prospect had her stopping with Tammy. She'd be home for spring break in a week and again over Easter. Perhaps by then the pain wouldn't feel sharp enough to cut her and she'd be willing to share with him then.

Reagan wiped the last of her tears and hardened her resolve. How had she let a man become so important that his rejection stung like a bullet to the chest? After all her hard work, *she'd* become the cliché. He'd jumped right into dating someone else, so knowing about her faith wouldn't have changed his mind. Four days ago, she'd woken up in his arms. Today he flaunted someone new in her face. Her first instinct had been correct: Dash Carter was a jerk.

Chapter Thirty-Six

Dash sat in the booth of his favorite pizza restaurant and tried to focus on the girl sitting across the table. Jessica prattled on about her hometown (somewhere in north Georgia), her major (journalism), her allergies (seasonal), and a hundred other ideas that popped into her pretty head. Dash struggled to pay attention.

On paper, Jessica ticked all the boxes. They met at church, where she'd been a regular attender since starting at ASU two years ago. Her father was a preacher, her older sister married and expecting a child, her mother a homemaker. Her *Just Jess* blog focused on holding onto her Christian faith during the college years and she'd just topped six hundred followers. Her shoulder-length brown hair, green eyes, and the smattering of freckles across her nose gave her an unpretentious look he found attractive.

Despite all the checked boxes, he knew this would be their second and final date. Just like Amanda, and Chloe, and Brittany. All pretty. All good Christian girls. All failed to capture his interest. Ever since he'd pulled that stunt in front of Reagan a month ago and crushed what was left of her faith in him to bits, he'd thrown himself into dating. There was someone out there for him who shared his beliefs and could make him forget about Reagan, and he'd never find her if he holed up in his apartment. But the more he dated, the less he believed that to be true.

He knew he had to stop comparing every girl he met to Reagan, but there was no comparison. No one had her fire, her wit, or the judgmental comments he found enjoyment in challenging. No one got his gears grinding the way she could with her cynical outlook and cunning intellect. And no one set his blood to boil the way Reagan could with just one look.

He sighed and realized Jessica watched him, waiting for some sort of response. Whoops. He should have paid attention to her instead of daydreaming about his neighbor.

"I'm sorry." He placed his napkin on the table. "Did you ask me something?"

"Your website," she said. "How's the blog going?"

"Oh, its …" He wasn't sure. He'd posted his blog for the past few months and hadn't thought much about it since. "Good, I guess. How do you gauge the success or failure of a website?"

"You're not analyzing your data?" she asked in the same shocked manner as if he'd confessed to not brushing his teeth.

"No. Should I?"

"Absolutely. Tell you what, I've got some great articles on SEO and data analysis I can send you. Or …" She gave him a sideways glance and batted her lashes. "I could come over some time and show you how to read your numbers."

She could, but that might qualify as a third date and he didn't want to lead her on. While boring, pretty Jessica didn't deserve for him to put ideas in her head. He bet Reagan could show him how to read his numbers. She knew all about his website … "I'd really appreciate the articles, Jessica, but I'm afraid I'm going to have to pass on your offer of help. We're tied up trying to get an EP ready for release, so I'm not sure when I'll find the time."

Her smile fell as if he'd kicked her cat. Better to let her down now before they spent any more time together. She deserved someone nicer than him, someone who would at least pay attention when she spoke.

"Okay. That's fine. I'll send them over sometime this week."

"Thanks," he said. After paying the bill, Dash drove Jessica home, walked her to her door, and gave her a chaste kiss on the cheek because a handshake felt inappropriate. As he leaned in and his lips grazed her smooth skin, he caught a whiff of her perfume. She smelled as clean and fresh as a cool spring day, but even that didn't ignite a spark. He'd done the right thing in letting her down.

Maybe dating wasn't the best way to get over Reagan. Maybe he needed to concentrate on his Axis kids and go deeper with his Bible study guys. Except for Mark, he'd only spent time with the other members while in group. Perhaps he'd suggest an outing where they could mingle in a social setting. With all his brooding, he'd forgotten the key to happiness was to focus on God, not people. God would provide a mate for him when God was ready, and no amount of manipulation on Dash's part could change the timing.

Resolved to wait on God's timing, Dash pulled into the apartment's parking lot and spotted Reagan walking purposefully toward her door, backpack slung over one shoulder, her hair swaying against her back. The fist of need landed a punch right to the center of his gut. Dash turned off the ignition and sat in his truck until she'd disappeared inside. He'd move out of the complex in the fall so he didn't have to suffer any more sightings in his final semester. Reagan could live her life however she chose, but he no longer wished to watch, want, and wonder.

When Dash's truck grumbled into the parking lot, Reagan fisted her backpack, quickened her pace, and refused to turn around. She didn't care where he'd been, what he'd been up to, or who he'd brought home. Her heart, her fragile, wounded heart, grieved for what might have been whenever she thought of him. She did her best not to think of him.

Her sweet friend Fallon from Bible study set a lovely example by praying for her abusive ex on a daily basis. Fallon found peace with her past through prayer and shared her story to encourage others. If only Reagan could find the maturity to pray for Dash. He'd hurt her, and in doing so had set her back. She fought daily with the old urges to do her best and to be the best to the detriment of everything and everyone else. Only by attending Bible study did she realize how destructive her behavior had been and how important it was to never slip back into old habits, no matter how comforting they appeared.

Despite the lingering pain, God kept nudging her to forgive Dash for the hurt he'd caused. Some days she felt ready. But then she'd glimpse him coming or going from his apartment, jogging around campus, or hear the rumble of his motorcycle engine and take twelve steps in reverse. She only had to think about the night they spent in Savannah, the hurtful words he'd said, or the classless wink he'd tossed her way while pursuing another girl, and any thoughts of forgiveness flew right out the window.

She took the stairs two at a time and escaped inside the apartment. Kayla sat on the couch when Reagan entered, twirling a lock of golden hair, a textbook on her lap. "Hey." She shut the book. "How was your test?"

"I think I did pretty well." Reagan leaned her backpack against the wall and plopped onto the couch, toeing off her shoes. "Won't know for sure until the grades come out."

Kayla nodded, distracted.

"You okay?"

Kayla sighed. "Do you remember the night you hooked up with Chad Ferguson?"

Reagan inhaled a sharp breath and absorbed the shock. Thank goodness her memory of that night remained fuzzy or she'd never be able to look herself in the mirror. Looking back, she could plot her mistakes and missteps so clearly. Her resentment toward her mother because her father never bothered to stick. Her pursuit of sweater vest-wearing, BMW-driving Chad Ferguson because she thought a guy like him could erase her humble past. Her dangerous drive to be the best at everything because she'd convinced herself anything less meant total failure. "Barely. Why?"

"Seems like a million years ago, doesn't it?"

It was the first time she'd talked to Dash—the day he'd offered to help, the day she'd practically spit in his face. Because Dash took her to church and pushed her to attend Bible study, she'd found a peace she'd never known existed. The Bible showed her she didn't have to feel ashamed of her circumstances. She didn't have to cuddle up to know-it-all jerks to forget her humble roots. She didn't have to push herself to succeed beyond her limits. God loved her just as he'd made her—in His image. Thankfully, God used her missteps and mistakes for His glory. No matter how she felt about Dash, she'd always feel grateful to him for leading her to Christ. In the end, that was enough reason to forgive him.

"Yes, it does."

"April's almost over," Kayla said. "Finals are just around the corner. Summer will be here before we know it."

"Why do you sound so sad?"

Kayla shrugged and tossed the book away. "I don't know. We're going to be seniors. It feels like time is moving so fast. Too fast."

"What does that have to do with Chad?"

Kayla scrubbed her hands over her face. "Nothing, I was just thinking back over the year. How is it working with him every day?"

Reagan lifted a shoulder. "It's fine. We basically ignore each other. He's always trying to one-up me in front of Mark, but I don't take the bait. It infuriates him, which makes me happy."

"You're a better person than I am," Kayla said. "I'd hate to work with someone I detest."

"It's not all his fault. It takes two to tango, and as embarrassing as it is to admit, I was as complicit as him."

Kayla stared at her. "You really have changed. You used to be really angry about things and carry all that baggage around with you."

"What baggage?"

"Your mistakes with Chad, how hard you had to work, bitterness toward those who had everything handed to them."

Reagan glanced around the quiet apartment. "Don't tell Shelby, but God knocked that chip right off my shoulder."

Kayla smiled and mimed turning a key to her mouth. "My lips are sealed."

"The ladies in Bible study have taught me not to judge a book by its cover. There's a lot of pain people carry around that no one can see. I'm not the only one who's had it tough. Besides, I'm in college, I have a mother who loves me, and good friends. I have a lot to be thankful for."

"Yep," Kayla stretched out along the couch and bumped Reagan's leg with her foot. "You've definitely changed. For the better."

Chapter Thirty-Seven

"Well, that was good timing." Connie approached Dash as he got out of his truck. He'd pulled in the driveway behind her garage where she'd just begun unloading a van full of groceries.

Dash took the grocery bags from her arms. "What army are you feeding?" He eyed the bags filled to bursting.

"The little army inside. They eat a lot. Plus I've got Bible study tonight and I want to try a new cookie recipe I found."

"Cookies?" Dash wagged his brows. "It just so happens I'm free to taste test."

She opened the door and he nodded his thanks. "No boys allowed." Connie slid her purse from her arm and placed her keys on the hook by the garage door.

After setting the groceries on the counter, Dash turned to face Connie. "Is Mark around? I want to talk to him about some fellowship ideas for our Bible study."

"Like what?" she asked.

"Like a bowling league or joining with another men's group to play softball."

Dash high-fived Jackson as he slid into the room in sock-covered feet. "Help me with the groceries, little man?" Dash opened the kitchen door for Jackson and followed him outside. Loaded with the last of the bags, Dash helped Jackson heft the grocery bags onto the island with a boost, and then patted his bottom as he ran off to find Lily.

Dash rummaged through the groceries. Crackers, apples, and of course, two bags of celery. Yuck! He spied a bakery box and lifted it to his nose.

"A bowling league sounds like fun." Connie grabbed the box of muffins out of his hand. "Those are for my Bible study."

Mark breezed into the kitchen and waved at Dash. "I forgot you have Bible study tonight."

"How come we don't get muffins and cookies at Bible study?" Dash asked Mark.

"Because if I served them to you, I'd never get any for myself."

Connie held up a frozen pizza and a bag of chicken fingers. "Pick your poison," she said to Mark.

Mark pursed his lips as if deciding on dinner were a monumental decision. "I think it's a pizza nigh—"

A scream sounded from the den.

Mark and Connie bolted from the kitchen into the den, and Dash followed. Lily lay next to the staircase, holding her eye as blood streamed down her face.

Connie crouched down, her hand shaking as she asked a sobbing Lily what happened. The girl was too shocked to answer.

Jackson crept forward from his spot along the wall. "We were playing chase and Lily slipped. Her head crashed into the stair."

"Let me see, Lily bear," Connie coaxed. "I can't help unless you let me see."

Lily peeled her hands away and Dash bit his tongue so as not to gasp. Blood was everywhere, pouring down her face and dripping onto her clothes, the source undetermined.

Mark ripped the shirt from his back and carefully cradled Lily's head, wiping the blood from her eye. After the first swipe, they spotted the deep gash in her eyebrow. "There it is." Mark's voice shook. "It's not her eye. Thank God."

"That's going to need stitches," Connie mumbled. Lily cried harder. "It's okay, Lil. The doctors are really good at fixing things up, and this needs to be fixed."

"I don't want to go to the doctor," Lily sobbed.

"We have to, honey," Mark said. "We don't have a choice."

Dash scooped Jackson into his arms. "Take Lily to the emergency room. I'll stay here with Jackson until you get back."

Connie nodded and helped Lily into the kitchen to clean up the blood. Mark stood up, the red hair on his torso shimmering in the light as his chest heaved. "Are you sure you don't mind? This could take a while."

"Go," Dash said. "I'll feed him, put him to bed." He patted Jack's back. "We'll have a man's night."

Mark cupped Jackson's cheek. "It's okay buddy. It wasn't your fault and Lily's going to be just fine."

The kid's lip pouted adorably, his eyes glistening with unshed tears.

"Listen to Dash. Mommy and Daddy will be home soon. I'll say goodnight when we get back. Be a big boy and say a prayer for your sister, okay?"

Jackson nodded as his dad bounded up the stairs, returning moments later wearing a clean shirt and a worried expression.

"Dash," Connie called from the kitchen. Dash shared a look with Jackson before jogging to her. "I need you to move your truck."

"Just take it," he pulled the keys from his pocket and tossed them at Mark. "That way I'll have your van with the booster seat for Jackson in case something comes up."

Connie nodded, so concerned for her whimpering daughter that she appeared confused. "Oh, right. Okay." She glanced around the kitchen, the bags of groceries, the ice cream on the counter.

"Just go. Me and Jack will unload the groceries and make dinner."

"Thanks," Mark called over his shoulder after ushering Connie and Lily out the door. "I owe you."

"Get out of here. We'll be fine."

He set Jackson on his feet and put his hands on his hips. "Let's get to work."

Dash's cell rang moments later. His stomach shot to his knees when he saw Connie's name on the display. "What's wrong?" he asked.

"I forgot about Bible study. Would you mind calling the girls and telling them what happened? There's a list on the side of the fridge."

"No problem. Let me know how Lily's doing."

Dash located the handwritten list hanging from a magnet. He unclipped the paper and set it on the counter. "Okay, bud.

Hand me that pizza box." He scanned the instructions, set the oven to bake, and lifted Jackson so he could set a box of pancake mix onto the top shelf of the pantry. They repeated the process, one box, one can, and one container at a time until all the bags were empty. Jackson stuffed them into a contraption on the back of the pantry door.

"Tell you what," Dash said. "I'll make these calls while we wait on the pizza. You can watch some TV."

Jackson scurried into the den and turned on the television, whooping at the chance to watch his favorite show at night during what Dash knew was usually the Adkins "Family Hour." Oh, well. Better for the kid to watch some TV rather than having to listen to Dash recount Lily's injury over and over. That would just get him worrying about his sister.

There were six names on the list. As he scanned the names his stomach glazed with sand when he saw Reagan Bellamy at the very bottom. Connie probably wrote her name in pencil because she knew her appearance in the group was temporary. Maybe they would have had a chance if she'd have stuck it out and explored the God he worshiped. Maybe. Shaking away the gloom, he started at the top and began making calls. If he lingered too long, he might not catch them before they left.

He'd just hung up with Kendra, explaining the story and asking for prayers when the timer sounded. "Jackson," he called after taking the pizza from the oven. "Dinner's ready. Shut the TV off and wash your hands, please."

The soundtrack of annoying music disappeared, leaving only the sound of sizzling cheese and the low hum of the refrigerator. Dash relished the quiet and the success of the evening. He'd called everyone on the Bible study list and prepared dinner. Now Jackson sat clean and happy at the kitchen island waiting for his two slices of pizza. No wonder his sister spent every weekend of her childhood watching the kids in the neighborhood. This babysitting thing was a piece of cake.

Dash settled beside Jackson and ruffled the kid's hair. "You want to say the blessing, Jack, or you want me to do it?"

Jackson's brow crinkled. "Dad always says the blessing. Since he's not here, I guess you should do it."

Dash bowed his head, recalled his childhood mealtime blessing—Good food, good meat, good God, let's eat!—and dismissed the idea. Jack's sister was injured and needed a serious prayer before they dug into their meal. "Heavenly Father, thank you for this meal, thank you for the many blessings you've bestowed upon us. Please hold Lily in your arms while she gets stitches, and please be with Mark and Connie as they endure the worry for their child. Give the doctor a steady hand and a good bedside manner. We ask this in the name of Jesus Christ, our Lord and Savior. Amen."

"Amen," Jackson said. "Dad always asks for prayers for those who suffer."

Dash huffed around his first bite. "Well, your dad's a lot smarter than me."

"He's the smartest guy in the world," Jackson said, dropping his piece comically. "That's hot."

"Let it cool for a second before you take a bite."

Jackson gulped from his glass of milk and wiped his mouth on the napkin at his side. "When will you be as smart as my dad?"

Dash choked out a laugh. "Probably never, but that's why I'm in school. To learn from guys like your dad so maybe someday I'll be as smart as them."

"It takes a long time." Jackson gave an affirmative nod. "Dad says he's still learning. He says every day is a chance to learn something new."

"He's right about that."

When the doorbell rang, Dash glanced at Jackson. "Your pizza should be cool enough now. Go ahead and eat and I'll be right back."

Dash spied dark hair and a curvaceous figure though the beveled glass door and wondered if Fallon's roommate hadn't given her the message about Bible study. He opened the door and nearly swallowed his tongue when he saw Reagan on the porch. "Reagan?"

"Umm …hi." From the look on her face—the blinking eyes and stiffening posture—she was as surprised to see him as he was to see her. "What … what are you doing here?"

"I'm …" *Shocked. Confused. Delighted.* "I'm watching Jackson." He noted the glow of embarrassment blossom along her neck and move up to her face, to the exact spot where he'd set his lips. He shook the memory away. "What are you doing here?"

"Watching Jackson?" she repeated. "For Bible study?"

"No." His brain couldn't function with her scent in the air. The cottony coconut smell left him incapable of processing anything but the answers to her questions. "Lily fell and cut her eyebrow."

Her hand flew to her mouth. "Oh no. Is she okay?"

"She'll be fine, but the cut's deep enough to need stitches." Why was Reagan here? She was holding some books against her chest. A lightbulb went off. "Are you dropping something off for Mark? I can give it to him when they get back."

"What? No." She shook her head and took a step forward so he had to back up and let her inside. "Can I come in for just a second? I really need to use the bathroom."

He held the door open for her and stared after her as she set the books on the table in the foyer and rushed to the half bath off the hallway to the den. He shook his head once, twice before shutting the door and glaring at the books. The one on top looked so much like the leather-bound journal he'd spotted in her room as she'd packed to go home that he stepped closer, nudged the cover open, and read a few lines from the page he'd exposed.

Everything in him went fuzzy just before the puzzle pieces in his brain solidified into a cohesive picture that had him hunching forward and flipping pages. What in the world …

Chapter Thirty-Eight

Reagan stared at her reflection in the mirror and cringed. Other than the pink blotches on her cheeks, she was deathly white, her eyes huge, her hair lying limp down her back. The old t-shirt she'd paired with holey jeans felt five sizes too small in the tiny, suffocating bathroom. She splashed water on her face, dabbed it off with a towel, and cursed her decision to attend Bible study sans makeup. Of all days to choose comfort …

She took a steadying breath and looked herself in the eye. She admonished her tiny bladder and gave herself a pep talk. *You can do this. You can face him again. Tell him the truth and get out of the house before he has a chance to grill you about not telling him sooner.*

With a fortifying breath, she exited the bathroom but stopped short when she spotted Dash looking through her journal where she'd left it on the table in the foyer. She crossed her arms and cleared her throat. "What are you doing?"

Dash dropped the cover but instead of acting embarrassed, he glared at her and raised his hands to his hips. "What is this?"

"Reagan!" Jackson shouted and ran from the kitchen, his mouth covered in red. He tumbled into Reagan's side, squeezing her tight, and leaving a streak of something on her shirt.

"Jack." Dash shook his head. "You just wiped your mouth on Reagan's shirt."

The boy looked down, frowned, and blinked up at her with pitiful eyes. "Sorry."

"That's okay." She tussled his hair. "It's an old shirt."

"I can fix it," Jackson said. He pulled Reagan into the kitchen, past the island where two plates with pizza slices sat abandoned, and into the adjacent laundry room. "Up there." He pointed to a high cabinet. "There's a stick Mom uses on my clothes when I get dirty."

Reagan reached up to open the cabinet and grabbed the stick, uncapped it, and swiped it along the red. She didn't have the heart to tell Jackson she didn't care half as much about the stain as she did about the fact that she'd caught Dash rummaging through her private thoughts. How dare he? And what was with that look he shot her? Shouldn't he feel guilty about getting caught instead of acting like she'd done something wrong?

"We're having pizza for dinner," Jackson said.

"So I see." She glanced at the two plates with slices and the half-empty milk glass before cutting her eyes back to Dash. He glared at her like a bug under a microscope. What was with him? "I hear your sister got hurt," she said to Jackson.

"Yeah." Jackson nodded his head and wrinkled his nose. "You should have seen all the blood."

"Glad I missed it." She smiled at him and then clapped her hands against her jeans. "Well, I'll get out of your hair. You two seem to have everything under control."

Dash wrapped his hand around her arm, stopping her from retreating back into the foyer. "We've got plenty of pizza. Why don't you stay and keep us company?"

"Yeah!" Jackson said. "Stay for dinner. Then you can read to me before bed. I'm in the middle of one of those books you told me about. It's awesome."

Reagan disengaged from Dash's hold as unobtrusively as possible so as not to alert Jackson of the tug of war occurring between the adults in the room. Dash stood with his legs spread, his arms crossed, and his eyes narrowed as if daring her to try and leave. She wouldn't have put it past him to tackle her if she tried. "I don't want to intrude."

"It's no intrusion." Dash's smile was totally fake. "In fact, you can fill us in on all the Bible study notes you've taken over the last couple of months. It's the book of John, right."

"That's right," Reagan said, her brows lifted, her stare accusing. If he wanted to play games in front of Jackson and pretend everything was hunky dory, she could play along too.

"And you've been studying it for how long now?" He tapped a finger to his lips, a picture of curious innocence. "I'm pretty sure Connie said the study would get the group through the entire spring semester."

"Yep. You've got the memory of an elephant." *And a chip on your shoulder about the same size.*

"Oh, you know." He gave her an angry grin that narrowed his eyes. "Details are kind of important to me."

"Details *are* important." She gave him an indulgent nod. "With Bible studies and …oh, I don't know … sabbaticals and stuff like that. Wouldn't you agree?"

He had the nerve to appear annoyed. "You're right. But so is the truth. Wouldn't you agree?"

"Of course the truth is important. It's also difficult to explain the truth to someone with a such a busy social life."

His flustered expression had her waving a mental fist in the air. *That's right. Take that and score one for me. Ha.*

Dash pressed closer, his voice edged with impatience. "Maybe I wouldn't have such a busy social life if someone had been honest with me about her faith."

Reagan's chin jutted up of its own violation. They stood so close she could feel his breath on her face and smell his woodsy scent. "It's hard to talk to someone who's been avoiding me for weeks. Oh, wait …" She clutched her chest. "I forgot. You've been so busy with class and the band." She counted with her fingers. "And the redheads and the blonds and the brunettes. Must be so taxing."

"Maybe I've been going out with all those girls because I couldn't—"

"Uh," Jackson stepped beside the them, his head bobbing from Reagan to Dash. "Can I eat?"

Reagan gathered a calming breath, eased back from the angry man in front of her, and softened her voice. "Of course you can. I'm sorry for our behavior. We're being silly."

"Sounds like you're fighting." Jackson scurried onto the stool and picked up a half-eaten slice of pizza.

"We're not fighting." Dash spoke over his shoulder as he retrieved a plate from the cabinet. "We're just talking."

Reagan took the plate he offered and squashed the urge to sling it into his chest like a Frisbee. Despite her childish thoughts and behavior, she could act like an adult in front of an eight-year-old. She grabbed a slice of pizza and sat as far away from Dash as possible. He sauntered around the island and took a seat as if he hadn't a care in the world.

"So, Jackson," Dash said. "Tell me about this book you're reading."

"It's a series. I'm reading the one about a bunch of boys who grew up to make a difference in the world through God."

"Really?"

Dash chewed and slid his eyes to Reagan, watching her in a way that made her pizza taste like sand. Was he going to condemn her for encouraging Jackson to read Christian stories?

"Maybe I can sit in while y'all read?" he said. "I love a good story."

"Sure," Jackson said. "I don't care if Reagan doesn't."

She wiped her mouth and swallowed a sarcastic retort. "The more the merrier."

When Dash's cell rang, he pulled the phone from his pocket, read the display, and tapped Jackson on the shoulder. "I'll be right back." As he eased into the other room and his voice faded to a low hum, Reagan exhaled the first full breath since the moment she'd walked inside the house. She didn't have a clue how to resolve things with Dash or even where things stood, but she knew one thing for sure—neither one of them would walk away unscathed.

"How's Lily?" Dash asked Mark as he stepped into the den and turned around to face the entrance. He didn't want anyone sneaking up on him and overhearing his conversation. He'd had more than enough surprises for one night.

"She's good. They applied some numbing jelly and we're just waiting for it to kick in before the doctor sews her up. Poor thing. She'll need a handful of stitches."

"Wow."

"It's a bad gash. She was lucky, though. It could have been so much worse if her eye had hit the corner of the stair. I can't even think about what would have happened."

Dash envisioned Mark pacing in the confined space, rubbing his hand over his face, desperate to help his little girl. "Praise God it wasn't worse."

"Amen to that." Mark sounded exhausted to the core. "How's Jackson?"

"He's good. Reagan's here and we're eating pizza."

"Reagan?"

"Yeah. She was on the Bible study list, but no one bothered to tell me she's been coming, so I didn't call her."

"Listen, Dash—"

"She's here," Dash said. This wasn't the time or the place to get into the depths and reasons for Mark's oversight. "Jack asked her to stay for dinner and read to him before bed. I just wanted to make sure that was okay with you and Connie."

"Of course, yes, that's fine, but—"

"No buts. Take care of Lily, and we'll sort this out later."

"I wanted to tell you."

"And you will." Dash's voice sounded harder than he'd intended. Mark had enough on his plate to worry about him now. "But Lily comes first. Tell her I think stitches are cool and I can't wait to see hers."

Mark sighed. "I will. Thanks. I'll shoot you a text when we're headed home."

When Dash walked back into the kitchen, Jackson and Reagan sat with their heads together, giggling about something he probably wouldn't understand. There was so much about her he didn't understand.

Her smile faded, and her eyes turned cool as he eased into their line of vision, breaking the spell of happy chatter. "That was your dad," Dash told Jackson. "Lily's fine. They're waiting on the doctor to stitch her up, and then they'll be home."

"Will she have to wear an eye patch?" Jackson asked. "Like a pirate?"

"No, you goof. They sew the wound together and in a couple weeks you won't even know it happened."

"She won't have a scar?" he asked.

"Why do you sound disappointed?"

"I want a scar on my face. That'd be so cool."

"Give it time," Dash mumbled. He had more scars on his body than he cared to count.

"How's Connie?" Reagan asked, pushing her plate away after only one piece.

"I don't know, but Mark sounded okay. Tired, a little impatient, but okay."

"Waiting around an emergency room must be driving him crazy." Reagan stood up and rinsed her plate in the sink. "He can't sit still for a second."

"He's got ants in his pants." Jackson said.

Reagan turned from the sink and laughed.

"That's what my teachers say about me."

Reagan's smile wavered as their gazes locked. The wounded look in her eyes made his chest ache. "The apple doesn't fall far," Dash said.

In his peripheral vision, he saw Jackson's head tilt. "What do ants have to do with apples?"

"It's just an expression." Dash couldn't look away from where Reagan's teeth pressed into her bottom lip, color flared to life along her neck, and her dusky almond eyes left him drowning in their depths.

Jackson solved the problem by yanking on his arm. "I wanna take a shower instead of a bath. Can you get the water right for me like Mom does?"

"Get the water right?"

"I think he means the temperature," Reagan said.

"Oh, yeah. Duh. I can get the water right." He turned to Reagan and hoped she recognized the plea in his voice. "We'll be back in a few. Make yourself comfortable."

She nodded, gathered the plates from the island, and turned back to the sink. As he and Jackson ascended the stairs, Dash prayed she'd still be there when they came back down.

Chapter Thirty-Nine

Reagan rinsed the dishes and shoved them into the dishwasher as fast as she could. Grabbing her purse, she made a beeline for the bottom of the stairs and, with phone in hand, listened for noises from the second floor. When the shower sputtered to life and Dash called for Jackson to hurry up and get in before the water went cold, Reagan paced into the den, sat on the chair facing the stairs, and pulled up her roommate's number.

"Hey," Kayla said. "What's up?"

"I need some advice."

"Why are you whispering?" Kayla asked.

"I'm at Connie's. Dash is here. It's a long story, and I don't have time to explain, but he knows I've been coming to Bible study."

"Well … that's good, right?"

"I'm not sure. He seems pretty mad."

"That's not your fault. You tried to tell him."

"I know."

"So what's the problem?"

Reagan sighed. She didn't have time to beat around the bush. "After all the girls I've seen him with in the past few weeks, I don't know what to hope for. Truth is, I'm mad at him."

"Has he explained?"

"No. We're kind of babysitting Jackson until Mark and Connie get home. We haven't had a chance to talk."

"The kid's got to go to bed sometime."

"That's what I'm afraid of." She pulled the phone from her ear to listen for the water running through the pipes. "I don't know what to say to him."

"Tell him the truth. Spell it out from the very beginning."

"I know I should, but I'm scared."

"Why? Do you think he's going to hurt you?"

"No. Maybe. I don't know. Every time I'm around him there's this weird pull between us. I just … If I tell him I'm a believer and he's still not interested, I think that'll hurt more than seeing him with other girls. He could reject me for real. I'm afraid of how that will feel."

Kayla clucked her tongue. "Well, if there's one thing I can tell you for sure, it's that feeling anything is better than feeling nothing. You can't expect someone to love you if you don't give them the chance to hurt you too."

Reagan rolled her eyes and wished for the millionth time Kayla wouldn't view everything through romance-colored glasses. "I'm not talking about love."

"I know, but you like him. You like him in a way I've never seen you like anyone else. He could hurt you, which makes you vulnerable."

"Yes."

"But think about how much you'll regret never giving each other the chance to explain and see what could be for you. You owe it to yourself to let this play out."

"You're right." Reagan let her eyes slip closed. "I know you're right."

"Trust God for putting you in this situation. He alone knows your future."

Those words were the exact reason Reagan called Kayla in the first place. Despite her proclivity for romanticizing every situation, she knew how to motivate a new believer. "I do trust God and I know He put us here for a reason."

"You can do this. You've faced a lot in the last few months. Telling Dash about your faith is a good thing. He'll be happy for you no matter what his feelings are. I know he will."

Reagan nodded. "Okay." She heard footsteps and her stomach pinwheeled. "I've gotta go. Wish me luck."

"You don't need luck," Kayla said. "Have faith."

Dash appeared at the bottom of the stairs and strode into the kitchen before Reagan could tuck her phone into her pocket. She stood up, walked into the foyer, and slowed her steps when she spied Dash with one hand against the island and the other rubbing his neck. She approached cautiously. "Hi."

He straightened and whipped around as if she'd startled him. "You're here."

"I said I'd stay. Did you think I'd left?"

He gave a half-hearted shrug. "Yeah."

"I told Jackson I'd read to him and I will. I know this is uncomfortable, but I'm not going to bolt on a little boy."

Dash inhaled a breath and let it out with a deliberate, appraising gaze. "He's ready to read. I told him I'd get you."

Reagan nodded but couldn't move from where his stare held her captive. What was he thinking behind those impassive hazel eyes? "You coming?" she asked.

"Yeah. I'll be up in a second."

"Okay." She climbed the stairs, grateful for the reprieve. She needed to calm down and get a grip on her emotions. This wasn't a life or death situation. They were two friends clearing the air. Nothing more. She needed to keep her thoughts focused on God and His plans for her life, and not her treacherous libido.

She found Jackson in his room, tucked under denim blue covers, his hair wet from the shower. He patted the bed when he saw her in the doorway. "Mom and I finished the second story last night, so we can start with the third."

"Why don't you read to me?" Reagan asked as she took a seat. "These stories are about boys. I think they'd sound better in your voice."

"I want you to read."

"How about we each read a page? That way it's fair."

He made a sour face but agreed nonetheless, handing her the book. "You go first."

Reagan had just passed the book back to Jackson when Dash appeared in the doorway, leaning against the frame, his hands resting in the pockets of his jeans. The look he gave her made her stomach quiver and her nerves spike to attention. Everything about him relaxed—the way he crossed one leg in front of the other and propped against the jamb—but his expression held questions too raw to answer. She forced herself to look away and zone in on Jackson.

They swapped the book back and forth through two stories until Jackson's eyes grew heavy and Reagan's stomach churned with dread. She couldn't keep the poor kid up all night just to avoid the inevitable.

"That's it for tonight." She closed the book and set it on his nightstand. "Did you brush your teeth?"

Dash stepped inside, startling Reagan. He'd been so quiet, and she'd done such a good job of pretending he wasn't there that his presence loomed large in the tiny blue room. "Teeth are brushed, book was read. Time to say your prayers and call it a night."

When Jackson lowered his head and brought his tiny hands into an angel's pose, Reagan bowed her head and closed her eyes.

"Dear God," Jackson said. "Please watch over my sister and Mom and Dad and all the people in the hospital. Please bless my grandparents, and I could probably use some help on my math quiz tomorrow. Amen."

"Did you have homework you didn't tell me about?" Dash asked.

"No," Jackson said. "I did it right after school."

Dash gave a noncommittal grunt before squeezing Jackson's foot through the covers. "Get some shut-eye. Your mom and dad are on their way home now."

Reagan rubbed the soft strands of his hair before standing up. Her feet like cinder blocks and her heart battered her ribcage while her cuticles suffered her nervous picking. She'd never wanted to leave a room less. "Good night, Jackson."

"Night."

It was a wonder Dash's hand didn't disintegrate when his fingers grazed her back as he led her out of the room and into the darkened hallway. They silently descended the stairs, her nerves popping like a hot wire and their footfalls echoing in her head like a nail gun. The front door opened as she hit the landing at the base of the stairs. Mark appeared, carrying Lily as if she weren't all limbs and torso.

"You're back," Dash said from behind her. She didn't dare turn and look at his face.

"Finally." Connie shut the door.

"I'm going to go put her down." Mark eased past them and up the stairs.

"I'm coming with you." Connie followed her husband. "We'll be right down."

Reagan nodded and watched them go as relief and worry created a nauseating brew in her gut. There'd be no time to talk with Mark and Connie home. "I'm going to go." She grabbed her books and keys from the foyer table and turned toward the door, but Dash anticipated her move and placed himself in front of her escape.

"What's your hurry?"

"No hurry, but since Mark and Connie are home, I don't see a need to stay."

"Reagan." Dash dipped his chin and lowered his voice. "We need to talk."

"Yes, we do. But not here. Not now. I'm tired, and I've got a test to study for. Text me, and we'll arrange a time."

"Text you?"

"Yes, Dash, text me. If you're not too busy with class and the band, text me and we'll set a time to talk."

She regretted her words when he grimaced.

"Please don't throw that at me again. I need to explain."

"And you will. So will I. Just not now. Tell Connie … tell her I'll be in touch."

She reached around him for the door, but he didn't budge. She couldn't leave with him blocking the exit. He looked down at her, his eyes pleading. "I'm sorry I hurt you. Please promise me you'll give me a chance to explain."

"You don't need to apologize."

"I do. We've got to talk about this, Reagan. There's so much I need to say to you, so much I need to understand."

Too flustered to speak, she only managed to nod. Dash eased back and opened the door for her.

She trotted down the porch stairs and jogged to her car, her fingers fumbling with the buttons on her key fob. She had to get out of there before she embarrassed herself any further by crying.

Dash stood rigid in her rearview, his hand on the doorknob as she punched the gas and fled.

"Did Reagan leave?" Mark asked as he entered the kitchen where Dash waited and stewed. He had to get a hold of his anger. Mark had been through enough with his daughter. He didn't deserve the onslaught of accusations building inside a friend.

"Yeah. How's Lily?"

"Exhausted." Mark rubbed his forehead, his gaze weary. "Look, Dash, I—"

"I'm not sure we should do this right now. It's not my habit to kick someone when they're down."

"I'd like to explain."

"Explain what?" Connie came into the kitchen with bare feet and tire eyes. Even ready to drop, she sensed the tension between them. "What's going on?"

"Dash didn't know Reagan's been coming to Bible study."

Connie gripped the back of an island chair, her head cocked to the side. "You didn't know?"

"I didn't tell him," Mark said.

"I thought she quit," Dash said. "You said you didn't expect her to come back after the Christmas break."

"I didn't. She shocked me when she showed up after Christmas and apologized. She's been here every week since. I …" She looked at Mark and sighed. "I thought you knew."

Dash watched Connie's lips move, but each word she spoke scrambled beyond meaning. Mark, his friend and mentor, had kept the truth from him for months. Even his wife appeared surprised. "Since Christmas?" He couldn't deal with Mark. Not when his need for information trumped his desire for understanding. "Is she … does she believe in God? Is she a skeptic or a follower?"

"She's a believer." Connie smiled. "She's accepted Christ. She's even talking about getting baptized."

All the blood in Dash's body flooded his heart leaving him dizzy and delighted. He'd never heard such amazing news. "That's …" He cleared the emotion from his throat. "That's awesome."

"Yeah," Connie agreed. "It is. She fought it tooth and nail, but she's all in. I'm proud of her. You should be too, since you're the one who brought her to God."

"Me?" Dash asked. "I did everything wrong."

"No," Mark said. "I did everything wrong. All I can say is I'm sorry." Every part of Mark sagged—his arms onto the counter, his face as if melting under a heat lamp, his shoulders as if weighted down by guilt. "I never intended to mislead you."

If Mark insisted on talking about this now, he'd get an earful. Dash gripped the counter with both hands and bit back an oath. "I can't believe you never told me!"

"I was going to—"

"When?"

"The night we met for dinner, when we bumped into Eli. You'd just told me how you'd decided to cool things between you and Reagan."

"Because I thought she wasn't a believer." He drove his hands through his hair and spun around. He couldn't look at Mark without wanting to hurt him. "Why would you let me think that when you knew?"

"She'd just come back from break." Mark's voice was laced with guilt. Dash faced him, watched as he struggled to justify his actions. "She'd just accepted Christ. I was going to tell you, then Eli interrupted, and I didn't. I figured you'd find out eventually, preferably after your sabbatical, and after she'd had some time to dig into being a Christian."

He tugged on the ends of his hair before letting go. The things he'd said to Reagan in Savannah came rushing back, the shattered look on her face like a reopened wound. "You've got to stop playing God with my life!"

"Dash, I—"

"No!" He backed up, needing distance. "I said things to her, mean, hurtful things. I flaunted other girls in her face to keep her away because I couldn't stop wanting her."

No wonder. How many times had he asked God to take the longing away, to stop the feelings if she wasn't the one? All the praying, all the pleading, all the sleepless nights. All the boring dates while the woman he wanted probably hated him.

"I was wrong and I'm sorry. I thought it was best at the time."

Connie came around the island and touched Dash's shoulder. "If it makes you feel any better, I think it would have hindered her walk with the Lord if you had known any earlier. She would have intertwined her feelings for you with her feelings for Christ and that's never a good thing." She sent a pointed stare at her husband. "Mark should have told you, but I do think it helped strengthen her faith having nothing and no one but God."

Connie was right, but that didn't lessen his anger or assuage his guilt. "Well, I can't be upset about how things worked out because she's committed to Christ. Knowing that, I wouldn't change what happened. I just wish I'd handled it better."

"I'll talk to her," Mark said. "I'll make sure she understands."

"No." Dash ran a hand over his face. "I'll do the talking from now on."

Mark stepped in front of him, his eyes sincere. "I hope you can forgive me."

Although disappointment curdled in his gut, Dash knew he couldn't hold a grudge. "I will."

"You will?"

"Eventually." Mark's grim expression almost made Dash laugh. Almost. "Don't look so down. Eventually might be tomorrow." He let out a sigh. "You've been there for me through the toughest days of my life. One bad decision doesn't erase that."

"I hope not."

"It doesn't. I just need some time to talk to Reagan. If she'll let me."

Connie walked over and pulled him into a hug. "God has a plan. If He'd wanted you to know before now, He would have made a way. Trust Him."

Dash squeezed her tight, grateful Reagan had a woman like Connie in her life. "I do."

Chapter Forty

Are you still up?

Reagan stared at the text from Dash as her stomach twisted and held. Of course she was still up. She'd changed into pajamas as soon as she'd gotten home and settled on the couch to study after filling her roommates in on the latest. Even with a test looming and the clock nearing midnight, there wasn't a chance she could rein in her feelings and find comfort in sleep.

"Why are you grimacing at your phone?" Shelby asked from her perch on the floor of the den.

"It's Dash. He wants to know if I'm still awake."

"Umm." Shelby nodded. "Those yes or no questions are real puzzlers."

Reagan reached behind her and threw a pillow from the couch at Shelby. Although she missed, she managed to scramble papers into disorder and annoy her roommate.

"What's the big deal?" Shelby asked.

"I'm not sure I'm ready."

"You've been mooning over the guy for months. You're beyond ready."

Kayla came out of her room, her hands clasped in front of her chest. "Talk to him. It's not like you're going to get any rest until you do."

Reagan sighed. "Fine." She texted

Yes

and set the phone aside. "I may as well get it over with."

"Ooh. The anticipation is killing me." Kayla clapped her hands. "What are you going to say?"

"I don't know. I figured I'd let him do the talking. Since he's so eager."

Three quick knocks had Reagan closing her eyes and praying for wisdom. *Please Lord, don't let me mess this up.* She glanced down at her pajama shorts and tank top as Shelby and Kayla twittered down the hallway to their rooms. And she thought her night couldn't get any worse than when she'd showed up at Connie's.

After edging the door open, Reagan spotted Dash leaning on the railing a few steps away, his brow furrowed, his expression guarded.

"Hi." She stepped outside, shutting the door behind her to ensure her roommates wouldn't eavesdrop.

"Hey." He stepped closer. "Sorry it's so late. I saw your lights on and figured I'd give it a shot."

She crossed her arms over her chest when his eyes mapped her from head to toe. "That's okay. I'm up."

"I know you're studying and I don't want to interrupt." He blew out a breath and ran his hands over his face.

His weary eyes and all the energy that usually radiated from him seemed to have evaporated and left him wilting. She'd been so wrapped up in her own emotions, she hadn't taken a moment to consider how he might feel other than mad at her. "Connie told me how you accepted Christ and I …" He swallowed, and her stomach tightened. "I'm so happy for you, Reagan. I know I mucked everything up in Savannah, and even before then, but I need you to know how thrilled I am for you."

She sucked in a breath. Connie told him, and he was happy?

"If you want to share, if you're willing to talk about your journey, I'd love to listen."

She shuffled her feet. Did he expect her to tell him now, standing outside in her bare feet in the middle of the night? "Well, it's kind of a long story."

His smile hitched, and a shadow of a grin flashed along his stubbled jaw when the spark between them ignited. "You don't have to tell me now, but I couldn't go to bed—I didn't want you to go to bed—thinking I was upset with you. Because I'm not. At all."

"Okay. Thank you for telling me. It does help." She looked at her toes, his shoes, and the concrete between them as a blush crept up her cheeks. The apology helped, but they still had ground to cover. "Full disclosure—I may still be a teensy bit mad at you."

His grin sizzled, and his eyes went smoky and soft. "I think that's warranted."

"I'm just being honest." And trying not to melt like an ice cream cone under the glare of his gorgeousness.

He stuffed his hands in his pockets and lifted his shoulders. Everything about him appeared lighter, less burdened. "I appreciate that. I expect nothing less."

"I'm glad we understand each other."

Dash nodded. "We're working on it, that's for sure."

She couldn't stand outside staring at him any longer. Every part of her wanted to lean in and rest her head on his chest, let him soothe her worry with his touch and forget about all the reasons they needed to talk. But they did need to talk and late at night on a moonlit balcony seemed the absolute wrong place to clear the air.

"I'd better get back inside," she said.

Dash touched her arm as she turned to leave. "Now that I'm not avoiding you, I'm pretty much going to bug you until you agree to meet. So we can talk. So I can listen. So I can explain."

His stalker tendencies shouldn't make her toes curl. "Okay."

"How does tomorrow sound?"

Reagan pinched the bridge of her nose and tried to focus around the swirling cloud of feelings. "Tomorrow sounds … busy. I've got class, work with Mark, and then a test."

Dash nodded, pressing his lips together. "I've got practice with the band tomorrow night, so that's not the best for me either. How about Saturday?"

Oh goodness. He was serious, and the intent look in his eyes meant she'd better clear the lust from her head and think about her schedule. "Saturday should be good."

Little butterfly wings of hope took flight in her chest at his smile. The flutter turned into a gale force wind when he leaned in and placed his lips on her forehead, warm and soft and enticing. "Goodnight Reagan."

She swallowed and watched him back against the railing before turning and walking to his apartment. They shared one long look before he moved to go inside. "Lock your door," he called.

Reagan nodded and scurried inside before she followed him home and stayed up all night … talking.

Reagan bit her tongue as Chad Ferguson reclined in Professor Adkin's chair, linking his fingers behind his head and setting his feet on the desk.

"I see you've finished another project," he said.

Reagan didn't pause in her filing. Since he'd adopted her organizational system, Professor Adkins counted on her keeping his desk free of unused files. "I just do what I'm told."

"Really?" Chad asked in his annoyingly nasal tone. "Is that why his desk is so clean he could eat off of it?"

"Yes." She knocked his feet off the desktop. "And he does, so keep your feet on the floor."

His comeback died as Mark whisked inside and stopped short. "You bored, Chad?"

Chad stood up so fast he nearly overturned the chair. "Uh, no sir. Just admiring Reagan's filing system."

"It's genius." Mark shooed Chad out from behind his desk. "Can you excuse us, please. I need to speak to Reagan. Alone."

She wanted to punch Chad in the face as he sneered at her as he left. What a jerk. But as soon as he'd left, her nerves sparked to life. "Is something wrong?"

"Yes, but I hope an apology will make it right."

"I … I'm sorry. I'm not sure what I did, but—"

Mark held up his hand. "Reagan, no. I'm the one who needs to apologize."

"You do?"

"About Dash."

Her face flared. Why would he bring up Dash when they'd always made a concerted effort not to talk about personal stuff in the office? "I don't understand."

"Dash didn't know you were coming to Bible study because I didn't tell him. I didn't want him to know."

Reagan sat down in his guest chair when her knees trembled. She took a deep breath, let it out, and began picking at her nails. "Okay."

Mark leaned against his desk and folded his arms across his chest. "You'd just come back to Connie's group and he'd told me he was cooling things with you because you weren't a believer. I had the chance to correct him and I didn't. I was wrong, and I'm sorry."

"That's …" Like a shotgun blast to the gut. She shrugged. "You did what you thought was best for him. I get that."

"Maybe it was best, maybe it wasn't. I should have told him. It had nothing to do with you, and everything to do with me. Truth is, I'm proud of him and his walk with God. I suggested the sabbatical, so my pride was wrapped up in his completion. You were the one thing I thought could derail him, and I made a choice. The wrong choice."

"You don't have to explain—"

"I'd like to." He unfolded his arms and stared at a spot above her shoulder, seemingly lost in thought. "Pride's a funny thing. It's a sin and I know that, but even knowing that, I didn't ask for

God's wisdom or guidance. I just did what I thought was best to get Dash across the finish line." His eyes locked on hers. "I thought it mattered to him, when in truth, it mattered more to me."

Reagan fought the urge to soothe his battered ego. As her boss, everything about their conversation felt upside down.

"It's okay. He knows now. We're going to talk and clear the air. There's no harm."

"Umm," Mark shook his head. "He told me he hurt you with his avoidance and in Savannah …"

Her face flamed. Dash told Professor Adkins about Savannah?

"… and I'm pretty sure that wouldn't have happened if I'd been honest. It wasn't my place to orchestrate his life. That's God's role. I hope you can find it in your heart to forgive me."

"Professor Adkins—"

"Mark, please."

"Mark. You don't need to apologize. You've given me an incredible opportunity to work here, and Connie's welcomed me into your home."

He glanced around the office. "You've more than earned your position."

"I hope so. I enjoy working for you and I hope whatever happens with Dash doesn't affect my job or our interactions."

"I'm sorry. I'm making you uncomfortable." He righted himself and put his hands on his hips. His 80s hair band t-shirt mocked the seriousness of their conversation. "No more personal talk at the office. I hope we can be friends outside the office. Connie thinks the world of you, and clearly so does Dash."

Reagan shrugged and looked away. How did she answer him? "Thank you."

"Listen." He moved around his desk. "Why don't you bug out of here early? Chad's obviously got nothing to do. I'll have him file the rest."

"I don't mind."

"Go on." He shooed her with his hand. "I'll see you next week."

She glanced around the office at the piles left to complete. Every fiber in her wanted to stay and finish the job, but she couldn't argue with her boss. Besides, escaping the weirdness between them sounded like the best idea. "Okay. Thank you."

She slung her backpack onto her shoulder and turned toward the door.

"Hey, Reagan," Mark said.

"Yes, sir?"

"Do me a favor and remember my role in this when you talk to Dash. The things he did, the way he acted—it all needs context."

"Okay. She stared at him—the disheveled orange hair, the faded black t-shirt—and voiced her thoughts. "You love him, don't you?"

"He's the little brother I never had." He shrugged. "An adopted son of sorts. Go easy on him."

And just like that the awkwardness disappeared. The one thing Reagan understood was the love and protectiveness of a created family. "I'll do my best."

Chapter Forty-One

Dash suggested they meet at a cafe just off campus at noon. At 11:45 he could have peeled his skin off. At ten to, he couldn't stop his knee from bobbing an anxious jig. By 12:02 when Reagan pulled into the lot, he jumped up to greet her and lost the table he'd arrived early to secure.

"You look great," Dash said as they stood in line to order. Her hair hung in loose waves, her lips shimmered with some kind of sexy gloss, and her eyes sparked with nervous energy. She would have looked fantastic in a paper bag, but her Sweetgrass Butcher t-shirt felt like a good sign. "I like your t-shirt."

"I found it in my mom's closet over break. She let me have it."

"I like your mom already." He wanted to punch himself for bringing up a sore subject, but she simply nodded and perused the menu. Interesting …

Dash needed caffeine about as much as he needed jet fuel, but he ordered sodas to go with their sandwiches and sucked his down while they waited for a table. Soon they were settling into a booth across from one another. Dash leaned in, so he could hear over the chatter of other students seeking food and company on a muggy Saturday afternoon.

As they ate, Reagan told him about the young preacher from her hometown who challenged her to explore the possibility of faith. Once she'd finished her food, she rested her hands on the table, scraping at her nails as she talked about her mom. Dash reached across and stilled her busy fingers. His touch became a rub, the rub turned into a hold. The feel of her skin in his palm was like coming home on Christmas morning.

He didn't have to pry for details. Whether it was the caffeine or his enthusiastic reaction, she talked openly about her feelings, her past, and the peace she'd discovered in the months while they weren't talking. At times he struggled to maintain his smile when inside his heart broke that he'd been MIA for the better part of her conversion. *Not my journey*, he reminded himself as her joyous tale unfolded.

"That's quite a testimony."

Reagan scoffed and took a sip of her drink. "When Connie asked everyone to give their testimony at the first Bible study I attended, I didn't even know what that meant."

"You've come a long way."

"Yeah, I guess I have. I feel good about where I'm at, and for once at peace with the future."

"It's nice to relinquish control to God," he said. "Before I submitted and let God take the reins, I never realized how freeing it could be."

"It's an amazing feeling." Her gaze slipped to the table and she drew her hand free, linking her fingers. "We need to talk about Savannah."

Dash waited for her to look at him. "I never should have touched you."

"I'm not talking about the physical." She blinked several times. "I get how that happened, and it wasn't just you."

Dash sighed. "I hurt you."

"Yes, you did. But Dash, you need to understand. Even though I was hurt by what you said, by what you insinuated about me, I'm proud of you for turning me away."

He shook his head. He couldn't have heard right. "What?"

"If you felt even a fraction of what I felt when we woke up… together, for you to choose your faith over that kind of crazy connection was an amazing act of conviction. I don't know that I could have done the same."

Would she ever cease to surprise him? "It was the hardest thing I've ever done."

Her head cocked adorably to the side. "Come on, Dash. You left your band at its most successful—"

"And pushing you away that morning was the hardest thing I've ever done. Hands down."

Even in the faded afternoon light, her color brightened. "Then I'm even more impressed. And proud, if you don't mind my saying so."

"I don't mind, but Reagan, I wish you'd told me."

She closed her eyes and tucked her lips between her teeth. "I tried. You were gone, and the receptionist said you'd checked out."

He could still summon the caged feeling of the hotel and his desperate need to flee and clear his head. "And at home?"

Her eyes flashed. "I was a coward, and you were avoiding me."

"I was avoiding you, but if you'd have pressed me I would have listened. What were you afraid of?"

Her face pinched tight and her color deepened. "That you'd reject me!"

"Reagan …" He shoved his hands through his hair.

"I had feelings for you Dash. I was afraid if I told you the truth it wouldn't matter."

"How could you have thought that? You knew how I felt about you."

"I suspected, and you'd certainly hinted. But when you dropped off the planet after Christmas, I assumed it was how you behaved with everyone."

"Seriously? You think I flirt like that with everyone?"

Her shoulder hitched, and she glanced away. "Well, yeah."

He sat back in his seat and waited for her to look him in the eye. "Okay, just so we're clear. I don't flirt like that with everyone. I'm a people person by nature, but there's always been something about you that's different from everyone else."

Her blush disappeared before her eyes clouded with hurt. "I didn't feel very different when I saw you with a new girl every week."

He deserved her censure as much as she deserved an explanation. "I talked to my mom over Christmas. She knew how much I liked you, and she sat me down and told me I'd come too far in my walk to forget my goals. She told me it'd be hard and that I'd feel guilty for leading you on, but she assured me it was for the best if we didn't share the same beliefs."

"Oh."

"So, after Savannah when I so ineptly explained my position, I thought it best for both of us if I focused my energy … elsewhere."

"Well …" She folded her hands on the table and rubbed her thumbs together. "You definitely don't have a focusing problem."

He stilled her movements by covering her hands with his. "The only thing I could focus on was how little interest I had in anyone but you." At her disbelieving stare he said, "Why do you think I got so mad when I realized you'd been coming to Bible study?"

She stared at him, her eyes open and clear, but full of questions. "So where does that leave us now?"

No more lies. No more half-truths. No more evading. "I can't speak for you, but I'm right where I want to be. Holding hands with a girl I'm falling for, hoping she feels the same."

Reagan swallowed and shook her head at Dash, at his vulnerable and open expression. He'd been honest with her—brutally honest—and he deserved the same in return. "You're not a beat-around-the-bush kind of guy."

"I don't see the point. I want to date you. Only you and see where this goes."

Her pulse spiked as her throat closed. He'd listened, explained, and laid it all on the line. There was no time to weigh the options or second guess, not with him staring at her with his heart in his eyes. She took a deep breath and told him the truth. "You scare me Dash. The way I feel about you scares me, but I want to date you, too. Only you. And see where this goes."

His smile bloomed, and his grip tightened almost painfully. They laughed at one another like goofy idiots until her face ached from smiling.

"Okay. Okay." He breathed a sigh. "Thank God."

She nodded and for the first time in hours, glanced around the restaurant. Other than the servers milling around, they were the only people present. "I guess we should get out of here."

Dash was as oblivious as she to the lateness of the hour, blinking at the empty tables as if coming out of a trance. "Yeah, I suppose we should."

He folded her hand into his the moment she stood up, and walked her to her car. "I'll see you at home."

Reagan could only nod at his smoldering look. If he kissed her now, standing beside her car in a parking lot not far from campus, she'd have melted into the blacktop never to be seen again.

She followed his truck back to the apartment, closed and locked her door, and met Dash at the base of the stairs. He grabbed her hand as they ascended and turned to face her at her door.

"I want to kiss you." He backed her against the plank boards. "And this time, there won't be any confusion about who made the first move."

She nodded as everything inside of her went fuzzy and soft. His lips hovered, his breath hitched, and his body pressed against hers from torso to toes. All the longing, all the doubt disappeared as he swiped his lips against hers feather light before grazing her lips with his teeth. Someone moaned—her or him she couldn't be sure—and the echo of it lit up her spine like a glow stick. The boy could kiss the wits right out of her mind.

They stood outside her apartment, lip to lip, heart to heart, and turned months of longing into a monster make-out session on the balcony by her door. The sky could have opened and breathed fire, the floor beneath them could have gave way and sent them tumbling to their death, and she wouldn't have noticed, so intent was she on Dash. When at last she pulled back to catch her breath, the look of wonder on his face had her knees going week. "Dash." She ran her hands over his face to be sure the moment was true.

"Reagan." Dash dropped his forehead to hers and closed his eyes. "You need to go inside."

All she wanted to do was sink back into him and fly and he wanted her to go? "I do?"

He nodded. "Yes. Go inside. If we're going to do this, we're going to do it right. I can't … I won't …"

"I get it." Although disappointed she knew he was right. They had to find a way to deal with their needs while getting to know each other the way God intended. Crazy attraction withstanding, they had lots to learn about each other and see where this could go.

He stepped back, running his hands down her arms and linking their fingers. "Go inside, talk to your friends, get some sleep. Will you be at church tomorrow?"

"Yeah." She squeezed his hands. "I'll be there."

"Okay." He rubbed his lips against hers once more before stepping back with a groan. "Will you wait for me after? Like before?"

"I'll wait for you." She turned and opened the door, smiling at him as he walked backwards towards his apartment. The sound of throats clearing behind her had her jolting and jerking around.

"Hello," Kayla said. Shelby sat on one side of her roommate, and Emily on the other. Dylan came out of the kitchen with a drink in his hand.

"Hey." Reagan closed the door at her back. "What's going on?"

"Oh, nothing much." Dylan sat next to Emily and slung his arm around her shoulders. "How was your lunch?"

The way they sat there staring at her, smug grins on all of their faces, meant she and Dash hadn't been as quiet as she'd hoped. "Lunch was delicious." She knew they were waiting for a blow-by-blow but decided to make them work for it. "I'm beat," she said. "My room's a mess. I'm going to clean up."

Kayla and Shelby stood up and blocked her passage from both ends of the couch. "Not so fast." Shelby crossed her arms against her chest. "Sit. Tell us everything."

Reagan bit her lip as she sank onto the couch. "What do you want to know?"

"What did he say?" Kayla asked.

"We cleared the air. He was avoiding me because he thought I wasn't a believer, and he got mad when he found out because … well, I mean …"

"He likes you," Emily said, "if that make-out session is any indication."

Reagan covered her face with her hands. "Tell me you didn't see that."

"Everyone saw that," Dylan said. "I walked in right beside you and neither one of you flinched."

"Oh no."

"Oh yes," Kayla said. "It's so romantic."

"It's actually pretty pathetic," Shelby said. "The guy lives by himself a few doors down."

Kayla popped her arm. "Leave her alone."

Reagan spoke through her fingers. "It was a goodbye kiss that got out of hand."

"Goodbye?" Emily asked, her brows winging upward.

Reagan dropped her hands and stared at her lap. "Goodbye until tomorrow. We're kind of dating now."

Kayla squealed and hopped up, grabbing Reagan's shoulders, and pulling her into a hug. "Our little girl in her first relationship! I'm so happy for you."

When Kayla released her, Reagan glanced at each of her roommates and made a solemn vow. "Despite what you just witnessed, I promise no more middle school PDA."

"I'm going to hold you to it." Shelby pointed at Emily and Dylan. "It's bad enough with these two molesting each other every time I turn around. I can only stomach so much."

Dylan grinned like a Cheshire cat. "I can't help it that Emily can't keep her hands off me." He grumbled as Emily's elbow found his stomach.

"I'm happy." Through God's love and abiding wisdom, Reagan was ready to take an emotional risk with Dash. "I don't know where we're headed, but it feels right to give it a try."

"You're taking a leap of faith," Kayla said. "Literally and figuratively."

"I guess we are," she said. "Y'all have been great to me this year, dealing with all this stuff."

"The year's almost over and now you start to date?" Emily asked. "What will happen this summer?"

Reagan sighed. She hadn't thought about summer break. She hadn't thought about much at all. "I don't know. I'm going home. I promised my mom, and I owe it to her not to break a promise."

"Will Dash be here, or is he going back to Atlanta?"

"I'm not sure." Reagan's bubble of happiness deflated just a bit. "We'll figure it out no matter where he is this summer."

Shelby scowled, pointing an accusing finger at Reagan. "You're being really calm about this. That's very unlike you."

Reagan shrugged. She did feel calm and she knew why. Giving God control meant she didn't have to obsess over life's details, but she knew better than tell Shelby God was the reason. "If there's one thing I learned this year it's that I can't plan everything."

"Amen to that." Dylan got to his feet. He reached down and pulled Emily up by her hands. "Come on, woman. You can kiss me goodbye like nobody's looking."

As Emily and Dylan left the apartment and Shelby went to her room, Kayla once again captured Reagan in a bone-crushing hug. "I'm so happy for you."

"I'm pretty darn happy too."

They walked down the hallway arm in arm. "You found God and found a boyfriend."

"I think God led me to a boyfriend." They stopped outside Kayla's door. "He's pretty great, Kay."

"You're pretty great too, so I'd say you're a perfect match."

"Perfect or not, it feels right. It scares me how much I like him."

"Scared is good. It would be weird if you weren't at least a little bit freaked out."

"I may need your help. I've never done this before."

Kayla rested her hands atop Reagan's shoulders. "You'll be fine. You've got God on your side. He's all the help you need."

Kayla was right. For the first time in her life, Reagan knew no matter what happened, if she kept her eyes on God, everything would be okay. "Amen to that."

Also by
CHRISTY HAYES

Discover Other Contemporary Romance & Women's Fiction Titles by Christy Hayes

Kiss & Tell Stories:

A Kiss by Design, Book 1, Kiss & Tell Series

A Kiss by the Book, Book 2, Kiss & Tell Series

Kiss & Make Up: A Kiss & Tell Novella

Golden Rule Outfitters Series:

Mending the Line, Book 1, Golden Rule Outfitters Series

Guiding the Fall, Book 2, Golden Rule Outfitters

Taming the Moguls, Book 3, Golden Rule Outfitters

Connected to GRO Series:

Dodge the Bullet

Shoe Strings

Connected Books:

Heart of Glass

The Sweetheart Hoax

Single Title:

Angle of Incidence

Misconception

The Accidental Encore

Short Story:

Good Luck, Bad Timing & When Harry Met Sally

The WG2E's Viva La Valentine Romance Anthology (*Good Luck, Bad Timing & When Harry Met Sally* originally appeared in the Valentine Anthology. The collection of Valentine stories makes a great gift and it's a great way to discover new writers*!)*

Lost Love Letters: An Indie Chicks Anthology

50 First Chapters: An Indie Chicks Anthology

About the Author

Christy Hayes lives outside Atlanta, Georgia, with her husband and dogs. When not writing, she's reading, walking dogs, or stalking her adult children on social media.

Please visit her website at
www.christyhayes.com
for more information.

CPSIA information can be obtained
at www.ICGtesting.com
Printed in the USA
BVHW080017281118
533674BV00007B/26/P

9 781625 720160